A Time of Exile

A Time of Exile

A Novel of the Westlands

BY
KATHARINE KERR

A FOUNDATION BOOK
Doubleday
New York London Toronto Sydney Auckland

DEDICATION

tibi, Dea, nominis pro gloria tuae

A FOUNDATION BOOK
PUBLISHED BY DOUBLEDAY
a division of Bantam Doubleday Dell
Publishing Group, Inc.
666 Fifth Avenue, New York, New York 10103

FOUNDATION, DOUBLEDAY, and the portrayal of the
letter F are trademarks of Doubleday, a division of
Bantam Doubleday Dell Publishing Group, Inc.

DESIGNED BY DOROTHY KLINE

Library of Congress
Cataloging-in-Publication Data

Kerr, Katharine.
A time of exile : a novel of the Westlands /
by Katharine Kerr. —
1st ed.
p.   cm.
"A Foundation book."
I. Title.
PS3561.E642T56   1990   90-3894
813′.54—dc20   CIP

ISBN 0-385-41463-3
ISBN 0-385-41464-1 (pbk.)

June 1991
1   3   5   7   9   10   8   6   4   2
FIRST EDITION

A Note on the Pronunciation of Deverry Words

The language spoken in Deverry is a member of the P-Celtic family. Although closely related to Welsh, Cornish, and Breton, it is by no means identical to any of these actual languages and should never be taken as such.

Vowels are divided by Deverry scribes into two classes: noble and common. Nobles have two pronunciations; commons, one.

A as in *father* when long; a shorter version of the same sound, as in *far,* when short.

O as in *bone* when long; as in *pot* when short.

W as the *oo* in *spook* when long; as in *roof* when short.

Y as the *i* in *machine* when long; as the *e* in *butter* when short.

E as in *pen.*

I as in *pin.*

U as in *pun.*

Vowels are generally long in stressed syllables; short in unstressed. Y is the primary exception to this rule. When it appears as the last letter of a word, it is always long whether that syllable is stressed or not.

THE PRONUNCIATION OF DEVERRY WORDS

Diphthongs generally have one consistent pronunciation.

AE as the *a* in *mane*.

AI as in *aisle*.

AU as the *ow* in *how*.

EO as a combination of *eh* and *oh*.

EW as in Welsh, a combination of *eh* and *oo*.

IE as in *pier*.

OE as the *oy* in *boy*.

UI as the North Welsh *wy*, a combination of *oo* and *ee*. Note that OI is never a diphthong, but is two distinct sounds, as in *carnoic* (KAR-noh-ik).

Consonants are mostly the same as in English, with these exceptions:

C is always hard as in *cat*.

G is always hard as in *get*.

DD is the voiced *th* as in *thin* or *breathe*, but the voicing is more pronounced than in English. It is opposed to TH, the unvoiced sound as in *th* or *breath*. (This is the sound that the Greeks called the Celtic tau.)

R is heavily rolled.

RH is a voiceless R, approximately pronounced as if it were spelled *hr* in Deverry proper. In Eldidd, the sound is fast becoming indistinguishable from R.

DW, GW, and TW are single sounds, as in *Gwendolen* or *twit*.

Y is never a consonant.

I before a vowel at the beginning of a word is consonantal, as it is in the plural ending *-ion*, pronounced *yawn*.

Doubled consonants are both sounded clearly, unlike in English. Note, however, that DD is a *single letter*, not a doubled consonant.

Accent is generally on the penultimate syllable, but compound words and place names are often an exception to this rule.

THE PRONUNCIATION OF DEVERRY WORDS

This is, of course, the same system of transcription used in the earlier volumes of these chronicles—a fact that may surprise some few readers. I refer to those scholars of Elvish, as well as one well-known Elvish scholar, who have taken time better employed elsewhere to criticize my decision to dispense with the vast apparatus of diacritical marks with which they attempt to render on paper that most nuanced of languages. No reader of popular fiction wants or needs to wade his or her way through a page where long names bristle with peculiar typefaces like some sort of verbal porcupines. In my approximations I have as before relied upon native speakers of Elvish in difficult or ambiguous cases; I trust that their judgment will eventually carry the day even in academic circles and that this tedious debate in the back pages of various linguistic journals will at last be put to rest.

Prologue

The Eldidd Border

1096

"AS THRIFTY AS a dwarf" is a common catchphrase, and one that the Mountain People take for a compliment. Although they see no reason to waste anything, whether it's a scrap of cloth or the heel of a loaf, they keep a particularly good watch over their gemstones and metals, though they never tell anyone outside their kin and clan just how they do it. Otho, the silver daggers' smith down in Dun Mannannan, was no different than any other dwarven craftsman, unless he was perhaps more cautious than most. His usual customer was some hotheaded young lad who'd dishonored himself badly enough to be forced to join the silver daggers, and you have to admit that a wandering swordsman who fights only for coin, not honor, isn't the sort you can truly trust with either dwarven silver or magical secrets.

During his long years among humans in the kingdom of Deverry, Otho taught a few other smiths how to smelt the rare alloy for the daggers, an extremely complicated process with a number of peculiar steps, such as words to be chanted and hand gestures to be made just so. Otho would always refuse to answer questions, saying only that if his students wanted the formula to come out right, they could follow his orders, and if they didn't, they could get out of his forge right then and spare everyone trouble. All the apprentices shut their mouths and stayed; they were bright enough to realize that they were being taught magic of some sort, even if they weren't being told what the spells accomplished. Once they opened shops of their own, they went on repeating Otho's procedures in the exact way they'd been taught, so that every dagger made of dwarven silver in Deverry carried two kinds of dweomer.

One spell Otho would acknowledge, especially to someone that he liked and trusted; the other he would have hidden from his own brother. The first produced in the metal itself an antipathy to the auric vibrations of the elven race, so that the dagger glowed brightly the moment an elf came within a few feet of it. The other, the secret spell, was its necessary opposite, producing an affinity, in this case to the dagger's true owner, so that if lost or stolen, sooner or later the magical currents of the universe would float that dagger home. The thing was, by "true owner" Otho meant himself, which meant that any lost dagger would eventually come home to him, no matter who had actually made it or how much its interim owner had paid for it. Otho justified all of this by thinking of the purchase price as mere rent, a trifling detail that he never mentioned to his customers.

Once and only once had Otho produced an exception, and that was by accident. Round about 1044, he made a dagger for Cullyn of Cerrmor, one of the few human beings he truly admired. In the course of things, that blade passed to Rhodry Maelwaedd, a young lord who was forced by political exile to join the silver daggers. As soon as Rhodry laid his hand on the dagger, it was obvious that his blood was a little rarer than merely noble—the blade blazed up and accused him of being half an elf at least. Grudgingly, and only as a favor for Cullyn of Cerrmor's daughter, Otho took off the denouncing spell. What Otho didn't realize, since his dweomer was a thing of rote memory rather than real understanding, was that he'd weakened the complementary magic as well. The dagger now saw Rhodry, not the dwarf, as its one true owner.

A silver dagger's life is never easy, and Rhodry's time on the long road was worse than most, and by one thing and another he managed to lose the blade good and proper, far away in the Bardekian archipelago across the Southern Sea, round about the year 1064. At the same time as Rhodry was killing the man who'd stolen it, the dagger itself fetched up in the marketplace of a little mountain town called Ganjalo, where it stayed for several years, stubbornly unsold. The merchant couldn't understand—here was this beautiful and exotic item, reasonably priced, that no one ever seemed to want to buy. Finally it did catch the eye of an itinerant tinker, who knew of a rich man who collected unusual knives of all sorts. Since this rich man lived in a seaport, the dagger allowed itself to be installed in the collection. Again, some years passed, until the collector died and his sons divided up the various blades. The youngest, who happened to be a ship's captain, felt drawn to the dagger for some irrational reason and traded another brother an entire set of pearl-handled fish knives for it. The next time this captain went to sea, the dagger went with him.

But not to Deverry. The captain sailed back and forth from Bardek proper to the off-lying islands of Orystinna, a lucrative run, and he saw no reason to consider making the dangerous crossing to the distant barbarian kingdoms. After some years of this futile east-west travel, the dagger changed owners. While gambling, the captain had an inexplicable run of bad luck and ended up handing the dagger over to a friend to pay off his debt. The friend took it to a northern seaport and on a sudden whim sold it to another marketplace jeweler, who bought it on the same kind of impulse. There it lay again, until a young merchant passed by and happened to linger for a moment to look over the jeweler's stock. Since this Londalo traded with Deverry on a regular basis, he was always in need of little gifts to smooth his way with customs officials and minor lords. The dagger had a barbarian look, and he bought it to take along on his next trading run.

Of course, poor Londalo didn't realize that in Deverry offering a silver dagger as a gift was a horrible insult. He found out quick enough in the Eldidd town of Abernaudd, where his ill-considered gesture cost him a trading pact. As he bemoaned his bad luck in a tavern, a kindly stranger explained the problem, and

Londalo nearly threw the dagger onto the nearest dungheap then and there, which was more or less what the dagger had in mind. Yet, because he also knew a lesson when he saw one, he ended up keeping it as a reminder to never take other people's customs for granted again. If silver could have feelings, the dagger would have been livid with rage. Back and forth it went between Bardek and the Deverry coast for some years more, while a richer, older Londalo became a respected and important member of his merchant guild, until finally, in the spring of the year 1096, he and the dagger turned up in Aberwyn, where Rhodry Maelwaedd now ruled as gwerbret. The magical currents around the dagger thickened, swirled, and grew so strong that Londalo actually felt them, as a prick of something much like anxiety.

On the morning that he was due to visit the gwerbret, Londalo stood in his chamber in the best inn Aberwyn had to offer and irritably applied his clan markings. Normally a trained slave would have painted on the pale blue stripes and red diamonds that marked him as a member of House Ondono, but it was very unwise for a thrifty man to bring his slaves when he visited the kingdom of Deverry. Surrounded by barbarians with a peculiar idea of property rights, slaves were known to take their chance at freedom and disappear. When they did, the barbarian authorities became uncooperative at best and hostile at worst. Londalo held his hand mirror at various angles to examine the paint on his pale brown skin and finally decided that his amateur job would have to do. After all, the barbarians, even an important one like the lord he was about to visit, knew nothing of the niceties of the art. Yet the anxiety remained. Something was wrong; he could just plain feel it.

There was a knock at the door, and Harmon, his young assistant, entered with a respectful bob of his head.

"Are you ready to leave, sir?"

"Yes. I see you have the proposed trade agreements with you. Good, good."

With a brief smile Harmon patted the heavy leather roll of a document case that he carried tucked under one arm.

6

As they walked through the streets of Aberwyn, Londalo noticed his young partner looking this way and that in distaste; occasionally he lifted a perfumed handkerchief to his nose as they passed a particularly ripe dungheap. There was no doubt that visiting Deverry was hard on a civilized man, Londalo reflected. The city seemed to have been thrown down around the harbor rather than built according to a plan. All the buildings were round and shaggy with thatch, instead of square and nicely shingled; the streets meandered randomly through and around them like the patterns of spirals and interlace the barbarians favored as a decorative style. Everywhere was confusion: barking dogs, running children, men on horseback trotting through dangerously fast, rumbling wagons, and even the occasional staggering drunk.

"Sir," Harmon said at last. "Is this really the most important city in Eldidd?"

"I'm afraid so. Now remember, my young friend, this man we're going to visit will look like a crude barbarian to you, but he has the power to put us both to death if we insult him. The laws are very different here. Every ruler is judge and advocate both as long as he's in his own lands, and a gwerbret, like our lord here in Aberwyn, is a ruler far more powerful than one of our archons."

In approximately the center of town lay the palace complex, or dun as the barbarians called it, of the gwerbret. The barbarians all talked about how splendid it was, with its many-towered fortress inside the high stone walls, but the Bardekians found the stonework crude and the effect completely spoiled by the clutter of huts and sheds and pigsties and stables all around it. As they made their way through the bustle of servants, Londalo suddenly realized that he was wearing the silver dagger on his tunic's leather belt.

"By the Star Goddesses! I must be growing old! I don't even remember picking this thing up from the table."

"I don't suppose it'll matter, sir. All the men around here are absolutely bristling with knives."

Although Londalo had never met this particular ruler before, he'd heard that Rhodry Maelwaedd, Gwerbret Aberwyn, was an honest, fair-minded man, somewhat more civilized than most of his kind. Londalo was pleased to notice that the courtyards were reasonably clean, the servants wore decent clothing, and the corpses of hanged criminals were nowhere in sight. At the door of the tallest tower, the broch proper, the aged chamberlain was waiting to greet them. In a hurried whisper Londalo reminded Harmon that a gwerbret's servitors were all noble-born.

"So mind your manners. No giving orders, and always say thank you when they do something for you."

The chamberlain ushered them into a vast round room, carpeted with braided rushes and set about with long wooden tables, where at least a hundred men, all of them armed with knife and sword both, were drinking ale and nibbling on chunks of bread, while servant girls wandered around, gossiping or trading smart remarks with the men more than working. Near a carved sandstone hearth to one side, one finer table, made of ebony and polished to a shine, stood alone, the gwerbret's place of honor. Londalo was well pleased when the chamberlain seated them there and had a boy bring their ale in actual glass stoups. Londalo was also pleased to see that the tapestry he'd sent ahead as a gift was hanging on the wall near the enormous fireplace. As he absently fingered the hilt of the silver dagger, he realized that his strange anxiety had left him. Harmon, however, was nervous, glancing continually at the mob of armed men across the hall.

"Now, now," Londalo whispered. "The rulers here do keep their men in hand, and besides, everyone honors a guest. No one's going to kill you on the spot."

Harmon forced out a smile, had a sip of ale, and nearly choked on the bitter, stinking stuff. Like the true merchant he was, however, he covered over his distaste with a cough and forced himself to try again. In a few minutes, two young men strode into the hall. Since their baggy trousers were woven from one of the garish plaids that marked a Deverry noble, and since the entire warband rose to bow to them, Londalo assumed that they were a pair of the gwerbret's sons. They looked much alike, with wavy raven-dark hair and cornflower-blue eyes. By barbarian standards they were both handsome men, Londalo supposed, but he was worried about more than their appearance.

"By the Great Wave-father himself! I was told that there was only one son visiting here! We'll have to do something about getting a gift for the other, no matter what the cost."

The chamberlain bustled over, motioning for them to rise, so they'd be ready to kneel at the proper moment. Having to kneel to the so-called noble-born vexed Londalo, who was used to voting his rulers into office and voting them out again, too, if they didn't measure up to his standards. As one of the young men strolled over, the chamberlain cleared his throat.

"Rhodry, Gwerbret Aberwyn, the Maelwaedd, and his son."

In his confusion, Londalo almost forgot to kneel. Why, this lord could be no more than twenty-five at most! Mentally he cursed the merchant guild for giving him such faulty information for this important mission.

"We are honored to be in your presence, great lord, but you must forgive our intrusion in what must be a time of mourning."

"Mourning?" The gwerbret frowned, puzzled.

"Well, when we set sail for your most esteemed country, Your Grace, your father was still alive, or so I was told, the elder Rhodry of Aberwyn."

The gwerbret burst out laughing, waving for them to rise and take their seats again.

"I take it you've never seen me before, good merchant. I've ruled here for thirty years, and I'm four and fifty years old. I'm not having a jest on you, either." Absently he looked away, and suddenly his eyes turned dark with a peculiar sadness. "Oh, no jest at all."

Londalo forgot his protocol enough to stare. Not a trace of gray in the gwerbret's hair, not one true line in his face—how could he be a man of fifty-four, old back home, ancient indeed for a barbarian warrior? Then the gwerbret turned back to him with a sunny smile.

"But that's of no consequence. What brings you to me, good sir?"

Londalo cleared his throat to prepare for the important matter of trading Eldidd grain for Bardekian luxuries. Just as he was about to speak, Rhodry leaned forward to stare.

"By the gods, is that a silver dagger you're carrying? It looks like the usual knobbed pommel."

"Well, it is, Your Grace." Mentally Londalo cursed himself all over again for bringing the wretched thing along. "I bought it in the islands many years ago, you see, and I keep it with me because . . . well, it's rather a long story . . ."

"In the islands? May I see it, good merchant, if it's not too much trouble?"

"Why, no trouble at all, Your Grace."

Rhodry took it, stared for a long moment at the falcon device engraved on the blade, and burst out laughing.

"Do you realize that this used to be mine? Years and years ago? It was stolen from me when I was in the islands."

"What? Really? Why, then, Your Grace absolutely must have it back! I insist, truly I do."

Later that afternoon, once the treaty was signed and merchant on his way, the great hall of Aberwyn fell quiet as the warband went off to exercise their horses. Although normally Rhodry would have gone with them, he lingered at the table of honor and considered the odd twist of luck, the strange coincidence, as he thought of it, that had brought his silver dagger home to him. A few serving lasses wandered around, wiping down tables with rags; a few stable hands sat near the open door and diced for coppers; a few dogs lay in the straw on the floor and snored. In a bit, his eldest son came down to join him. It was hard to believe that the lad was fully grown, with two sons of his own now and the Dun Gwerbyn demesne in his hands. Rhodry could remember how happy he'd been when his first heir was born, how much he'd loved the little lad, and how much Cullyn had loved him. It hurt, now, thinking that his firstborn was beginning to hate him, and all because his father refused to age and die. Not that Cullyn ever said a word, mind; it was just that a coolness was growing between them, and every now and then Rhodry would catch him staring at the various symbols of the gwerbretal rank, the dragon banner, the ceremonial sword of justice, with a wondering sort of greed. Finally Rhodry could stand the silence no longer.

"Things are quiet in the tierynrhyn, then?"

"They are, Father. That's why I thought I'd ride your way for a visit."

Rhodry smiled and wondered if he'd come in hopes of finding him ill. He was an ambitious man, Cullyn was, because Rhodry had raised him to be so, had trained him from the time he could talk to rule the vast gwerbretrhyn of Aberwyn and to use well the riches that the growing trade with Bardek brought it. He himself had inherited the rhan half by accident, and he could remember all too well his panicked feeling of drowning in details during the first year of his rule to allow his son to go uneducated.

"That's an odd thing, Da, that dagger coming home."

"It was, truly." Rhodry picked it up off the table and handed it to him. "See the falcon on the blade? That's the device of the man you were named for."

"That's right—he told me the story. Of how he was a silver dagger once, I mean. Ye gods, I still miss Cullyn of Cerrmor, and here he's been dead many a long year now."

"I miss him too, truly. You know, I think I'll carry this dagger again, in his memory, like."

"Oh here, Da, you can't do that! It's a shameful thing!"

"Indeed? And who's going to dare mock me for it?"

Cullyn looked away in an unpleasant silence, as if any possible mention of social position or standing could spoil the most innocent pleasure. With a sigh he handed the dagger back and picked up his tankard again.

"We could have a game of Carnoic?" Rhodry said.

"We could, at that." When Cullyn smiled at him, all his old affection shone in his dark blue eyes. "It's too muggy to go out hunting this afternoon."

They were well into their third game when Rhodry's wife, the Lady Aedda, came down to join them at the honor table. She sat down quietly, even timidly, with a slight smile for her son. At forty-seven she had grown quite stout, and there were streaks of gray in her chestnut hair and deep lines round her mouth. Although theirs was a politically arranged marriage, and in its first years a miserable one, over time she and Rhodry had worked out a certain accommodation to each other. He felt a certain fondness for her, a gratitude that she had given him four strong heirs for Aberwyn.

"If my lady wishes," Rhodry said, "we can end this game."

"No need, my lord. I can watch."

And yet, by a common, unspoken consent they brought the game to a close and put the pieces away. Aedda had asked for so little from both of them over the years that they were inclined to give her what small concessions they could. As the afternoon wore on in small talk about the doings of the various vassals in the demesne, Rhodry drank more and more and said less and less. The heat, the long silences, the predictability of his wife's little remarks all weighed him down until at last he got up and strode out of the hall. No one dared question him or follow.

His private chamber was on the third floor of a half-broch, a richly furnished room with Bardek carpets on the floor and glass in the windows, cushioned chairs at the hearth and a display of five beautifully worked swords on one wall. Rhodry threw open a window and leaned on the sill to look down on the ward and the garden, where the dragon of Aberwyn sported in a marble fountain far below. One old manservant ambled across the lawn on some slow errand; nothing else moved. For a moment Rhodry felt as if he couldn't breathe. He tossed his head with an oath that was half a keening and turned away.

For over thirty years he had held power, and for most of them he had loved it all: the symbols and pageantry of his rank, the tangible power that he wielded in his court of justice and on the battlefield, the subtle but even greater power he exercised in the intrigues of the High King's court. As he looked back, he could remember exactly when that love turned sour. He had been at the royal palace in Dun Deverry, and as he entered the great hall, the chamberlain of course announced him. At the words "Rhodry, Gwerbret Aberwyn," every other noble-born man there turned to look at him, some in envy of one of the king's favorites, some in subtle calculation of what his presence would mean to their own schemes, others with simple interest in the sight of so powerful a man. All he felt in return was irritation, that they should gawk at him as at a two-headed calf in the market fair. And from that day, some two years earlier, Rhodry had slowly come to wonder when he would die and be rid of everything he once had loved, free and shut of it at last.

He left the window and sat down in a half-round rosewood chair, intricately carved with interlace wound about the dragons of Aberwyn, to draw his newly returned silver dagger and study it. Although the blade looked like silver, it was harder than the best steel, and it gleamed without a trace of tarnish. When he flicked it with a thumbnail it rang.

"Dwarven silver," he muttered to himself. "Ah, by the lord of hell, I must be going daft, to wish I was out on the long road again!"

He owned another piece of dwarven silver, too, a ring he always wore on the third finger of his right hand, a simple band of elven workmanship, engraved with roses on the outside and a line of elven writing on the in. Just as he held up his hand to look at the ring, a page opened the door.

"Your Grace? Am I disturbing Your Lordship?"

"Not truly."

"Well, Your Grace, there's this shabby old herbwoman at the door, and she's insisting on speaking to you. One of the guards was going to turn her away, but she gave us this look, Your Grace, and I . . . well, I was frightened of her, so I thought I'd best tell you."

Rhodry's heart pounded once.

"Did she give you her name?"

"She did, Your Grace. It's Jill."

"I'll receive her up here."

The lad frankly stared, then bowed and trotted away.

While he waited for the woman he once had loved more than life itself, Rhodry paced back and forth from window to door. He hadn't seen Jill in thirty years, not since the night when she left him, simply rode out of his life without a backward glance—or so he assumed—to follow a Wyrd even stranger than his own. At first, he thought of her constantly, wondered if she missed him, wondered if her studies in the strange craft of the dweomer were bringing her the happiness she sought. Yet as the years passed and his wound healed, he let her memory rest except for an idle wondering every now and then if she were well. Although she did come to Aberwyn to tend her dying father, Rhodry was at court in Dun Deverry at the time. Every now and then, some news of her doings came his way, but never in any detail. Now she was here. He was dreading seeing her, because she was only a few years younger than himself, and he hated the thought of seeing her beauty ravaged by age. When he heard her crisp voice thanking the page, his heart pounded once again. The door opened.

"The herbwoman, Your Grace."

In strode a woman dressed in men's clothing, a pair of dirty brown brigga and a much-mended linen shirt, stained green in places from medicinal leaves and stems. Her hair, cropped like a lad's, shone a silvery gray, and crow's-feet round her blue eyes ran deep, but she seemed neither young nor old, so full of life and vigor that it was impossible to think of her as anything other than handsome. Beautiful she wasn't, not any longer, but as he stared at the face which coincided with the one belonging to his lovely young lass of past years, he found that it fit her better than the beauty he was remembering. Her sudden smile could move him still.

"Aren't you going to say one word to me?" she said with a laugh.

"My apologies. It's just a bit of a shock, having you turn up like this."

"No doubt. You're in for a worse shock than that, I'm afraid."

Without waiting to be asked she sat down in one of the chairs by the hearth. He took the other facing, and for a few moments the

14

silence deepened around them. Then he remembered that his silver dagger must have been coming home at the same time as she was riding into Aberwyn, and he shuddered, feeling a cold touch of Wyrd that made the hairs on the nape of his neck bristle.

"And what is this shock?"

"Well, for starters, Nevyn's dead."

Rhodry grunted as if at a blow. He'd known Nevyn, her teacher and master in the craft of magic, very well indeed—in fact, Rhodry owed him his life and his rhan both.

"May the gods give him rest in the Otherlands, then. Somehow I thought the dweomer would keep the old man alive forever."

"He was beginning to wonder himself." She grinned so broadly that it seemed inappropriate. "He was glad to go, when the time came."

"How did it happen? Was he ill, or was there an accident?"

"What? Oh, naught of that sort. It was time, and he went. He made his goodbyes to all of us and lay down on his bed and died. That's all." Her smile faded. "I'll miss him, though. Every hour of every day."

"My heart aches for you, truly."

As if to share his sympathy Wildfolk came, sprite and sylph and gnome, materializing like the fall of silent drops of rain to float down and stand around them. When a skinny gray fellow climbed into Jill's lap and reached up to pat her cheek, she smiled again, shoving the mourning away. The sight of the Wildfolk reminded Rhodry of his own problems. Whatever else Jill might have been to him, she was a dweomermaster now, the possessor of strange powers and even stranger lore.

"I've got a question for you," he said. "How long does an elven half-breed like me live, anyway?"

"A good long while, though not so long as a true elf. I'd say you've got a hundred years ahead, easily, my friend. When I'm buried and gone, you'll still look like a lad of twenty."

"By all the ice in all the hells! That can't happen! How long will it be before all of Aberwyn figures out that I'm no true Maelwaedd, then?"

"Not very, truly. The common folk are already whispering about you, wondering about dweomer and suchlike. Soon enough the noble-born will, too, and they'll come to you with a few hard questions about exactly how much elven blood there is in the Maelwaedd clan, and whether or no those old rumors about elves living forever are true. If someone found out who your true father was, it would be a nasty blow to your clan's honor."

"There's a cursed sight more at stake than the honor of the Maelwaedds. Can't you see, Jill? My sons disinherited, and civil war in the rhan, and—"

"Of course I see!" She held her hand up flat for silence. "That's the other reason I've come."

He felt the cold again, rippling down his back. Thirty years since he'd seen her, and yet they still at times shared thoughts.

"I had an omen," she went on. "It was right after we buried Nevyn—me and the folk in the village where we lived, that is—and I went walking out to a little lake near our home, where there's a stand of rushes out in the water. It was just at sunset, and there were some clouds in the sky. You know how easy it is to see pictures in sunset clouds. So I saw a cloud shape that looked just like a falcon catching a little dragon in her claws. Oho, think I, that's me and Rhodry! And the minute I thought it, I felt the dweomer cold, and I knew that it was true. And here I am."

"That simple, is it? You think of me, and here you are?"

"Well, I had to ride to Aberwyn like anyone else."

"Not what I meant. Why did the omen in the clouds make you come here?"

"Oh, that! None of your affair."

He started to probe, but her expression stopped him: unsmiling, a little cool, like the cover of a book abruptly slammed shut. He could remember Nevyn turning that same blank stare on questioners who pried into things they weren't meant to know. Gwerbret or not, he would only be wasting his time if he should ask more.

"I don't suppose you could cast some dweomer on me to make me age."

"You're still a ready man with a jest, aren't you? I can't, and I wouldn't if I could. The way out's obvious, anyway. You'll have to turn the rhan over to your eldest lad and leave Eldidd."

"What? That's a hard thing for a man of my rank to do."

"If you give up the rhan, your son will keep it. If you try to keep it, your son will lose it."

"It's not just the blasted rhan! You're asking me to leave blood kin behind. Jill, by the gods, I've got grandsons."

"Do you want to see them murdered to wipe out the last traces of a bastard line?"

With a groan he buried his face in his hands. Her voice went on remorselessly.

"Once the first whispers go round that you might not be a trueborn Maelwaedd, you'll have to settle them by the sword, and honor duels have led to wars before, especially with a rich prize like Aberwyn at stake. If you lose the civil war, your enemies will hunt down every child who could even remotely be considered your heir, even Rhodda's lad."

"Oh, hold your tongue! I know that as well as you do."

"Well, then?"

He looked up to find her watching him with a calm sort of wondering. For a moment he hated her.

"It's all well and good to talk of me leaving Eldidd, but I'm not an exile or a shiftless younger son anymore. If I present a petition to the king to allow me to abdicate, the rumors will pile up like horse dung in a winter stable. Besides, what if our liege asks me my reasons outright? I could try to lie, but I doubt me that I'd be convincing. The king knows me cursed well."

She frowned at the hearth while she considered.

"You're right, aren't you? I'll have to think about that." Abruptly she rose. "If anyone asks you why I came here, tell them I wanted to tell you about Nevyn, because that's true enough in its own way. I'll see you again, and soon."

Then she was gone, out and shutting the door before Rhodry

could rise from his chair. For a while he tried to convince himself that he'd been having a strange, drunken dream, but the elven ring gleamed on his finger to remind him of the truth, that he would have to leave his clan behind for the sake of his love for it. Besides, the dweomer had saved his life several times over in the past, and he knew, with a sudden cold certainty, that the time had come to repay his debt.

Bred and born to rule, carefully trained to impose his will on others while following every nicety of courtesy, Cullyn Maelwaedd was unused to feeling guilt, and he hated this constant nag of conscience. Every time he looked at his father, it bit deep and gnawed him that at times he wished that Rhodry were . . . not dead, no, never that, but perhaps showing some signs that he might indeed die at some point. In a way, his dilemma was unique. Because Rhodry had refused to send Cullyn into fosterage as custom demanded and had taken the unheard-of step of raising his son himself, Cullyn was one of the few noble lords in Deverry who honestly loved his father. Every time he caught himself wondering if he'd ever actually inherit Aberwyn and felt the accompanying bite of guilt, he saw the wisdom of fosterage in a world where a son's power depends on his father's death.

Cullyn also was fairly certain that his father suspected him of wishing him gone. After the first few days of his visit, Rhodry became more and more withdrawn, spending long hours alone either riding through the demesne or shut up brooding in his private chamber. Cullyn considered simply going home, but since he'd said that he'd stay for ten days, he was afraid that leaving ahead of schedule would seem suspicious. On the fifth morning he came down for breakfast only to find that Rhodry had already left the dun. He went out to the stable to question the groom, but the gwerbret hadn't said a word about where he was going. As he made his way through the clutter of sheds behind the broch, he noticed two serving lasses gossiping furiously about something, an activity that would have meant nothing if they hadn't suddenly fallen silent at the very sight of him. He walked on past, tormenting himself by wondering if even the wretched common-born servants knew his secret.

Later, as he was going up to his chamber in the broch, a similar thing happened, two pages, this time, who stopped talking the moment they saw him. Cullyn grabbed one of them by the shirt collar.

"And just what are you saying that's unfit for my ears?"

The two boys went dead white and looked as if they wanted to run, but whether or not he would ever be gwerbret, Cullyn was a powerful lord and no man to argue with.

"Begging your pardon, my lord, please, it was naught."

"Indeed? Then why have you gone as white as milk?"

The second page was older and obviously a bit wiser. He stepped forward with a passable bow.

"My lord, we mean no offense. We were talking over this strange rumor. Maybe you should know about it, my lord. Then you can stop people from repeating it."

"Indeed? And just what have the townsfolk been saying?"

"Well, you know, my lord, how the gwerbret looks so young? We heard an old woman in the marketplace saying it was all because of dweomer. She said some old wizard cast this spell on him years and years ago, that he'd never get old, but then he'd have to die all of a sudden, like, to pay back the spell. The old woman said there's a gerthddyn in town spreading the tale. He heard it up north or somewhere." He paused, sincerely troubled. "My lord, that's not true, is it? His grace is splendid, and I don't want to see him die."

"Here, that can't be true, indeed. Don't you bother your heart with it."

Yet he hesitated, troubled himself, remembering all the tales whispered among his clan that Rhodry's life had been touched more than once by dweomer. And what if this strange story were true? Although by that time most people in Deverry knew that magic existed, few knew much about its true powers and capabilities, so Cullyn was ready enough to believe that it could keep his father unnaturally young. He summoned four men from his warband as an escort, then went into the town. By asking round in the market square he found out that the gerthddyn had been staying at the Green Goose, the best inn in Aberwyn, but when he went there, the tavernman told him that the gerthddyn had ridden out that very morning.

"I'll wager, my lord, that he knew he couldn't stay here long, what with him spreading them nasty tales about your father. There's not a vain bone in the gwerbret's body, my lord. Why would he be making pacts with sorcerers just to keep his looks?"

"Well spoken, truly. What was this fellow like?"

"His name was Salamander, my lord, and he was a skinny sort of fellow with yellow hair. Oh, he was a splendid talker, my lord, when he was telling his tales, so it's no wonder this wretched rumor's spreading itself around. Now, wait, my lord." He paused to suck his brown stumps of teeth in thought. "Salamander didn't rightly say the rumor was true, like. He said he heard it up in Belglaedd and asked if we thought there was any truth in it."

"I see. Well, he's gone and no more trouble to us, then."

When Cullyn returned to the great hall, Rhodry was sitting at the head of the table of honor and drinking alone. He waved his son over with a smile that made him look more his normal self than he had in days.

"There you are, lad. I've been thinking. Shall we go hunting on the morrow? I rode out to the forest preserve today, and the gamekeeper tells me we've got a pair of young stags. We could cull one easily and help the old stag keep his dominion for another spring."

"Gladly, Father."

Cullyn motioned a page over to pour him ale. As they talked about the hunt to come, he forgot all about strange rumors in the normality of the moment.

Just at dawn on the morrow, Cullyn joined his father and the kennelmaster in the courtyard, where the well-trained dogs lay still but excited, ears pricked, tails thumping the cobbles. When the men mounted for the ride to the forest, the dogs leapt up and swarmed round the kennelmaster, who trotted along with them on foot as the party set out. In the brightening day the hunt left Aberwyn behind and went north along the bank of the river Gwyn, which churned white and swollen with the spring runoff. About eight miles on they reached the preserve, a smallish stand of timber compared with the vast gwerbretal hunting park at Belglaedd farther north. While they ate a cold breakfast and let the dogs rest, Alban the gamekeeper appeared out of the forest and sat down with them, a gnarled and wind-chapped man as tough as an oak root. Since he was nearly as shy as the deer themselves, it took him a long time to bring out the various scraps of news he had for the gwerbret; he would say one thing, then withdraw into himself before he brought out the next. Rhodry listened with an amazing patience.

Since Cullyn loved the hunt, he was almost as excited as the dogs by the time they finally got underway. So early in the year the trees were only just leafing out, and the bracken and ferns still low. Ducking and dodging the occasional branch, they rode through the widely spaced oaks behind the kennelmaster and his pack. The deerhounds coursed this way and that, sniffed the wind more than the ground, then suddenly broke, baying off to the left. With a laugh Rhodry spurred his horse after them, and Cullyn followed, catching up with the hounds, who turned abruptly and headed off in the general direction of the river.

All at once, Cullyn's horse stumbled slightly, forcing him to let it slow to regain its balance and calm down. When he headed after the hunt, it was a good ways ahead of him. He could just see them through the trees. Then he heard the barks turn to yelps of terror, and the kennelmaster scream. Spear at the ready, he kicked his horse hard, dodged through at a dangerous gallop, and burst into a clearing to see a wild boar, flushed by accident but furious nonetheless, making a straight charge at the pack. Dogs scattered and the kennelmaster yanked himself into a tree barely in time. Cullyn found himself swearing with every foul oath he knew.

They had no boarhounds—worse yet, no boar spears with the

essential guards on the haft. Already his horse was tossing its head in fear as the massive, reeking boar charged one of the hounds. As Cullyn kicked his horse forward, Rhodry appeared, raced between the boar and the dog, and stabbed down at it as he passed. Enraged, the boar swung after him and let the dogs be. With a battle cry Cullyn charged after as Rhodry led the boar along. He could see what his father had in mind—keep sticking the slower-moving boar, keep it running and bleeding until they wore the thing out and could make a safe kill. Since by its snarls he could tell that the boar was deep in rut, he knew they had a long, hard fight ahead.

But they had forgotten about the river. Just as Cullyn caught up, their strange hunt burst out of the forest to the cleared roadway along the riverbank. Yelling for Cullyn to stay back, Rhodry tried to turn his horse, but the mount got a good look at the boar following and reared—then slipped and went down. Rhodry rolled clear easily, unhurt, but the boar was turning and charging.

"Da!" Cullyn's voice was the shriek of a child. "Da!"

Half to his feet, Rhodry threw himself to one side and rolled straight into the river. Blind with fury, the boar hurled itself in after him. Cullyn could never remember dismounting, nor could he remember stripping off his hunting leathers; all he knew was that suddenly he was in the river and swimming, desperately coursing from bank to bank, letting the current carry him downstream until at last, utterly exhausted, he heard Alban screaming at him from the bank.

"To shore, my lord! I beg you, come ashore!"

With the last of his strength Cullyn fought the current to the bank and grabbed the butt of the spear that Alban was holding out. It took both their strengths to haul him up onto land.

"I never saw them," Cullyn gasped.

"No more did I, Your Grace."

The sound of that honorific knocked the last bit of breath out of him. When he looked up, he saw the gamekeeper's face streaming tears, and the sight made him burst out sobbing, half keening, half choking as he gasped for breath. All his suspicions, all his envy and his fears were at last at an end, but he would have spent a year in the hells just to have his father back again.

"By every god and his wife," Salamander whispered, and his face was white with fear. "I never dreamt your lad would try to fetch you out again like that."

"No more did I, or I'd never have agreed to this daft scheme!" Rhodry felt like hitting him. "Aberwyn could have lost two gwerbrets in one misbegotten day! Ye gods, did you have to make that cursed boar so terrifying? I never knew you could make an illusion smell like that."

"You don't understand, O brother of mine." Salamander passed the back of his hand over his sweaty forehead. "That boar was none of my work. It was real, a solid, corporeal, existent, and utterly unplanned accident."

Rhodry felt the color drain from his own face. He was about to say something particularly foul when Jill came crawling back into their hiding place, a bracken-filled ditch on the other side of the river.

"He's safe," she whispered. "The gamekeeper and the kennelmaster are with him, and all the dogs, too. They've gotten the horses under control, and no doubt they'll be riding home soon. We'd best get out of here before every man in your warband comes out to search for your corpse."

"They're not my men anymore."

"Well, true enough, and we've got only the grace of the gods to thank that they ride for your eldest son and not the second." She turned on Salamander. "You and your wretched, blasted, rotten, and foul elaborate schemes!"

"You were the one who insisted there be witnesses, and you agreed to this scheme at the time. Berate me not, O princess of powers perilous, for I put not that stinking boar in their path."

Although Jill growled under her breath, she let the matter drop. For some minutes they lay there, waiting until the remnant of the hunting party should leave. While Salamander's dweomer could turn one man invisible as he crawled out of a river, he couldn't hide a party of three horsemen, a mule, and two packhorses. Now that he knew Cullyn was safely on land, Rhodry felt heart-wrung and numb, hating the irony of it, that he would find out how much his son loved him when he'd never see the lad again.

Eventually the hunting party gave up their last futile search and rode back to Aberwyn, leaving them in sole possession of the woods. Rhodry was more than glad to change out of his damp clothes into the things he'd smuggled out in readiness: a pair of plain gray brigga, an old linen shirt with no blazons, a cheap belt with his silver dagger on it.

"So here I am, a silver dagger again, am I?"

"Not for long," Salamander said. "We'll be in the elven lands soon enough."

"Provided no one catches us."

"Don't fret about that," Jill broke in. "Salamander can make sure no one recognizes you, even if they're staring right at you."

"Well and good, then. We'd best be off."

"Just that. Our father should be waiting near the border."

"And that's going to be a strange thing, meeting my true father after all these years, and him a bard at that."

"Mam, I tried to save him, truly I did." Cullyn sounded like a little boy again.

Aedda caught his hands in hers and squeezed them gently.

"Of course you did. I know you did."

For his sake, out of pain for his pain, she managed to do the proper thing and weep, but there was no mourning in it. For years she had tried very hard not to blame Rhodry; after all, she wasn't the first lass in Deverry who'd been given away to cement a treaty, and she wouldn't be the last. Yet still, he had taken her maiden-head, her youth, her life, truly, while keeping her always to one side of his affairs, and then, the final bitter thing, he had taken her sons from her, too. They always loved you more than they loved me, she thought. By every fiend in hell, I'm glad you're dead.

Although they never found the gwerbret's body, they did put up a stone to mark his passing, out in the sacred grove where his ancestors lay. On it they carved this englyn:

> This grave marks Aberwyn's grief.
> A wild wolf in the battle-strife,
> Rhodry laughed when he took your life.

And that was the first death of Rhodry Maelwaedd and the vindication of the old hermit who, years and years before, had told him he would die twice over.

Keeping to country lanes and open lands, buying food from farmers and shunning the duns of the noble-born, Rhodry, Salamander, and Jill traveled west and south for ten days until they reached the large stream or small river known as Y Brog, marking what most human beings considered the Eldidd border, since only elves lived beyond it. During Rhodry's rule, the Westfolk, as Eldidd people called the elves, had started becoming a little friendlier than they'd been in times past. Every now and then a trading party would show up in the border towns of Cannobaen or Cernmeton to offer their beautiful horses in return for ironwork and glasswares; even more rarely, an embassy would appear in Aberwyn itself with tokens of friendship and alliance for the gwerbret. Yet they were still strange and alien, still frightening to most people. It was one of Rhodry's regrets that he'd never been able to make his subjects welcome the Westfolk in the rhan. Since he'd always raised his sons to like and admire them, he could at least hope that they would continue to be welcome in the dun.

"I suppose I'll get word now and then of how things fare in

Aberwyn," he remarked one evening. "Especially if Calonderiel goes to pay his respects to the new gwerbret."

"Of course he's going." Salamander was kneeling by their campfire and feeding in sticks. "That was part of the scheme. He'll be waiting to have a chat with us, and then he'll head east. What's wrong? Worried about your holdings? Well, your former or late lamented holdings, I should say."

"It's strange, truly. I can't stop thinking about Aberwyn. I keep drafting mental orders, you see, about the way things should be run, and every now and then I actually find myself turning round to call a page or suchlike to carry a command for me."

"You'll get over it in time. Think of rulership as a fever. It'll pass off as your health returns."

"Well and good, then. Maybe I need some strengthening herb water or suchlike."

They shared a grin. Although they were only half brothers, they looked a good bit alike in everything but coloring. Salamander's hair was as ash-blond pale as Rhodry's was dark, but they had the strong jut of their jaw and the deep set of their eyes in common, as well as a certain sharpness about the ears that marked them as half-breeds.

"Where's Jill, anyway?" Salamander stopped fussing with the fire and came to sit down beside him.

"I don't know. Off meditating or whatever it is you sorcerers do, I suppose."

"Do I hear a sour note marring your dulcet tones? A touch of pique, a nettlement, if indeed such a word exists, a certain jealousy or resentment of our demanding craft, or mayhap a . . ."

"Will you hold your tongue, you chattering bastard?"

"Ah, I was right. I did."

At that moment Jill appeared on the other side of the fire. They were camped near a little copse, and in the uncertain light it seemed she materialized right out of the trees like one of the Wildfolk.

"You two look as startled as a pair of caught burglars. Talking about me?"

"Your ears were burning, were they?" Salamander said with a grin. "Actually, we were just wondering where you were, and lo, our question is answered, our difficulty solved. Come sit down."

Smiling, but only a little, Jill did so.

"We should be at the ruined dun on the morrow," she remarked. "That's where the others are meeting us. Do you remember it, Rhodry? The place where Lord Corbyn's men tried to trap you during that rebellion."

"Ye gods, that was years and years ago, but remember it I do, and that dun will always be dear to my heart, because it was there that I first saw you."

"You chatter like your wretched brother, don't you?" She got up and walked away, disappearing noiselessly back into the copse and gone.

Rhodry winced and stared into the fire.

"I think, O brother of mine, that there's somewhat you don't quite understand." Salamander paused for dramatic effect. "Jill's beyond you now. Beyond us both, truly, for I'll admit that there was a time or brief season in my life when I was madly in love with her myself—without the slightest result, let me hasten to add, but a cold and most cruel rejection, a sundering of my heart and the smashing to little bits of my hopes."

"Oh. Who is he, then?"

"Not who, O jealousy personified. What. The dweomer. It takes some people that way. Why, by every god in the sky, do you think she left you in the first place? Because a love of dweomer is a burning twice stronger than lust or even sentiment, which it ofttimes overpowers."

Rhodry and Jill had parted so long ago that Rhodry quite simply couldn't remember its details, but he could remember all too well his bitterness.

"I didn't understand then and I don't understand now, and cursed if I even want to."

"Then there's naught I can say about it, is there? But I warn you, don't let yourself fall in love with her again."

Rhodry merely shrugged, wondering if the warning were coming too late.

On the morrow morn they splashed across Y Brog and left the settled lands behind. All that day they rode through fallow grasslands, dotted here and there with copses or crossed with tiny streamlets; that night they camped in green emptiness. Yet early on the next day Rhodry saw rising on the horizon a broken tower, as lonely in the endless grass as a cairn marking a warrior's grave—which, he supposed, it might well have been.

"Did this dun fall to the sword?"

"I haven't the slightest idea," Jill said. "Calonderiel might know."

The elf in question, an old friend and a warleader among his people, was waiting for them near the empty gap in the outer walls that once had held wooden gates. They saw his horse first, a splendid golden gelding with a silvery mane and tail, tethered at his leisure out in the grass. Calonderiel himself was pacing idly back and forth in the ward, where grass grew round the last few cobbles and a profusion of ivy was sieging the broch itself. A tall man but slender, as most of his people were, the warleader had dark purple eyes, slit vertically like a cat's, moonbeam-pale hair, and, of course, ears as long and delicately pointed as a seashell.

"So there you are!" he sang out in Deverrian. "I thought Salamander had gone and gotten you all lost."

"Spare me the implied insults, if you please." Salamander made him a sketch of a bow. "You must have been talking with my father, if you'd think so ill of me. Which reminds me. Where is the esteemed parent? I thought he'd be eager for a first look at this other son of his."

"No doubt he will, when he finds out you've ridden west." Calonderiel turned to Rhodry. "My apologies, but Devaberiel's gone off north somewhere with one of the alarli. I've got my men out riding, passing the word along and looking for him. He'll turn up."

"Blast and curse it all!" Jill got in before Rhodry could say a word. "I wanted to speak with him before I rode on, and now I'll have to sit around here and wait."

"Impatient, isn't she?" Calonderiel was grinning. "You should be used to elven ways by now, Jill. Things happen when they happen, and not a moment before."

"Well," Rhodry said. "I'll admit to being a bit disappointed myself."

"And you must admit, Cal," Salamander broke in, "that my father can take his sweet time about things. He calls his progresses stately or measured; I call them dilatory, tardy, lackadaisical, or just plain slow."

"Well, you've got a point." The warleader glanced Jill's way. "Aderyn's at the encampment."

"That'll make the waiting easier, truly. How far away is everybody?"

Not very far at all, as it turned out. A couple of miles to the west the camp sprawled along a stream: some twenty brightly colored round tents, a vast herd of horses, a small flock of sheep, a neat stack of travois poles, all scattered through the tall grass in a tidy sort of confusion. As they rode up, a rush of children and dogs came yelling and yapping to meet them; about thirty adults strolled more slowly after.

Over the years Rhodry had picked up a fair amount of Elvish, more than enough to greet everyone and to understand the various speeches of welcome that came his way. He smiled and bowed and repeated names that he forgot a moment later. When Calonderiel insisted that the two brothers share his tent, there were plenty of willing hands to carry their gear and to take their horses. Skins of mead and bowls of food appeared as the camp settled in around the main fire for a celebration. Everyone wanted to meet Devaberiel's son and tell him about the major feast planned for the evening, too. In all the confusion it was some hours before Rhodry realized that he'd lost track of Jill.

About half a mile away from the main camp, Aderyn's weathered tent stood alone near a stand of willows at the stream edge. It was mercifully quiet there, except for the trill of birds in the willows. Jill tethered her horse out with Aderyn's small herd, then carried her gear round to the tent flap. Just as she was wondering whether to call out a greeting, the flap rustled open, and Aderyn's new apprentice, a pale-eyed young elf named Gavantar, crawled out. He was even more slender than most of his people, and pale-haired, too, so that Jill found herself thinking of him as more a spirit than a man. But his hands were strong enough as he snatched her burdens from her.

"Let me carry that gear for you, O Wise One of the East. You might have let me tend your horse."

"I'm not some withered old woman, lad, not yet, anyway. Is your master here?"

"Of course, and waiting for you."

Although the day was warm, the tent was dim and cool, the air sparkling from the rush and bustle of elemental spirits that always surrounded Aderyn. Wildfolk crouched or lounged all over the tent, sprawling on the floor, clinging to the walls, perching on the many-colored tent bags hanging from the poles. A small fire smoldered under the smoke hole in the center, and the dweomer-man himself was sitting cross-legged nearby on a pile of leather cushions. He was a small man, fully human, with enormous dark eyes in his slender, wrinkled face, and dead-white hair, which swept up from his forehead in two peaks like the horns of an owl. When he saw Jill, he grinned in honest delight and rose to catch her hands in his.

"Ah, it's good to see you in the actual flesh! Come sit down. Can I offer you some mead?"

"None for me, thanks. I don't have your head for the stuff. I wouldn't mind a cup of that spiced honey water the Westfolk make, though."

The apprentice put the saddlebags down and hurried out again, heading for the main camp to fetch a skin of the drink in question. Aderyn and Jill sat down facing each other, and she began pulling some cloth-wrapped bundles out of her gear. A gaggle of gnomes clustered round to watch, including the small gray fellow that followed Jill everywhere.

"Nevyn wanted you to have these books." She handed Aderyn a pair of ancient folios with crumbling leather bindings. "Though what you're going to do with a matched set of Prince Mael's writings, I don't know."

"Lug them around with all due honor and respect, I suppose. Actually, these particular volumes mean somewhat to me. The man who gave them to Nevyn was someone I much admired." He ran slender fingers over the stamped decorations, flecked here and there with the remains of gold leaf, a roundel enclosing a pair of grappling badgers, and under it a motto: "We hold on." "But fancy him remembering that, after all these years! I'm quite surprised that I do, actually."

"And here's a trinket from Brin Toraedic. He said to tell you that since it was older than both of you put together, it was a marvel indeed."

Aderyn laughed and held up the golden cup, made of beaten metal and decorated with a ridged pattern utterly unlike any made by human or elf. Jill found herself studying the old man; he seemed no older, no weaker than he ever had, but still she worried. He picked up her thought.

"My time won't be for a little while yet. I have Gavantar to train, and he's just begun his studies."

"Ah. I just . . . well, wondered."

"Things have been hard for you with Nevyn gone." It was not a question.

"They have. It's not just the missing of him, though that's bad enough. I feel so wretchedly inadequate, little more than an apprentice myself, truly, and not fit to be the Master of the Aethyr."

"Oh, here, we all go through that! You'll grow into the job. It's like becoming captain of a warband, I suppose. All that responsibility at first—why, it must overwhelm a man, thinking of all those lives that depend on his decisions."

"True-spoken. But I've got Nevyn's work to finish. I keep feeling that I've absolutely got to do it right for his sake."

"Wait a moment now! It's not his work, any more than it's your work. Don't let that kind of vanity enter in or you'll find yourself worrying indeed. It's all *our* work, and the work and will of the Great Ones. Think of it as an enormous tapestry. We each weave a little piece, what small amount we're capable of, then hand the grand design on to the next worker. No one soul could possibly finish the entire thing by himself."

"You're right enough, aren't you?" Jill smiled, feeling her dark mood lift. "I'll drink to that! Here comes your Gavantar now."

Carrying a leather bottle that was dripping wet and smelling of Bardek cinnamon and cloves, Gavantar ducked through the flap and joined them. Once the drink was poured round, he sat down by the door on guard, and with a shy duck of his head refused to move closer even when Aderyn invited him. He was new to the dweomer, Jill supposed, and still in awe of what he considered strange and mighty powers. Soon enough, when he came to see how natural in their way Aderyn's magicks were, he would begin to feel at ease.

"Is Rhodry still with Calonderiel?" she asked.

"He is, O Wise One. The whole camp wants to meet him."

"Good. Then he'll stay out of trouble for a few hours, anyway." She turned back to Aderyn. "Rhodry is one of the things that are vexing me."

"Ah. He's still in love with you?"

"That, too, I suppose, but that's not the important thing. I wonder what's going to happen to him now, mostly. No, I worry about him, worry badly. We've snatched him away from everything he knows and loves, which is harsh enough, and then beyond that, there's his Wyrd. For so long his whole life was ruled by that prophecy, and now he's fulfilled it, and well, what's going to become of him?"

"Prophecy?"

"The one Nevyn received all those years ago. Don't you remember it? Rhodry's Wyrd is Eldidd's Wyrd, it ran."

"Oh, that! Of course—he became gwerbret in the nick of time, didn't he?"

"You seem to take it all blasted lightly, but so he did. Look, there would have been a long and ghastly war in Eldidd if Rhodry hadn't been there to inherit the rhan."

Aderyn merely nodded. Jill supposed that he was so old, and had seen so many wars, that one more conflict would have meant nothing to him.

"And then there's the rose ring, too," she went on. "I've been vexing myself about that bit of jewelry for months now. That's why I want to talk to Devaberiel, you see, to ask him about it and that rather odd being who gave it to him. I'll wager he wasn't an ordinary elf."

"You're right about that." Aderyn's voice had gone tense and strange. "I've got my own ideas about who that mysterious benefactor was."

"I want to hear them. And what about that wretched inscription? If we knew what it meant, we might be able to unravel the entire mystery."

Although she was expecting him to tell her his ideas or at least acknowledge that she'd spoken, Aderyn sat for a long time merely staring out into space. At last, though, he spoke in a voice that was half a whisper, half a sigh.

"The ring—that cursed ring! Dwarven work, and it had a life of its own, just like their trinkets always do. Stranger than most, this one, and I'll wager its work isn't over yet." He shook his head, then went on in a normal voice. "But, oh yes, the prophecy . . . so a man of elven blood finally ruled in Eldidd! Fancy that!"

"Well, you know, his son has a good dollop of elven blood in his veins, too. Young Cullyn." Jill had to smile at his expression. "Here, Aderyn, you look shocked to the very heart!"

The old man shrugged and looked away, and at that moment the weight and sadness of all his long years seemed to press him down. Wildfolk clustered round, patting his hands, climbing into his lap, glaring at Jill as if accusing her of causing their friend pain. In spite of his shyness Gavantar inched himself closer, looking back and forth between the two masters of his craft with a worried little frown.

"Well, the land did belong to the People once," Jill went on. "I'd like to see them welcome there again. Or is it a wrong thing for men and elves to mix their blood like this?"

"Not in the least." Aderyn threw off the mood and half the Wildfolk with a shrug and a wave of one hand. "And it would be splendid, in my opinion, anyway, for the People to have some say in ruling Eldidd, too. It's just hard for me to believe when I remember some of the things that have happened over the years. There's been a lot of bad feeling, Jill, just a terrible lot of bad feeling between my two tribes. That's how I always think of elves and men, you see, as both mine now, though once, truly, I hated thinking that I might still be a human being. Of course, Rhodry's the one who's really caught between the two worlds, isn't he? It's not going to be easy for him, either. I can testify to that, from my own experience." He paused for a long moment. "Well, it's going to be much worse for him, truly. There are things that have happened to him in other lives that are bound to come to a head now. That's one reason I made sure to be here on the border when he came."

"Indeed? What sort of things?"

"Well, it's a long and winding tale, truly, and one that runs hundreds of years, all told, though I think me that we're about to get to the end of it at last. You do remember, don't you, that his soul in another body was my father?" The old man grinned. "If anyone can remember that far, way back in the mists of time when I was born."

Jill smiled with him, but she felt a touch of dweomer eerie run down her back. She had, after all, in another body been his mother. Aderyn was too courteous to mention the point.

"But Gweran—my father, that is, and Rhodry in another flesh —was the most human man I've ever seen."

"But he was a bard. You're forgetting that. There's a touch of . . . well, what? madness? the Wildlands? . . . somewhat strange and magical and crazed and inspired, all at once, in the soul of every bard."

"Well, so there is. I hadn't truly thought of it that way before. Wyrd and the tangles of Wyrd! They always say that no man can know the truth of it."

"Or woman either, but we've all got to try to untangle our own."

"Just so, and we were speaking of other people's work earlier, weren't we? But Rhodry might well be my work now—no need for you to bother and all—though I might end up needing your help one fine day. After Gweran died, I doubt me if you were involved in much of this." He thought hard, chin in hand. "You've always belonged to the human race, Jill, not to the Elcyion Lacar like I do —not that Rhodry's soul was ever supposed to be so mixed up with the elves, either, truly, bard or not. It's an odd thing, how tangled a man's Wyrd can become, and all through muddles and blunders. But you don't need to trouble your heart over it. Truly, I don't think you *were* involved, except in the most casual way."

And in spite of herself Jill was vexed that there was some deep part of Rhodry's soul and Rhodry's Wyrd that had nothing to do with her.

Part One

Deverry and Eldidd

718

IN THE COLD gray morning, when the mists rose from the surface of Loc Tamig, one could understand why the local farmers thought it haunted. All Aderyn could see of the lake surface was a few patches of rippled water, broken by a drowned tree and four steel-gray rocks, while on the far shore the pine-black mountains rose up in peaks and shadows. The sound of a hundred waterfalls chattered and murmured through the mists like spirit voices. At the moment, though, Aderyn was more worried about the coming rain than possible ghosts. He was, of course, still a young man then, with his hair a nondescript brown and always hanging in an untidy lock over his forehead rather than swept up in the owl shape it would later assume, and he was even skinnier, too, because half the time he forgot to eat when he was deep in his dweomer studies. That particular morning he was down on his knees in the tall spring grass, digging up valerian roots with a small silver spade.

Wildfolk clustered round to watch him work—two small gray gnomes, skinny and long-nosed, three blue-green sprites with pointed teeth and pretty faces. Just like children, they crowded close, pointed mute questions, and generally got in the way. Aderyn named everything they pointed at and worked fast with one eye on the lowering clouds. Just as he was finishing, a gnome picked up a clod and threw it at his fellow. Snarling and baring their teeth, the sprites joined in a full-scale dirt fight.

"Stop it! Your great lords would find this most discourteous!"

One sprite pinched him on the arm. All the Wildfolk vanished with little puffs of air and dust and a gust of smell like clean leaf mold. Aderyn gathered up his things and ran for shelter in the spattering rain. Down among a stand of trees was the round stone hut he shared with his master in the dweomercraft. Two years before, he and Nevyn had built the hut with their own hands and made a small stable for their horses and mules. Out in back was their garden, where practical beans and cabbages grew as well as exotic cultivated herbs, and a flock of chickens had their own little house. Most of their food, though, came from the farming villages at the north end of the lake, where the local people were glad to trade supplies for medicine.

When Aderyn dashed into the single round room, he found Nevyn sitting by the fire circle in the center and watching the play of flame. A tall man, with a thick thatch of white hair and deep-set blue eyes, Nevyn was close to a hundred years old, but he had more vigor than most men of twenty, a striding walk and the erect carriage of the great prince of the realm that once he had been.

"Back just in time, you are. Here comes the storm."

A gust of wind eddied smoke through the drafty hut as the drops began pattering on the roof. Nevyn got up and helped Aderyn lay the valerian to dry on clean cloths. The roots had to be sliced thin with a small silver knife, a nose-wrinkling smell, and they had to wear fine leather gloves, too, lest the strong juices poison them.

"Nevyn? Will we be leaving Loc Tamig soon?"

"You will."

Aderyn sat back on his heels and stared at him.

"It's time for you to go off on your own. I've taught you all I know, and your Wyrd runs different than mine."

Every though he'd always known this day would come, Aderyn felt close to tears. Nevyn laid down one last slice of root and turned to look at him, his piercing blue eyes unusually gentle.

"It'll ache my heart to see you go. I'll miss you, lad. But it's time. You've reached the third nine of your years now, and that age marks a turning point for everybody. Come now, you know it, too. You've got your herbcraft to feed and clothe yourself, and I've opened the gates of the dweomer for you as far as I can. Now you have to walk through those gates and take up your own Wyrd."

"But what will my Wyrd be?"

"Oh, that's not for me to say. No man can see another's Wyrd. You have the keys to open that door. It's time for you to work a ritual and use them. The Lords of Wyrd will reveal what you need to know—and not a jot more, doubtless."

On the morrow, when the rain stopped, Nevyn took his horse and two pack mules and rode off to the villages to buy food. He told Aderyn that he would stay away three days to leave him alone for the working, but as to what that working would be, he said nothing at all. Only then did the apprentice realize that the most important moment of his life was strictly in his own hands. He would have to draw on all his knowledge and practice to devise a ritual that would open his Wyrd and put him in contact, at least for a few brief moments, with his secret and undying soul, the true core of his being that had invented and formed the young man known as Aderyn for this lifetime the way a potter takes clay and makes a bowl. As he stood in the doorway and watched Nevyn ride away, Aderyn felt a panic tinged with excitement, an exultation touched with dread. It was time, and he felt ready.

That first day, while Aderyn did his usual chores in the garden and hut, he kept thinking about the task ahead. He had at his disposal a vast amount of ritual lore—tables of correspondences, salutations to the gods, invocations and mighty calls to the spirit world, signs, sigils, and gestures to set in motion streams of force and direct inner energies. In his excitement, his first thought was to use them all, or at least as many as possible, to create a ritual that would sum up and climax all rituals, as elaborately decorated, braided, laced, and spiraled as a beautiful brooch fit to give a king. While he weeded cabbages, his mind raced this way and that, adding a symbol here, a prayer there, trying to fit twenty years of work into a single mighty pattern. All at once he saw the irony: here he was, grubbing in the dirt like a bondsman and making grandiose plans. He laughed aloud and contemplated his mud-stained fingers, callused with years of menial work such as this. The Great Ones had always accepted his humble status and lowly sacrifices before. No doubt a simple ritual would be best now. With the insight came a feeling of peace, because he'd passed the first test.

But just as with a simple meal or a simple garden, every element would have to be perfect of its kind and perfectly placed. The second day, Aderyn worked furiously all morning to finish his chores by noon. He ate a light meal, then went outside to sit under a willow tree by the shore of the lake, sparkling in the soft spring sun. On the far shore the stony, hard mountains rose dark against a blue sky. He looked at them and thought over his lore, rigorously pruning instead of proliferating it. A simple approach to a central symbol—he looked at the peaks and smiled to himself. For the rest of the day he practiced every word and gesture he would use, mixing up the order so no true power would run through them. In the evening, by firelight he prepared his magical weapons—the wand, cup, dagger, and pentacle that he had made and con-secrated years before. He polished each one, then performed the simple rituals of consecration again to renew their power.

On the third day, he was quiet as he went through his work. His mind seemed as still as a deep-running river, only rarely dis-turbed by what most men would call a thought. Yet in his heart he renewed, over and over, the basic vows that open the secret of the dweomer: I want to know to help the world. He was remembering many things, sick children he'd helped heal, children who died because they were beyond the help of herbs, bent-back farmers who saw the best of their harvests taken by noble lords, the noble lords themselves, whose greed and power-lusts drove them like spurs and made them suffer, though they called the suffering glory. Someday, far in the future, at the end of the ages of ages, all this darkness would be transmuted into light. Until that end, he would fight the darkness where he found it. The first place he would always find darkness would be in his own soul. Until the light shone there, he could do little to help other souls. For the sake of that help, he begged for the light.

At sunset, he put his magical weapons in a plain cloth sack and set off for the shore of the lake. In the twilight, he made his place of working, not a rich temple glittering with golden signs and perfumed with incenses, but a stretch of grassy ground. He used the dagger to cut a circle deosil into the turf, then laid his cloth sack down for an altar in the middle. On the sack he laid the dagger, the wand, and the pentacle, then took the cup and filled it with lake water. He set the cup down among the other objects and knelt in front of the sack to face the mountains. Slowly the twilight deepened, then faded as the first few stars came out, only to fade in turn as the full moon rose, bloated and huge on a misty horizon. Aderyn sat back on his heels and raised his hands, palms flat upward, about shoulder high. As he concentrated his will, it seemed the moonlight streamed to him, tangible light for building. He thrust his hands forward and saw to the east of his rough altar two great pillars of light, one all pure moon-silver, the other as dark as black fire shining in the star-strewn night. When he lowered his hands, the pillars lived apart from his will. The temple was open.

One at a time, he picked up each weapon, the dagger for the east, the wand for the south, the cup for the west, and the pentacle for the north, and used it to trace at each cardinal point of the circle a five-pointed star. Above and below him he finished the sphere, using his human mind alone to trace the last two stars, the reconcilers of the others. When he knelt upon the ground, he saw the temple glowing with power beyond his ability to call it forth. The Lords of Light were coming to meet him. Aderyn rose and raised his hands to the east between the pillars. Utterly calm, his mind as sharp as the dagger's point and deep as the cup, he made light gather above him, then felt and saw it descend, piercing him through like an arrow and rooting itself in the ground. His arms flung out as he felt the cross shaft pierce him from side to side. It seemed he grew huge, towering through the universe, his head among the stars, his feet on a tiny whirling sphere of earth far below, enormous, exalted, but helpless, pinned to the cross of light, unmoving and spraddled, at the mercy of the Great Ones.

The voice came from everywhere and nowhere.

"Why do you want knowledge?"

"Only to serve. For myself, naught."

With a rush like cold wind, with a dizzying spin and fall, he felt himself shrink back until he stood on the damp grass and saw the temple around him, the pillars glowing, the magical weapons streaming borrowed light, the great pentangles pulsing at their stations. He nearly fell to his knees, but he steadied himself and raised his hands in front of him. In his mind he built up the vision between the pillars—a high mountain covered with dark trees and streaked with pale rock under a sunswept sky—until it lived apart from his mind and hung there like a painted screen. Calling on the Lords of Light, he walked forward and passed through the veil.

Pale sun glinted on flinty rock. The path wound steeply between dead shrubs, twisted through leafless trees, and over everything hung the choking smell of dust. Aderyn stumbled and bruised himself on rock, but he kept climbing, his lungs burning in the thin cold air. At last he reached the top, where huge boulders pushed out from gray soil like the bones of a long-dead animal. He was afraid. He had never expected this barrenness, this smell of death as thick as the dust. Although the wind was cold, he began to sweat in great drops down his back. It seemed that little eyes peered out at him from every rock; little voices snarled in cold laughter. He could feel their hatred as they watched him.

"Would you serve here?" the voice said.

Aderyn had to force the words from his lips.

"I will. I can see there's need of me."

There was a sound—three great claps of thunder booming among the dead rocks. As they died away, the eyes and the voices died with them. The mountaintop was lush with green grass; flowers grew, as vivid as jewels; the sun was warm.

"Look down," the voice said. "Look west."

Aderyn climbed to the top of a boulder and looked out, where it seemed the sun was setting on a smooth-flowing wide river. Oak forest stretched on the far bank.

"West. Your Wyrd lies west. Go there and heal. Go there and find those you will serve. Make restitution."

As Aderyn watched, the sun set over the river. The forest went dark, disappearing under vast shadows. Yet he could hear the water flowing. With a start he realized he was kneeling in the dew-soaked grass and hearing the hundred water-voices of Loc Tamig. In the west, the moon was setting. He rose and walked back between the pillars, then knelt again before the altar to raise his hands and prayed aloud in thanks to the Lords of Light. As he finished, the pillars disappeared, winking out like blown candles. He withdrew the five-pointed stars into himself and erased the magic circles.

"And any spirits bound by this ceremony, go free! It is over. It is finished."

From the lake came three hollow claps of thunder in answer. Aderyn stood and stamped three times upon the ground, then fell to his knees, sweating with exhaustion, trembling so hard from the spent forces that he could do nothing but kneel and shake until the first pale gray of dawn cracked in the east and brought him some of his strength back with the sunlight. He gathered up his magical weapons, put them in the sack, then rose to see Nevyn striding across the grass toward him.

"Oh, here! Have you been close by all this time?"

"Did you truly think I'd leave you to face this alone? You've done well, lad."

"I heard the voices of the Great Ones. I'll never forget this."

"Don't. It would go hard with you if you did. You've had your great vision, but there will be plenty of other little ones. Never forget this, either: you've just begun."

Aderyn slept all that day and through most of the night. When he woke, a few hours before dawn, he knew that the hour had come for him to leave. As he lay in darkness and considered routes west, he was calm, knowing, without knowing how he knew, that he would see Nevyn again, many times, no doubt, over the years ahead. His grief at leaving his beloved master was only another test; he'd had to believe that he would lose Nevyn in order to see if he would ride out even in grief. You're not an apprentice anymore, he thought, not a master, either, mind—but the journeyman is ready to go look for his work.

In the center of the hut, a fire flared, revealing Nevyn beside it.

"I figured you were awake," the old man said. "Shall we have one last meal together before you go?"

"We will. I know I don't need to, but I wish I could pour my heart out in thanks for all you've done for me."

"You were always a nicely spoken lad. Well, then, in thanks, do one last thing that I charge you: go say farewell to your family before you head west. I took you from them, after all, and I feel I should send you back one last time."

All of Aderyn's new confidence dissolved in a sudden stab of anxiety. Nevyn grinned at him as if he knew exactly what was happening.

"Oh, I'll do it!" Aderyn snapped. "But I'd hoped to spare them that."

"Spare yourself, you mean. And how can you handle the mighty forces of the universe if you can't even face your own father?"

After they ate, Aderyn saddled his riding horse and loaded up his mule. He had only a few things of his own—a bedroll, a spare shirt, a cloak, his magical weapons, the cooking pots and implements he needed for camping by the edge of the road—but he did have a great store of herbs, roots, salves, and other such medicines, all of which needed to be carefully stowed in the canvas panniers. Nevyn also insisted on dividing their small store of coins and giving him half.

"You've earned it as much as I have. Ride out in the light. We'll meet again one of these days, and if the need is great, we can scry each other out through the fire."

"Well, so we can." Aderyn felt a definite lump in his throat. "But I'll miss you anyway."

As he rode out, leading his mule, Aderyn turned in the saddle and looked back. Nevyn was standing by the door of the hut and watching. He waved once, then turned back inside.

On a day warm with the promise of coming summer, Aderyn reached the village of Blaeddbyr and Lord Maroic's dun, where his father, Gweran the bard, served the White Wolf clan and where Aderyn had been born and raised. To his surprise, the ward and the familiar buildings seemed much smaller than he'd remembered them. Near the broch tower he dismounted and looked round the dusty ward. A few curious servants stopped to look him over; a couple of the riders came strolling over as if to ask him his business there. All at once he heard a woman's voice.

"Ado, Ado, thank the gods!"

It was his mother, Lyssa, laughing and weeping at the same time as she threw herself into his arms. Close to tears himself, Aderyn hugged her tight, then set his hands on her shoulders and smiled at her. She'd grown stout but was still beautiful, her raven-dark hair barely touched with gray, her wide blue eyes bright, her cheeks barely marked with wrinkles.

"It's so good to see you," Lyssa said. "Truly, I was wondering if we would ever see you again. Can you stay with us a while?"

"I will, if Lord Maroic allows. But, Mam, this is the last visit I'll ever make. I want you to know that now."

Lyssa caught her breath sharply, but he knew there would be no tears or recriminations. In a sweep of laughter, the rest of his family came running from the broch and clustered around him— his younger brother, Acern, training to take his father's place as bard, his sister, Araena, married to the captain of Maroic's guard and with a baby of her own, and finally his father, Gweran, as tall and imposing as always with his blond hair heavily laced with silver. In a chattering crowd they escorted him inside, where the aging Lord Maroic rose from his carved chair and announced that Aderyn was going to take his meat and mead for as long as he wanted to stay. The dailiness, the cheer, the mundanity of the visit broke over Aderyn like a wave, as if the dweomer were only some dream he'd once had. Being surrounded by his family made him realize why he had a lonely road ahead: the strange lore that mattered to him could never be shared. It set him apart like walls even as he talked and gossiped and shared heavy meal after heavy meal with them all in the long drowsy days of his visit.

Gweran went out of his way to spend time with Aderyn, much more than usual. Aderyn supposed that Lyssa had told him that his firstborn son would never ride home again. She'd always been the link between them, keeping them at peace, telling them things that they could never voice themselves. There was good reason for their distance. Looking at his father's silvery hair, his straight, almost regal bearing, his rich clothing that he wore like the honor it was, Aderyn found it hard to remember that Gweran was a murderer who had used the very law itself as a weapon. At times he wondered if Gweran even remembered the young rider, Tanyc, whom he'd so cleverly trapped twenty years before. Perhaps he did, because even though their talks rambled through Aderyn's childhood, every time they came close to Aderyn's seventh year, when the murder had happened, Gweran would shy away and find a distant topic to discuss. Aderyn was more than willing to let the subject stay closed. Even though he'd only been a child and spoken in all innocence, still he felt he shared his father's blood guilt. Seven years old or not, he'd blurted out the information that had sent Gweran hunting revenge. "Tanyc's always looking at Mam, Da." Even at this lapse of years, he could hear his small boy's voice pronouncing an unwitting death sentence.

Since he'd done much meditation work to heal that old wound, Aderyn was surprised the way the murder rose to haunt him. Doubtless it came from being in the dun, whose walls had once displayed his private horror. He remembered it vividly: climbing out of bed on a sunny morning, throwing open the shutters at the window, and seeing, just down below his tower room, Tanyc's body hanging by the neck from the ramparts. He was bound hand and foot, his head flopping like a rag doll's, and already the ravens were wheeling in the sky. Aderyn could only think there'd been some ghastly accident. He started screaming for his mother, who ran to him, looked out the window, and in a moment of horrified honesty, blurted out, "Your da's killed him!" Later, she tried to recant, but by then Aderyn knew that his father had goaded the young warrior into drawing a sword against him, a bard, a capital crime under Deverry laws. In his child's way, he knew his mother had told him the truth that first time.

Aderyn wondered if Lyssa felt she shared their guilt. After all, Gweran and Tanyc had been fighting over her. During the visit, Lyssa said little, merely listened to him and his father talk while she watched Gweran with a patient devotion. Her man was a good husband who still loved her; he was famous, with young disciples clamoring to study with him; his skill kept her in comfort. Perhaps she'd carefully forgotten that he'd murdered a man for her sake. Perhaps.

On the last day of the visit, Aderyn and Lyssa walked down to the Nerraver as they'd so often done when he was a child. The river ran full between lush green banks and sparkled in the sun with little fish-scale ripples of silver. When they sat down for a rest, Lyssa hunted through the grass and picked a few daisies like a young girl.

"Ado? Do you remember the year of the Great Drought?"

"I do." That was the year of the murder, too. "Did you know it was Nevyn's dweomer that set it right?"

"Of course. It was one reason I let you go as his apprentice."

"And do you regret that decision now?"

"Well." Lyssa looked at her daisies. "If a mother is any kind of mother at all, she knows her sons will leave her. I have your sister and her babies nearby."

"Well and good, but, Mam, truly I'll miss you."

Lyssa shrugged, turning the flowers this way and that between her fingers, fighting to keep back tears.

"Do you think you'll ever marry on this strange road of yours?" she said at last.

"I doubt it. It wouldn't be much of a life for a woman, living out of a mule's pack and sleeping by the road."

"True enough, but here—don't tell me the dweomer lets a man carry on with tavern lasses and suchlike."

KATHARINE KERR

"It doesn't, but then I've got no intentions of doing anything of the sort."

Lyssa considered him, her head a bit to one side.

"You don't care much for women, do you, Ado?"

"Care? Of course I do. Truly, Mam, I prefer their company and talk to that of men most of the time."

"That's not what I meant."

When he understood, Aderyn felt distinctly squeamish—after all, she was his mother.

"Well, I don't, not in that way. But, Mam, don't trouble your heart over it. I don't care for other lads or suchlike."

"That wouldn't have bothered me. It's just that I've always felt you didn't have much of a taste for that sort of thing with anyone. Do you feel you can't trust us women?"

"And why would you think that?"

"Oh, you saw a bit too much, maybe, when you were a lad."

Aderyn hesitated, then decided it was time for the truth.

"You mean Tanyc."

"Just that." Lyssa was studying the daisies. "He died because of me, no matter whose fault it was." She looked up sharply. "I'll swear it to you, Ado. I never gave him a word of hope or encouragement."

"I never thought you did. But it's not that, Mam. It's the dweomer. It's taken my whole life. Everything I would have given to a woman I've spent on the dweomer, heart and soul both."

Lyssa sighed in honest relief, as if she'd been blaming herself for her son's celibacy. Later, when he was alone, Aderyn wondered if in one way her fear was justified. He'd never blamed her, the woman in the case, for one wrong thing, but the murder had left him with doubts about being a man. To become obsessed with a woman the way Tanyc was seemed to lead to death; to love a woman the way his father did seemed to tempt crime. He decided that he'd better meditate on the subject and untangle this knot in his mind. It might interfere with his work.

All that summer, Aderyn made his way west, going from village to village, supporting himself nicely by selling his herbs—or

50

nicely by his standards, since he was content with two spare meals a day and the occasional tankard of ale in a clean tavern. At times he settled for a week or two to gather fresh herbs or to tend to some long illness, but always he moved on, leaving grateful farmers and villagers behind. Every night when he performed his ritual meditations, he would brood on his Wyrd and wonder where it lay. Gradually his intuition grew that he should turn southwest in his wanderings, but no other signs or hints came to him, at least not in any simple way. When the first clue was given, it took him a long time to unravel it.

Near the western border of the kingdom was one last river, the Vicaver, where Aderyn went simply to take a look at it. Rather than the oak forests of his visions, however, he found the river bordered by farms, pastures, and the occasional stand of willow trees. Aderyn crossed it and rode to the village of Ladotyn, a straggle of some fifty houses scattered among poplar trees, though it did have a proper inn. The innkeeper told him that they got merchant caravans coming through the town, on their way to and from the kingdom of Eldidd to the west.

"And if you're thinking of riding west through those mountains, good sir, you'd best see if you can join some other travelers. Those louse-ridden savages up in the hills are always causing trouble."

"Well, I don't intend to stay here all winter, caravan or no."

"It's your burying, not mine—well, if you even get a burial in the ground and not in their stomachs, if you take my meaning, like."

Although a caravan did indeed appear at the inn, it turned out that it was coming home to Deverry from Eldidd, and the caravan master, Lillyc, doubted very much if Aderyn would see one going the opposite way so late in the season. As they stood talking together out in the innyard, Lillyc remarked that he'd been trading in some towns that lay on a river called the El.

"Now that's a strange name," Aderyn remarked. "I don't think I've ever heard it before."

"No doubt." Lillyc gave him the grin of a man with a secret

joke. "It's not a Deverry word, nor an Eldidd one, either. The name comes from the Westfolk. They live off to the west of Eldidd, you see. Used to range farther east, but now the place is getting properly settled."

"Indeed? Are they some of the Old Ones, then?"

"If you mean the squinty-eyed, dark-haired bondsfolk, that they aren't. Oh, the Westfolk are a different lot altogether, and a strange bunch. They won't settle in proper farms and towns. They wander around with their horses and sheep, just where the fancy takes them." Lillyc paused for a small frown. "But they've helped me and many a merchant make his fortune. They love iron goods —can't work the stuff themselves, I suppose. How could you, riding around with never a proper forge? They trade us horses. Look."

At that moment one of Lillyc's men walked by leading a pair of the most beautiful horses Aderyn had ever seen. They were both mares, but they stood sixteen hands easily, and their wide, deep chests and slender legs bespoke good wind and good speed both. The most amazing thing, however, was their color, a dark rich gold like fresh clay dug from a riverbank while their manes and tails were as silvery pale as moonbeams.

"Gorgeous, good sir!" Aderyn said. "I'll wager any noble lord in Deverry would give you a small fortune for breeding stock like that."

"Just so, just so. But I had to spend most of a small fortune to get them, let me tell you."

A strange folk, then, these Westfolk, and perhaps with strange lore to match. The very thought made a cold shudder run down Aderyn's back as he wondered if they were in some way linked to his Wyrd.

"Here, I'm determined to go west. Think the weather will hold up in the mountains for a few more weeks?"

"It's not the weather you've got to worry about, it's the savages. If I were you, lad, I'd wait. A herbman's a valuable sort of man to have around. We'd all hate to lose you, like."

Aderyn merely smiled. Waiting was not one of his strong points.

Since he was going to be traveling farther than he'd previously planned, Aderyn decided that he'd best consult with Nevyn. That night, he went up to his chamber and built himself a small fire in the hearth. When he called upon his old master, the image built up fast, Nevyn's face floating in the flames and scowling at him.

"So, you deigned to contact me, did you? I've been worrying myself sick."

"My humble apologies, but truly, everything's been fine."

"Good. Well, now that you've made the first link, I can contact you again without wounding your dignity, I suppose, but kindly don't let me brood about you for months at a time, will you?"

"Of course not. And you have my heartfelt apologies."

"That's enough humility for now, please. What have you been doing with yourself?"

Aderyn told him what little there was of interest in his summer's wanderings, then turned to his plan of traveling to Eldidd. As the old intimacy between them reestablished itself, Nevyn's image grew in the fire, until it seemed that they were standing face to face, meeting in gray void swirled with violet mists.

"Well, it seems that Eldidd would be as good a place to go as any," Nevyn said at last.

"Do you know of any others of our kind there?"

"I don't, but that doesn't mean there aren't any. Keep your eyes open, lad, and see what you find. Remember what I've always told you: in these things, there's no need for hurry."

"What do you think about this strange tribe, the Westfolk?"

"Very little, because I've never heard of them before. If naught else, this is all very interesting."

At that time Eldidd was an independent kingdom, whose rulers were ultimately descended from the legendary warriors known as the Hippogriff and the Dragon, the two foster brothers of King Bran himself who joined him for the Great Migration. In the year 297, after a bitter struggle over the kingship of Deverry, Cynaeval and Cynvaenan, their descendants and the current leaders of the two clans of the Dragon and the Hippogriff, with all their allies, kinsmen, supporters, and dependents, left Deverry to sail west and found their own throne and royal city. For years, the small colonies eked out a precarious existence along the seacoast, but in time the Hippogriff's people flourished and spread up the great river valleys of the Dilbrae and the El, while the Dragon clan spread north from their town of Aberwyn up the Gwyn and the strangely named Delonderiel. In the year when Aderyn crossed the mountains of the Belaegyrys range into Eldidd, the kingdom boasted a respectable two hundred thousand people.

Because he needed to gather more medicines, Aderyn avoided the sandy coast road and chose the easy northern pass through the mountains. On the western side, he reached rolling hills, brown and scruffy with frostbitten grass, and there he stumbled upon a tiny village in a secluded valley. The small square huts, roofed with dirty thatch, were made of rough-hewn wood packed with mud to keep out the chill. Grazing on the brown and stubbled grass were goats and a few cows. The village belonged to some of the Old Ones, those unfortunate folk who'd lived in the land before the bloodthirsty Deverrians had ridden their way to seize it from them. Dark-haired, on the slender side, they had their own immensely complex language, or rather a mutually incomprehensible group of them, which in the settled parts of Deverry and Eldidd were forbidden by the laws of their conquerors but were kept alive by stealth. When Aderyn rode up to the huts, the folk came running out to stare at him and his fine horse and mule. In a group, the eight men of the village advanced upon him with their rough spears at the ready, but when Aderyn spoke in their language and explained that he was a herbman, they lowered the weapons. Dressed in a long brown tunic, a man of about forty stepped forward and introduced himself as Wargal, the headman.

"You'll forgive our greeting, but we have great reason to fear these days."

"Indeed? Are the men of Eldidd close by?"

"The despicable blue-eyed ones are always too close by."

For a moment they contemplated each other in an uneasy silence. Wargal's eyes flicked back and forth between his folk and the stranger. He had a secret, Aderyn supposed, and he could guess it: the village was sheltering a runaway bondsman.

"Are there any sick in your village?" Aderyn said. "I have many herbs, and I'll gladly help anyone who needs them in return for some fresh milk and a night's shelter."

"Any stranger is welcome to milk from my flock. But if you can spare some medicine, one of our women has a bad case of boils."

The villagers tended Aderyn's horse and mule while Wargal took him to his own home, which had no furniture except for three big pottery jars near the tiny hearth and the straw mattress he shared with his wife. Hanging on the wall were a few bronze pots, a couple of knives of the same metal, and some rough cloth sacks. Aderyn sat down next to Wargal in the place of honor by the hearth while villagers crowded in for a look at this amazing event, a stranger in their village. After some polite conversation over bowls of goat's milk, the woman with boils was duly treated in the midst of the curious crowd. Other villagers came forward to look over the herbs and ask shy questions, but most were beyond his help, because the real plague in this village was malnutrition. Driven by fear of the Eldidd lords, they eked out a miserable living on land so poor that no one else wanted it.

Although Aderyn would have preferred to eat his own food and spare theirs, Wargal insisted that he join him and his wife in their dinner of goat's-milk cheese and thin cracker bread.

"I'm surprised you don't have your winter crops in yet," Aderyn remarked.

"Well, we won't be here to harvest them. We had a long council a few days ago, and we're going to move north. The cursed Blue-eyes get closer every day. What if one of their headmen decides to build one of those forts along the road?"

"And decides you should be slaves to farm for him? Leaving's the wise thing to do."

"There's plenty of open land farther north, I suppose. Ah, it's so hard to leave the pastures of your ancestors! There's a god in the spring nearby, too, and I only hope he won't be angry with us for leaving him." He hesitated for a moment. "We thought of leaving last spring, but it was too much of a wrench, especially for the women. Now we have another reason."

"Indeed?"

Wargal considered him, studying Aderyn's face in the flickering firelight.

"You seem like a good man," Wargal said at last. "I don't suppose you have any herbs to take a brand off a man's face?"

"I only wish I did. If you're harboring a runaway, you'd best move fast in case his lord comes looking for him."

"So I told the others. We were thinking of packing tomorrow." Wargal glanced around the hut. "We don't have much to pack or much to lose by leaving—well, except the god in the spring, of course."

Aderyn felt a sudden cold shudder of dweomer down his back. His words burned in his mouth, an undeniable warning that forced itself into sound.

"You *must* leave tomorrow. Please, believe me—I have magic, and you must leave tomorrow and travel as fast as you can. I'll come with you on the road a ways."

His face pale, Wargal stared at him, then crossed two fingers to ward off the evil eye, in case Aderyn had that, too.

On the morrow, leaving took far longer than Aderyn wanted. Although the village's few possessions were easily packed onto bovine and human backs, the goats had to be rounded up. Finally a ragged group of refugees, about eight families with some twenty children among them, the cows, the herd of goats, and six little brown dogs to keep the stock in line, went to the holy spring and made one last sacrifice of cheese to the god while Aderyn kept a fretful watch on the path behind them. By the time they moved out of the valley, it was well after noon, and the smaller children were already tired and crying from the smell of trouble in the air. Aderyn piled the littlest ones into his saddle and walked, leading the horse. Wargal and a young man, Ibretin, fell in beside him. On Ibretin's cheek was the brand that marked him as a lord's property.

"If you think they'll catch us, O Wise One," Ibretin said to Aderyn. "I'll go back and let them kill me. If they find us, they'll take the whole tribe back with them."

"There's no need for that yet," Wargal snapped.

"There never will be if I can help it," Aderyn said. "I'd be twice cursed before I'd let a man be killed for taking the freedom that the gods gave him. I think my magic might make us harder to find."

Both men smiled, reassured by Aderyn's lie. Although he could control his aura well enough to pass unnoticed and thus practically invisible, Aderyn couldn't make an entire village disappear.

For two days they went north, keeping to the rolling hills and making a bare twelve miles a day. The more Aderyn opened his mind to the omens, the more clearly he knew that they were being pursued. On the third night, he scried into a campfire and saw the ruins of the old village, burned to the ground. Only a lord's warband would have destroyed it, and that warband would have to be blind to miss the trail of so many goats and people. He left the campfire and went to look for Ibretin, who was taking his turn at watching the goats out in the pasture.

"You've called me Wise One. Do you truly think I have magic?"

"I can only hope so. Wargal thinks so."

It was too dark under the starry sky to see Ibretin's face. Aderyn raised his hand and made the blue light gather in his fingers like a cool-burning torch. Ibretin gasped aloud and stepped back.

"Now you know instead of hoping. Listen, the men chasing you are close by. Sooner or later, they'll catch us. You offered to die to save your friends. How about helping me with a little scheme instead?"

At dawn on the morrow, while Wargal rounded up the villagers and got them moving north, Aderyn and Ibretin headed south. Although Aderyn rode, he had Ibretin walk, leading his pack mule as if they'd been traveling together for some time as servant and master. About an hour's ride brought them to the inevitable warband. They were just breaking their night's camp, the horses saddled and ready to ride, the men standing idly around waiting for their lord's orders. The lord himself, a tall young man in blue-and-gray-plaid brigga, with oak leaves embroidered as a blazon on his shirt, was kicking dirt over a dying campfire. When Aderyn and Ibretin came up, the men shouted, running to gather round them. Aderyn could see Ibretin shaking in terror.

"Oh, here," a man called out. "This peddler's found our flown chicken! Lord Degedd will reward you for this, my friend."

"Indeed?" Aderyn said. "Well, I'm not sure I want a reward."

With a signal to Ibretin to stay well back, Aderyn swung down from his horse just as Degedd came pushing his way through his men. Aderyn made a bow to him, which the lord acknowledged with a brief nod.

"I've indeed found your runaway bondsman, but I want to buy him from you, my lord. He's a useful man with a mule, and I need a servant."

Caught utterly off guard, Degedd stared for a moment, then blinked and rubbed his chin with his hand.

"I'm not sure I want to sell. I'd rather have the fun of taking the skin off his cursed back."

"That would be a most unwise pleasure."

"And who are you to tell me what to do?"

Since Aderyn was not very tall, the lord towered over him with six feet of solid muscle. Aderyn set his hands on his hips and looked up at him.

"Your men called me a peddler, but I'm nothing of the sort. I'm a herbman, traveling in your country, and one who knows the laws of the gods. Do you care to question me further?"

"I do. I don't give a pig's fart whether you're a learned man or not, and anyway, for all I know, you lie."

"Then let me give you a sample of my learning. Enslaving free men to work your land is an impious thing. The gods have decreed that only criminals and debtors shall be bondsmen. That law held for a thousand years, back in the Homeland, and it held for hundreds here, until greedy men like you chose to break it."

When his men began muttering, shamefaced among themselves at the truth of the herbman's words, the lord's face turned purple with rage. He drew his sword, the steel glittering in the sun.

"Hold your ugly lying tongue and give me back that bondsman! Be on your way or die right here, you scholarly swine!"

With a gentle smile, Aderyn raised his hand and called upon the spirits of fire. They came, bursting into manifestation with a roar and crackle of bright flame on the sword blade. Howling, Degedd struggled to hold on to the hilt, then cursed and flung the flesh-branding metal to the ground. Aderyn turned the flames to illusions and swung around, scattering bright but harmless blue fire into the warband. Yelling, shoving each other, they fell back and ran away to let their lord face Aderyn alone.

"Now then, I'll give you two copper pieces for him. That's a generous price, my lord."

His face dead white, Degedd tried to speak, failed, then simply nodded his agreement. Aderyn untied his coin pouch and counted the coppers into the lord's broad but shaking left hand, as the right seemed to pain him.

"Your chamberlain will doubtless think you've made a fine bargain. And, of course, if you and your men return straight to your lands, there's no need for anyone to ever hear this tale."

Degedd forced out a tight sour smile. Doubtless he didn't care to be mocked in every tavern in Eldidd by the story of how one herbman had bested him on the road, especially since no one would believe that the herbman had done it with magic. With a cheery wave, Aderyn mounted his horse and rode away, with Ibretin and the mule hurrying after. About a mile on, they looked back to see Lord Degedd and his warband trotting fast—away back south. Aderyn tested the dweomer warnings and felt that indeed, all danger was over. At that he laughed aloud.

"If nothing else," he told Ibretin, "that was the best jest I've had in a long time."

Ibretin tried to smile but burst into tears instead. He wept all the way back.

That night there was as much of a celebration in the camp as their meager provisions would allow. Aderyn sat at the biggest fire with Wargal and his wife while the rest of the villagers squatted close by and stared at him as if he were a god.

"We have to let the goats rest a day or they'll stop giving milk," Wargal said. "Is that safe, Wise One?"

"Oh, I think so. But you'd best travel a long ways north before you find a place to settle down."

"We intend to. We were hoping you'd come with us."

"I will for a while, but my destiny lies in the west, and I have to go where my magic tells me."

After three more days of slow, straggling marching, the luck of Wargal's tribe turned for the better. One afternoon they crested a high hill to see huts of their own kind spread out along a stream, prosperous fields, and pastures full of goats. When they came up to the village, the folk ran to meet them. There were only seven huts in the village, but land enough for many families. After a hasty tribal council, their headman, Ufel, told Wargal that he and his folk were welcome to settle there if they chose.

"The more of us, the better," Ufel said. "Our young men are learning a thing or two from the cursed Blue-eyes. Someday we'll fight and keep our lands."

Wargal tossed back his head and howled a war cry.

Their journey over, the refugees camped that night along the streambank. The villagers brought food and settled in for talks to get to know their new neighbors. At Ufel the headman's fire, Wargal and Aderyn drank thin beer from wooden cups.

"I take it your folk have lived here for some time," Aderyn said. "May you always live in peace."

"So I hope. We have a powerful god in our valley, and so far he's protected us. If you'd like, I'll show you his tree on the morrow."

"My thanks, I would." Aderyn had a cautious sip of the beer and found it suitably weak. "I don't suppose any of the Blue-eyes live near you?"

"They don't. And I pray that our god will always keep them away. Very few folk of any kind come through here—one of the People every now and then, that's all."

"The who?"

"The People. The Blue-eyes call them the Westfolk, but their own name for themselves is the People. We don't see many of them anymore. When I was a little child, they brought their horses through every now and then, but not recently. Probably the demon-spawn Blue-eyes have tried to enslave them, too, but I'm willing to bet that they found it a very hard job."

"From what I've heard, the Eldidd men have some kind of trade with them—iron goods for horses."

"Iron goods? The idiot Blue-eyes give the People iron?" Ufel rose and paced a few steps away from the fire. "Trouble and twice trouble over that, then!"

"What? I don't understand. The Westfolk seem to want the iron and . . ."

"I can't explain. For a Blue-eye you're a good man, but telling you would be breaking geis."

"Never would I ask you to do such a thing. I'll say no more about it."

On the morrow, Aderyn rose before dawn and slipped away before the village was truly awake to spare everyone a sad farewell. He followed an ancient trail that wound through the barren pine-stubbled mountains without seeing a soul, either good or bad, until he rejoined the road. Even though the fields were plowed and ready for the fall planting, and orchards stood along the road, the houses were few and far between, and villages rare, unlike in Deverry. As he came closer to the river El, the real spine of the country, the houses grew thicker, clustering in proper villages.

Finally, after six days on the road, he reached Elrydd, a proper town where he found an inn, not a cheap place, but it was clean, with fresh straw on the tavern-room floor.

Aderyn paid over a few of his precious coins for the lodging, then stowed his gear in a wedge-shaped chamber on the upper story. The innkeep, Wenlyn, served a generous dinner of thick beef stew and fresh bread, topped off with apple slices in honey. He also knew of the Westfolk.

"A strange tongue they speak. Break your jaw, it would. A jolly sort of folk, good with a jest, but when they come through here, they don't stay at my inn. Don't trust 'em, I don't. They steal, I'm cursed sure of it, and lie all the time. Can't trust people who won't stay put in proper villages. Why are they always riding on if they don't have somewhat to hide, eh?" Wenlyn paused to refill Aderyn's tankard. "And they've got no honor around women. Why, there's a lass in our very own town who's got a bastard by one of them."

"Now here, plenty of Eldidd men sire bastards, too. Don't judge the whole herd by one horse."

"Easy enough to say, good sir, and doubtless wise. But there's just somewhat about these lads. The lasses go for them like cats do for catmint, I swear it. Makes a man nervous, it does, wondering what the lasses see in a bunch of foreigners. Huh. Women have got no sense, and that's all there is to that."

Aderyn smiled in bare politeness while Wenlyn sucked his teeth and sighed for the folly of lasses.

"Tell me, good sir," Aderyn said at last. "If I ride straight west on the king's road, will I eventually meet up with some of these folk?"

"Oh, no doubt, but what do you want to do that for? If you do, be cursed careful of your mule and horse. They might take a fancy to them, like. But as to where, let's think—never been there my-self—but Cernmeton, that region, that's where our merchants go to trade."

"My thanks. I'll be leaving on the morrow, then. I've just got a fancy to take a look at these folk."

Wenlyn stared at him as if he were daft, then left Aderyn to finish his meal in peace. As he sopped up the last of his stew with a bit of bread, Aderyn was wondering at himself. He felt something calling him west, and he knew he'd better hurry.

Out on the grasslands the seasons change more slowly than they do in the mountains. At about the time when Aderyn was seeing omens of autumn up in the Eldidd hills, far to the west the golden sunlight still lay hazy on the endless-seeming expanse of green. When the alar rode past a small copse of alders clustered around a spring, the trees stood motionless and dusty in the windless heat, as if summer would linger there forever. Dallandra turned in her saddle and looked at Nananna, riding beside her on a golden gelding with a white mane and tail. The elder elven woman seemed exhausted, her face as pale as parchment under her crown of white braids, her wrinkled lids drooping over her violet eyes.

"Do you want to rest at the spring, Wise One?"

"No need, child. I can wait till we reach the stream."

"If you're sure—"

"Now don't fuss over me! I may be old, but I still have the wit to tell you if I need to rest."

Riding straight in the saddle for all her five hundred years, Nananna slapped her horse with the reins and pulled a little ahead. With her second sight, Dallandra could see the energy pouring around her, great silver streams and pulses in her aura, almost too much power for her frail body to bear. Soon Nananna would have to die. Every day Dallandra's heart ached at the thought of losing her mistress in the craft of magic, but there was no denying the truth.

Their companions followed automatically as they rode on. Earlier that morning, their alar had hurried ahead with the flocks and herds and left them a small escort of others who needed to move slowly. Enabrilia came first, leading the packhorse that dragged the heavy wooden travois with the tents. Her husband, Wylenteriel, their baby in a leather pack on his back, rode some distance behind and kept the brood mares with their young colts moving at a slow but steady pace. His brother, Talbrennon, rode point off to one side. In the middle of the afternoon Nananna finally admitted that she was tired, and they made camp near a scattering of willow trees. Normally, since they were only stopping for one night, they wouldn't have bothered to unpack the tents, but Dallandra wanted to raise one for Nananna.

"No need," Nananna said.

"Now here, Wise One," Wylenteriel said. "Me and Tal can have it up in no time at all."

"Oh, children, children, it's not time for me to leave you yet, and when it's time, you can fuss all you like, but it won't give me one extra hour."

"I know that's true," Dallandra said. "But—"

"No buts, child. If you know it, act on it."

Wylenteriel, however, insisted on a compromise: he and Tal set up a small lean-to keep the night damp off and unpacked cushions from the travois to lay on the canvas ground cloth. Dallandra helped Nananna settle herself, then knelt and pulled off the old woman's boots. Nananna watched with a faint smile, her thin, gnarled hands resting on her frail knees.

"I'll admit I could use a bit of a nap before dinner."

Dallandra covered her with a light blanket, then went to help set up the camp. The men were already watering the horses at the stream; Enabrilia was sitting on the ground by a pile of dumped gear and nursing Farendar, who whimpered and fussed at her breast. He was only a year old, still practically a newborn by elven standards. Dallandra wandered downstream, driven by a sudden stab of omens. Even in the bright sunlight she felt cold, knowing that warnings were trying to reach her like slivers of ice piercing the edge of her mind, an image of winter, when something would tear her life in half and change her irrevocably. Nananna's death, probably. With a shudder she ran back to the safe company of friends.

That night, while the others sat around a small campfire, Dallandra went to the lean-to. Nananna made a large ball of golden light and hung it on the ridgepole, then rummaged through her saddlebags for the small silver casket that guarded her scrying stones. There were five of these jewels, each set in a small silver disk graved with symbols: ruby for fire, topaz for air, sapphire for water, emerald for earth, and finally, the largest of them all, an amethyst for aethyr. Nananna laid the disks on a cushion and frowned at them for a moment.

"I had a dream while I was napping, and I need to see a bit more. Hum, the amethyst will do."

Carefully Nananna wrapped the other jewels up in bits of fine silk cloth, then laid the amethyst disk in the palm of her right hand. Dallandra knelt beside her and looked into the stone, where a small beam of light gleamed in the dead center, then swelled to a smoky void—or so it seemed to Dallandra. Nananna, however, watched intently, nodding her head every now and then at some detail. Finally she spoke the ritual word that cleared the stone of vision.

"Now that's interesting," Nananna said. "What do you think of it?"

"Nothing. I couldn't see."

"A man of magic is coming to us from the east. His destiny lies here, and I'm to take him in."

"Not one of those smelly Round-ears?"

"Any man who serves the Light is welcome in my tent."

"Of course, Wise One, but I didn't think a Round-ear would have the wits for magic."

"Now, now! Harsh words and prejudice don't suit a student of the Light."

"I'm sorry."

"I don't like the Round-ears much either, mind. But I'm trying. Do your best to try, too."

In the middle of the next afternoon, they rode into the alardan, the great camp where the People meet at the end of the summer after a long season's wandering with their flocks and herds. That year the banadars of the scattered tribes had chosen the Lake of the Leaping Trout, the most southerly of a chain of lakes along a wide river which the Eldidd men, with a characteristic lack of imagination, called simply Aver Peddroloc, the four-lake river. To the south stood a vast oak forest, tangled and primeval, that was a burying ground held sacred by the People for a thousand years. From the north shore spread an open meadow, where now hundreds of brightly painted tents rose like flowers in the grass. Out beyond were flocks of sheep and herds of horses, watched over by a ring of horsemen.

As their little group rode up, Talbrennon peeled off to drive their stock into the communal herds. Dallandra led the others down to the lakeshore and found an open spot to set up camp. As they dismounted, ten men came running to do the heavy work for the Wise One and her apprentice. Dallandra led Nananna away from the bustle and helped her sit down in the grass, where Enabrilia and the baby joined them. Farendar was awake, looking up at his mother with a wide toothless grin.

"Look, sweetie, look at the camp. Isn't it nice? There'll be music tonight, and you can listen."

Farendar gurgled, a pretty baby, with big violet eyes, a soft crown of blond hair, and delicate ears, long and tightly furled, as all babies' ears were. They would begin to loosen when he was three or so.

"Give your aunt Dalla a kiss." Enabrilia held him up. "Malamala's sweetest love."

Obligingly Dallandra kissed a soft pink cheek. There was a definite odor about the child.

"He's dirty again."

"Oh, naughty one!"

Enabrilia knelt down in the grass and pulled up his little tunic to unlace the leather diaper and pull it off. The diaper was stuffed with long grass, definitely well used; Enabrilia shook it out and began to pull clean. All the while she kept up a running stream of sweet chatter that vaguely turned Dallandra's stomach. Her friend gushed over the baby no matter what he did, whether soiling his diapers or blowing his snotty little nose. At times it was hard for Dallandra to believe that this was the same girl who used to train for an archer and race her horse ahead of the alar across the grasslands, who used to camp alone in the forest with Dallandra, just the two of them. Every child, of course, was more precious than gold and twice as rare among the People; every elf knew that, and Dallandra reminded herself of it often. When Enabrilia started to put the grass-filled diaper back on, Farendar proceeded to urinate all over himself and her hand, but his mother just laughed as if he'd done something clever.

"I think I'll walk back to the camp," Dallandra said. "See if the tent is ready."

The tents were indeed standing, and Halaberiel the banadar was waiting in front of Nananna's with four members of his warband. Louts, Dallandra considered the young men, with their long Eldidd swords at their sides and their swaggering walk. Halaberiel himself, however, was a different matter, a farseeing man and a skilled judge for the alarli under his jurisdiction. When Dallandra held up her hands palm outward, he acknowledged the gesture of respect with a small firm nod.

"I'm glad to see you, Wise One. I trust Nananna is well."

"A bit tired. She's down by the lakeshore."

"I'll go speak with her." Halaberiel glanced at his escort. "You all stay here."

The four of them obligingly sat down in front of the tent. The worst four, Dallandra thought. Calonderiel, Jezryaladar, Elbannodanter, and Albaral—they were all staring, hungry-eyed and smiling. She felt like kicking dirt in their faces. As she followed the banadar, Calonderiel got up and ran after, catching her arm and bobbing his head to her.

"Please, Dalla, won't you take a little stroll with me? Oh, by the gods who live in the moon, I've dreamt about you every night for weeks."

"Have you?" Dallandra shook her arm free. "Then maybe you've been drinking too much Eldidd mead before you go to bed. Try taking a herbal purgative."

"How can one so lovely be so cruel? I'd die for you. I'll do anything you say, fight a thousand Round-ears or ride alone to hunt down the fiercest boar! Please, won't you give me some quest? Something dangerous, and I'll do it or die all for your sake."

"What a lardhead you can be!"

"If I talk like a madman, it's because I'm mad all for the love of you. Haven't I loved you for years? Have I ever looked at another woman in all that time? Haven't I brought you gifts from down in Eldidd? Please, won't you walk with me a little ways? If I die for lack of your kisses, my blood will be on your head."

"And if I get a headache from listening to you babble, then the pain will be in my head, too. Cal, the alardan's full of prettier women than me. Go find one and seduce her, will you?"

"Oh, by the gods!" Calonderiel tossed his head, his violet eyes flashing with something like rage. "Doesn't love mean anything to you?"

"About as much as meat means to a deer, but I don't like to see you unhappy. We've been friends for ever so long, since we were children, truly."

Just seventy that year, Calonderiel was a handsome man, tall even for one of the People, towering a full head above her, his hair so pale it seemed white in the summer sun and his eyes as deep-set as a dark pool among shade trees. Yet Dallandra found the thought of him kissing her—or worse yet, caressing her—as repellent as the thought of biting into meat and finding a maggot.

"Besides," she went on, "how would your pack of friends take it if I chose you?"

"They'd have to take it. We threw knucklebones to see who'd get the first chance to court you, and I won."

"You what?" Dallandra slapped him so hard across the face that he reeled back. "You beast! You gut-sucking sheep worm! Am I supposed to be flattered by that?"

"Of course you are. I mean, aren't you glad to have four men all ready to die for you?"

"Not if they dice over me first like a piece of Eldidd iron-ware."

"I didn't mean it like that!"

"Horse turds."

When Dallandra started to walk away, he grabbed her arm again, bobbing his head and ducking before her like a bird drinking from a stream.

"Please, wait! At least tell me this: is there someone you love more than me? If there is, then I'll ride off with a broken heart, but I'll ride."

"Since I don't love you at all, it wouldn't be hard to find someone I loved more, but actually, I haven't even looked. Why don't you believe me, you cloudbrain? I don't love you. I don't love anyone. I don't want to get myself a man. Plain truth. No more to say. There you are."

Rage flared in his eyes.

"I *don't* believe it. Come on, tell me: what can I do to make you love me?"

She was about to swear at him, then had a better idea.

"I'll never love any man who isn't my match in magic."

"What a rotten thing to say! What man's ever going to match you? That's a woman's art."

"It doesn't have to be." Dallandra gave him a small smile. "A man could learn it, too—if he had the guts, and most of you don't."

This time, when Dallandra shook free and walked on, Cal stayed behind, savagely kicking at a tuft of grass with the toe of his boot. She hurried on to the lakeshore, where Nananna and Halaberiel were sitting in the long grass in the shade of a willow tree, their heads together and talking urgently.

"I've asked the banadar to do us a small favor," Nananna said. "Concerning yesterday's vision."

"Of course I'll go look for this man, Wise One. I'll take my escort with me, too." He thought for a moment. "Let's see—the last of the Round-ear merchants is still here. I could ask him if he's seen anything of a stranger."

"No," Nananna said. "I know this is only making your task harder, Banadar, but I'd prefer that you speak to the Round-ears as little as possible."

Halaberiel shot her a troubled glance, then nodded his agreement.

"Take Cal with you, will you?" Dallandra broke in. "I want him out of my sight."

"Oh, now now." Halaberiel gave her an infuriatingly paternal smile. "He's a decent boy, really, if you'd only give him a chance."

When Dallandra crossed her arms over her chest and glared at him, Halaberiel hastily looked away and made the sign against the evil eye with his fingers. Although the evil eye was only a myth, most dweomerfolk found it a useful one.

"Very well, Cal will ride with me," Halaberiel said. "Now, about this Round-ear we're fetching, can you give me a sign to look for, O Wise One?"

"Come to my tent after dark. I'll give you a riddle to ask him, too, just to make sure you've cut the horse out of the herd of cows."

"Good." Halaberiel rose, bobbing his head at her. "Shall I escort you to your tent?"

"No, but thank you. I think I'll take a bit of sun."

Nananna waited until the banadar was out of earshot before she spoke.

"And why are you breaking poor Cal's heart?"

"I don't love him."

"Very well, then, but there's nothing wrong with your finding a nice young man to keep you warm in the winter."

Dallandra wrinkled her nose and shuddered. Nananna laughed, patting Dallandra gently on the arm with one frail hand.

"Whatever you want, child. But a cold heart may find it hard to work magic as it grows older and more chill."

"Oh, maybe so, but I hate it when they hang around me, yapping like dogs around a bitch in heat! Sometimes I wish I'd been born ugly."

"It might have been easier, but the Goddess of the Clouds gave you beauty, and doubtless for some reason of her own. I wouldn't argue with her now that you have it."

That night was the first in what promised to be a long series of feasts. Each alar made up a huge quantity of a single dish and set it out in front of their tents—Dallandra stewed up a vast pot of dried vegetables heavily spiced with Bardek curries—and the People drifted from one alar to another, sampling each dish, stopping to talk with old friends, then moving on to the next. Dallandra took a wooden bowl and trotted back and forth from alar to alar to fetch a selection of favorite treats for Nananna, who sat regally on a pile of cushions by a campfire and received visitors while she ate. By the end of the alardan she would have seen everyone at the meeting and dispensed wise advice, too, for most of their problems. Someday this role of wise woman would be Dallandra's, but she was filled with the dread that she was too young, not ready, nowhere near Nananna's equal. Her worst fear was that she would somehow betray her people's trust in her.

Slowly the night darkened; a full moon rose bloated on the far empty horizon. Here and there, music broke out in the camp, as harpers and flute players took out their instruments and started the traditional songs. Singing, or at least humming along under their breath, the People drifted back and forth through the light from a hundred campfires. Just as the moon was rising high in the sky, the Round-ear merchant came to pay his respects to Nananna. Since she was supposed to be polishing her knowledge of the Eldidd tongue, Dallandra moved close to listen as Namydd of Aberwyn and his son, Daen, made Nananna low bows in the Round-ear fashion and sat down at her feet. The merchant was a portly sort, graying and paunchy, and his thin wisps of hair made his round ears painfully obvious. Daen, however, was nice-looking for one of his kind, with a thick shock of blond hair to cover what Dallandra thought of as his deformity.

"I'm most grateful you'd speak with me, O Wise One," Namydd said in his barbarous-sounding speech. "I've brought you a little gift, just as a token of my respect."

Daen promptly handed over a cloth-wrapped parcel, which his father presented to Nananna with as much of a bow as he could manage sitting down. With a small regal smile, Nananna unwrapped it, then held up two beautiful steel skinning knives with carved bone handles.

"How lovely! My thanks, good merchants. Here, Dallandra, you may choose which one you want."

Eagerly Dallandra took the knives and studied them in the firelight. One knife was decorated purely with interlacements and spirals; the other had a picture of a running horse in the clumsy Eldidd style. She chose the abstract one and handed the other back to Nananna.

"My thanks, good merchants," Dallandra said. "This is a truly fine thing."

"Not half as fine as you deserve," Daen broke in.

Dallandra realized that he was staring at her with a besotted smile. Oh no, not him, too! she thought. She rose, made a polite bob, then hurried to the tent on the excuse of putting the new knives away.

By the time the moon was at her zenith, Nananna was tired. Dallandra shooed the last visitors away, then escorted Nananna to their tent and helped her to settle into bed. In the soft glow of the magical light, Nananna seemed as frail as a tiny child as she lay wrapped in her dark blue blanket, but her violet eyes were still full of life, sparkling like a lass's.

"I do love an alardan," Nananna said. "You can go watch the dancing if you'd like, child."

"Are you sure you won't need me for anything?"

"Not while I sleep, no. Oh—I forgot all about Halaberiel. Here, go find him and tell him I'll speak to him in the morning."

Shortly after dawn on the morrow, Halaberiel appeared at their tent with the four young men who were to ride with him. They all sat on the floor of the tent while Nananna described the young Round-ear she'd seen in her vision—a slender man, much shorter than one of the People, with dark hair and big eyes like an owl. He was traveling with a mule and earning his living as a herbman.

"So he shouldn't be too hard to find," Nananna finished up. "When I scried him out, he was leaving Elrydd and making his way west. Now, the rest of you leave us while I tell the banadar the secret riddle."

Carefully avoiding Calonderiel, Dallandra left the tent along with the men and went over to Enabrilia's tent, which stood nearby. Enabrilia was cooking soda bread of Eldidd flour on a griddle while Wylenteriel changed the baby. Enabrilia broke off a bit of warm bread and handed it to Dallandra.

"I've got something to show you later," Enabrilia said. "We traded a pair of geldings for some marvelous things yesterday. A big iron kettle and yards and yards of linen."

"Wonderful! I should take some of our extra horses over to the Round-eyes, too."

The Eldidd merchants left the alardan the next day, taking away fine horses and jewelry and leaving behind a vast motley assortment of iron goods, cloth, and mead. The alardan settled down to its real business—trading goods among itself, and sorting out the riding orders for the long trips ahead to the various winter camps. Just at twilight, Dallandra took an Eldidd-made ax and walked about a mile to a stand of oaks where she'd spotted a dead tree earlier. In the blue shadows under the old trees, all tangled with underbrush, it was cool and quiet—too quiet, without even the song of a bird. Suddenly she was aware of someone watching her. She raised the ax to a weapon posture.

"All right," Dallandra barked. "Come out."

As quietly as a spirit materializing, a man of the People stepped forward. Dressed in clothes pieced out of animal skins, he carried a long spear with a chipped stone blade, the shaft striped with colored earths and decorated with feathers and ceramic beads. Round his neck on a thong hung a small leather pouch, also elaborately decorated. One of the Forest Folk, come so close to a gathering—Dallandra lowered the ax and stared in sheer surprise. His smile was more a sneer as he looked her over.

"You have magic," he said at last.

"Yes, I do. Do you need my help for anything?"

"Your help?" The words dripped sarcasm. "Impious bitch! As if I needed your help for one little thing. That axhead is made of iron."

Dallandra sighed in sudden understanding. The Forest Folk

clung to ancient taboos along with ancient ways—or so the People saw it.

"Yes, it is, but it hasn't hurt me or my friends. Honest. No harm's come to us at all."

"That's not the issue. The Guardians are angry. You drive the Guardians away with your stinking filthy iron."

To Dallandra the Guardians were a religious principle, not any sort of real being, but there was no use in arguing philosophy with the Forest Folk.

"Have you come to warn us? I thank you for your concern, and I shall pray for forgiveness."

"Don't you mock me! Don't you think I can tell you despise us? Don't you dare speak to me as if I were a child, or I'll—"

When he stepped forward, raising the spear, Dallandra threw up one hand and summoned the Wildfolk of Aethyr. Blazing blue fire plumed from her fingers with a roaring hiss. The man shrieked and fell onto his knees.

"Now," she said calmly. "What do you want? If you just want to lecture me, I'm too busy at the moment."

"I want nothing, Wise One." He was shaking, his fingers tight on the spear shaft for comfort. "I brought someone who does need your help."

When he called out, a human man crept forward from the underbrush. His dark hair was matted; his tattered brown rags were filthy. He fell to his knees in front of her and looked up with desperate eyes. He was so thin that she could see every bone in the hands he raised to her.

"Please help me," he stammered out in the Eldidd tongue.

Dallandra stared at his dirty face. On his left cheek was a brand, bitten deep into his flesh, the mark of some Round-ear lord. A bondsman—fleeing for freedom and his life.

"Of course we'll help you," Dallandra said. "Come with me. Let's get you fed first." She turned to the spearman. "You have my sincere thanks. Do you want to eat with us, too?"

For an answer he rose and ran, slipping back into the forest like a deer. Weeping a low animal mutter under his breath, the

Round-ear staggered to his feet. When they reached the alar, the People clustered round with shouts and oaths. Wylenteriel pressed a chunk of bread into the man's filthy hands and got him a bowl of ewe's milk to drink—the roast lamb and spiced food would have only made him vomit.

"One of the Forest Folk brought him in," Dallandra said. "They must have been waiting for the merchants to leave."

"I heard your people help such as us," the bondsman stammered. "Oh, please, I can't bear it anymore. My lord's a harsh man. His overseer flogs us half to death whenever it suits him."

"This lord is probably coming after him, too," Dallandra said to the crowd in Elvish. "I wish Halaberiel were here, but we'll have to work something out without him."

"My alar's riding west." Gannobrennon stepped forward. "We'll take him with us, and we'll leave tonight."

"Good, but what if the Round-ears ride in looking for him?" Elbaladar said. "We'd better break up the alardan."

At this a round of arguments, suggestions, a babble of good advice and drawbacks, broke out. Slowly Nananna came out from the tent and walked over. At the sight of her, everyone fell silent.

"Elbaladar is right," Nananna said. "We'd better break camp tonight. I can contact Halaberiel through my stones and tell him the news." She paused, looking around at the assembled people. "I need four or five young men to join my alar. We can't ride fast, and so the Round-ears might catch up with us."

Quickly the news spread through the alardan: they were rescuing a Round-ear slave, and the Wise One had given her orders. The People gobbled down the feast, then packed up gear and struck tents by firelight and the rising moon. A few at a time, the alarli cut their stock out of the common herds and disappeared, moving on fast into the silent dark grasslands, until the vast meadow stood empty with only the crushed grass and various leavings to show where the alardan stood. Just after midnight four young men brought their stock and their possessions over to join the Wise One's group, the last two tents left of hundreds.

"I can ride for a few hours tonight," Nananna said. "I want to turn back east. If the Round-ear lord finds anyone, it had best be me."

They made a hasty, sparse camp two hours later on the banks of the river that flows out of the Lake of the Leaping Trout. In the morning they forded the river and turned dead south through the grasslands. Enabrilia and Dallandra led the travois horses while Wylenteriel, Talbrennon, and one of their new recruits herded the stock in the rear. The other three rode in front, hands on sword hilts, eyes constantly sweeping the horizon, ready to ride between any Round-ear and Nananna. Toward noon, the trouble came. Dallandra saw a puff of dust heading toward them that soon resolved itself into six horsemen, trotting fast over the grasslands.

"Good," Nananna said. "Let's pull up and let them catch us. Dalla, you do the talking."

Dallandra handed her the rope of the travois horse and rode up to the head of the line. The horsemen shouted and turned their horses, galloping the last half mile up to the alar. At their head was a heavyset blond man in the plaid brigga that marked him as an Eldidd lord; behind him were five of his warband, all armed and ready. The lord checked his men some twenty feet away from the alar and rode on alone to face Dallandra. He looked sourly over the small party; she could see him noting well the armed men—six of them, counting young Talbrennon.

"My lord! Shall we charge?"

"Hold your tongue!" the lord yelled. "Can't you see the women with them? And one of them's old at that."

Dallandra relaxed slightly; so he had a bit of his kind of honor. The lord edged his horse up close to hers.

"Now, can any of you speak my language?"

Dallandra gave him a wide-eyed stupid stare.

"Eldidd." He sighed and pointed to himself. "I'm a lord. I lost a bondsman. Have you seen him?"

"Bondsman?" Dallandra said slowly. "What is bondsman? Oh —farmer."

"That's right." The lord raised his voice, as if she would understand if only he shouted. "A kind of farmer. He has a brand here."

He pointed to his cheek. "A mark. He's my property, and he ran away."

Dallandra nodded slowly, as if considering all of this.

"He's a young man, wearing brown clothes," the lord bellowed at the top of his lungs. "Have you seen him?"

"That I not. No see farmers."

The lord sighed and looked doubtfully at the alar's gear, as if a bondsman wrapped in blankets might be hidden on a travois.

"Which way have your people ridden? North? South?" He pointed out the various directions. "Do you understand? Where have you come from?"

"North. No see farmers. No farmers in north grass."

"Well, you would have seen him out in those dismal plains."

"The dis . . . what?"

"Oh, never mind." The lord made a vague bow in her direction, then turned and yelled at his warband. "All right, men, we're riding east. The bastard must have doubled back."

As soon as the warband was out of sight, the alar burst into howls and cackles. Dallandra leaned into her saddle peak and laughed till her sides ached.

"Oh, a splendid jest," Wylenteriel gasped with his perfect Eldidd accent. "No see farmer! By those hells of theirs, Dalla!"

"No speak good. Me simple elf. Hard of hearing, too."

On a wave of laughter the alar rearranged their riding order and continued their slow trip south.

About four days' ride west of Elrydd, Aderyn came to a tiny lake fringed with willow trees. In a nearby farming village were a woman ill with shaking fever and a man with a jaw abscessed from bad teeth. Aderyn made a camp on the lakeshore with a proper fire circle of stones, a canvas lean-to for covering his gear, and a neat stack of firewood donated by the grateful villagers, and rode daily into the village to care for his new patients. Once they were out of danger, he lingered to gather and dry wild herbs. On his tenth night there, as he was eating bread and cheese by his fire, he heard his horse whinny a nicker of greeting to some other horse, but one he couldn't see or hear. When the mule joined in, Aderyn felt profoundly uneasy. He was a good two miles from the village, far away from help if he should need it.

Off among the willows a twig snapped; then silence. Aderyn spun around and stared into the darkness. He thought he saw something moving—too slender for a deer—no, nothing but tree branches. Now here, he told himself, you're letting your nerves run away with you. But in the distance he heard another sound—a footfall, a twig. He retreated close to the fire and picked up the only weapon he had, a table dagger.

The five men materialized out of the willow trees and stepped quietly into the pool of firelight. While he gawked, too frightened to speak, they ringed him round, cutting off any escape. All five of them had pale blond hair, like moonlight in the fire-thrown shadows, and they shared a certain delicate kind of good looks, too, so that Aderyn's first muddled thought was that they were brothers. They were dressed differently than Eldidd men, in tight leather trousers instead of baggy brigga and loose dark blue tunics, heavily embroidered, instead of overshirts, but they all carried long Eldidd swords.

"Good evening," one of them said politely. "Are you the herbman the villagers told us about? Aderyn, the name was."

"I am. Do you need my help? Is someone sick?"

The fellow smiled and came closer. With a twitch of surprise Aderyn noticed his ears, long, delicately pointed and curled like a seashell, and his enormous eyes were slit vertically like a cat's.

"My name is Halaberiel. Answer me a riddle, good herbman: where have you seen the sun rise when you see with your other eyes?"

"At midnight, but that's a strange riddle for a man to know."

"It was told me by a woman, actually. Well, good herbman, we truly do require your aid. Will you ride west with us?"

"And do I have any choice about that?"

"None." Halaberiel gave him a pleasant smile. "But I assure

you, we mean you not the least harm. There's a woman among my people with great power in what you Round-ears call dweomer. She wants to speak with you. She didn't tell me why, mind, but I do what Nananna wants." He turned to one of the others. "Calonderiel, go fetch his horse and mule. Jezry, bring our horses."

The two melted away into the darkness with hardly a sound.

"I take it we're leaving tonight," Aderyn said.

"As long as you're rested, but we won't go far. I just want to put a little distance between us and the village. The villagers might go running to their lord with tales of Westfolk prowling around." Suddenly he laughed. "After all, we are actually thieving tonight, stealing the herbman away."

"Well, the herbman is curious enough to come with you on his own. I'm more than willing to speak to anyone who has dweomer."

"I can't tell you how glad I am to hear that. It would have ached my heart to tie you up, but we couldn't have you taking wing and flying away the minute our backs were turned."

"Flying? Not quite, but I have ways of moving in the dark, true enough."

"Ah, you're only an apprentice, then. Well, no doubt Nananna can teach you a thing or two."

Halaberiel spoke so matter-of-factly that the implication was unmistakable. Could this Nananna fly? Did all the dweomermasters of the Westfolk have a power that was only a wistful dream for those of the human sort? Aderyn's heart started pounding in sheer greed. If Halaberiel had somehow changed his mind and tried to keep Aderyn away, he would have had a nasty fight on his hands. Aderyn's kidnappers-cum-escort saddled his horse, loaded up his mule, then put out and buried his fire for him. As the horses picked their way across the dark meadow, Halaberiel rode beside Aderyn.

"I'll tell Nananna tonight that we've found you."

"You can scry, I take it."

"I can't. She'll come to me in a dream, and I can tell her then."

Just after midnight, Halaberiel ordered his men to make a rough camp by a riverbank. Aderyn judged they'd gone about ten miles. In the darkness, he could see nothing, but in the morning, he woke to the sight of a swift-flowing, broad river and, beyond on the farther bank, a primeval oak forest. He jumped up and ran to the water's edge. It had to be—he knew it deep in his heart—it was the river of his vision. With a little yelp of sheer joy he jigged a few dancing steps there on the riverbank.

"Is somewhat wrong?" Halaberiel came up beside him.

"Not in the least. Quite the contrary, in fact. You don't need to worry about me trying to escape or suchlike, believe me."

After a meal they forded the river and walked the horses slowly into the forest, which soon turned so thick and tangled that they had to dismount and lead their mounts along a deer track. In a few miles the trail disappeared, leaving them to thread their own way through the trees. For three agonizing hours they picked their way west, stopping often to urge on the balky horses or deliberate on the best way to go. Finally, just when Aderyn was ready to give up in frustration, they came to a road: a proper, hard-packed, level dirt road about ten feet across, running straight as a spear through the forest.

"Here we are," Halaberiel remarked. "Few of the Round-ears would push on long enough to find this, you see."

"I take it you don't trust my kind."

"And how should I?" Halaberiel considered him with cool violet eyes. "No offense, good sir, to you as a man, but first we gave the Round-ears the coast; then they started pushing up the rivers; now I see them breeding like rats and swarming all over the country. Everywhere they go, they make slaves out of the Old Ones who were here before them. Where will they stop? Anywhere? Or will they keep on pushing north and west, plowing up the grasslands for their fields and killing the grass for our horses? Are they going to look at us and covet us for slaves one fine day? They've already broken at least one treaty with my kind that I know of. Trust them? I think not, good sir. I think not."

"I assure you, those of us who serve the dweomer hate slavery as much as you do. If I could free every bondsman in the kingdom, I would."

"No doubt, but you can't, can you?" With an irritable shrug,

Halaberiel turned away and called to his men. "Let's get on the road. We can rest the horses when we come to the big spring."

The spring turned out to be some two miles farther west, a stone pond with a stone culvert that led the overflow down to a stream among the trees. Inside the stone wall water welled up clear and noiselessly from the sandy bottom. Before anyone drank, Halaberiel raised his hands over the water and called out a short prayer in a soft musical language to thank the god of the spring. Then they unsaddled their horses, let them roll, and watered them before sitting down to their own meal of smoked fish and soft ewe's-milk cheese. Aderyn was beginning to be able to tell the young men apart: Calonderiel, taller than the rest; Elbannodanter, as delicately handsome as a lass; Jezryaladar with a quick flash of a grin; and Albaral, who said very little and ate a lot.

"Banadar?" Calonderiel said. "Has Nananna told you where she is?"

"Not far beyond the forest. She and her escort met up with a couple of big alarli yesterday, and they're all camping together by the haunted pool. The rest of our warband's on the way to join them, too. We'll all move down to the winter camp together."

When he finished eating, Aderyn went for a closer look at the spring. The stonework was carved with looping vines and flowers, and peering out from among them were the little faces of the Wildfolk.

"Halaberiel?" Aderyn said. "Your people do beautiful stonework."

"Well, they used to. This is over eight hundred years old. There's not a man or woman alive now who could do as well."

"Indeed? Here, your men call you banadar. Is that like a lord or prince?"

"In a way, but only in a way. We'll have to start teaching you our speech, Aderyn. Most of us here in the east know a bit of the Eldidd tongue, at least, but farther west the People don't care for the barbarous languages."

Late in the afternoon they followed a little stream out of the forest into the grasslands and made their night's camp. As he was unloading his mule, Aderyn realized that he was completely lost, cut off from Eldidd and everything he'd ever known. Perhaps he might have been able to find his way back through the forest to the river on his own—perhaps. Later, when the others were asleep in their bedrolls, Aderyn sat by the dying campfire and thought of Nevyn. The old man's image built up instantly, smiling at him.

"Did I wake you?" Aderyn thought to him.

"Not at all. I was just sitting here wondering about you. Where are you? Still in Eldidd?"

"I'm not. Strange things have been happening."

Carefully and in some detail Aderyn told him about his forced trip to see Nananna. His eyes thoughtful, Nevyn's image grew stronger above the fire.

"Strange things indeed. Now fancy that—I never knew another race lived to the west. I think me that King Bran and Cadwallon the Druid led their folk to a stranger place than ever they could have guessed. I'll have to meditate on this, but from what you say, I think that these elves originate in a different part of the Inner Lands than men do."

"So it would seem. I truly wonder what kind of dweomer they have."

"So do I. I trust you'll tell me when you find out. It seems the Lords of Light have warned this Nananna of your coming. Interesting, all of it."

"I truly wish you were here to see for yourself."

"Well, who knows? Maybe someday I'll ride west. Until then, be careful, will you? Don't go rushing into anything unwise just out of lust for secret lore."

Then he was gone, the contact broken and cold.

Toward noon on the next day they reached the camp. They came to the sheep first, a huge flock, watched over by dogs and mounted shepherds, one of whom was a woman, dressed in the same leather trousers and dark blue tunic as the men, but with long hair in one thick braid hanging down to her waist. About an hour's ride on they reached a herd of some sixty horses on long tethers, among them the rich yellow-golds with silvery manes and tails so highly prized by Eldidd men. Just beyond the herds were the tents, along a stream and among the willow trees there. Each was a swirl and splash of bright color—animals, birds, leaves, tendrils—all intertwined but so solid and realistically painted that it seemed the birds would fly away. Out in the middle was a big cooking fire, where men and women both were working, cutting up lamb, stirring something in a big iron kettle. Other elves stood round, talking idly. When Halaberiel called out, the folk came running, all talking at once. Aderyn heard his name mentioned several times, and some of the folk openly stared at him. In a flood of laughter and talk, the men began to help them unsaddle their horses.

Off to one side Aderyn noticed a young woman whose hair, as pale as silver, hung to her waist in two long braids. Her face was a perfect oval; her enormous eyes were as dark and gray as storm clouds; her mouth was as delicate as a child's. When she walked over to speak to him, he felt his heart pounding like a dancing drum.

"Aderyn? My name is Dallandra, Nananna's apprentice. My mistress is resting, but I'll take you to her later. My thanks for coming to us."

"Most welcome, but the banadar didn't give me much choice."

"What?" Dallandra turned on the banadar. "What did you do, kidnap him like a lot of Round-ear bandits?"

Although Halaberiel laughed, he stepped back a pace from her anger. She's splendid, Aderyn thought, and by every god, she must have a dweomer, too! All at once he was aware of Calonderiel watching him narrow-eyed, his arms folded over his chest. Aderyn's heart sank; he should have known that a woman like this would be long spoken for. Then he caught himself. What was he doing, him of all people, acting like some stupid young lad bent on courting? Hastily he recovered his dignity and made Dallandra a bow.

"There's no need to chide the banadar. I'd gladly travel a

thousand miles for the sake of the dweomer. In fact, I already have."

She smiled, well pleased by his answer.

"Where shall we put you? You don't have a tent of your own."

"I'll take him with me," Halaberiel said. "Truly, good Aderyn, my tent is yours if it pleases you."

The banadar's tent, a blue-and-purple monster some thirty feet across, stood at the edge of the camp. Lying around on the floor were piles of blankets and saddlebags. Halaberiel found a bare spot near the door and gestured to Aderyn to lay down his bedroll.

"The unmarried men in my warband shelter with me, but I promise you'll find them better-mannered than a Round-ear lord's warriors."

Jezryaladar brought in Aderyn's mule packs and dumped them unceremoniously on the ground near his bedroll. Apparently the elves considered this all the unpacking that was necessary; Halaberiel took his arm and led Aderyn outside to introduce him to the crowd round the cooking fire. A young woman, carrying a baby on her back in a leather-and-wood pack, handed Aderyn a wooden bowl of stewed vegetables and a wooden spoon, then served the banadar. They stood up to eat off to one side of the fire and watched as the young men of the warband lined up for their share.

"That lamb will be done later, I suppose," Halaberiel said vaguely.

"Oh, this is fine. I don't eat much meat, anyway."

As the afternoon wore on, everyone was perfectly friendly, and most of the people spoke the Eldidd tongue, but on the whole, Aderyn was ignored or, rather, taken for granted in a way that made him feel slightly dizzy. After they ate, Halaberiel sat down on the ground in front of one of the tents and started an urgent conversation in Elvish with two men. Aderyn wandered through the camp, looking at the paintings on the tents, and watched what the people were doing in a vain attempt to fit into their pattern. The People strolled around, talking to whomever they met, or perhaps taking up some task, only to drop it if they felt like it. Aderyn saw Jezryaladar and another young man bringing a big kettle of water up from the stream to the fire; it sat there for a long time before Calonderiel put it on the iron tripod to heat; then it sat some more until a pair of the lads got around to washing up about half of the wooden bowls. When Aderyn wandered off, he found a young woman sitting on the ground behind one of the tents and talking to a pair of sleek brown dogs; she lay down, fell asleep, and the dogs lay down with her. Later, when he strolled back that way, they were gone.

Finally, toward twilight, the roast lamb was done. Two of the men took it off the spit and slung it down on a long wooden plank, while others kicked the various dogs away. Everyone gathered round and cut off hunks of meat, which most of them ate right there, standing up and talking. Aderyn saw Dallandra putting a few choice slices on a wooden plate and taking them away to a tent painted with vines of roses in a long, looping design.

"Nananna must be awake," Halaberiel said with his mouth full. "She's very old, you see, and needs her rest."

Privately Aderyn wondered if it might be days before Nananna got around to remembering she'd had him brought here. As it grew dark, some of the elves built a second fire, then sat around it with wooden harps that looked somewhat like the ones in Deverry but which turned out to be tuned in quarter tones; they had long wooden flutes, too, that gave out a wailing, almost unpleasant sound for a drone. They played for a few minutes, then began to sing to the harps, an intricate melody in the most peculiar harmonies Aderyn had ever heard. As he listened, trying to figure them out, Dallandra appeared.

"She's ready to see you. Follow me."

They went together to the rose-painted tent. Dallandra raised the flap and motioned him to go in. When he crawled through, Aderyn came out into a soft golden light from dweomer globes hanging at the ridgepoles. All around were the Wildfolk: gnomes curled up like cats or wandering around, sprites clinging to the tent poles, sylphs like crystal thickenings of the air. On the far side, perched like a bird on a pile of leather cushions, was a slender old woman, her head crowned with stark-white braids. Aderyn could feel the power flowing from her like a breath of cool wind hitting his face, a snap and crackle in the air to match the life snapping in her violet eyes. When she gestured to him to sit down by her feet, he knelt in honest respect. Even when Dallandra joined her mistress, Aderyn couldn't take his eyes from Nananna's face. When she spoke, her voice was as strong and melodious as a lass's.

"So, you're the dweomerman from the east, are you?"

"Well, I'm *a* dweomerman from the east. I take it you had some warning of my coming."

"I saw somewhat in my stone." Nananna paused, leisurely studying his face. "In truth, I asked for you."

Dallandra caught her breath with a small gasp.

"I'll die soon," Nananna went on. "It is time, and Dallandra will have my tent, my horses, and my place among our folk." She laid a bony, pale hand on the lass's shoulder. "But I leave her a bitter legacy along with the sweet. I am old, Aderyn, and I speak bluntly. I do not like your people. I fear their greed and what it will do to us."

"I fear it, too. Please believe me—I'd stop them if I could."

Nananna's eyes bored deep into his. Aderyn looked back unflinchingly and let her read the truth of what he said.

"I have heard of the dweomer of the east," she said after a moment. "It seems to serve the Light I serve, only after its own manner."

"There is only one Light, but a rainbow of a thousand colors."

Pleased by the answer, Nananna smiled, a thin twitch of bluish lips.

"But one of those colors is the red of blood," she said. "Tell me somewhat: will your people kill mine for their land?"

"That's what I'm afraid of. They've killed others for theirs—or enslaved them."

"No one will ever enslave an elf," Dallandra broke in. "We'd die first, every last one of us."

"Hush, child!" Nananna paused, thinking. "Tell me, Aderyn. What sent you to us?"

"Just this spring I left my master and received my vision. In it I saw a river, far to the west. When Halaberiel brought me to you, I crossed that river."

"And do you want to go back across it to your own kind? I can have the banadar escort you."

"Wise One, there are some rivers that can never be recrossed."

The old woman smiled, nodding her agreement. Aderyn felt cold with excitement, a sweet troublement. He could hear the distant singing, drifting in from the night with the wailing of flutes.

"If you asked for me, and if I've been sent to you," Aderyn said, "what work do you want me to do?"

"I'm not truly sure yet, but I do want Dallandra to have a man of your people at her side who understands your ways as she understands ours. I see blood on the grasslands, and I hear swords and shouting. It would be a shameful thing if I didn't even try to stop it. Will you ride with us for a while?"

"Gladly. How can I stand by and let my folk do a murdering thing to haunt their Wyrd forever?"

"Nicely spoken. Tell me, Dalla—can you work with this man?"

Dallandra turned her storm-cloud gaze Aderyn's way and considered him for so long that his heart began pounding.

"Well," she said at last, "I'd work with the Dark Fiends themselves if it would help my people. He'll do."

"Well and good, then, as your folk would say." Nananna raised a frail hand in blessing. "Ride south with us, young Aderyn, and we'll see what all our gods have in store."

THE COLD AUTUMN rains slashed down over the town of Cernmeton and sent water sheeting across the cobbles and pooling in the gutters. Wrapped in his heavy winter cloak of dark blue wool, Cinvan rode fast through the twisting streets and left it up to the few townsfolk abroad to get out of his horse's way. He clattered through the gates of the tieryn's dun, a walled compound centered round a stone broch, rode round to the back stables, and yelled for a groom. A stable boy came running.

"So you're back, are you? How was your visit home?"

"As good as it needed to be. Did I miss any excitement?"

"You didn't, unless you count getting drunk in our lord's hall as excitement." He sighed in a melancholy way. "We've got a tournament going on Carnoic. So far Edyl's ahead by six games."

"I'll see if I can give him a run for his coin, then."

In the great hall smoke from the two huge hearths drifted in blue wisps across the round room. On one side the warband of thirty-five men was sitting and drinking at their tables. Up by the honor hearth, Tieryn Melaudd was slouched in his carved chair and drinking with his two sons, Waldyn and Dovyn. The tieryn was a florid-faced, raven-haired man, heavy with middle age but still capable of swinging steel. Of the sons, Waldyn, the elder, had the blond hair he'd inherited from his Deverry mother, but the

younger looked much like a slender version of his father. Everyone knew that Dovyn was his father's favorite son, too—a pity,
since under the new laws he could never inherit a share of the
demesne. Cinvan knelt before the tieryn, who gave him leave to
speak with a wave of his hand.

"I've returned to your service as I pledged you, my lord. A
thousand humble thanks for giving me leave."

"Welcome, lad. And how fares your kin?"

"They're doing well, my lord." Cinvan was lying, but he saw
no need to burden the tieryn with a problem he could do nothing
about.

"Good, good. Get yourself some ale and join your comrades."

Cinvan rose, bowed, and made his escape from the awesome
presence of the noble-born. He dipped himself a tankard of ale
from the open barrel in the curve of the wall, then strolled over to
join the warband. Most of the men were watching Edyl and Peddyc play Carnoic, a board game where the players moved black or
white stones along a pattern of triangles in attempts to capture
each other's men. Every move the two of them made was slow,
studied, and accompanied by either cheers or oaths from the rest
of the warband. As Cinvan stood watching them, Garedd came
over and laid a hand on his shoulder.

"So our falcon's flown back to the nest, has he? Pity—I was
hoping you'd drown on the road."

Cinvan threw a mock punch his way.

"Bastard! Anything happen while I was gone?"

"Naught. And how was Elrydd?"

"As well as it needed to be."

Garedd shot him a look of honest sympathy. They took their
tankards and sat down at a table far from the crowd around the
game.

"And your sister?" Garedd said.

"That's the cursed worst thing of all. By the hells, I was
minded to beat her black and blue. First she has to go and get
herself a bastard, and now she's given it up."

"She what?"

90

"Gave the babe up. To her rotten cat-eyed man. He rides in and wants the little lass—because she'll only be a burden on our Dewigga, or so he says, and so she up and lets him take her away." Cinvan slammed the tankard down on the table. "And Da was too cursed drunk to know or care. Ah, horseshit!"

"Now here, maybe it's for the best. Your sister's got a chance at a decent marriage someday now."

"Ah, that's what she said, blast her! But the shame of it, my own niece, one of my blood kin, riding with the Westfolk! What's her da going to do, I says to Dewigga, teach her to steal? And she's got the gall to slap me across the face and tell me to hold my tongue! Women!"

Garedd nodded in silent sympathy. Cinvan drew his dagger and began fiddling with it, just for comfort. On the hilt was graved his personal mark, the striking falcon that had earned him his nickname in the warband. He ran a heavily callused thumb over the mark and had thoughts of slitting this Gaverenteriel's throat for him one sweet day.

"And you know what else Dewigga had the gall to say? She's always known her man was going to take the babe when she was old enough. 'You're cursed lucky you didn't let me know,' says I. 'Why do you think I held my tongue?' says she. 'Cursed good thing,' says I, and she slaps me again."

"Why didn't you beat her black and blue?" Garedd said.

Cinvan shrugged, laying the dagger down on the table and picking up his tankard. The truth was too bitter to tell: he'd seen too much of that already, with his father beating his mother half to death every time she looked at the old man wrong. Her sobs still echoed through his dreams.

"Ah, wouldn't be worth the trouble," Cinvan said. "I just tell her that if she has another bastard, don't come running to me for coin for the midwife this time, and she flounces out of the room like a highborn lady with her nose in the air."

"Good for you. Women need to be kept in their place."

"Cursed right."

They finished their ale in silence. At the far table, Edyl's howl of rage—he always was a rotten loser—announced that Peddyc had won the game. Amid laughter and jests, coin changed hands all around the warband.

"And here's our falcon back," Ynryc called out, pocketing a silver piece from the defeated side. "Come on, Cinvan—give Peddyc here a game. You've got a good hand with the stones."

"Maybe I will, if he'll take me on."

"Oh, I'm always game," Peddyc said, grinning. "Let's see if I can keep my winnings."

Edyl rose from his place at the board.

"Welcome back, falcon. And has your sister given you a nephew yet? But with proper ears this time?"

The world went red. Cinvan stepped forward, hit Edyl hard in the stomach with his right, and swung up to clip his jaw with his left. Edyl went down like a sack of grain as the hall exploded in shouting. Cinvan felt men grabbing his arms, heard Garedd yelling at him to calm down. Abruptly the red fog cleared. Cinvan knelt to his lord in a cold, shaking sweat.

"And what's all this? By the hells, you haven't been back for one wretched hour, Cinvan."

Cinvan nodded in dumb agreement. He was so sure that he was in for a flogging that he could already feel the whip on his back. Young Dovyn caught his father's arm and whispered something to him.

"Oh." Melaudd turned to Peddyc. "Did Edyl make remarks about Cinvan's sister?"

"He did, my lord."

"Well, then, he's gotten what he deserved. Tell him I said so when you bring him round. But here, Cinvan, try to keep peace in my hall, will you? If you'd only ignore these stupid foul jests, they'd stop making them after a while."

"True-spoken, my lord, and my apologies."

Later that day, when Melaudd and Waldyn's wives and their serving women came down from the women's hall to sit with the noble lords at the table of honor, Dovyn came to drink with his father's warband. Cinvan wondered if he felt more at home with the men now that his brother had an infant son, another heir between him and Cernmeton.

"Good to see you back, falcon."

"My thanks, my lord. For a lot of things."

"Most welcome, truly. I've got somewhat to ask you. I'll be riding down to Aberwyn soon. My father's given me leave to take some of his men along for an escort. I was thinking of you, Garedd, Peddyc, and Tauryn. Are you game for a wet ride?"

"Gladly, my lord. Your father's a generous man with his ale, but time hangs heavy in winter."

"Just that." Dovyn gave him a grin. "We might have a bit of sport in the spring, though. Here, I'll tell you the news. I'm riding to Aberwyn to lay claim to some of that empty land up by the Peddroloc. If I can gather the farmers and suchlike, by the gods, why shouldn't I have land and a dun of my own?"

"Why not?" Cinvan pledged him with his tankard. "Good for you, my lord. I take it your father's sponsoring you."

"Just that." Dovyn's smile was full of boyish hopes and pride. "He says he'll back me with the warband if any of the cursed Westfolk try to argue about it. I can fancy myself spreading the Bear clan's name a little farther west."

"And your clan's glory." Cinvan had a swallow of ale. "May the Bear roam where he will."

Two days later, when the storm broke, Lord Dovyn and his escort set out for Aberwyn. All along the way, Melaudd's personal vassals and allies gave them a roof over their heads and ale to drink, which was all that mattered to Cinvan. Dovyn was full of his plans, chattering about them in a most unlordly manner. Since the Old Ones had already fled this part of the country, his new demesne would have to be tilled by free farmers, but there were plenty of younger sons among the Eldidd freemen. Among the commoners, a freeman could divide his property up among his heirs when he died, but who would settle for some part of a farm when he could win a whole one? With a noble lord and his warband to protect them against the Westfolk, they would be glad to move and break new land, which would become theirs in freehold in return for dues. (Back in the Homeland, the noble-born had always divided their property, too, but here in the new and hostile country, with empty land all around them, they preferred to keep holdings strong by passing them intact to one heir.) Lord Dovyn would be a poor lord at first, but his wealthy father was willing to tide him over with cattle and extra horses until the crops—and the taxes—began coming in.

About halfway through the trip, they stayed with Tieryn Braur of Belglaedd, who greeted Dovyn warmly and made sure his men had shelter in the barracks instead of the stables. At dinner that night, the four Bear riders were given decent seats at a table near the fire and all the meat and mead they wanted, though Cinvan drank little. Up at the table of honor, the young lord was talking with his host and a pretty young woman who seemed to be the tieryn's daughter. From their long distance away, Garedd watched them with a sentimental smile.

"I think our Dovyn's picked out the lady of this new demesne."

"Huh?" Cinvan said. "Who?"

"The daughter, you dolt! Look."

Obligingly Cinvan looked. Dovyn and the lass were smiling at each other's every word.

"Now, that warms a man's heart." Garedd paused to belch. "What do you wager he had no chance of winning her before? But now he'll have land to offer."

"You're drunk."

"I am, but so what? It's just like somewhat in a bard's tale. He'll win the land and all for her sake."

Cinvan ignored him and had another swallow of mead.

Since the men of the Bear were direct personal vassals of the princes of Aberwyn, Dovyn and his escort sheltered in the royal dun itself, a vast many-towered broch in the middle of Aberwyn. At meals, the Bearsmen sat at one side of an enormous great hall that had room enough to seat two hundred and watched their lord, far away at the other side near a hearth made of fine pale stone, all carved with the princely dragons of the rhan. During the day, they had leave to wander round the town, which with its twenty-thousand inhabitants was the biggest place Cinvan had ever seen. Every morning he and Garedd walked down to the harbor, where the prince's four war galleys rode at anchor and merchant ships came and went. In the afternoon they would go to one of the taverns that the prince's men recommended and pick up a couple of cheap whores, or sometimes only one to spare the extra cost. As Garedd remarked one day, life in Aberwyn was a cursed sight more amusing than playing Carnoic in Melaudd's hall or badgering a kitchen maid into taking a tumble with them out in the hayloft.

Unfortunately, every earthly paradise comes to an end sooner or later. On their last day in Aberwyn, Cinvan and Garedd went down to their favorite tavern to say a sentimental farewell to the lasses there. As they were sitting over a couple of tankards, a stout gray-haired fellow in red-and-white-checked brigga came into the room. Uneasily he threw his fur-lined cloak back from his shoulders and looked with disdain at the chipped tables, straw-strewn floor, and blowsy wenches.

"Now, what's he doing in here?" Garedd said.

"Looking for us. See? Here he comes."

The merchant strode over to their table with a friendly, if somewhat fixed smile.

"My name's Namydd. I see you ride for the Bear clan."

"Well, so we do," Garedd said, and he was the one who went on talking to the merchant while Cinvan sat and glowered. "And what can we do for you, good sir?"

Namydd brushed off the wooden bench with the side of his hand, then sat down and ordered ale all round. When the wench brought it, he inspected the rim of his tankard and wiped it on his sleeve before he drank.

"Now, I've heard an interesting piece of news about your Lord Dovyn. Some of my connections in the prince's court tell me he's filed a claim to land around the Four Lakes."

"He has. What's it to you?"

"A matter of great profit and one to your lord as well. I'm a merchant, you see, and I'd be willing to pay him for the rights to have a trading depot in his village."

"Well, he doesn't have a village yet, good sir. But he'll probably need the coin."

"Most lords in his position do. Now, I'd like to approach him about this, but I wanted to have a word with one or two of his men first. Tell me, is your lord the approachable sort?"

"He is. As decent a young man as you could ask for."

"Splendid! How soon will he be making his move on the land?"

"Oh, sometime in the summer. As far as I understand these things, anyway, they've got all sorts of legal matters to tend to first. Why don't you ride to Cernmeton later in the winter? Doubtless he can tell you more then."

"I will, I will."

Namydd smiled all round, but Cinvan kept on scowling. Although he couldn't say why, he was sure this merchant had some game of his own afoot, and one that might not be to his lordship's advantage.

For some weeks the elves drifted south, heading for the warmer seacoast and the winter camps. Although Aderyn slept in Halaberiel's tent, he rode with Nananna and Dallandra, ate with them at meals, and spent most evenings, too, at the Wise One's side. Starting at first principles, they compared their two systems of magic a piece at a time—or, to be exact, Aderyn had a system of magic, while Nananna had a body of lore. Her dweomer was all of the greatest power, mind, and in line with the true principles of the universe, but there was no doubt that it was a thing of pieces and fragments. For instance, she knew nothing about astrology and only scraps of information about the levels of the universe beyond the astral. When it came to walking the secret paths, her lore was all jumbled, based only on the raw experience of her teacher and herself. He finally realized, in fact, that Nananna's teacher had discovered the technique very late in her life and almost by accident. One evening, using every bit of tact he possessed, he asked Nananna if she realized that the fabric of her magic was a bit frayed. Rather than being offended, she laughed with an earthy good humor.

"Frayed, young Aderyn? Shredded and full of holes, more like, I'd say. It's because of the Great Burning, of course. We lost all our books then, and along with them such niceties as tracts on the motions of the stars and long tables of ritual correspondences."

"Burning? Did someone just burn all the magical books?"

"A bit more than the books. Oh, of course, you wouldn't know about that, would you?" She paused for a long moment, and grief bit deep into her face. "Maybe my broken dweomer suits us, because the People, young Aderyn, are naught but a remnant themselves. Long, long ago we lived in cities, the seven cities of the far mountains, ruled over by a council of seven kings. There were paved streets and big houses, beautiful temples and libraries filled with books that everyone was allowed to read, or so I've been told—I've never seen such things myself, mind. Old as I am, it was before my time, a good eight hundred years ago now when the Hordes came. They were demons, some say, ugly, squat, hairy creatures with fangs and big noses. I suspect they were real flesh and blood myself. Be that as it may, they came by the hundreds of thousands, fleeing south from the northern forests for some reason of their own, and as they came they burned and looted and killed. They destroyed the cities in a few short years, and all that's left of the People is this remnant, wandering the grasslands. We're the children of those who managed to get away in time, you see, and our families were all country people, farmers, most of them, or we never would have survived at all. Two women learned in magic managed to escape the burning of the cities and reach the grasslands, where the other refugees took them in, but they didn't bring any books and so on with them. They were lucky to escape with their heads still on their shoulders, and they didn't have time to pack properly, you might say, before they left."

"Two? That's all?"

"That's all, out of all the grand schools and the temples. They did their best to pass on what they knew, but among us, as among you, talented sorcerers aren't exactly as common as sheep in a fold. One of them was old, too, and died soon, worn out by the horrors she'd seen. My teacher studied with the other."

"But these Hordes—why? Why did they just destroy everything?"

"I only wish I knew. No one does."

"Uh, you said somewhat about these Hordes taking heads. I, er, well, wonder, er, does anyone remember what they looked like exactly?"

Nananna laughed, a bitter mutter under her breath.

"They may not have been actual demons, but they weren't your people, young Aderyn, so rest your heart about that. All the old tales agree that they only had three fingers on each hand, for one thing, and that their faces, especially round the jaws, were all swollen and deformed, for another. Now, when I was a lass I heard one of the elders talk about those deformed faces, and he said it looked to him like they were actually covered with scar tissue in some kind of ritual pattern, maybe with some charcoal powder added in, like, to make the scars more prominent. I've never heard of a Deverry man doing such a thing."

"And we all have five fingers, too. I can't tell you how happy I am—for a moment I was sure that we were all somehow to blame."

"Indeed? Why? Your folk's general nature?"

"Well, that, too, but when I had my vision, I heard a voice telling me to go west. And it said, 'Make restitution.' So I thought, well, maybe we owed you somewhat."

"Eldidd men owe us a great deal, but not because of the Burning, not as far as I know, anyway." Nananna paused abruptly. "What's all that noise out there?"

Aderyn heard urgent voices and footsteps. Just as Dallandra rose to go look, Halaberiel pushed open the tent flap.

"Wise One, my apologies for disturbing you, but Namydd the merchant is here with talk of trouble."

When Dallandra spoke in Elvish, Nananna made an impatient wave in her direction.

"Aderyn has to understand this, too. Speak in his tongue. If you would, Banadar, bring Namydd to me."

In a few minutes Halaberiel returned with a paunchy graying man in the checked brigga and elaborate shirt of a merchant. He was obviously exhausted, his eyes dazed, his movements stiff as he bowed to Nananna.

"My thanks for seeing me, Wise One," Namydd said. "I've brought you some gifts, just tokens of my respect, but my son is still unloading our horses. We've ridden night and day to reach you."

"Then sit down and rest. Dalla, fetch the poor man some mead. Banadar, stay with us. Now, what brings you here in such a hurry?"

"Great trouble, O Wise One," Namydd said. "One of the northern lords, Dovyn of the Bear by name, is laying a formal claim to the lands by Loc Cyrtaer—the very place where we meet to trade every fall."

"Oh, is he now?" Halaberiel broke in. "And does he think he's going to cut the trees on our death-ground, too?"

"I know these lands are sacred to your people." Namydd paused to take a wooden bowl of mead from Dallandra. "The merchant guild of Aberwyn is totally on your side. We tried to intervene with the prince, but all he'd say is that you'll have to come to his court and file a legal counterclaim."

When Halaberiel swore in Elvish, Nananna scowled him into silence.

"Then we shall do just that," Nananna said. "I'm sure the prince will agree when he sees the justice of the thing. Now here, Namydd, has this lord chosen the death-ground itself?"

"Land that's very close, but I think—I hope and pray—that the prince will listen to reason about such a sacred thing. Now, the guild sent me here with offers of aid. Your people can shelter with us if you come to Aberwyn. We have a man trained in our laws to act as your counsel—all at our expense, of course."

KATHARINE KERR

"My thanks," Nananna said with one of her wry smiles. "I
forget sometimes how rich trading with us has made you."

Namydd winced.

"Well, so it has. The Wise One is wise enough to know that
when a man's self-interest is at stake, he's most trustworthy. If the
banadar agrees, I think he'd be the best one to ride to Aberwyn.
Our people have a great respect for those of high standing."

"So they do," Aderyn put in. "And even greater respect for
those of royal blood. Hal, you wouldn't happen to be descended
from the kings of the seven cities, would you?" He glanced at
Nananna. "There were seven, didn't you say?"

"There were." Halaberiel forgot himself enough to interrupt
the Wise One. "Ye gods, you must have a grand sort of magic if you
could see that in me! For what it's worth, I am indeed—a pitiful
sort of inheritance, but mine."

"Then if you'll listen to my humble council, I think you'd best
travel as a prince—in the fullest sense of the word."

Halaberiel looked briefly puzzled, then grinned.

"It might be amusing to try a bit of the pomp and mincing that
pleases the Blue-eyes," Halaberiel said. "What does the Wise One
think?"

"Oh, I agree. Banadar? Take poor Namydd to your tent so he
can get some sleep. Then return to me so we can plan things out.
Namydd, you and your guild have my deep and heartfelt thanks."

Namydd bowed, nearly fell from weariness, then let Halaberiel lead him away. Once they were gone, Nananna turned to
Aderyn.

"Will you ride with the banadar?" Nananna said. "I'd be grateful if you would. I can give you a scrying stone so you can send me
news, and I think it would be wise to have a man who understands
the Light along on this little matter."

"Gladly, Wise One."

"But let me give you a warning. You can never truly desert
your own kind, no matter how much loyalty you give to us. You
must be scrupulously fair, not partisan. Do you understand? If the

100

Lords of Light had wanted you to be an elf, you would have been born in an elven body."

"I do understand that, O Wise One, and I'll think well about what you say."

Almost against his will, Aderyn glanced at Dallandra. Her storm-gray eyes were distant, cool, judging him, as if she were wondering if he could truly live up to his fine words. Aderyn vowed to do the best he could, and all for her sake.

By morning, the news was all over the camp. Young men and women hefted weapons and swore bloody vengeance if the Round-ears so much as touched the death-ground. The older members of the group flocked round Halaberiel and offered advice, warnings, and general opinions. Every man and woman who owned horses had a right to speak out about such an important matter, but finally, by nightfall, they reached a decision. The camp went through its material goods and donated twenty-one matched golden horses, twenty-one fancy saddles and bridles, a heap of new clothes and all the jewelry they owned to make Prince Halaberiel and his escort look as rich as the Dragon Throne itself. Halaberiel himself owned a gem that impressed even Aderyn, an enormous sapphire as blue as the winter sea, set in a pendant of reddish gold some three inches across and ornamented with golden roses in bas-relief. When the warband saw him wearing it, they fell silent; Jezryaladar even held up his hands and nodded to the pendant in a sign of respect.

"It belonged to my grandfather, Ranadar of the High Mountain," Halaberiel said to Aderyn. "For all the good it ever did him."

As a last touch, Aderyn took the warband aside and instructed them in the courtesies that a Round-ear warband would show a man of royal blood. Finally they chose some packhorses—duns and roans, these—and a couple of young men to come along and pretend to be servants. Since Aderyn himself would be the prince's councillor, he too got fancy clothes but a silvery-gray horse to ride.

On his last night in camp, Aderyn and Dallandra wrapped themselves in heavy cloaks and walked a little ways away through the silent grasslands. The night was clear, streaked with moonlight, and so cold that their breath puffed as they walked.

"Be careful, won't you, Aderyn?" Dallandra said abruptly. "I've got a bad feeling about all of this."

"A dweomer warning?"

"I don't know if I'd call it that. Just a bad feeling. I'm sorry, but I just don't trust your people."

"I can't say I blame you. Ye gods, it makes me sick, thinking about how much you've all lost already, and now my folk come riding in trying to take away what little you've got left."

"There's plenty of land for all of us, though. That's the sad thing. There truly is plenty for all, if the Round-ears would only see that. The grasslands stretch way far away to the west, and way up north, too, before you come to the mountains."

"How far away were the seven cities?"

She shrugged, thinking hard.

"I have no idea. Months' worth of riding, I guess. We never go there anymore."

"Why not? Are the ruins haunted or suchlike?"

"Most like, but that's not why. Wait—I heard some old tale about a plague—that's right! At the end, it was plague that destroyed the Hordes, and the bards say that their corpses choked the gutters and paved the streets. If you want to know about all that old stuff, you should ask a bard at the winter meetings. They keep the lore alive."

"You don't seem to care much about it, do you?"

"Ye gods, I grew up hearing about the Burning till I was sick of it. So we lived in splendor once! Who cares? The past is dead, say I, and we've got to make the best of what we've got now."

Yet her voice cracked with bitterness and regret.

Since Lord Dovyn and his escort left Aberwyn before the merchant guild sent its representatives to the prince, they rode back home thinking that the matter of Dovyn's new lands was settled. Life for Cinvan and the warband settled into a drowsy autumn routine: exercising their horses in good weather, and in bad, gathering in the great hall to drink ale and keep the Carnoic tournament going, which by then was a close and heated affair. Garedd marked one of his silver pieces and kept a record of its progress through the wagers—sure enough, every time he lost it, it eventually came back to him. Cinvan took up the battle in earnest and fought his way to the front rank of contenders. He liked the cold pure strategy of the game, where a single mistake was fatal, and had put in long hours studying the various moves and tactics. Often on the long afternoons, while the wives were up doing whatever it was that women did in the women's hall, Melaudd, Waldyn, and Dovyn would stroll over, tankards in hand, to watch the games and lay an occasional wager themselves.

When the message arrived, they were all gathered at the riders' side of the hall. Cinvan was playing a particularly difficult game with Peddyc, who was almost his equal. He was debating whether to sacrifice one of his stones in order to jump and capture two of Peddyc's when there was a bustle at the door. The gate-keeper came running in with an exhausted rider, his cloak pinned with the dragon brooch of Aberwyn.

"My lord Dovyn, an urgent message for you."

Swearing under their breath, Peddyc and Cinvan stopped their game. A servant hurried off to find the scribe, who duly appeared to take the piece of parchment and read it aloud. The warband clustered round to hear.

"To Dovyn, lesser lord of the Bears, newly designated lord of Loc Cyrtaer, I, Addryc, prince of Aberwyn by the grace of his highness, Waryn, king of Eldidd, send greetings," the scribe began. "My lord, a matter of great difficulty has been set before me by Prince Halaberiel, son of Berenaladar, son of Ranadar, a king of the Westfolk. The land on which you laid recent claim in my court is under prior claim to said Halaberiel as part of his royal hunting preserve. Certain sections of said land have also served as tribal burial ground for the ancestors of the Westfolk since time immemorial. I most urgently summon and request you to appear in my palace so that this matter may be discussed and settled in my court of law under my personal arbitration. Under my seal and mark, Addryc, prince of Aberwyn."

"Oh, by the asses of the gods!" Dovyn burst out. "Those cursed Westfolk! The gall! Prince, is he? I'll just wager!" He turned to his father in mute appeal.

"Whether he's a prince or not, Addryc's a prince for sure," Melaudd said. "We'd best ride south and take a look at this."

Dovyn began pacing restlessly back and forth.

"Why didn't this cursed horse herder come forward before? The rotten gall! This is going to delay everything."

"Maybe it will, maybe it won't," Waldyn put in. "Now calm yourself, brother. No need to draw steel and strike sparks until you see how the prince's judgment goes."

"Just so." Melaudd turned to the messenger. "Did this Halaberiel ride in with an armed escort?"

"He did, my lord. Twenty men."

"Well and good. Then we'll take twenty of mine and leave the rest with Waldyn."

Much to their delight, Cinvan and Garedd were chosen to be part of the escort and have another chance at the marvels of life in Aberwyn. At the meal that night, while the men who were going to be left behind grumbled, swore, and generally cursed the others for their good fortune, Cinvan and Garedd pumped the messenger for every scrap of news he had, which, as a common rider like themselves, was little enough.

"Well, here," Garedd said at last. "Do you think this Hala what's-it is truly a prince?"

"Well, now, I know this isn't a friendly sort of thing to say, but I wouldn't doubt it. I've never seen so many jewels on a lord! And this escort of his is always bowing and scraping around him, saying 'my prince this' and 'my prince that,' fetching him mead and bringing him cushions. You know, there's one good thing you've got to say about the Westfolk—they blasted well can hold their mead. I've never seen a man drink the way this prince can."

"I'm more interested in how they hold their swords," Cinvan said.

"Now listen, lad." The messenger shot him a sharp glance. "Naught's going to come to bloodshed in Aberwyn's court. A man who draws steel there gets twenty-five lashes, and if he's still alive when they're done with him, they throw him out of the warband onto the roads to starve."

"I know that as well as you do," Cinvan snapped. "I was just wondering if things would come to a war."

"Now here," Garedd broke in. "That's for the lords to decide. If Dovyn takes the judgment, then he'll be looking for land elsewhere, that's all. God knows, there's enough of it, out to the west."

Cinvan turned to look across the hall to the table of honor, where Melaudd and Dovyn were talking urgently, heads together, and Melaudd's lady watched, shredding a piece of bread with frightened fingers.

Halaberiel and his retinue had been gone three days before Nananna heard from Aderyn. Impressively enough, he could reach her mind directly, rather than wait for a dream. One evening Dallandra was adding a few twigs and chips of wood to their tiny fire when the old woman suddenly went still and stared off into midair.

"Everything's going smoothly so far," Nananna said at last. "They crossed into Round-ear territory with no trouble, and now they're about a day and half's ride from the city itself."

"Is Aderyn all right?"

"Of course, or he could hardly contact me, could he?"

"I'm sorry. I'm just so worried, thinking they'll be poisoned or ambushed or murdered by the Round-ears one way or another."

"Have you had a true dream or a vision?"

"No, it's just my fears talking to me. I even know it, but I can't seem to stop."

"Don't try to stop. Let the voices talk, but ignore them."

Nananna tilted her head to one side to study her apprentice. "You're coming to like Aderyn, aren't you?"

"Oh, he's nice enough." She kept her voice casual. "For a Round-ear. No, that's mean of me. He's been a good friend so far, and whether or not he's a Round-ear has nothing to do with it."

"That's better, yes. I like him myself, but even more to the point, he's willing to help us beyond measure. He has knowledge that's been lost to the People for eight hundred years, and he's willing to share it for the asking. I call that admirable myself."

"So do I, Wise One. Maybe I've misjudged the Round-ears. Let's just hope that there's more men like Aderyn in Eldidd."

On the trip south, Melaudd kept the warband riding fast from dun to dun of his allies and vassals. Everywhere they stopped, the lords offered encouragement and support. The consensus seemed to be that these blasted Westfolk had caused enough trouble, and the sooner they were shoved back to open land, the better. But when they reached Aberwyn, they had a nasty surprise waiting for them. They would, of course, be staying in the dun of the Dragon Prince, but so, it turned out, was this prince of the Westfolk and his escort. Out of simple fairness, Addryc had offered Halaberiel his shelter and protection. Every man in the warband saw this courtesy as a betrayal. Dovyn was furious enough to talk openly in front of the men.

"What do you wager those cursed merchants are behind this? Piss-poor coin polishers!"

"Now here, lad," Melaudd said, and sharply. "Trade's important to Aberwyn. I'm as angry as you are, but you have to understand his highness's position. Watch your tongue while we're here."

"How can you insult our prince, Father? Do you really think he values coin more than honor?"

"I said, hold your tongue! You're a young cub yet and not quite licked into shape, so you leave all the talking to me."

When the Bear's warband came into the hall for dinner, they found their rivals there ahead of them, seated as far across the riders' side of the hall as possible and surrounded by Aberwyn's men. Another portion of Addryc's warband surrounded the Bears —in the friendliest possible way, of course—and sat them down. Cinvan accepted a tankard of ale from a servant girl and peered across the vast smoky hall to the honor hearth, where the noble-born and their guests were drinking mead. Prince Addryc was seated at the head of the table with Melaudd and Dovyn to his left and the elven leader at his right. The fellow was tall, even for one of the Westfolk, and he certainly looked like a prince; it wasn't just his finery, Cinvan decided, it was the way he moved and talked with the ease of someone who's used to being obeyed. Next to him sat a slender young man, quite human-looking, with untidy brown hair and dark eyes, who seemed to be included in whatever important conversation was going on. Cinvan tapped one of the Aberwyn men on the shoulder.

"Who's that next to that Halaberiel fellow?" Cinvan said. "The skinny fellow swimming in his fancy shirt."

"The prince's councillor, Aderyn. Everyone says he's got dweomer."

"Ah, horseshit. Old wives' tale."

"Oh, is it now? I wouldn't be so sure, lad."

Cinvan turned to Garedd, who merely shrugged in suspended judgment. Cinvan felt a small cold fear at the very possibility of dweomer. It was as if he should remember something, or know something, or take some warning—he simply couldn't understand his own thoughts. Fortunately the servants came to the table with roast beef and bread to distract him from the unfamiliar and painful process of introspection.

Later that night, though, Cinvan came face to face with this mysterious young councillor. He went out to the ward to relieve himself of some of the prince's ale, and as he was coming back in, he met Aderyn going out, doubtless for the same reason. Just in case this unprepossessing lad did have some kind of magic, Cinvan made him a civil bow and stepped aside. Aderyn nodded pleasantly, then stopped to look him full in the face. As he stared into those owl-dark eyes, Cinvan turned cold. He felt pierced and pinned to the wall behind him like a rabbit skin stretched out to dry. At last Aderyn smiled and released him.

"Here, good sir," Cinvan stammered, "do I know you from somewhere?"

"Oh, you do indeed, but you won't remember."

Aderyn walked on, leaving Cinvan shaking behind him. Cinvan hurried back to the table and the comfort of Garedd's company. He picked up his tankard and drank a good bit of it straight off.

"What did the councillor say to you?" Garedd said. "There at the door, I mean."

"Oh, naught that counted for much, but he's got dweomer, sure enough."

Dinner that night at the prince's table was a tense affair, with conversation not likely to help one's digestion. With the roast pork Addryc demanded and got statements from both claimants, then let them glare at each other while he considered the matter. With the baked apples he remarked that he was sure that some treaty or another could be worked out, once he'd consulted the priests on the laws.

"A treaty, Your Highness?" Halaberiel remarked. "We've had experience of your treaties before, I'm afraid."

"And what do you mean by that, my prince?" Addryc said in a smooth and level voice.

"The matter of the lands beyond that village of yours, the one called Cannobaen."

Addryc winced and considered his apple, swimming in cream in a silver bowl.

"My heart aches with shame over that matter, but there was naught I could do. I forbade the lords in question to settle out beyond the treaty boundary."

"Then why, pray tell, are they still there?"

"Because they removed themselves from my jurisdiction and bound themselves in personal fealty to my father, the king. I was furious, frankly, but what could I do? Declare war on my own father? That was my only choice."

Halaberiel raised one eyebrow in polite disbelief, but he did allow the prince to change the subject.

Rather than prolong the agony of having rivals eating at his table, Prince Addryc held malover on the disputed land near Loc Cyrtaer the morning after the Bears' arrival. They met in a half-round of a room where the dragon banner of Aberwyn and the hippogriff blazon of all Eldidd draped damp stone walls. Bronze charcoal braziers, glowing cherry red against the chill, stood as common as chairs. The prince sat at a narrow writing desk with the ceremonial sword of Aberwyn in front of him and a scribe with pens and parchment at his right hand. Behind him stood two councillors and a priest of Bel, there to advise on the holy laws. In front of him, Aderyn and Halaberiel had chairs to the right while Melaudd and his son sat off to the left. Although the prince was an imposing man, sitting straight and tall, with touches of wisdom's gray in his raven-dark hair and the snap of command in his dark blue eyes, Aderyn felt sorry for Addryc, who was also intelligent enough to see that any decision he made would be the wrong one, caught as he was between the powerful merchant guild on the one hand and his noble vassals on the other. In hopes of bringing the banadar to a mood to compromise, Aderyn had told him the truth, that if Addryc ruled totally in favor of the Westfolk he would be sowing the seeds of a possible rebellion. The legal councillor for the merchant guild had tried to counsel patience, but Aderyn doubted that the banadar had paid much attention to either of them. As they sat together and waited for the proceedings to begin, Halaberiel's face was set, neither pleasant nor unpleasant, merely distant. It was impossible to tell what he might be thinking. Melaudd and his son, however, were as open as the meadowlands —a barely controlled fury showed in every line of their faces, that anyone, for any reason at all, should cross their will.

"Very well, my lords," Addryc said at last. "We discussed this matter extensively last night. I see no need to chew over the stale meat of the case again."

Halaberiel and the two lords nodded their agreement.

"I have consulted also with his holiness here." Addryc indicated the priest. "He tells me that it would be a grave and impious thing for any man to settle upon, cut wood upon, or plow a sacred burial ground. No doubt the gods of the Westfolk would join great Bel in cursing such an action."

When Dovyn began to speak, Melaudd glared him into silence.

"I assure Your Highness and his holiness both that never would my son or I commit such an impiety," Melaudd said. "If his highness, the prince of the Westfolk, will see to it that the limits of this sacred ground are clearly marked, I will see to it that no man steps upon it unless for some sacred purpose."

"Well and good, then." Addryc turned to Halaberiel. "And will his highness so undertake to mark the land?"

"I will," Halaberiel said. "With swords, if need be."

Addryc winced. Melaudd rose from his chair.

"And does the prince doubt my word?"

"Never," Halaberiel said calmly. "But my lord will not live forever, and who knows what men will come after him?"

The moment was saved. Melaudd bowed and sat back. The two Aberwyn councillors sighed in relief. Aderyn himself found that he'd been holding his breath and let it out again.

"Very well, then," Addryc said. "I shall have a formal writ drawn up, declaring the sanctity of those forests, and posted publicly in both Cernmeton and Elrydd for all to see."

The scribe dipped a pen in an inkwell and wrote a few notes, the pen scratching painfully loud in the silence.

"Now, to turn to the remainder of the land under dispute," Addryc said. "My lord Dovyn, the prince has offered you a compromise, land that you may settle upon farther north and east."

"And why should I compromise?" Dovyn snapped. "Does he claim every bit of land in Eldidd?"

Melaudd forgot himself enough to slap his son on the shoulder, but the damage was done. Halaberiel rose and looked the young lad over.

"My lord, I own nothing," Halaberiel said, "any more than any noble lord of your people owns the land lent to him by the gods. The only property that either of us may claim with any certainty is the six feet of land that your kin will use to bury you someday, and the single tree that my kin will cut to burn me in that same future. There is, however, land that the People use, and land that we never travel upon. I merely suggest to your arrogant soul that you might take land that's of no use to other men and thus spare us all a good deal of trouble."

Dovyn flushed a scarlet red. Halaberiel sat back down and looked the prince's way.

"My prince Halaberiel." Addryc shot a nervous glance at Melaudd. "I've explained the laws of Eldidd to you. If you wish to make certain your claim to this hunting preserve is honored by our laws, then you must be in residence upon the land for a certain portion of every year. A man who lets land lie unused forfeits all claims to it."

"I understand, and it's a sensible ruling in its way. You'll find me there every spring."

"Done, then." Addryc turned to Melaudd. "My lord, there is land for the taking just north of your demesne along the banks of the Gwynaver. May I ask why your son didn't put in a claim to that empty land?"

"Because he wanted to settle on the lakeshore, Your Highness," Melaudd said. "There aren't any settlements on the lakes, and it's rich land and a strong defensive position." He shot Halaberiel a daggered glance. "The day may come when Your Highness wishes there were a strong and loyal dun there."

Addryc blinked twice. The priest looked as if he were silently praying.

"And I'll say something else, by your leave," Melaudd went on. "I've never heard of Westfolk having kings until we received your message, and I'll wager you never did either. It strikes me as strange that you'd turn away from the men who've served you loyally for so long in favor of a stranger."

"And have I turned away from you yet?" Addryc said levelly. "I have yet to pronounce my judgment."

Abashed, Melaudd looked away.

"My prince." Addryc turned to Halaberiel. "I'm considering asking you to surrender land for Dovyn's demesne at the lakeshore. In return, I'll grant you and your people a clear, formal, and indisputable title to the land along the west bank of the Gwynaver. With my seal upon the charter, this matter will never rise again. The burying ground and the north shore of the lake will be yours. The south shore and a dun at the river's mouth will be Dovyn's. All the land between the lake and the Gwynaver will be yours to hunt in or to fortify as you think fit."

"With Bears on the south shore, fortification might be in order," Halaberiel said. "Your Highness, I realize that this is a difficult judgment for you. You have offered a generous settlement, one which I'm minded to take. On the other hand, I have vassals just as you do. No one among my people will give up the south shore easily—I warn you. You're sitting there squirming, wondering if your lords will cause you trouble if you favor me. I'm sitting here squirming just as hard, wondering what my people will think of me if I take this bargain. Do you understand?"

It was so high-handed, foreign, and utterly honest that the councillors and priests gasped aloud. Addryc leaned back in his chair and sighed, running his fingers over the hilt of the ornate ceremonial sword—he understood all too well. Halaberiel turned to Aderyn with one pale eyebrow raised.

"And what does my honored councillor advise?" Halaberiel said.

For privacy Aderyn rose, bowed to the prince, and led Halaberiel outside to the hall.

"I think we should take it, Hal. It's the best we're going to get, and Nananna will work on keeping down resentment. You're not truly the kind of prince who has to worry about rebellions, and Addryc is."

"Poor old Addryc. Well, we've saved the death-ground, and truly, that was first in my mind. I don't trust these Bears, though. How long will it be before they push their greedy snouts northward? That young cub needs to be turned over someone's knee and spanked."

"Well, you're right enough, but if you turn down the judgment, then it's war. Melaudd can rally the prince's other vassals against you because you've refused the prince's judgment."

"Indeed?" Halaberiel considered for a moment. "Well, let me see if I can wring one more concession out of his harried highness."

They returned to the dead-silent room. Halaberiel bowed, then stayed standing to address his royal counterpart.

"Your Highness, your judgment seems fair to me, except for one small point. Will you guarantee me and my people access to the northern lands from the south? The best ford lies in the land you would give the Bears."

"I see no reason why you can't have road rights. The road should be a public one, anyway, so the merchants can use it."

When Dovyn started to speak, his father laid a warning hand on his arm.

"That seems only just, Your Highness," Melaudd said. "If the prince will guarantee the good conduct of his people as they pass through. I know they travel with sheep and horses, and farmers can't afford the loss if stock wanders off into their fields."

"We shall make a formal pact," Halaberiel said. "Any trampled grain shall be paid for in mutton and wool."

Pleased, Melaudd nodded; the prince smiled; the councillors gave Aderyn small nods of satisfaction that reason had prevailed.

"And what about when your people steal mine blind?" Dovyn snapped.

Every seated man in the room rose. The priest of Bel stepped forward, watchful to prevent bloodshed. Halaberiel shook off Aderyn's restraining hand and strode over to face Dovyn.

"Just what are you calling me?"

"Everyone knows the Westfolk are a pack of thieves. Why shouldn't you be a prince of thieves?"

With a startled gasp, Melaudd threw himself forward, but too late. Halaberiel slapped Dovyn backhanded across the face so hard that the lad staggered back. Halaberiel turned to the prince in appeal.

"So this is the kind of court you keep in Eldidd," Halaberiel said. "Where a man who puts himself under your judgment must listen to insults and lies."

"Naught of the sort," Addryc said levelly. "Lord Dovyn will tender you a formal apology. I trust his father agrees with me on this."

"His father does indeed, Your Highness." Melaudd's voice shook. "And I'll tender my own apology first and freely."

Everyone was watching the two princes, suddenly united against this presumption of a lesser lord. Aderyn felt a cold dweomer touch and turned to see Dovyn sliding his sword free of its sheath.

"Don't!" Aderyn yelled. "Hal, watch out!"

Halaberiel spun around just as Dovyn drew and swung. Aderyn threw himself forward and took a blow on his left hand—mercifully only a glancing one as Dovyn tried to hold up, or he would have been known as Aderyn One-hand forever after. He heard the crack of breaking bone and stared numbly at a surge of blood as the room exploded—yelling, swearing, scuffling among the onlookers, the princes shouting for order, the priest invoking Bel's name. Melaudd made a frantic grab at his son, pinned him from behind, and shook him so hard that Dovyn dropped the sword. Halaberiel caught Aderyn's shoulder, steadied him, and swore at the sight of the wound. The priest of Bel ran forward and grabbed Aderyn's arm just as the door flew open and the prince's guard shoved their way in. His face purple with rage, Addryc waved them back, but they stood ready out in the corridor.

"So, Melaudd," Addryc growled, "is this how you raise your sons—drawing on a man in my hall? My hall? By the name of every god of our people! In my very chamber of justice!"

Melaudd tried to answer, but he was shaking too hard. Dovyn broke free and threw himself down at the prince's feet.

"I beg your forgiveness, Your Highness. I . . . I . . . I just forgot myself."

Halaberiel left Aderyn to the priest and stepped forward. "And how soon would you remember his highness's judgment, then? Your Highness, do you truly expect me to strike a bargain with men like these?"

Aderyn suddenly realized that he was close to fainting, a luxury that he couldn't afford in this dangerous pass. He staggered to a chair and sat down hard. The priest knelt beside him and tried desperately to stanch the running wound with a scarf that the scribe handed him.

"Look at this!" Addryc's voice growled with indignation. "He's wounded a councillor and an unarmed man! Guard! Run and fetch the chirurgeon!"

"I'll be all right in a minute," Aderyn gasped.

Although the white scarf was soaking with bright red blood, and his fingers stuck out at an unnatural angle, Aderyn felt no pain. His mind noted his own symptoms from a detached distance: shaking, chills, a dry mouth—oh, he was in shock, all right. He looked up and tried to concentrate on the strange tableau in front of him: Dovyn scarlet with shame at the prince's feet; Halaberiel frozen with rage: Melaudd pale, his mouth working as if he were praying to the gods to let him wake from what had to be a nightmare.

"Your Highness," Aderyn whispered, "please don't make a decision in fury. My prince, that goes for you, too."

Then he fainted dead away. He seemed to be standing in a swirling dark void, flecked with gold light like fish scales. In the midst of a rushy hiss of noise, he heard someone call his name, and Nananna came striding out of the mists. Here on the inner planes, her image was young and beautiful, her stance that of a warrior.

"What have they done to you? Does the banadar still live?"

"He does. I just fainted, that's all. The lad who hurt me has been arrested."

Although Aderyn tried to tell her more, he began floating away, swimming up from the bottom of a dark gold-flecked river.

The rushy hiss grew louder and louder; then suddenly he broke the surface and found himself awake, lying on a feather bed. A heavyset man with a blond mustache was bandaging his splinted fingers. Aderyn smelled the clean sharp scent of bruised comfrey root packed in his wound.

"Should heal up fine," the chirurgeon was saying over his shoulder. "A superficial slice. These things cut a lot of minor blood vessels, looks like the third hell, but nothing dangerous. Now, as for the fingers, he's got two broken, but it's a clean fracture."

"Just so," Aderyn gasped out. "I need water to restore my humors, too."

"Aha, you're awake, are you? They told me you were a physician of sorts."

The chirurgeon gave him a friendly pat on the shoulder and stood up to make room for Halaberiel, who brought Aderyn water in a silver goblet. He sat down on the bed, slipped one arm under Aderyn's shoulders, and helped him drink.

"You took the cut intended for me. I'll never forget this. You're a friend of the People now and forever."

"Most welcome." Aderyn was still too groggy to appreciate the force of that promise. "What did you and the prince determine?"

"Naught yet." Addryc himself stepped forward. "Prince Halaberiel and I decided to take the last bit of wise advice you gave us. Lord Dovyn is shut up in a chamber under house arrest. His father gave me a personal pledge of security for him. Here, Aderyn, Melaudd is a good man, and he's truly shattered by his son's arrogance."

"No doubt," Aderyn said. "My heart aches for any father with a son like that."

Aderyn drank several goblets of water, then lay back exhausted on the pillows. He was in Halaberiel's luxurious chamber, he realized, and it was full of people. Over by the unglazed windows the other elves were sitting on the floor in grim silence. Two of the prince's guard were standing in the doorway to wait upon their liege's orders. At the polished wood table, the chirurgeon was packing up his gear and talking quietly to his young apprentice.

"I'll make a decision about young Dovyn tonight," Addryc said. "The chirurgeon tells me you'd better rest for a while, and I want you there to testify as the victim of this outrage."

"Well and good, Your Highness, but what about the land?"

The prince turned to Halaberiel, who merely shrugged.

"If naught else," Addryc ventured, "my decree about the sacred burial ground will stand in all perpetuity."

"Indeed?" Halaberiel turned to Aderyn. "I'll consider the matter later."

Addryc nodded in defeat. For a few moments he hovered there uneasily, then took his leave with a gracious bow and a few muttered words about letting Aderyn rest. Once the chirurgeon was gone, too, the other elves got up and moved closer to Aderyn's bedside, all twenty of them in a disorderly circle.

"I say we ride out of here and go burn Melaudd's dun," Calonderiel said. "That blow was intended for the banadar."

There was a muttered chorus of agreement.

"Oh, hold your tongue, Cal!" Halaberiel snapped. "Since when do we visit the son's crime on the mother? And there's more than one woman in that dun."

"Well, true, but it would have been satisfying, somehow, to see his tents go up in flames."

"We should just move to the west and let them have the rotten land," Jezryaladar put in. "Who wants a cursed thing to do with men like this?"

"What?" Albaral snarled. "And let the horse turds win?"

Eight or nine men began talking and arguing at once. Halaberiel shouted them into silence.

"Now listen, I'm minded two ways. It depends on what Addryc does to atone for Dovyn's crime. If he offers me fair justice, well, then, I say we take the compromise. We're not doing this just for ourselves. The People need the merchants and their iron and grain, and we have to be able to guard that death-ground. There's a lot more of the Round-ears than there are of us. They can afford a wretched war a lot better than we can."

Calonderiel started to speak, then thought better of it. Everyone else nodded in agreement as Halaberiel went on.

"But what we do next depends on what happens with young Dovyn. If I decide to take the compromise, think of it this way: if we control the Gwynaver, we control one of their main routes north. If they want to ride up our river, we can say no and have their prince behind us."

"That river turns west a ways up north," Calonderiel expanded the thought. "If we can block a main route west, so much the better."

"Good, Cal. Now that's thinking." He glanced at Aderyn. "You're dead pale, Councillor."

"I need to sleep. Take the lads away, will you, but please, by the gods of both our peoples, keep them out of trouble."

Close to sunset, Aderyn woke from the pain of his wound. He found strong wine in a flagon by his bed, drank some to ease the ache, then lay quiet for a while, watching the late golden sun cast long shadows across the Bardek rugs on the polished floor. He was just considering getting up and trying to light some candles when there was a timid knock at the door.

"Come in."

Much to his surprise, Cinvan the Bearsman hurried into the room and knelt beside the bed in sincere humility. As he looked down into Cinvan's hard young face, Aderyn was remembering looking up at this same soul in another body—Tanyc as a seemingly giant young man, and him a small boy of seven. It was a shock to run across Tanyc's soul at all, and even more of one to find him reborn so soon.

"And what can I do for you, lad?" Aderyn said.

"Well, I don't truly know. I shouldn't be here at all, I suppose. Am I tiring you? I can just go away."

"If you're troubled enough to come here, then I'll certainly listen. I take it the news of what happened in the chamber of justice has gotten itself spread around."

"Just that, but I'll wager you don't know the half of it yet. Garedd said I shouldn't be bothering you like this. Garedd's somewhat of a friend of mine, you see, and he usually does the thinking for the pair of us, but I had to come ask you. You see, they say Addryc's as mad as mad at Lord Dovyn, and he wants to have him flogged like a common rider for drawing on you."

"You're right—I hadn't heard that."

"So, well, you see, our young lord saved me from getting flogged once, and so I thought, well, maybe, you being a councillor and all, you'd see things a bit different than most, and speak up for mercy, like."

"I usually speak up for mercy whenever I can, so you can put your heart at rest about that. But I'm afraid that the matter's likely to be out of my hands."

Cinvan nodded, thinking this over. He was much like Tanyc, Aderyn decided, probably as arrogant in normal circumstances. Yet Aderyn was touched that he would break all protocol to plead for mercy for his young lord.

"How's that cut?" Cinvan said. "From what I hear it'll heal up clean, but it ached my heart, to think of my lord dishonoring himself by hurting an unarmed councillor. Uh, well, I mean, I'm sorry you're hurt, too."

"My thanks." Aderyn began to see why this Garedd generally did the thinking for Cinvan. "Well, maybe the prince will think differently about flogging your lord tonight, when his rage has had a chance to cool. He's not going to want to offend Lord Melaudd, after all."

And yet it turned that this reasonable statement was overly optimistic. After the evening meal, the prince called a meeting in his chamber of justice. By candlelight they assembled, Aderyn and Halaberiel, Melaudd and Dovyn, the grave gray councillors, the priest of Bel, the nervous young scribe. Addryc laid the ceremonial sword of Aberwyn onto the writing table to open the court. Candlelight sparked on the golden blade and glittered on the jeweled hilt and the hand guard, formed into a dragon shape.

Addryc sat down behind the table and motioned to Dovyn to kneel in front of him, a harsh gesture that made Melaudd wince. "We are here to consider what to do with you, Lord Dovyn. Let me remind you of your fault. Just when the victory you desired was within your grasp, you turned it to defeat. You insulted a man of royal blood. You broke every law of order by drawing your sword in my presence and my dun. In your clumsiness, you wounded not your target, which would have been grave enough, but an unarmed man who had no chance to defend himself. You spilled blood in the prince's chamber of justice. You have brought a grave shame to your father's heart. You have disgraced your kin and clan. If your father were to pronounce you exiled, I would put my seal on his decree without a moment's thought."

Dovyn slumped almost to the floor, his head bowed, his face drained of all color.

"Do you have anything to say in your own defense?" Addryc said.

"Naught, Your Highness," Dovyn whispered.

"So I thought. Tieryn Melaudd, do you have aught to say for your own son?"

"Naught, Your Highness, except that I love the young cub." He paused, honestly baffled, staring around the chamber as if he still couldn't believe that he was here to witness his son's disgrace. "Truly, I've tried to raise him right. I feel his shame as mine. Freely will I offer to pay the prince the full blood-price for his councillor, just as if my son had killed the man, not just wounded him."

"You what, my lord?" Halaberiel sat straight up in his chair. "Is it the custom of your country to buy justice, then?"

"My prince, please," Aderyn said. "You don't understand the laws of Eldidd. He's not trying to buy justice, but to fulfill it. Every man has his lwdd, his blood-price. If he's killed or maimed, the criminal's kin must pay that price to his clan. Melaudd is being incredibly generous to offer so much without even waiting for the prince's decree."

"I see." Halaberiel turned to Melaudd. "Then my apologies, my lord, for my misunderstanding."

Melaudd only nodded as if he no longer cared what the prince might or might not do. A faint look of disgust lingered around Halaberiel's mouth, as if he'd bitten into rotten fruit.

"You're truly fortunate, my prince," Addryc said, "to have such a wise man of our people to advise you. But in my heart I agree with you. The lwdd is indeed fit recompense for the wrong done Councillor Aderyn, and in his name, I accept it from you, Melaudd." He jerked his head at the scribe, who began writing. "But there remains the fact, Lord Dovyn, that you broke geis by drawing steel in my dun. If this offense had happened in the great hall, when you and the prince had been drinking mead, well, then, I'd be minded to mercy. But in cold blood, in perfect sobriety, you drew a blade in the very chamber of justice, and you did so in front of your outraged father's very eyes."

Dovyn was slumped so low that his forehead almost touched the floor. Melaudd leaned back in his chair, his hands twisted together, the broad knuckles bloodless.

"Therefore," Addryc went on, "I demand a recompense for this fault beyond the wounding of Councillor Aderyn. The laws have no lwdd to pay for their bleeding, Tieryn Melaudd. The penalty for this offense is twenty-five lashes in the public ward."

"Your Highness." Melaudd rose and flung himself down beside his son in the same smooth motion. "I'll beg of you, if ever I've served you, to spare him the shame of it. Not the lashes so much, Your Highness, but the shame—strung up in the ward like a common rider."

"I fear he's comported himself like a common rider, Tieryn Melaudd."

"Your Highness?" Aderyn rose and bowed. "I, too, will beg for mercy. The lad is very young."

"Old enough to know the laws. This injury doesn't concern you, good councillor."

"Your Highness?" Halaberiel rose and bowed. "Never would I question the wisdom of your judgment, but may I ask one thing?"

"You may, my prince."

"Is the penalty for this offense death?"

"It's not."

"But the lad's young and might well die from so many lashes."

"Just so," Addryc said with a nod. "Very well. I hereby lower the penalty to fifteen. Dovyn, raise your head and look at the man you thought your enemy. He's brought you mercy."

Slowly Lord Dovyn raised his head and turned Halaberiel's way, but his cornflower-blue eyes, blackish in the candlelight, burned with hatred.

Prince Addryc picked up the ceremonial sword and flipped it point upward, holding it high.

"Hear then my decree," Addryc said. "Tieryn Melaudd will pay the full lwdd for Councillor Aderyn's wound. Lord Dovyn will receive fifteen lashes in the public ward from my executioner tomorrow at dawn." He lowered the sword and rapped the pommel three times on the table. "So be it."

Melaudd began to weep, a little sob under his breath, the rusty tears of a man who hasn't wept since he was a little lad. At Addryc's call, two guards stepped in, hauled Dovyn to his feet and marched him out, with Melaudd trailing after. Halaberiel caught Aderyn's elbow and helped him bow to the prince; then they left Addryc alone with his righteous rage.

"How do you feel, Ado? Well enough to come to my suite for a goblet of mead?"

"I'm not a drinking man, but tonight I will. But I have to go down to the great hall first—there's someone I need to see."

In the great hall, they found the various human warbands drinking quietly, free of elven presence, as Halaberiel had told the men of the Westfolk to stay up in their own quarters. Off to one side Aderyn found Cinvan sitting with a beefy blond lad whom he introduced as Garedd.

"I'm sorry, lad," Aderyn said. "I tried to speak for mercy, but the prince judged otherwise. I'm afraid they're going to flog your lord tomorrow."

"So we heard. The guards came out and told us the news. It aches my heart, but I'm no man to question a prince."

"It aches mine, too," Garedd said. "Here, sir, is it true that your prince spoke for mercy?"

"It is. It's thanks to him that the lad will get only fifteen strokes."

On the morrow, Aderyn stayed in his chamber when the prince's justice met Dovyn's bare back. From his refuge up in the main broch, he heard the distant noise of the various warbands being marched out to witness what happened to a man who broke the prince's discipline. Then there was a deadly silence. Once he heard a faint sound that might have been a scream. Aderyn did his best to think of other things until he heard the crowd breaking up down below. In a few minutes, Halaberiel and the rest of the elves came up and crowded into his chamber.

"I've never seen such a barbarous thing," Halaberiel said.

Jezryaladar untied a skin of mead, took a long swallow, and passed it to the prince, who downed a good bit of it before he passed it on. Halaberiel began pacing back and forth in silence. The skin of mead went round till it was empty.

Late that morning, a page came, asking the prince and his councillor to attend upon Addryc. Aderyn and Halaberiel followed the lad into the prince's private chambers in one of the secondary towers. This was a comfortable room, furnished with carpets and tapestries, carved chairs set by a small hearth of pink sandstone, and windows open to a view of a garden. Goblet of mead in hand, Addryc was standing by the hearth, and Melaudd was sitting slumped in one of the chairs. Addryc had the page serve Halaberiel and Aderyn mead, then sent the lad away. During all of this, Melaudd never moved or took his eyes from the floor.

"I see no reason to drag this discussion into open court," Addryc said. "Now, as far as I'm concerned, Lord Dovyn has paid the price the law demands, and that matter is over and done with. Do you and your councillor agree, my prince?"

"We do," Halaberiel said. "Tieryn Melaudd, you have my honest sympathy."

Melaudd turned his way slack-eyed. He seemed to have aged ten years in this single morning.

"I suppose I should thank you, but I can't find it in my heart."

Addryc went tense and stepped forward.

"Well, by the hells! What am I supposed to do—mince and grovel before the cause of my son's shame? Before this prince rode in, everything was as smooth as cream, but now I see the man I serve twisted this way and that by a foreigner!"

"Tieryn Melaudd." Addryc's voice was silky. "You forget yourself."

Melaudd opened his mouth to reply, thought better of it, and rose to bow to the prince.

"Now, here, my lord," Aderyn said to Melaudd. "We still need to reach accommodation over the matter of the land."

"Perhaps. But I wonder in my heart why I should be forced to accommodate."

"Do you?" Halaberiel snapped. "Now you listen to me! That land is ours, not yours, not the prince's, not any man in Eldidd's. Do you understand me, Melaudd? The only claim you have is the one I allow you to have."

"Oh, is it now? For years and years I haven't seen one man or woman either on that land. It's been lying there going to waste—"

"Melaudd!" Addryc took another step forward. "We determined the question of use in the malover."

Melaudd swallowed his words with a dagger glance at both princes. Halaberiel nodded Addryc's way, then went on.

"I came in here willing to offer your cursed whelp a demesne out of my ancestral territory, and all I get is arrogance. Very well, then. A prince of my line can be just as arrogant when he needs to be. If your son or one of his blasted riders sets one horse's hoof on that land, then some of my people will be there to spear him off his wretched saddle."

The tieryn turned to Addryc with a snarl.

"And I suppose I'm expected to take this in your palace, Your Highness?"

Addryc hesitated, a man walking the edge of a sword with bare feet.

"I've given my judgment. If the prince of the Westfolk withdraws the matter from my arbitration, there's naught I can do."

"Naught?" Melaudd's word was a howl of rage.

"Just that. I can neither furnish you with aid nor stand in the way of what you see fit in this matter. But the decree about the burial ground still stands. If ever that sacred ground is despoiled, my personal guard will deal with the criminals, and I will lead them myself."

"Indeed?" Halaberiel said. "My respect for Eldidd justice has just shattered, Your Highness, no matter what fine words you use. You're giving Melaudd the right to wage war on my folk."

"I'm giving him naught of the sort! You don't understand! By relinquishing my jurisdiction, I've opened the way for you to appeal directly to my father, the king, himself. I'll see to it that he takes the matter up straightaway."

"The king!" Melaudd sputtered. "You'd let this . . . this creature go to the king!"

Addryc flung up one hand for a slap, caught himself, and froze.

"Don't distress yourself over it, Melaudd," Halaberiel said. "I have no desire to deal with weasels any longer, not even the king of weasels. Well and good then, Prince Addryc. You've made your decision, and I've made mine. We will be leaving your hospitality this very afternoon. I only wish now that you'd given Dovyn the full twenty-five strokes."

Motioning to his councillor, Halaberiel strode out of the chamber. When he looked back, Aderyn saw Addryc grabbing Melaudd's arm; then a page closed the heavy door with a bow. As they made their way through the twisting corridors of Aberwyn's broch, Halaberiel said not a word, and Aderyn was afraid to speak to him. When they got back to his suite, though, they found Namydd waiting anxiously among the elves.

"My thanks for your help, good merchant," Halaberiel said. "But the weasels have found a nice hole in the fence. I warn you—

if you come to the Lake of the Leaping Trout to trade, ride prepared to find yourself in the middle of a war."

Namydd groaned aloud. Halaberiel paced back and forth as he told the story, pausing often to curse by elven gods, while the others merely listened, hands on sword hilts.

"Hal, please!" Aderyn said at last. "Try to understand Addryc's position. Deverry lords like to bluster about Great Bel's will, but they don't rule by some kind of divine right, you know. Even high kings have been overthrown before, and they doubtless will be again. The prince can't risk open rebellion in the north."

"Oh, I understand perfectly. It's because I understand that I see no use in dealing with him further or with his blasted father, the king, either. He sees the honorable thing but he simply won't do it. All of the Round-ears are that way. This is the Cannobaen Treaty affair all over again. They speak fine words, but when it comes to giving up one little thing they want, well, then, they're ever so sorry, but . . . it's always but, isn't it? It would be better if they gobbled openly like the swine they are, instead of mincing around and giving themselves airs. I've tried to mince around like they do, and now I'm sick of it. We'll mark the death-ground and see if the good prince honors his most noble pledge. We'll also see what Dovyn does. We may have to teach him a lesson. And then, good Namydd, we shall see what happens next."

The twenty men jumped to their feet and cheered, but Halaberiel cut them short with a wave of his hand.

"We're discussing death. Don't act as hungry for it as the wretched Round-ears. Go on—start getting your gear together. We're leaving this stinking hole this very afternoon."

His eyes bright, Garedd leaned close to Cinvan to whisper. "It's all getting blasted interesting."

"Is there going to be war? That's all that interests me."

"Just like a falcon—your mind always on meat. But listen, Cinno, when I was down at the stables this afternoon, I heard our

Melaudd talking with Lord Ynydd of the Red Lion. Melaudd's sounding his allies out, like, trying to see how far they'll back him and Dovyn against these cursed Westfolk."

"Indeed? And what did Ynydd say?"

"Blasted little. He's playing it cautious, like, saying Dovyn got himself into it, so he'll have to get himself out. But I'll wager he's just afraid of the prince."

"Huh." Cinvan glanced around the luxurious great hall. "Then the sooner we're out of Aberwyn, the better. Men have got more guts farther north."

"They're leaving Aberwyn now," Nananna said. "There's been trouble."

The old woman slumped forward over her scrying stones. With a little cry Dallandra caught her in her arms, but Nananna raised her head and managed a faint smile.

"I'm not dying yet, child, but I'll admit to being very tired. Will you help me to my bed?"

Dallandra got her settled among the cushions, spread a fur robe over her, then dismissed the dweomer light when Nananna fell straight asleep. After she put the scrying stones away, she lingered, feeling helpless, for a few minutes; finally she left the tent lest her very anxiety wake the old woman. Outside, the alar was at its communal dinner. When Dallandra joined them, Enabrilia handed her a wooden bowl of venison stew.

"How's the Wise One?"

"Very tired. Bril, there's been trouble. The men are on their way home as fast as they can ride."

The talk and the singing died abruptly. Dallandra felt more helpless than before.

"That's all I know. Aderyn couldn't spare a moment to tell us more."

"And just how do we know we can trust this Round-ear sorcerer?" Talbrennon snapped.

"Because Nananna said we could, you moldy horse apple!" Dallandra was shocked by the rage in her own voice. "Ye gods, don't we have enough trouble on hand without you looking for more?"

In the deepening silence the crackling of the fire sounded like the rage of a forest in full flame. Dallandra handed the bowl back to her friend, then turned and ran out of the camp. She had to be alone.

Earlier that evening, their alar, in the company of several others they'd met, had camped about eighty miles south of the Lake of the Leaping Trout. Although they were out on the high plateau of the grasslands, the edge of the primeval forest lay only a few miles away, down in the lowlands that also held the farms of the Round-ear lords. With a flock of Wildfolk darting around her, Dallandra wandered downhill, heading to the forest for comfort as even the most civilized elves are prone to do in troubled times. Once she was well among the scrubby new growth, mostly beeches and bracken, at the forest edge, she sat down on a fallen log and opened her mind to thoughts of Aderyn. She could pick up his existence dimly—very dimly—as a feeling of dread for the future and a very much present pain in his hand; once she received a brief visual impression of him clinging to the saddle as the warband rode hard through the dark. That was all, and as much as she hated to admit that she could care about a Round-ear, she felt sick with worry.

All at once she realized that she wasn't alone. The night was far too quiet: no owls called, no animals were abroad and moving in the undergrowth. She was miles from camp without even a knife. As she stood up, the Wildfolk vanished in a skittering of fear. Dallandra took a deep breath and tried to ignore her pounding heart; if the Round-ears were prowling around, the only weapon she had was her magic. Although she thought of running, movement and noise would give her away. Off to the south she saw a bobbing sphere of light, heading her way; twigs cracked; shrubs whispered against passing bodies. A hunting horn blew, clear and melancholy. Suddenly the light split, multiplied into a line of lights dancing along like a parade of torches, and singing drifted through the chilly air as the procession came closer, circled round, ever nearer, the singing louder—definitely Elvish, but wild, somehow, and hard to follow—the lights blinding as they ringed her round and flared up.

Out of the circling light stepped a woman. She was tall, even for one of the People, and slender, with her silver-pale hair cascading wild down to her waist. Her yellow eyes were huge and slit with emerald pupils. At first Dallandra thought that she was wearing a dress made of beaten gold, but it must have been some trick of the light, because suddenly it seemed that she was wearing only a knee-length tunic of some coarse linen. Her hair seemed darker, too, almost blond. In her hands she carried a slacked bow, and at her hip was a quiver of arrows.

"Do you know who I am?"

"I . . . I . . . I've heard tales of the Blessed Court. The ghosts of the seven kings and the faithful who died with them."

The woman laughed, a peal of scorn. She was wearing a golden diadem round her forehead, jewels winked at her throat, and her dress gleamed again with gold. The bow was gone.

"Tales and nothing more, girl, tales and nothing more. We *are* the Blessed Court, sure enough, but we were here long before your kings and their stinking iron and their ghastly cities." She turned to address someone over her shoulder. "Do you hear that? Do you hear how our fame suffers? Reduced to being labeled ghosts and nothing more and by our own people at that."

Rage howled and pealed through the forest on a blast of icy wind. Strain her eyes as she might, Dallandra could see nothing beyond the circle of torches. When the woman turned back, she was wearing the rough tunic again and hunting boots; the bow in her hands was drawn, a silver-tipped arrow nocked at the ready.

"Tell me our name, or we'll hunt you through the forests like a beast, girl. You stink of the demon metal."

What struck Dallandra the hardest was the irony of it, that she was going to die before Nananna, when all along she'd been bracing herself for her teacher's death. The woman smiled, revealing long pointed teeth like a sprite's. Dallandra tried to speak, failed, swallowed, and blurted the only answer she could think of.

"The Guardians."

The woman laughed, the bow gone, her dress now of silk and a deep soothing blue.

"Right you are. Remember us."

With a howl and an upflung arm she turned and plunged through the circle of torches. Whoever the others were, they laughed and howled and sang with her as the procession rushed off, as fast and smooth as if they floated above the ground. Perhaps they did. Dallandra was shaking too hard to speculate. She sank to her knees and trembled while the lights bobbed away, farther and farther, the song fading, the laughter only a sigh of wind: then gone. Finally Dallandra forced a few words through dry lips.

"I'm sorry I ever doubted you."

With one last convulsive shudder she looked around her and saw, sticking point down into the earth, an arrow. When she drew it out she heard the woman's voice whispering from the wind.

"A gift for you. Remember."

Dallandra ran all the way back to the comfort of the fire and the camp. Still shaking, still gasping for breath, she stammered out the story between gasps while everyone crowded round and passed the silver-tipped arrow from hand to hand.

"After all," Wylenteriel remarked, "we'd better take a good look at it now, because it'll probably turn into a twisted stick or something when the sun comes up."

Only then did Dallandra remember all the old stories about the Guardians that she'd heard as a child, "fantastic tales for the little ones," or so they'd always been called. Now she knew that in some measure at least they were true. Yet, when the sun came up on the morrow, the arrow was still an arrow, beautifully worked from some dark wood and fletched with blue feathers from, most likely, a jay. Dallandra took it in to show Nananna along with breakfast.

Nananna was slow to wake that morning. As she sat up, she plucked at the cushions with frail and clumsy fingers as if they annoyed her. For the briefest of moments she couldn't remember her apprentice's name. Dallandra felt tears spring to her eyes from fear as well as grief. She turned away and hid them.

"What's this arrow?" Nananna's voice was suddenly full again, and in control. "It's got a dangerous dweomer upon it."

"Dangerous?"

"Deadly to the likes of us, child. I can feel a destiny upon it. It will kill a shape-changer as he flies and turn his body to elven form, too, when he falls dying from the sky."

"I didn't know, Wise One, but truly, I never did trust the giver of it. A strange thing happened to me last night."

When Dallandra started to tell the story, Nananna was all attention, but in a bit her mind seemed to drift away. She ran slow fingers over the polished shaft, then let it fall from her lap.

"Well, child, this puzzle is yours, not mine," she said at last. "I . . . I know nothing of these things."

The fear turned to a presence, cold and menacing behind her, as if a murderer had crept into the tent.

"Well, it probably doesn't mean much." Dallandra forced herself to sound brisk and cheerful. "Would you like some porridge? Namydd the merchant brought us some nice Eldidd oats the last time he came."

Later, when she was alone, Dallandra wept for hours.

Just north of Cannobaen, Halaberiel's warband crossed a shallow stream with no name (although it was known the Badger in later years) which should have marked the limits of Eldidd territory, or so the prince told Aderyn, even though some twenty-odd miles west stood the dun and farms of the treaty-breakers' holdings. Aderyn, however, never saw that dun, because they turned north, heading for the forest edge, long before they reached it. By then Aderyn was exhausted, riding wounded and worried for long hours as Halaberiel pushed both his men and his horses hard. Tree and meadow, rock and road—they all blurred together into the endless ache of that long ride. Finally they reached a camp, though not Nananna's, and Aderyn was bundled off to a tent to sleep on leather cushions while the prince talked with the leaders of the various alarli.

In the morning when they rode out, twenty more warriors came with them and a herd of extra horses, too. Aderyn was shocked when he realized that some of those warriors were women. At noon that day they met up with a single alar, heading south, which donated six fighting men, three women archers, and a horse laden with arrows. At sunset, they rode into Nananna's camp to find it huge. Other dweomermasters had heard Nananna's call for help and sent their people, among them sixty warriors with spare horses and weapons both. After all, Halaberiel remarked, they were going to need every sword they could get.

"Our longbows are just hunting weapons. I don't imagine they'll be much good against Eldidd armor. I don't know, of course —we've never tried it."

"Ah." Aderyn tried to nod sagaciously, then fainted dead away.

He woke to find himself lying on his back on a spread of cushions in Halaberiel's enormous tent. Dweomer light shimmered near the smoke hole. At first he thought his injured hand was bleeding badly; then he realized that it was draped into a wooden bowl of warm herb water to soak. When someone knelt beside him he turned his head to find Dallandra, her beautiful eyes all grave concern. He thought that all his pain was well worth it, just to see her worried about him.

"That rotten Round-ear chirurgeon did a clumsy enough job on your hand," she snapped. "We're just lucky that the humors haven't turned foul."

"Well, I didn't exactly follow his orders. Ye gods, my mouth! Is there water?"

She handed him a wooden cup of spring water and watched while he drank it all, then refilled it from a skin lying nearby.

"How do you feel other than your hand?"

"A little tired, but I'll be all right. It's just that the beastly thing aches so much."

She got up and moved round to lift his hand out of the water and dry it off on a scrap of clean cloth. Her touch was so light that he felt no pain, not even in his splinted fingers.

"I've gotten the bindings wet," she remarked, "so they'll shrink as they dry and pull the splints tighter." With a little frown she laid her hand on his and stared at the splints, her lips a little parted in hard thought. The pain seemed to run out of the wounds like spilled water. "There. Better?"

"Much! My thanks, truly, a thousand times over."

"When it starts hurting again, come to me and I'll do it again." Gently she laid the hand down on a cushion and picked up the bowl of filthy herb water. "I'll just throw this away."

As she left, Aderyn heard her speak with someone; in a moment Halaberiel came in. The prince had traded his fine clothes for a pair of tight leather trousers, a plain shirt, and a heavy leather jerkin that looked as if it would turn a blade or two.

"Dallandra says you'll recover. I'm glad to hear it."

"My thanks, Banadar. I hear a lot of noise outside. Have more men ridden in?"

"Fifteen, that's all. But we've got a good-sized warband now, and we may pick up a few more as we ride north. I imagine Melaudd's scraping up every man he can, too. I've sent a scouting party ahead to the lake. The rest of us will leave tomorrow."

"I'll come with you."

"Are you sure? There's no need . . ."

"There is. I'm a herbman, aren't I? If things come to battle, you'll need me more than five swords."

"Done then, and my thanks."

As it turned out, Aderyn wasn't the only healer and dweomer-master who insisted on riding with the army. That night, when Dallandra came in to tend his wounds again, she was close to tears.

"What's so wrong?" Aderyn said.

"Nananna. She's coming with you to the Lake of the Leaping Trout."

"What? It's going to be a forced march. She'll get exhausted."

"She's exhausted already. It's time. She's going to die."

Dallandra wept, her face running tears while her whole body shook in silent grief. When Aderyn scrambled to his feet and flung his good arm around her in a clumsy attempt to comfort her, she pulled away.

"It's wrong of me to weep like this. It's her time, and that's that." She busied herself in wiping her face on her sleeve. "I should accept it and be done with it."

"Easy to say. Not so easy to do."

She nodded a distracted agreement.

"Are you coming with her?" Aderyn said. "And us, I mean?"

"Of course. Do you think I'd let her go alone?" She turned on him with an expression so fierce that he stepped back. "Oh, I'm sorry I snapped at you. I'm all to pieces over this."

"As well you might be. It's all right. I was just worried about her."

"So am I. I'm bringing Enabrilia along, too, to help me tend her. She's sending the baby and her man off with the others. I'm sorry, Ado. I meant to tell you earlier."

He hugged it to himself like a treasure: she'd used his nickname, just casually, as if they'd known each other a good long time.

During the long, hard march to the lake, Aderyn traveled at the rear of the line with the two elven women. Thanks to Dallandra's healing dweomer, his wounded hand bothered him hardly at all, but even if it had pained him, he would have ignored it in his concern for Nananna. Often he wondered if the old woman would live to reach the burial ground. In the mornings she mounted her horse easily enough, but after a few hours her energy would ebb, and she would ride hunched over, clinging to the saddle with both hands, her frail fingers like the talons of some ancient bird, gripping its perch in a desperate fear of falling. By their late camps she would be unable to dismount—Aderyn and Dallandra would lift her down from her horse and carry her like a child to her blankets. Since she could barely eat, she grew lighter every day, all bone and sheer will.

"I'll live long enough to see the death-ground," she would say. "Don't fuss over me, children."

In the end, she was right. Just at noon on a late autumn day, warm and hazy with false summer, Halaberiel led his army—because an army of some two hundred warriors it was by then—up a low grassy rise. Riding in the rear, Aderyn heard sudden yells. Since he couldn't understand the words, he thought the men in the van were seeing the enemy, drawn up and ready for them.

"Stay here with Nanannal!" he yelled at Dallandra.

He turned his horse out of line and rode hard, heading for the head of the line. As he rode, the shouts resolved themselves, then spread down the line of march: dal-en! dal-en! the lake! the lake! Just at the crest of the rise Aderyn came up to Halaberiel, who was calling for a temporary halt. Far down the green slope lay the silver lake, a long finger of water caught in a narrow valley pointing southeast to northwest. To the north a thick forest spread along the valley floor, the dark pines standing in such orderly rows that obviously they were no natural growth. Halaberiel waved his hand in their direction.

"The death-ground. And the trees of my ancestors."

They set up camp that afternoon between the forest and the north shore of the lake in a grassy meadow clearly planned as a campground: there were stone fire pits at regular intervals and small sheds, too, for keeping firewood dry and food safe from prowling animals. After he helped Dallandra make camp—as best he could with his clumsy broken hand—Aderyn joined the council of war, consisting of Halaberiel and ten other elves, hastily elected squad leaders and temporary captains. For over an hour they argued strategy in Elvish while Aderyn tried to pick out the few words he knew; eventually he gave it up and drowsed. After the council disbanded, some of the men from the banadar's personal warband joined them and, out of deference to the dweomerman, spoke in Deverrian. After more talk of arrows, Calonderiel said something so odd that it caught Aderyn's attention.

"How many trees should we cut, Banadar?"

"I don't know. A lot. Too many—ah, by the Dark Sun, far too

many no matter how few it is! We need to go into the forest and see how much stacked wood's there already, I suppose." Halaberiel caught the puzzlement on Aderyn's face and smiled, a painful twist of his mouth. "Come with us. There's somewhat you need to see."

In the last of the afternoon sun, they left the camp and crossed the neatly tended boundary of the forest into the dark and spicy-scented corridors of trees. In a clearing, not ten yards in, stood a structure of dry-walled stone and rough-cut timber about thirty feet on a side. When Halaberiel pushed open the creaking wooden door, Aderyn could see that it was stacked about a third full with firewood. Since by then he'd grown used to the parsimonious elven fires of dried horse dung and twigs, he stared at the wood as if it were a dragon's hoard of gold and jewels.

"When one of the People dies," Halaberiel said, "we take some of this seasoned wood to burn the body. Then we cut a tree to replace it and plant a new one. So, every time one of the People dies, a tree dies, too, and another is born. Normally, it all works out. Now, though, there's going to be a war."

"And you'll need dry wood." Aderyn felt abruptly weary. "Lots of it."

"Just so. But it's going to be a problem. Even if we start cutting tomorrow, the wood's going to be green for a long time. Ah, by the gods of both our people! If this place weren't so sacred, I'd just withdraw and let the rotten-hearted Round-ears have the lakes."

"Never!" Calonderiel's voice was a snarl. "Banadar, how could you even say it?"

With a shrug Halaberiel shut the doors again and turned away, waving to the others to follow him. They were almost back to the camp when they saw Dallandra's friend Enabrilia racing toward them, her long hair streaming behind her, her hands waving as she called out.

"Aderyn, Aderyn, hurry! Nananna's dying!"

Aderyn was running before he quite realized it. Following Enabrilia, he dodged through the camp and came panting at last to Nananna's tent. When he ducked through the flap, Enabrilia stayed outside. He could hear her ordering other people to stand back and keep quiet; then her voice faded away. Inside the tent, a pale dweomer light cast soft shadows. On a heap of leather cushions Nananna lay, her head cradled in Dallandra's arms, her white hair unbound and streaming over her shoulders like a drift of snow. The old woman's face was as pale and dry as parchment, the skin stretched tight over bone, her eyes huge and staring and dark as her cat-slit pupils strained to catch the fading light.

"Here's Aderyn," Dallandra whispered. "He'll get out his medicines and help you."

"There's no need of that." Nananna's voice was a rasp of whisper. "Come here, child."

Aderyn knelt in front of her and took one withered hand in both of his.

"Tell me, Aderyn, will you stay with us?"

"I will. My Wyrd lies here. I know that, even though I'm not sure what it is."

"I know." Her voice was faint, drawing him closer. "I've had one last dream. Teach my people, Aderyn. Teach them your dweomer to mend their shattered magicks. Teach them herb lore, too, to replace the physicians they lost so long ago."

"Gladly, Wise One. Everything I know will be theirs."

She smiled, a draw of bloodless lips, and rested for a long moment before she spoke again.

"Dalla, you shall teach him how to grow a pair of wings like yours. That will be his payment, to fly where he wills."

"Done, then." Dallandra's voice was steady, but when Aderyn looked up, he saw tears streaming down her face. "Everything I know will be his."

"Good." Nananna's breath came in a long sigh. "There must be no secrets between you, none, do you hear? Only with the dweomer can our two races meet in peace, and naught must be held back."

"Well and good, Wise One," Aderyn said. "But what do you mean, grow wings?"

"Our dweomer has a strange trick or two to show you." Nananna managed a smile. "Dallandra and I are shape-changers. Someday you, too, will learn to take on the body and flight of a bird —an owl, I think, to judge from those big eyes of yours."

Aderyn caught his breath with a gasp.

"A thousand thanks. I swear I'll be worthy of it, and only use it to serve the Light."

"Good. Very well, then. I have set you both on your course. It's time for me to depart. Child, let me lie down now."

Dallandra settled her on the cushions and moved aside to kneel by Aderyn. For a moment Nananna lay still, gathering her energy; then slowly, softly under her breath, she began to chant, and her voice took on a last brief flower of strength.

"The river opens before me. I see the light upon the river. It is time to sail to the sea."

When Dallandra sobbed aloud, Aderyn realized that she was too distraught to fulfill the ritual, and that he would have to take her rightful place.

"May the sun shine on you as you sail the river," he whispered. "May the current be fast."

"The sun gathers around me. I step into the boat at the river-bank."

"I see the silver river flowing west, the dark rushes and the boat, ready for you."

As he spoke, Aderyn did indeed see in his mind the vision that they were building together as they went on speaking, describing the scene back and forth to each other. Wrapped in the golden light of the sun, the soul stepped into it—a pale flame of silver light, flickering at first, then towering up strong, far different from a human soul.

"Sun and moon, shine upon her!" Aderyn cried out. "Bring her to the sea of light, love, and life."

The boat was drifting downriver, the silver flame glowing as she rode proudly on. He seemed to drift above it on a bird's wings and see, in the gleaming sunset ahead, Others coming to meet them on a vast wave of light. Nananna rose free of the boat and flew to join them in a sudden blaze that left him blind. Blinking his physical eyes and shaking his head, he brought himself back to find her body lying dead on the cushions.

"It is over," Aderyn called out. "She has gone to her true home."

Like thunder came a booming hollow drumbeat in answer, three great knocks rolling over the camp. From outside he heard a shout, then voices raised in keening, a high and musical wailing for the dead. Aderyn slapped his open palm once on the ground to earth the final force. It was finished. Her trained soul had no need to hang around near its corpse for three days; she had left cleanly and gone free. Aderyn crossed the frail arms over the slender chest and closed the eyes that the soul no longer needed for seeing.

"We should burn the body soon," Aderyn said. "Or do your people lay out the dead to weep over them?"

Dallandra looked at him, then threw back her head and howled. Tears ran down her face as she keened over and over, reaching up, pulling at her hair, unloosening the braids in a silvery spill of mourning, rocking herself from side to side so violently that Aderyn threw his arms around her and pulled her tight. She wept against him, sobbing like a child, her pale soft hair like a cloud over his arms, while outside the People sang in a long wail of grief.

"Hush, hush, it was time."

As violently as it had come, her weeping left her. He could see her wrench her will under control as she looked up, her eyes as calm and gray as fog over sea.

"So it was. And someday we'll meet again in some land or another."

"Just so. Have faith in the Light."

In simple exhaustion, Dallandra leaned her head against his shoulder. As Aderyn held her, his heart pounding, he realized that he'd fallen in love.

That night they burned Nananna and scattered her ashes under the trees of the sacred grove, in a spot where the moon fell through the branches and touched the ground with silver. On her grave Halaberiel swore an oath that never would the race of men defile this spot. All night, the People wept and sang songs of mourning, but when the sun rose, their grief was gone.

There was nothing left but to wait and see what move the Bear clan made next.

"Four hundred men!" Garedd said. "I never thought our lord could raise so many."

"I told you that the men of the north had guts, didn't I?" Cinvan said. "We'll shove those stinking Westfolk off Lord Dovyn's land, sure enough."

They were standing on the roof of Tieryn Melaudd's dun, ostensibly on guard duty, but they'd spent most of the afternoon leaning on the railing and watching the last preparations for the march west. In those days, four hundred men was a sizable army, and the ward below was a cram and clutter of horses, supply wagons, and men, the servants rushing back and forth loading provisions, the lords and riders standing around and talking over the campaign ahead.

"Tomorrow," Cinvan said. "We ride tomorrow. Cursed well about time, too."

"I'm just glad we didn't draw fort guard."

"Cursed right. The sooner we get the fighting started, the better."

Garedd nodded his agreement, then went back to watching the bustle below. Cinvan walked across the tower roof and looked off to the west, where, far out of sight, the enemy lay, no doubt waiting for them. Normally, on a night before a march to battle, he would have been as eager as he was trying to act, but this time, he was troubled by thoughts that he could barely understand. As a matter of course he wanted battle glory, and he wasn't afraid of battle pain—that wasn't the problem. He was simply having trouble convincing himself that he hated the Westfolk as much as he should, considering that they were now his sworn lord's enemies.

No matter how hard he tried to banish the memory, he kept thinking of Prince Halaberiel, demanding and getting mercy for Lord Dovyn. And what about his sister's man, too? What if Gaverro was part of the elven warband? Cinvan cordially hated the elf, but what about his little daughter, so far away from her mother now? What if his own niece ended up an orphan after this fight? Back and forth Cinvan prowled, struggling with an utterly unfamiliar conscience. Finally, when the sunset was turning the west a gilded pink, he reminded himself that as an oath-sworn rider there was absolutely nothing he could do about anything except follow his lord's orders.

"We're off watch," Garedd called out. "You coming? What's wrong with you, anyway?"

"Naught. I'm on my way."

Yet he paused for one last look to the west, and he shuddered, wondering for the first time in his life if he might die in a coming war. Then he shook the feeling off and clattered downstairs to the warmth and noisy cheer of the great hall.

Three days after Nananna died, the first scouts came in. Aderyn was having dinner with Prince Halaberiel when they arrived at the camp; at the sudden gleeful shouts the banadar left his meal and hurried to meet them, with Aderyn trailing after. Although Aderyn couldn't understand the Elvish reports, in time Calonderiel remembered his manners and translated for him.

"The Bears are here, camping down on the strip of land that Dovyn wanted. They've sent out scouts of their own. Our men spotted a couple of them crashing their way through the woods and killed them. When they don't come back, the Bears should be able to guess that we know they're here. They let a third Round-ear live, so he could tell the Bears about the terrain. That was Halaberiel's orders, you see, to let one live. Why, I don't know."

"How many men does Melaudd have?"

"About four hundred."

"Oh, ye gods."

"Bad odds, sure enough." Calonderiel paused, rubbing his chin. "Well, if we die defending the death-ground, it'll have a certain poetry to it." He caught Aderyn's arm and began leading him away from the others. "Will you promise me somewhat? When the battle starts, you and Dallandra will be in camp, waiting to heal the wounded, right?"

"That's our plan, truly."

"Well and good, then. If our line breaks, and we're all slain, will you make sure she gets to safety?"

"I will. I promise you on the gods of my people."

"My humble thanks. I know she'll never love me, but at least I can die content, knowing she'll live."

"You might not die at all, dimwit." It was Jezryaladar, strolling over to them. "The banadar has a trick planned. That was the reason they let one scout get away, as you might have known if you'd only listened more carefully."

"With these odds, a trick's not going to do much good, no matter how clever it is, and don't you call me a dimwit."

"My humble apologies." Grinning, Jezryaladar sketched a bow. "And your intellect does seem to be catching fire, truly, if you realize that you've got no chance with Dalla."

Calonderiel howled and slapped him across the face so hard that he staggered back. Before he could recover or speak, Calonderiel had stalked off into the night. Jezryaladar rubbed his face and swore softly to himself.

"Are you all right?" Aderyn said.

"I am, and you know, I deserved that. We're all on edge tonight, I'm afraid."

"Do you think Cal's right, and things are hopeless?"

"I don't, but blast me if I can tell why. I've just got this certainty deep in my heart that somehow or other Halaberiel's going to get us a victory out of this, but I doubt me if the banadar believes it himself."

The valley that sheltered the Lake of the Leaping Trout fell steeply to the water along its eastern side, but on the western, gentle hills rolled down, forming a strip of fairly flat ground, at least twenty yards wide, often wider, edging the entire length of the lake. When the lone scout came back with the news that the Westfolk were camped up at the far end, Melaudd and his allies automatically decided to move up on this flat ground, where they could ride three and four abreast in battle order, safe from some sudden ambush.

"Not that there's going to be an ambush," Garedd remarked. "From what I hear, the Westfolk only have about eighty riders with swords."

"That troubles my heart," Cinvan said, and he meant it. "I hate to fight with this kind of odds on our side. I'm an oath-sworn warrior, not a pig butcher."

"Well, Melaudd's an honorable man. He won't let all four hundred men charge a tiny warband like that. Probably just half of the army will ride in the first wave, and then we'll see what happens."

"That's a little better, anyway."

As the Bear clan's sworn men, Cinvan and Garedd were in that first wave when the army rode out on the morrow. Four hundred horseman jammed onto a narrow strip of ground tend to spread out, and the day was hot with the last of false summer, too, making the animals a little lazy and the men overconfident, with the end result that the line of march was over a quarter mile long as it wound its way toward the battle. At the time, since everyone assumed that the men in the rear would take no part in the fighting, it worried no one that they had no way of seeing what was happening in the van, if indeed anyone even thought of it. Cinvan and Garedd, riding some twelve ranks behind Tieryn Melaudd and Lord Dovyn, had as much of a view as they needed, especially since their route rose and fell to give them the occasional high ground. It was on one of these small rises, in fact, that they got their first good look at the elven line.

"Are they daft?" Melaudd said it so loud that Cinvan could hear him over the muffled clop of hooves on grass and the clinking of battle gear.

"Must be," Garedd muttered in an answer unheard by their lord.

The elven swordsmen were dismounted. In regular ranks they stood some hundreds of yards ahead in a crescent formation, its open and embracing end toward the oncoming Bears. To one side of them was the lake itself, and on the other, a line of sharpened wooden stakes pounded at regular intervals into the slope, with the points slanting uphill.

"Clever, that," Cinvan said grudgingly. "We can't outflank them and ride them down."

"Just so. But wait a minute, what's that behind them? Looks like a crowd of women."

"With stakes in front of them, too. What?! By all the ice in all the hells, what are those females doing there? Are they going to cheer their men on?"

"Savages, these people. That's all I can say. Howling savages."

"Look." Cinvan pointed uphill. "There's some more men, running into position, but they're not swordsmen. Oh, ye gods, they're carrying bows."

"So what?"

All this time, the army had been traveling forward, a little faster now, the men pressing their horses to close the line and bunch together into a tight formation. Cinvan saw silver wink as Tieryn Melaudd blew his horn for his men to draw swords and ride ready to charge. Up ahead the elven line held steady, waiting, the swordsmen rock-still as the horsemen trotted forward, and forward again, until they were only some hundred yards from the mouth of the crescent. All at once a distant voice cried out in Elvish; at the signal it seemed that a wind swept through the waiting Westfolk and made the line shudder in a long flex like grass before a storm. Bows swung up, arrow points winked and glittered, there was a sound, a rushy hiss, a whistle, a flutter, as over a hundred cloth-yard arrows arced up high, then plunged down at full force into the mail-clad riders and their unarmored horses. Screams burst out as horses reared and staggered, and men fell, some bucked off, others stabbed and bleeding right through their mail. Again came the hiss and rush of death; Lord Dovyn's horn blew in a long sob for a charge, then cut off in mid-wail as a third rain stabbed into the ranks. Horses were panicking, and worse yet, falling; charging was impossible as the dead or merely wounded bodies of men and beasts alike began to litter, then block the road. Carrying an empty, blood-streaked saddle, young Lord Dovyn's horse burst free of the mob at the van and staggered uphill. Again the arrows, ever again—screaming out every foul oath he knew, Cinvan tried to force his horse through the mob by sheer will to reach the wounded tieryn's side. All around him riders were trying to break free, to turn out to go up the hill or splash through the shallow edge of the lake, but inexorably behind came the press of their own allies, who could see nothing of the slaughter ahead, who only knew by the sound of things that the Bear clan was in danger and who out of sheer force of a deadly honor were rushing forward to join the battle and thus to trap the men they were trying to save.

Again the arrows, again and again, and now the Westfolk were cheering and screaming. As he reached the front rank and caught up with Melaudd, Cinvan saw that the women he'd so despised were archers, too, raining death down as hard as their men as they aimed at the exposed positions to the flanks. He wanted to weep—there was no time—the sword in his hand was useless—he went on cursing as the arrows came flying, again and again and again.

"Cinno! They're trying to desert us!" Garedd yelled. "The allies! They're pulling back!"

Cinvan turned his head to shout an answer just in time to see Garedd die, spitted through the chest by a broad-head arrow that snapped the rings of his mail front and back. With a cough and bubble of blood he fell sideways, only to be trampled by the horses of other Bearsmen as they desperately tried to turn and flee.

Hissing and whistling, the deadly rain came again. Cinvan's horse screamed and reared, kicking, as hard iron grazed its flank, but it came down able to stand. Silver horns rang out: retreat, retreat! in a blare of hysteria. Still untouched, Cinvan wrenched his horse around and kicked it into one last burst of gallop. He could see Tieryn Melaudd's broad back just ahead and followed it blindly, unthinkingly, right into the shallow water at the lake edge. Behind him he could hear a few more men cursing and yelling as they splashed after to skirt the battle and turn round the archers' position.

"To their camp!" Melaudd screamed. "Trample it! Vengeance! To their camp!"

Then the tieryn laughed, a madman's howl, a keen of grief, equally mad. Out of loyalty alone Cinvan followed his lord while his mind screamed against the dishonor of such a low trick.

As best he could with his left hand, Aderyn was organizing his packets of herbs to treat the wounded when he heard the horses coming. His first thought was that the elven side had lost and was retreating; then he heard the battle cries, Eldidd voices, shrieking in rage and hatred. Dallandra screamed and came running toward him.

"The Bears! They're heading here!"

"Get into the forest. Run!"

She obeyed without a moment's thought, racing through the tents. Aderyn started to follow, then turned back. If he abandoned his medicinals, wounded men would die. He could see the horses by then, a squad of some fifty out of an army of four hundred, heading in a cloud of dust straight for the defenseless camp. Distantly he could hear elven war cries, chasing after. He grabbed his heavy packs, then froze in sudden panic as the lead horsemen swung round and headed straight for him, swords flashing, slashing the tents, hooves pounding, kicking, trampling bedrolls and cooking pots alike in empty revenge. Aderyn knew he should run, could hear his own voice speaking aloud and begging himself to run, but the panic bit deep and froze the blood in his veins like snakebite as two horsemen charged, closer, closer, closer.

"Not the councillor!" A third horseman burst past a tent and swung by him at an angle to meet the others. "Turn off!"

Swords flashed; one of the charging men screamed and pitched over his horse's neck.

"I said turn off!"

The second horseman did just that, dodging back the way he came, only to meet elven riders as Halaberiel led his swordsmen, mounted now, into camp. Dust plumed with the battle cries as the last few Bearsmen fled, screaming and cursing as they headed south. Aderyn's rescuer turned his horse to follow, then pulled his blowing horse to a stop and slumped in the saddle. Aderyn ran to him just in time to catch him as he slid to the ground in a welling of blood. An arrow had pierced his mail just at the armpit, where the arteries were pumping his life away. Aderyn pulled off his pot helm and eased the padding back from his death-pale face: Cinvan.

"A councillor and an unarmed man," the lad whispered. "Couldn't let my lord disgrace himself a second time."

Then he died with a stiffening and a shake of his whole body.

"Are you all right?" It was Halaberiel, rushing over, bloody sword in one hand, helm in the other, blood flecking his face and pale hair.

"I am. Are we retreating?"

"Retreating?" Halaberiel howled with laughter. "We've carried the day, man! We slaughtered the ugly lot of them!"

Aderyn wept like a child, but as he looked into Cinvan's glazed eyes, he wasn't sure if his tears were joy or grief.

In that last battle in the camp, fought against men sworn in their hearts to die and put an end to shame, the elven forces took casualties, but with only nine elven dead and some twenty wounded against the hideous human losses, Halaberiel was right enough to claim a complete victory. All that day Aderyn and Dallandra worked over the wounded with a swarm of volunteers to help them until the two of them were as gory as corpses themselves. By moonlight they swam in the lake shallows to wash themselves clean, then returned to the camp to find the dead laid out, ready for cremating on the morrow. Dallandra was so weary and heartsick that she crept into her tent to sleep without even a bite to eat, but Aderyn, who was used to battle wounds from his apprenticeship, joined in the victory feast. Since in honor of the battle Halaberiel decided that they could squander seasoned wood and build a proper bonfire, light blazed and danced through the camp along with music from drum and harp. Drunk and howling, the banadar's own warband ran from group to group of celebrating elves, while Halaberiel himself sat off to one side on a pile of cushions and merely watched. When Aderyn joined him, Halaberiel handed him a skin of mead. Aderyn had a few cautious sips to ease his aching muscles.

"Over a hundred Round-ears escaped," Halaberiel said abruptly. "All men from the rear of the line, so they were probably Melaudd's allies rather than Bearsmen. Think they'll raise an army and come back for revenge?"

"I don't. Melaudd's other son will rage and bluster and try to call in alliances, but who's going to join him after this? And he himself can't have more than a handful of men left—the ones that stayed behind on fort guard, no more."

"Good. We'll leave marking the death-ground for later, then. I want to ride before the winter rains come in earnest."

"Indeed? Ride where?"

"South." Halaberiel gave him a tight and terrifying smile. "To wipe out that settlement west of Cannobaen."

Aderyn stared in helpless confusion.

"I've learned somewhat today," Halaberiel went on. "These bows of ours are good for bringing down more than the gray deer. Never again am I going to creep around and humble myself to the dog-vomit Round-ear lords. Eldidd they may have, but no more." He threw back his head and laughed aloud. "Not one stinking cursed inch more, by every god of both our peoples!" Then he let his face soften. "My apologies, Aderyn. I forget that I'm talking about your folk. There's no reason for you to ride south with us when we go. You and Dallandra can just rejoin the alar and wait for us there."

Aderyn rose, staring blankly into the leaping fire.

"Unless you'll be leaving us?" Halaberiel got up to join him. "Never would any man of the People nor a woman either stop you if you choose to ride away, even if you go right to our enemies and warn them."

Aderyn turned and walked off, heading blindly for the meadow beyond the campground, only to stop abruptly when he reached it. Out on the flat the warbands were dancing, winding in long lines through a scatter of tiny fires. The People danced single-file, arms held rigid shoulder-high, heads tossed back while their feet skipped and stamped through intricate measures in time to the drum and harp. Over the music wailed voices, half a keen of grief tonight, yet half a cry of triumph. When the revelers drew close he could see sweaty, impassive faces bob by in a surge of quarter tones, wavering and rising like the firelight; then with a sway and shudder the dancers spun past and were gone. Halaberiel came up behind him and laid a paternal hand on his shoulder.

"I'm sorry," the warleader said. "But that dun has to be destroyed. We'll spare the women and children, of course, and every man's life that we can."

"I know." Aderyn found his voice at last. "What can I say? I've already seen my people muster an army to attack you, haven't I? If it weren't for your longbows, they would have slaughtered you like cattle."

"Just so. But you didn't ride west to watch men die, either. Do you want to go back to Eldidd? I'll give you an escort if you do."

For a moment Aderyn wavered. Even though he'd promised Nananna that he'd stay, he knew that she never would have held him to the promise under these circumstances, when the action at Cannobaen might lead to a full-fledged war. If it did, he belonged with his own kind, he supposed. His revulsion welled up, almost physical: his own kind, who broke their word and murdered and swaggered and enslaved and stole other men's land all in the name of honor? He saw then that he could never go back to Deverry and take up some sort of community life, not even as a healer and herbman. But what else was left for him? The life of a hermit on the edge of the wilderness? He could see himself turning into a recluse, hoarding his secret knowledge for its own sake until the knowledge turned bitter and drove him mad. Halaberiel waited patiently, his eyes shadowed in the flickering light.

"You're my people now," Aderyn said. "Here I stay."

Then he strode forward and took a place at the end of a line of dancers. Although the only steps he knew were from Deverry ring dances, they fit in well enough as the line swept him away across the meadow. All through the long fire-shot night he swayed and bobbed to the wail and the pounding of the music until it seemed in his exhaustion that he had no body left at all, that he floated with the elven warriors far above the grassy meadow and the dark. Yet toward dawn, when he was stumbling toward his tent, Aderyn realized that he would stay behind when the warband rode south. There were other healers among the elves; one of them would have to take his place for the slaughter out west of Cannobaen.

Everyone slept late that day, then woke, cursing and weeping, to the grim task of burning their own dead and giving Melaudd's army a decent burial in long trenches—after the bodies of men and horse alike had been stripped of every bit of metal, whether armor or tool. Out of respect for the prejudices of the noble-born, Halaberiel ordered Melaudd, his son Dovyn, and the two allied lords who'd died with them buried in a separate grave, though he did make sharp remarks about the foolishness of men who worried about their corpses. They packed and sodded a shallow mound over all the burials, too, and chipped the story of the battle onto a rough stone plaque. The job took days, and all during it, scouts rode out to the south and east to keep an eye on the Round-ears. Aderyn and Dallandra worked from dawn to dusk and then worked some more by torchlight as they tried to save the wounded horses as well as the wounded men. The elven casualties would mend fast, especially compared with the human beings, and without a trace of infection in all but the worst cases. The riders who had once ridden for Tieryn Melaudd were another matter entirely. Their worst cases all died; the rest were as sullen and misery-wrapped as only defeated men living on the charity of the enemy can be. Aderyn tended them alone to spare Dallandra the job.

"And I appreciate it, too," she remarked one morning. "But what are we going to do with them? They're prisoners, I suppose. Is Halaberiel going to use them to bargain terms or suchlike?"

"There's naught he wants to bargain for, he says, so he'll just release them." Aderyn hesitated, studying her pale face and the dark shadows smudging under her eyes. "How do you fare, Dalla? You've been working yourself blind."

"It keeps me from missing Nananna. And if I'm tired enough, I don't have bad dreams."

"Dreams about her, you mean?"

"Not truly." She turned away and seemed to be studying the white clouds billowing up from the south. "I hope we leave here soon. Winter's on the way, sure enough."

Aderyn saw that he'd been shut out of some mental chamber as surely as if she'd slammed a door in his face.

When the camp did break, Halaberiel divided his forces. The least-skilled warriors escorted the prisoners south to the Eldidd border, where they'd leave them before turning west to rejoin their alarli. The best of the fighters went with the banadar on a forced march for the treaty-breaking dun beyond Cannobaen. Aderyn, Dallandra, the elven wounded, the injured horses saved from the battle, and a small escort of those archers who were simply sick of fighting headed back west to the place where they'd left the rest of the alarli—left them years ago, or so it seemed to Aderyn, back in some other lifetime. The day they marched, it rained, and it kept raining, too, a good long period of drizzle every day as wave after wave of clouds swept in, dropped their burden, then rolled on. Since with so many injured people and animals along, their small column moved a scant twelve miles a day, by the time that they did rejoin the alarli, those waiting for them were frantic for news. When they rode up, in fact, a huge wail of grief went up from the camp, because everyone assumed that they were the only survivors of some horrible defeat. Once the truth went round, everyone was as much furious as relieved.

"Isn't that just like the wretched banadar!" Enabrilia snapped. "He never even sent them a message!"

"My apologies, truly," Aderyn said. "If I'd known, I would have sent someone on ahead. We just assumed—"

"That Halaberiel had thought to tell them. I know, I know. Not your fault. The grazing's getting really poor around here, by the way."

"Well, we'll move out tomorrow. The banadar wanted everyone to head for the winter camps. He said he'd find us there."

"Good. With this rotten weather we've been having, winter can't be far away."

At that point Aderyn realized that she and the others in the camp were treating him as Halaberiel's second-in-command and taking his orders without question, just as they took Dallandra's. Whether he felt himself worthy or not, these people now considered him a Wise One.

Far to the west of Cannobaen the seacoast turns jagged, rising into precarious cliffs, reaching long fingers of hill out into the ocean, and sinking into deep canyons where the winter rains flow into rocky riverbeds. These canyons provide some shelter from the constant wet winds, and here, at the time of which we speak, the People set up their semi-permanent winter tents, even though changing shifts of horsemen still had to ride guard on the grazing herds up in the exposed grasslands, because the fodder in the canyons themselves was sparse. Aderyn and Dallandra got their people settled safely in one of these camps some four nights before Halaberiel and the warband caught up with them. Exhausted men and horses both dragged into camp late on a day turned foul and dark by a slantwise drizzle. Although there were eight fewer swordsmen than had ridden out, and some twenty wounded archers, even in their weariness they crowed with victory: in a surprise attack they'd wiped out the lord and his warband, then forced the dun to surrender. Aderyn was kept so busy tending the wounded that he didn't see the banadar until late that night, when Halaberiel summoned him to a council in his tent. Although six elven leaders sat round the fire, Halaberiel spoke in Deverrian for Aderyn's sake.

"We need your advice. Do you think the prince is going to send an army against us in the spring?"

"I doubt it very much. I suspect that Addryc is pouring vinegar into his vassals' wounds right now, pointing out what happens to men who disobey their prince's decrees. You've punished his rebels for him, and on top of that, you've gotten rid of that dun. Do you think he liked having men loyal to another overlord out on his western flank?"

"But that overlord was Addryc's own father."

"Among the noble-born that kind of sentiment counts for very little."

Halaberiel considered for a long moment.

"Well and good, then," he said at last. "I'll send him some kind of formal apology the next time we meet a Round-ear merchant— I don't trust the Eldidd lords enough to send them a messenger. And when spring comes we'll ride to the lake and mark the death-ground. After all, it was part of the settlement I made with the prince, that I'd make sure the Round-ears saw me on my land."

"Just so, and I'm willing to bet that it'll settle the matter."

"Good. I did send Addryc one message. I gave it to the refugees who were going to Cannobaen. Just a little note, truly, asking him what he thinks of the Westfolk's style of justice." He smiled gently. "It seems to be a good bit more rigorous than his own."

Part Two

The Elven Border

719–915

THE HORROR OF first the battle, then the aftermath of the slaughter and the long withdrawal with the wounded had so filled Dallandra's mind and heart that she'd never had a proper moment alone with her mourning, or so it seemed to her. Once Halaberiel and the men returned, the life of the winter camps slipped gradually into its normal rhythms, and she felt Nananna's loss like a fresh stab to the heart. She took to going off alone for long hours, either riding far along the wild seacoast or assuming her bird-form and soaring high above the emerald-green grasslands during the intervals between storms, when the sky was cold and pure and the wind a highroad for her wings.

Although she knew that Aderyn was eager to learn how to fly, she put off teaching him on various excuses. In the winter camps were a number of other dweomerworkers, all of whom were impatient to meet him and to hear about the lore preserved in Deverry though lost in the west. Learning to fly in the bird-form was a long, hard job, requiring perfect concentration, solitude, and, quite simply, good weather. The fledgling dweomerman could no more learn to fly in a storm than a fledgling bird could. Yet at heart, she knew that she was putting off teaching him simply because she didn't want to. Sooner or later, she would honor her promise to Nananna and give him the lore, but until she absolutely had to, she wanted to keep it private, hers alone, the last vestige of the spiritual adventures she and Nananna had shared.

Dallandra's bird-form was an odd one. Normally, when masters of the craft finally achieved their goal and shape-changed, they found themselves in a bird-form modeled on some real species, though they couldn't truly choose which one. The process of finding one's form was basically an elaboration on constructing a body of light, in which the magician makes a thought-form as a vehicle for his or her consciousness out on the etheric plane. Although at first he has to imagine this form minutely every time he wishes to use it, eventually a fully realized body, identical to the last one, will appear whenever the magician summons it, out of no greater dweomer than "practice makes perfect," in exactly the way a normal memory image, such as the memory house a merchant uses to store information about his customers, becomes standardized after a long working with it. The elven shape-changer would start by imagining a simple bird shape, all one color and with generalized features. Once that image was clear and steady in her mind, she would transfer her consciousness over to it in exactly the same way she'd transfer to the body of light, then practice scrying on the etheric in this birdlike form.

Eventually, of course, came the true test, using this etheric form as a mold in which to pour the actual substance of her physical body until no trace of an elf remained on the physical plane, and an actual enormous bird flew free in the solid air. Some died while working this stage for the first time; a few even died thereafter, out of carelessness more than any other cause. Most students, however, neither died nor succeeded. Those few who did achieve the transfer over to the physical received a further surprise. When they opened their eyes and looked down at feather, not smooth flesh, they found themselves a very specific bird indeed rather than the generalized image of their mental efforts, a species that was somehow chosen for them by the deepest set of their unconscious mind and thus appropriate to their nature.

All except Dallandra. Learning the procedure had taken her a long, frustrating year; if it hadn't been for Nananna's faith in her abilities, she would have given up after six months. Finally, however, after a long, hard night's work, just when she was about to quit with a howl of frustration, she'd slipped over and felt her arms lengthen and lighten, her body turn full and strangely smooth, then opened new eyes to find herself perching on clawed feet. She'd become a—just what had she become? A bird, certainly, but an amorphous sort of species, a solid dove gray, even to her feet and eyes, with the powerful wings and smooth head of a raptor but a straight beak more like a linnet's. Nananna had never seen any bird quite like it; later, when they consulted with other dweomerwomen, none of whom had ever seen such a bird either, they realized that Dallandra had manifested her idealized form, a thing that had never happened before. Since she could fly with the best of them, however, no one but Dallandra had worried about it or even given it much weight. What counted was that she could make the transformation. Dallandra herself felt that she'd been given a troubling and deeply unusual omen, and not even Nananna could talk her out of her dread.

Dread or not, she loved flying, and in those long weeks when her grief for Nananna turned the whole world bleak, she took refuge in the wind as often as she could. It was on one of these solitary flights that she met the Guardians again. For weeks now, all during the hideous aftermath of the battle, they had haunted her dreams, coming to her in a swirl of bright colors and lights and music to utter strange warnings or make even stranger jests, none of which she could ever remember when she woke of a morning. On an afternoon when a pale and lowering sun struggled to burn off the morning's mist, she was swooping over a canyon when she saw three pure-white swans flapping along, legs dangling awkwardly, long necks bobbing in and out. Swans were so out of place in the grasslands that she darted after them, only to realize that they were as large as she was and thus no true birds at all. Since she knew of no dweomermasters who flew as swans, she followed when they circled down to land, splashing and bobbing, in a shallow backwater of the river below. She herself landed on the ground and hopped, suddenly clumsy, to the water's edge. When they spoke, the words came directly to her mind without effort or sound, and wrapped in their dweomer, she found she could answer the same way.

"So," the largest swan, who seemed to be male, remarked. "Our little sister can fly, can she?"

"Who ever would have thought it?" said the larger female. "Do you still have that arrow I gave you, girl?"

"Yes, of course. But how did you recognize me?"

On a ripple of amusement the swans flew up with a trail of real water splashes, then settled in a flurry of light on the ground nearby. All at once they were elven figures, and dressed in green clothing, rough tunics, leggings, and the younger woman had a short green cloak. To her horror Dallandra found herself in her own true form, but quite naked.

"Things seem much more difficult for you than for us." The younger woman took off the cloak and tossed it to her. "Here. You look cold."

Dallandra snapped the cloak out and wrapped it around her in one smooth gesture. She was sure that her face was scarlet.

"Thank you," she said with what dignity she could muster. "Do you have a name?"

"Of course, but I'm not going to tell you. We've just met."

"In my country it's the custom to exchange names when you meet someone."

"Foolish, very foolish," the elder woman said. "I'd never do such a thing, and I suggest that you don't, either, girl. Now, I want to ask you a question, and it's a very important one, so listen carefully. Why do your people insist on using iron when you know we hate it?"

"Well, first off, why should we care whether or not you hate it?"

"Very good, answering a question with another one. I think you're getting the hang of this. But I'll give you an answer. Because we're the Guardians. That's why."

"And if we stopped using iron, would you do something for us or help us in some way?"

"We did before, didn't we?"

"I don't know. I wouldn't remember. I mean, that was years and years ago, and I wasn't even alive then."

This answer shocked them. In a confused outburst of sound, they looked back and forth at each other—and disappeared, taking the cloak with them. Dallandra threw a few choice curses into the void after them, then concentrated on the laborious task of changing back into bird-form. Once she was safely settled, she flew straight home. She had a lot of questions to ask of the older dweomermasters in the camp.

And yet no one seemed to know much about the Guardians, because no one had ever considered before that they might be real rather than part of some old folktale. That they were spirits rather than incarnate beings seemed obvious enough, but no one knew where their true home in the universe might be, not even Aderyn.

"You know, we have tales about beings much like these Guardians," he remarked one afternoon. "My people must have met them somehow in their travels. But our lore about them is all bits and pieces, a tale here and there, much like yours is."

"They insist that they belong to the People, and they seem to be bound to the same lands. And they're more complex than planetary spirits or suchlike. They have faces and hearts—oh, that doesn't make sense."

"It does, truly. You mean they feel like real individuals."

"Just that. But unformed or unfinished or suchlike. Oh, I don't know! We'll have to wait till you see them, too, and then we can puzzle out more. They're fascinating, though."

"They are that. I hope I get to meet them."

Yet it seemed that they were avoiding him; indeed, they came to Dallandra only when she was alone. When she was out riding, she would see them only from a distance. Usually she'd hear strange music, turn to look, and see one of their processions jogging along at a great distance across the grasslands. Whenever she tried to gallop and catch them, they simply disappeared. When she was flying in the bird-form, though, they would often come as swans or ospreys to fly along with her, usually without sharing a word or thought. Finally it occurred to her that they shunned her in her real form because she generally carried iron with her—a knife at her belt, the bit in her horse's bridle, or the bars in her stirrups.

One cold but sunny day she decided to ride out bareback with only a rope halter to guide her horse, and she left her knives at home. Sure enough, as soon as she was well out of sight of the camp, the two women and their male companion appeared, riding milk-white horses with rusty-red ears.

"So," the elder woman remarked. "You've left your demon metal behind."

"Well, yes, but I honestly don't understand why you hate it so much."

The man frowned in thought. Although his face was both exceptionally handsome and elven, his hair was as yellow as a daffodil, his lips were a sour-cherry red, and his eyes were sky blue—colors as artificial as the tent paints that the artisans ground out of earths and barks.

"We don't understand, either," he said at last. "Or we'd tell you outright. Listen, girl, see if you can solve the puzzle for us. When there's iron around we can't come through to your world properly. We swell and shift and suffer. It hurts, I tell you."

"Through to our world? And where's your world, then?"

"Far away and over the sky and under the hill," the young woman said, and eagerly, leaning forward in her saddle. "Would you like to see?"

Dallandra felt a danger warning like a slap across the face.

"Someday maybe, but I've got to get home now and tend my herds."

She swung her horse's head around, kicked him mercilessly, and galloped away while their laughter howled round her head and seemed to linger in her mind for a long, long time.

Thanks to the male Guardian's frankness, Aderyn could unravel a bit of the puzzle, or rather, his old master, whom Aderyn contacted through the fire, did the unraveling when Aderyn discussed the information with him.

"He says they must be halfway between spirits and us," Aderyn reported. "The bodies we see are really just etheric substance, come through to the physical, and not flesh at all. They must be able to cast a powerful glamour over themselves as well to change their appearance and all, but Nevyn says that there has to be some sort of real substance for them to work with. Do you know what a lodestone is?"

"I don't."

"It's a thing Bardek merchants invented. They take an iron needle and do somewhat to it so that it soaks up an excess of aethyr. I don't know what they do—the sailing guilds keep it secret, you see. When they're done with it, it attracts tiny iron filings—oh, it's a strange thing to watch, because the filings cling to the needle like hairs on a cat! But the important thing is, after they've done this, one end of the needle always points south. They use it to navigate."

"By the Dark Sun herself! A wonder indeed! But what does this have to do with the Guardians?"

"Well, Nevyn says that iron would soak up aethyr from their presence and become much like a lodestone. Then it would either attract or repel the etheric substance they're made of."

"Making them shrink or swell, just like that fellow said."

"Just so. As to their true home, it might lie on the etheric, but they're not part of the Wildfolk. Then again, Nevyn says it might lie in some part of the universe that we don't even know about."

"And a great lot of help that is! But it doesn't matter where they belong. What counts is what they want with us. They claim they've served the People in the past. Do you think they're like your Lords of Light, the Great Ones? I mean, souls like us who've gone on before us to the Light?"

"I asked Nevyn that, and he said he doubted it, just because the Guardians seem so odd and arbitrary and, well, so dangerous."

"Well, then, maybe they're meant to come after us."

"But that's the Wildfolk's Wyrd, to grow under our care and become truly conscious. What I wonder is why the Guardians always appear as elves and ape elven ways. I don't trust them, Dalla, and I wish you wouldn't go off alone to meet them."

"But if I don't, how are we going to find out anything about them?"

"Couldn't we just ask the Forest Folk when we ride east in the spring?"

"The only thing the Forest Folk ever say about the Guardians is that they're gods."

Dallandra suddenly realized that Aderyn's warning was irritating her. How dare he tell me what to do! she thought. But she knew that in truth the Guardians were so fascinating that she simply didn't want to give them up. That very afternoon she left all iron behind, took her favorite mare, and rode out to the grasslands. Not far from the winter camp was a place where three rivulets came together to form a stream, and according to the "children's tales" the joining of three streams always marked a spot favored by the Guardians. In the spirit of testing a theory Dallandra rode straight there. She saw the horse first, a white gelding with rusty-red ears, then its rider, dismounted and lounging in the soft grass on the other side of the water-joining from her. When she rode up and dismounted, he got to his feet and held out his hand. In the cold winter sun his impossibly yellow hair seemed to glow with a light of its own.

"Come sit with me, little sister." His voice was as soft as the sounding of a harp.

"Oh, I think I'll stay on my side of the water, thank you. After all, sir, I don't even know your name."

He tossed his head back and laughed.

"Now that's one up for you! You can call me Evandar."

"I don't want a name I can call you. I want your true name."

"Another one up for you! What if I told you it was Kerun?"

"I'd say you were lying, because that's the name of a Round-ear god."

"And you score the third point. If I tell you my true name, will you tell me yours?"

"That depends. Will you tell the others my name, even though I won't know theirs?"

"My woman's name is Alshandra, my daughter's is Elessario, and I actually and truly am Evandar. It was going to be a jest, you see, to tell you my true name and have you think it false, and in your thinking it false it would have had no power, though power it should have had, and so it all would have been satisfying, somehow. For a jest, that is."

If he had been elven, he would have been daft, she decided, but since he was his own kind, who knew if he were daft or sane? A bargain, though, was a bargain.

"My name is Dallandra."

"A pretty name it is. Now come join me on my side of the stream, because I've told you my name."

"No, because I've given you my name in return."

He laughed with another toss of his head.

"You are truly splendid." Like a wink of light off silver, he disappeared, then reappeared standing beside her on her side of the water. "So I shall come to you instead. May I have a kiss for crossing the water?"

"No, because I've already done you the favor you asked me. I've found out about the iron."

Although he listened gravely, his paintpot blue eyes all solemn thought, she wondered if he truly understood her explanation, simply because it seemed so abstract.

"Well," he said finally, "I've never seen one of these lodestones, but I'll wager it would only pain me if I did. Thank you, Dallandra. You're clever as well as beautiful."

His smile was so warm, his eyes so intense, that she automatically took a long step back. His smile vanished into a genuine melancholy.

"Do I displease you so much?" he said.

"Not at all. It's just you strike me as a dangerous man, and I wouldn't care to cross Alshandra's jealousy, either."

"More than clever—wise!" He grinned, revealing sharp-pointed teeth. "We never mean to hurt you people, you know. In

165

fact, we've tried to help you more often than not. Well, most of us try to help. There are some . . ." He let the words trail away, stared down at the grass for a long moment, then shrugged the subject away. "We need you, you see."

"Why?"

"To keep from vanishing."

"What? Why would you vanish?"

"I think . . . I think . . ." He looked up, but he stared over her shoulder at the sky. "I think we were meant to be like you, but we stayed behind, somehow. Truly, I think that's it. We stayed behind. Somehow."

And then he was gone, and his horse with him, though the grass was flattened down where they'd stood. Dallandra felt suddenly cold and close to choking, so badly so that it took her a moment to realize that she was terrified, not ill. She mounted her horse and rode home fast. About half a mile from camp, she met Aderyn, walking by the river and obviously lost in thought. At the sight of him she almost cried in utter relief: he was so ordinary and homely and *safe*, a Round-ear maybe, but since he had the dweomer, he shared a deeper bond with her than any man of the People ever could. When he saw her, he smiled in such sheer pleasure that she suddenly wondered if he loved her, and she found herself hoping that he did, because for the first time in her life she realized that a man's love could be a refuge rather than a nuisance. She dismounted and led her horse over to him.

"Out for a ride?" he said.

"I was." She realized that he was simply not going to ask her about the Guardians, and she almost loved him for it. "I've been spending too much time alone, I think."

"Do you?" He grinned in relief. "I didn't want to say anything, but . . ."

"But, indeed. You know, it's really time we started teaching you to fly."

"I'd like naught better."

So close that their shoulders touched, wrapped in their conversation, they walked back to camp together, but it seemed to her that she heard the mocking laughter of the Guardians in the cry of distant seabirds. When she shuddered in a sudden fear, he reached out and caught her hand to steady her.

"What's so wrong?"

"Oh, naught. I'm just very tired."

When he released her hand, he let his fingers slip away so slowly, so reluctantly, and his eyes were so rich with a hundred emotions, that she knew he did love her. Her heart fluttered in her throat like a trapped bird.

"Are you sure you're all right?" he said.

"I suppose so. Ado, when I was riding today, I met a man of the Guardians, and he told me some strange things. I really need your help."

"Well, then, you shall have it, every scrap of it I can give you. Dalla, I'd do anything for you, anything at all."

And she knew that, unlike all those other young men who'd courted her, he meant it.

As the wet and drowsy winter days rolled past, Aderyn realized that being a man of the dweomer among the Westfolk brought more than honor with it. Dallandra had inherited all of Nananna's possessions—the tent and its goods, twenty horses, a flock of fifty sheep—but she did none of the work of tending them. Although she cooked her own food, and Aderyn's too, now, because she enjoyed cooking, the rest of the People did all her other chores; they would have waited upon her like a great lady if she'd let them. Since he, too, had the dweomer, Aderyn found himself treated the same. As soon as the People saw that he had no wealth of his own, presents began coming his way. Any animal that was in some way unusual—all lambs born out of season, any horse with peculiar markings, even a dog that showed a rare intelligence—seemed to the People to belong to those who studied equally strange lore and were turned automatically into the herds belonging to the Wise Ones. As Aderyn remarked to Nevyn one night, when they were talking through the fire, his new life had advantages over traveling as a herbman.

"Well, advantages of a sort," Nevyn thought to him, and sourly. "Always remember that you're there to serve, not to be waited upon. If you get a big enough swelled head, the Lords of Wyrd will find some way to shrink it for you."

"Well, true enough, and I do have a fair bit of real work to do, so you can put your mind at ease about that. There's so much teaching been lost out here, Nevyn. It's heartbreaking, truly. I only wish I was a real scholar, not just the clumsy journeyman I am. I'm terrified of failing these people."

"The thing about the dweomer teaching is, once you've got the rootstock, the plant will grow again on its own. Teach them what you know, and they'll recover the rest. Besides, someday soon I might ride your way, and I can bring books if I do."

"Would you? Oh, that'd be splendid! And you could meet my Dallandra."

Nevyn's image smiled.

"That would gladden my heart, truly," the old man said. "But I can't make any promises about when I'll come."

Every afternoon Aderyn and Dallandra would retire to her tent, where she began teaching him the mechanics of the shape-change and the Elvish language as well. His mind and his heart were so full that he was hardly sure if he loved her so much because she was dweomer or if her dweomer was only one more splendid treasure to be found in his beloved. He supposed that Dallandra knew he loved her, but neither of them said one explicit word. Aderyn himself was sure that she would be uninterested in a homely man like him but too kind to say so and break his heart. Since he had never been in love and never expected to be, he was caught by his own utter naïveté about human women, much less elven ones. He had never even kissed a lass, not once, not even in jest.

On a still night that was a little warmer than usual, Aderyn and Dallandra left the camp and walked alone to the seashore to practice a simple ritual. They had no plans of working any great dweomer or invoking any true power; they merely wanted to practice moving together in a ritual space and making the proper gestures in unison. When the moon broke free of the earth and flooded the water with silver, they took their places facing each other and began to build the invisible temple by the simple method of first imagining it according to formula, then describing to each other what they saw. With two trained minds behind them, the forces built up fast. The cubical altar, the two pillars, the flaming pentangles appeared at the barest mention of their names and glowed with power. Aderyn and Dallandra took positions on either side of the altar—he to the east, she to the west—and laid their hands on a glowing cube of astral stone that only eyes such as theirs could see. For the first time Aderyn actually felt it, as solid and cold as real stone, under his trembling fingers.

Dallandra raised her head and looked him full in the face. Although they had yet to start any invocations, suddenly he saw a female figure standing behind her, a gauzy sort of moonlight shape. At first he thought it might be one of the Guardians; then she stepped forward, burst into light and power, stood solid and real, grew huge until she seemed to swallow up the actual elven woman standing beside her. Her pale hair spread out like sunlight, flowers bloomed in garlands, her smile pierced his heart but so sweetly that he cried out and trembled as the scent of roses filled the air.

"What do you see?" It was Dallandra's voice, but as vast as a wave booming on the shore.

"The Goddess. I see her, and she stands upon you."

Barely aware of what he was doing, Aderyn sank to his knees and raised both hands in worship as the Goddess seemed to merge again with the moonlight and blow away in the wind. When she was gone, he felt like weeping with all the grief of a deserted lover. Dallandra called out and stamped upon the ground. With a snap of withdrawn power, the temple vanished, and Aderyn jerked forward and nearly fell, because he'd been leaning against the astral altar for support. Half spraddled on the wet sand, he was too exhausted to do more than watch while Dallandra formally closed the working and banished the invisible forces. Only when she'd finished did he hear again the sound of the ocean, crashing heavy waves nearby. She knelt down beside him and caught his hands in hers.

"I've never felt such power before. I don't know what went wrong—well, if you could call it wrong."

"Of course it was wrong!" Aderyn snapped. "I owe you a hundred apologies. I got completely out of control. By the hells, you must think me a rank beginner."

Dallandra laughed, a soft musical note.

"Hardly that!"

In the darkness, a faint glow still hung around her face. Suddenly, and for the first time in his life, he felt lust—not some sentimental warm desire, but a sheerly physical hunger for her body. He could think of nothing else; he wanted to grab her and take her like the worst barbarian in the world. Sharply he drew in his aura and pulled himself under control, but she had already seen the violence of the feeling playing across his face.

"We broke the ritual too soon." Dallandra's voice shook. "I owe you the apology. We should have let the force finish itself out."

"That would only have led to somewhat worse."

Aderyn dropped her hands and stood up, turning his back on her in a sick kind of shame. When she laid a timid hand on his shoulder, he turned and knocked it away.

"You'd best get back to your tent."

Biting back tears, she ran for the camp. He walked down to the water's edge, picked up a flat stone, and skipped it across the surface like a young lad. As it sank, he imagined his lust and made the feeling sink with it.

In the morning, when they met to continue their studies, Dallandra acted as if nothing unusual had happened the night before, but Aderyn could see that she was troubled. They spent an uncomfortable, distant hour discussing the proper visualization of the bird-form while from outside the noise from the alar filtered in —children yelling, dogs barking, Enabrilia's voice giggling as she discussed something with another woman, a brief yelling match and fistfight between two young men, the shouting as the rest of the alar ran to break it up. After they'd been interrupted for the tenth time, Aderyn's frustration boiled over.

"By the Lord of Hell himself, why can't they be quiet for two stupid minutes?"

"I don't know." Dallandra considered the question seriously. "It's an interesting point in a way."

Aderyn almost swore at her, too, but he restrained himself.

"It's not the noise that's bothering you," she said at last. "You know it and I know it."

He had the most unmagical feeling that he was blushing. For a brief moment she looked terrified of her own words, then forced herself to go on.

"Look, the more we work together, the more the forces will draw us together. We have to face up to that sooner or later."

"Of course, but then—well, I mean I'm sorry, I truly am, but—it would hardly be a good idea for us to—I mean . . ." Aderyn's words failed him in a celibate's fluster.

For a long time she stared at the floorcloth of the tent, and she seemed as miserably shy as he felt. Finally she looked up with the air of a woman facing execution.

"Well, I know you love me. I have to be honest—I don't love you yet, but I know I will soon, just from working with you, and I like you well enough already. We might as well just start sharing our blankets."

When Aderyn tried to speak, the only sound that came to him was a small strangled mutter. He felt his face burn.

"Ado! What's so wrong?"

"Naught's wrong. I mean, it's naught against you."

When she tried to lay her hand on his arm, he flinched back.

"I don't understand." Dallandra looked deeply hurt. "Was I wrong? I thought you wanted me. Don't you love me?"

"Of course I do! Oh, by the hells—I'm making a stinking botch of everything."

Like a panicked horse, Aderyn could only think of getting on his feet and running. Without another word, he left the tent, dodged through the camp, and raced down to the beach. He ran along the hard sand at the water's edge until he was out of breath, then flung himself down on the soft, sun-warmed beach closer in. So much for having great power in the dweomer, he told himself. You stupid lackwit dolt! He found an ancient fragment of driftwood and began shredding it, pulling the rotting splinters to fiber. He had only the faintest idea of how a man went about making love to a woman—what was she going to think of him—how could he sully someone as beautiful as she—what if he did it all wrong and hurt her somehow?

The wind-ruffled silence, the warm sun, the beauty of the dancing light on the ocean all combined to help calm his racing mind and let him think. Slowly, logically, he reminded himself that she was doubtless right. If they were going to generate such an intensity of polarized power between them, the only thing to do with it was to let it run its natural course and find its proper outlet—an outlet that was as pure and holy as any other part of his life. The dweomer had never expected him to live like a celibate priest of Bel. He honestly loved her, didn't he? And she was honestly offering. Then he remembered how he'd left her: sitting there openmouthed, probably thinking he was daft or worse, probably mocking him. He dropped his face in his hands and wept in frustrated panic. When he finally got himself under control, he looked up to find her standing there watching him.

"I had to come after you. Please, tell me what I've done to offend you."

"Naught, naught. It's all my fault."

Her lips slightly parted, Dallandra searched his face with her storm-dark gray eyes, then sat down next to him. Without thinking he held out his hand; she took it, her fingers warm and soft on his.

"I truly do love you," Aderyn said. "But I wanted to tell you in some fine way."

"I should have let you tell me. I'm sorry, too. I've had lots of men fall in love with me, but I've never wanted anything to do with any of them. I'm frightened, Ado. I just wanted it over and done with."

"Well, I'm frightened, too. I've never been with a woman before."

Dallandra smiled, as shy as a young lass, her fingers tightening on his.

"Well, then we'll just have to learn together. Oh, by those hells of yours, Ado, here we've studied all this strange lore and met spirits from every level of the world and scried into the future and all the rest of it. Surely we can figure out how to do what most people learn when they're still children!"

Aderyn laughed, and laughing, he could kiss her, her mouth warm, delicate, and shy under his. When she slipped her arms around his neck, he felt a deep warmth rising to fight with his fears. He was content with her kisses, the solid warmth of her body in his arms, and the occasional shy caress. Every now and then she would look at him and smile with such affection in her eyes that he felt like weeping: someday she would love him, the woman he'd considered unreachable.

"Shall I move my gear to your tent tonight?" he said.

She had one last moment of doubt; he could see it in her sudden stillness.

"Or we could let things run their course. Dalla, I love you enough to wait."

"It's not that." Her voice was shaky and uncertain. "I'm just afraid I'd be using you."

"Using me?"

"Because of the Guardians. I feel sometimes that I could drift into their sea. I want an anchor, Ado. I need an anchor, but I—"

"Then let me help you. I said I would, and I meant it."

With a laugh she flung herself into his arms and clung to him. Years later he would remember this moment and tell himself, bitterly, that he'd been warned.

Yet he could never blame himself—indeed, who could blame him?—for ignoring the warning when he was so happy, when every day of his new life became as warm and golden and sweet as a piece of sun-ripened fruit, no matter how hard winter roared and blustered round the camp. That afternoon he carried his gear over to Dallandra's tent and found that among the People this simple act meant a wedding. In the evening there was a feast and music; when Aderyn and Dallandra slipped away from the celebration, they found that their tent had been moved a good half mile from camp to give them absolute privacy, with everything they owned heaped up inside.

While she lit a fire for warmth as well as light, Aderyn laced the tent flap. Now that they were alone, he could think of nothing to say and busied himself with arranging the tent bag and saddle packs neatly round the tent. He moved them this way and that, stacked them several different ways, as if it truly mattered, while she sat on the pile of blankets and watched him. Finally, when he could no longer pretend that he had anything worthwhile to do, he came and sat beside her, but he looked only at the floorcloth.

"Well, uh, I don't know," he said. "Shall I tell you how much I love you?"

He heard her laugh, then a little rustling sound, and looked up to find her untying and unbraiding her hair. Her slender face seemed almost lost in that pale thick spill of silver waving down to her waist. When he risked running a gentle hand through it she smiled at him.

"We've laced the tent flap," she said. "No one will dare bother us now."

Smiling, Aderyn bent his head down and kissed her. This time she turned into his arms with a shy desire that sparked his own.

From that day on, everyone treated him as though he'd always lived among the People and always been Dallandra's man, just as she became his woman, so naturally, so easily, that he felt as if his heart would break from the joy of it, the first truly human joy he'd ever known in life, that of being part of a pair and no longer lonely. Even Calonderiel accepted the situation, although, just after the shortest day of the year, Cal did leave the banadar's warband and ride away to join another alar. Aderyn felt guilty over that and said as much to Halaberiel.

"Don't worry about it," the banadar said. "He'll reconsider when his broken heart heals. At his age, it'll probably heal quickly, too."

Halaberiel was right enough. When the winter camps were breaking up in the first of the warm weather, Cal came riding back, greeted everyone, including Aderyn, as a long-lost brother, and stowed his gear in its former place in the banadar's tent without a word needing to be said by anyone. As the alarli moved north, heading for the Lake of the Leaping Trout, other warriors came to join them, swordsmen and archers, men and women both, until an army rode into the death-ground to camp and wait for news from Eldidd. Since the dweomer sent Aderyn no warnings of danger, he doubted if there was going to be war, but Halaberiel spent long restless nights, pacing back and forth by the lakeshore, until at last a merchant caravan rode in with Namydd at its head to announce that there would be nothing but peace.

Even though Melaudd's elder son, Tieryn Waldyn now, had cried revenge and spent the winter riding all over the princedom trying to raise men to seek it, he'd failed ignominiously. Prince Addryc refused his aid, of course, on the grounds that the Bear's had violated his decree of sanctity for the elven burial ground. None of the other lords wanted either to displease the prince or to face the longbows of the Westfolk, and Waldyn's potential allies found an absolute army of reasons to avoid doing so, especially once the news from Cannobaen spread north, that a band of Westfolk had fallen upon the west-lying settlements without warning and wiped them out.

"So Waldyn can mutter over his ale all he wants," Namydd finished up. "But he's not getting any vengeance this summer, leastaways. Besides, Banadar, there's trouble along the Deverry border now. The king of Eldidd's collected the rights and dues from the mountain passes for as long as anyone can remember, but the Deverry gwerbret in Morlyn's started claiming them. There'll be blood over this, there will."

"Splendid," Halaberiel said. "They won't be encroaching upon our lands if they're fighting among themselves. May their gods of war lead them in a long, long dance."

The People spent just over a month at the Lake of the Leaping Trout, digging stones from the hills and using them to make a rough boundary line, rather than a wall, around the sacred territories. No one, it seemed, remembered how to make the mortar that had once held together the fabled cities of the far west, but as Halaberiel remarked, they'd be riding back often enough to keep the boundary in repair even without a proper wall. All during the construction Aderyn continued his teaching, since several of the dweomerworkers had followed them, and it was there, too, that Nevyn found him for his promised visit. Not only had the old man brought books of lore—three whole volumes of precious writings, including *The Secret Book of Cadwallon the Druid*—but he also had a mule pack filled with rolls of parchment, big blocks of dried ink, and special slate trays for grinding the ink into water. Pens, of course, they could cut from any bank of water reeds.

"How did you get the coin for all of this?" Aderyn said, marveling at the ink. Each block was stamped with the pelicans of the god Wmm. "Or did the temple just give it to you?"

"The ink was a gift, truly, but I bought the rest. Lord Maroic's son paid me handsomely for saving his new lady's life." Nevyn's face turned suddenly blank. "Ado, I've got news of a sort for you. Come walk with me."

When they left the tent, Dallandra hardly seemed to notice, so lost in the books was she. In the long sun of a hot spring afternoon they walked along the lake, where tiny ripples of water eased up onto clear white sand.

"Somewhat's wrong, isn't it?" Aderyn said.

"It is. There was fever, bad fever, in Blaeddbyr last winter. Your father and mother are both dead. So is Lord Maroic and most of the elderly and all of the babies in the village, for that matter."

Aderyn felt his head jerk up of its own will. He wanted to weep and keen, but he couldn't speak, couldn't move. Nevyn laid a gentle hand on his shoulder.

"It aches my heart, too, Ado. I felt it would be better to tell you myself rather than merely pass the news on through the fire."

Aderyn nodded his agreement, wondering at himself and at the grief that seemed to have torn out his tongue. They're not truly dead, he told himself. They've just gone on. They'll be born again. You know that.

"It was a terrible thing, that fever." Nevyn's voice was soft and distant, as if he were talking to himself alone. "But at least it was quick. I think Lyssa might have pulled through if it weren't that Gweran had already died. I don't think she truly wanted to live without him."

He nodded again, still unable to speak.

"There's no fault or shame in tears, lad. They've gone on to new life, but who knows if ever you'll see them again?"

At that, finally, he could weep, tossing his head back and sobbing aloud like one of the People. Nevyn patted him on the shoulder repeatedly until at last he fell quiet again, spent.

"I'll miss them," Aderyn said. "Especially Mam. Ye gods, Nevyn, I feel so lost! Except for you, I really don't have any people but the People now, if you take my meaning."

"I do, and you're right enough. But that's your Wyrd, lad. I'd never presume to guess why, but it's your Wyrd, and you've taken it up well. I honor you for it."

Since in his grief the noisy camp seemed too much to bear, Aderyn led Nevyn on a long, silent walk halfway round the lake. Having his old teacher there was a comfort more healing than any herbs. When the sun was getting low they started back, and Aderyn made an effort to wrench his mind away from his loss.

"And what do you think of my Dallandra?"

Nevyn grinned, looking suddenly much younger.

"I'm tempted to make some smart remark about your having luck beyond your deserving, to find a beautiful woman like this, but truly, her looks are the least of it, aren't they? She's a woman of great power, Ado, very great power indeed."

"Of course."

"Don't take it lightly." Nevyn stopped walking and fixed him with one of his icy stares. "Do you understand me, Aderyn? At the moment she's in love with you and in love with playing at being your wife, but she's a woman of very great power."

"Truly, I'm aware of that every single day we're together. And there's another thing, too. Don't you think I realize that she's bound to live hundreds of years longer than I will? No matter how much I love her, I'm only an incident in her life."

"What? What are you saying?"

"Forgive me, I forgot that you wouldn't know. The People live for a long, long time indeed. About five hundred years, they tell me, out on the plains, though when they lived in cities, six or seven hundred was the rule."

"Well, that'll keep a man honest out here." Nevyn hesitated in sheer surprise. "But, Ado, the envy—"

"I know. It's somewhat that I'll have to fight, isn't it? My own heart-aching envy."

That night the three of them sat together in Aderyn and Dallandra's tent. Since it was too warm for a fire, Dallandra made a dweomer globe of yellow light and hung it at the tent peak. Wildfolk swarmed, the gnomes hunkering down on cushions, the sprites and sylphs clustering in the air; a few bold gray fellows even climbed into Nevyn's lap like cats.

"Aderyn's been telling me about the Guardians," Nevyn said to Dallandra. "This is a truly strange thing."

"It is," Dallandra said. "Do you know who or what they are?"

"Spirits who've never been born, obviously."

Both Aderyn and Dallandra stared.

"Never been incarnated, I mean," the old man went on. "But I get the distinct feeling that they're souls who were destined to incarnate. I think, Dalla, that this was what Evandar meant by 'staying behind.' That they should have taken flesh here in the material world but refused to do it. The inner planes are free and beautiful and full of power—a very tempting snare. They're also completely unstable and fragile. Nothing endures there, not even a soul that would have been immortal if it had undergone the disciplines of form."

"Do you mean that the Guardians really will fade and simply vanish?" She was thinking hard, her eyes narrow.

"I do. Eventually. Maybe after millions of years as we measure time, maybe soon—I don't know." Nevyn allowed himself a grin. "It's not like I'm an expert in this subject, you know."

"Well, of course." Dallandra thought for a moment before she went on. "Evandar said that they were meant to be 'like us.' Are they elven souls, then?"

"Mayhap. Or it might well be that they belong to some other line of evolution, some other current in the vast river of consciousness that flows through the universe, but one that's got itself somehow diverted into the wrong channel. It doesn't much matter, truly. They're here now, and they desperately need a pattern to follow."

"But Evandar said his people could help us, do things for us."

"No doubt. They have all sorts of dweomer power at their disposal, dwelling on the inner planes as they do. I couldn't even begin to guess what all they may be able to do. But I'd be willing to wager a very large sum on this proposition: they have no wisdom, none. No compassion, either, I'd say. That's the general rule among those who've never known the material world, who've never suffered in flesh." Nevyn leaned forward and caught Dallandra's gaze. "Be careful, lass. Be on your guard every moment you're around them."

"I am, sir. Believe me. And truly, I don't want anything to do with them from now on. If it's my Wyrd to learn about them or suchlike, it can just wait till I've got the strength to deal with it properly."

"Well, I think me that in this case at least, your Wyrd should be willing to do just that."

And Nevyn smiled in relief, as if he'd just seen a horse jump some dangerous hurdle and come down safe and running.

It was some three years before Dallandra spoke with the Guardians again. In the first year of her marriage to Aderyn, she deliberately kept herself so busy learning what he had to teach and teaching him what lore she could pass on that she had few moments to think of that strange race of spirits. She also refused to go anywhere alone, and sure enough, they avoided her companions, if indeed they weren't avoiding her. By a mutual and unspoken agreement, she and Aderyn never mentioned them again, and they grew clever at changing the subject when one of the other dweomerworkers did bring the Guardians up. Her love for Aderyn became exactly the anchor, as she'd called it, that she wanted. He was so kind, so considerate of her, that he was an easy man to love: warm, gentle, and rock-solid reliable. Dallandra was not the sort of woman to demand excitement from her man; in her work she dealt with enough excitement to drive the average woman, whether human or elven, daft and gibbering. Since Aderyn was exactly what she needed, she did her best to give him everything he might need from her in return.

Yet, by the end of the second year, Dallandra began to see the Guardians again, though only at a distance, because they sought her out. When the alar was changing campgrounds, and she was riding at the head of the line with Aderyn or Halaberiel, occasionally she would hear at some great distance the melancholy of a silver horn and look up to see tiny figures in procession at the horizon. If she tried to point them out to her companions, the figures would be gone by the time they looked. When she and Aderyn went flying together—and by then he'd learned to take the form of the great silver owl—she would sometimes see the three swans, too, keeping pace with them but far off in the sky. Whenever she and Aderyn tried to catch up with them, they merely disappeared in a swift flicker of light.

Then, in the third spring after her marriage, the dreams started. They came to her in brief images, using the elven forms she'd seen before, Evandar, Alshandra, and Elessario, to reproach her for deserting them. At times, they offered great favors; at others, they threatened her; but neither favors nor threats held any force. The reproaches, however, hurt. She could remember Evandar vividly, saying that his people needed hers to keep from vanishing, and she remembered Nevyn's theories, too, as well as Nevyn's warnings. She told herself that the Guardians had made their choice when they'd refused to take up the burdens of the physical world; as the elven proverb put it, they'd cut their horse out of the herd—now they could blasted well saddle it on their own. Provided, of course, Nevyn's theories were right. Provided they'd known what they were doing.

Finally, after a particularly vivid dream, Dallandra haltered her mare and rode out bareback and alone into the grasslands. She did take with her, however, a steel-bladed knife. After about an hour of riding, she found a place that seemed to speak of the Guardians: a little stream ran at one point between two hazel trees, the last two left of a stand that must have been cut by an alar in some desperate need. Dallandra dismounted several hundred yards away, tethered out her mare, then stuck the knife, blade down, into the earth next to the tether peg so that about half the handle protruded but the blade was buried. Only after she'd made sure that she could find it again did she walk on to the paired hazels.

Sure enough, a figure stood on her side of this otherworldly gate: Elessario. If it had been Evandar, Dallandra would have turned back immediately, but she trusted another woman, especially one who appeared young and vulnerable, barely out of her adolescence. She had her father's impossibly yellow hair, but it hung long and unbound down to her waist; her eyes were yellow, too, and slit catlike with emerald green.

"You've come, then?" Elessario said. "You heard me ask you?"

"Yes, in my dreams."

"What are dreams?"

"Don't you know? That's when you talk to me."

"What?" Her perfect, full mouth parted in confusion. "We talk to you when you come into the Gatelands, that's all."

"Oh. Your father told me your name, Elessario."

She jerked up her head like a startled doe.

"Oh, the beast! That's not fair! I don't know yours."

"Didn't he tell you? He knows it."

"He does? He's never very fair, you know." She turned suddenly and stared upstream, between the hazels. "Mother's worse."

"You call them Mother and Father, but they never could have birthed you. Not in the usual way, anyway."

"But when I became, they were there."

"Became?"

Elessario turned both palms upward and shrugged.

"I became, and they were there."

"All right, then. Do you know what I mean by being birthed?"

When she shook her head no, Dallandra told her, described the entire process as vividly as she could and described the sexual act, too, just to judge her reaction. The child listened in dead silence, staring at her unblinking with her yellow eyes; every now and then, her mouth worked in disgust or revulsion—but still she listened.

"What do you think of that?" Dallandra said at last.

"It never happened to me, all that blood and slime!"

"I didn't think it had, no."

"But why? What a horrible thing! Why?"

"To learn this world." Dallandra swept her arm to point out sky and earth, grass and water. "To learn all about it and never ever vanish."

For a moment Elessario considered, her mouth working in thought this time, not disgust. Then she turned, stepped into the stream between the hazels, and was gone. That will have to do for now, Dallandra thought to herself. We'll see if she can even remember it. As she was walking back to her horse, she was thinking that Nevyn's theory of never-incarnate spirits seemed more and more true. She had just reached the tethered mare when she felt a presence behind her like a cool wind. She spun around to see Alshandra, towering and furious, carrying a bow in her hands with a silver-tipped arrow nocked and ready. Suddenly Dallandra remembered the arrow she'd been given and remembered even more vividly that it was no etheric substance but real, sharp wood and metal.

"Why are you angry?"

"You will not come to us in our own country."

"If I did, would I ever come back to my own country?"

"What?" Alshandra's rage vanished; she seemed to shrink down to normal size, but still she clasped the bow. "Why would you want to?"

"This is where I belong. What I love dwells here."

Alshandra tossed the bow into the air, where it disappeared as if it had tumbled through an invisible window into some hidden room. Dallandra's blood ran cold: these were no ordinary spirits if they could manipulate physical matter in such a way.

"You will take my daughter from me, girl. I fear you for it."

"What? I don't want to steal your daughter."

Alshandra shook her head in a baffled frustration, as if Dallandra had misunderstood her.

"Don't lie—I can see it. You will take my daughter. But I shall have a prize in return. Remember that, girl."

Swelling and huge, she rose up, her hands like claws as she reached out. Dallandra dropped to her knees, grabbed the hilt of the buried knife, and pulled it free, rising again in one smooth motion. Alshandra shrieked in terror and fell back. For one panicked moment they stood there, staring at each other; then Alshandra's form wavered—and bulged out, as if some invisible force from the knife blade was pushing against her midriff and shoving it back. She looked exactly like a reflection on the surface of a still pool when a puff of breeze moves the water: all wavering and distorted. Then she was gone, with one last shriek left to echo round the grasslands and make Dallandra's mare kick and snort in fear.

That night Evandar appeared in Dallandra's dreams and said one simple thing: you should never have done that. She didn't need him to tell her what action he meant. What he couldn't understand was that she felt not fear but guilt, that she'd caused Alshandra such pain.

In the morning, as they sat in their tent eating wild berries and soft ewe's-milk cheese, Dallandra broke their unspoken rule about mentioning the Guardians and told Aderyn what had happened. She was utterly stunned when he became furious.

"You said you'd never go see them again!" His voice cracked with quiet rage. "What, by all the hells, did you think you were doing, going off alone like that?"

She could only stare openmouthed. He caught his breath with a gasp, swallowed heavily, and ran both hands over his face.

"Forgive me, my love. I . . . they terrify me. The Guardians, I mean."

"I don't exactly find them comforting myself, you know."

"Then why—" He checked himself with some difficulty.

The question was a valid one, and she gave it some hard, silent thought, while he waited, patient except for his hands, which clasped themselves into fists as they rested on his thighs.

"It's because they're suffering," she said at last. "Evandar is, anyway, and his daughter suspects that something's very wrong with their people. They do need help, Ado."

"Indeed? Well, I don't see why you should be the one to give it to them."

"I'm the only one they've got, so far at least."

"Well, I need you, too, and so do the rest of the People."

"I know that."

"Then why do you keep hunting these demons down?"

"Oh, come on, they're not demons!"

"I know, I know. I'm sorry. I just don't like them. And besides, it isn't all pity on your part, is it? You seem to find them fascinating on their own."

"I've got to admit that. It's because they're a puzzle. We've searched out all the lore we can, from your old master and his books, from all the other dweomerworkers among the People, and we still don't know what they are. I'm the only one who has a chance of finding out."

"It's all curiosity, then?"

"Curiosity?" She felt a surge, not of anger, but of annoyance. "I wouldn't dismiss it that way."

"I never meant to dismiss it."

"Oh, indeed?"

And they had the first fight they'd ever had, hissing the words at each other, because back and forth outside the tent the rest of the alar kept going past on their morning's chores. Finally Dallandra got up and stormed out of the tent, ran through the camp, and kept running out into the grasslands. When she slowed to a walk and looked back, she was furious to see that he hadn't followed her. She caught her breath, then walked on, heading nowhere in particular and circling round to keep the camp in sight as a distant jagged line of tents on the horizon.

"Dallandra! Dallandra!" The voice seemed far away and thin. "Wait! Father told me your name."

She spun around to see Elessario running to meet her. As she came close, the grass parted around her as if she did indeed have physical substance and weight, but her form was slightly translucent and thin. Smiling, she offered one hand, bunched in a fist to hide something.

"A present for you."

When Dallandra automatically held out her hand, Elessario dropped a silver nut onto her palm. It looked much like a walnut in a husk, and it had a bit of stem and one leaf still attached, but all of silver, solid enough to ring when Dallandra flicked the husk with her thumbnail.

"Well, thank you, but why are you giving this to me?"

"Because I like you. And as a token. If you ever want to come to our country, it'll take you there."

"Really? How?"

"Touch it to your eyes, and you'll see the roads."

Again, automatically, Dallandra started to do just that, then caught herself in the nick of time. With a shaking hand she stuffed the nut into her trousers pocket.

"Thank you, Elessario. I'll remember that."

The child smiled, and she looked so happy, so innocent in her happiness, that it was impossible to suspect her of guile. Evandar, of course, was another matter.

"Did your father give you this to give to me?"

"Oh yes. He knows where they grow."

"Ah. I rather thought so."

Elessario started to speak, then suddenly yelped like a kicked dog.

"Someone's coming! Him! Your man!"

Elessario disappeared. Dallandra spun around and saw Aderyn hurrying toward her. When she went to meet him, he smiled in such relief that she remembered their quarrel.

"I'm sorry I ran out like that," she said.

"Well, I'm sorry I said all those things. I love you so much."

She flung herself into his arms and kissed him. With his arms tight around her, she felt safe again, warm and secure and even happy. But somehow, she forgot to tell him about the silver nut; when she found it in her pocket, she wrapped it up in a bit of rag and hid it at the bottom of one of her personal saddlebags, where he'd never have any reason to look for anything.

It was some months later, when the days were growing shorter and the alar was beginning to talk about heading for the winter camps, that Aderyn realized Dallandra was seeing the Guardians regularly. Although she would ride off alone at least three afternoons a week, both of them needed so much time alone, for meditation as well as certain ritual practices, that at first he thought nothing of it. His own teaching work took up so much of his attention that he was in a way grateful that she was occupied elsewhere. Later he was to realize that he'd also been refusing to believe that his woman would coldly and deliberately do something against his wishes; certainly no Deverry woman would have, and in spite of his conscious efforts to the contrary, in his heart he thought of Dallandra as a wife much like the one his mother had been. Besides, she always took her usual knife with her, and her horse had its usual bridle with an iron bit and cheekpieces, and iron stirrup bars and buckles on its saddle, a surety of sorts against the appearance of the Guardians. Eventually, of course, he realized that she could easily leave the horse and the knife behind somewhere and walk out to meet her friends.

What finally made him face the truth was her growing distraction. At the autumn alardan, when the People brought their problems to her in her role as Wise One, she spent as little time on them as possible; if she could do it without offending anyone, in fact, she turned these mundane matters over to Aderyn. When they were alone, she was lost in thought most of the time; holding any sort of a real conversation with her became next to impossible. Yet in his mind he went on making excuses for her—she's thinking about her meditations, she's working on some bit of obscure lore—until he happened to have a conversation with Enabrilia when they met by chance out by the horse herd.

"Is Dallandra sick?" she asked him.

"No. Why?"

"She's so distracted all the time. This morning I ran into her down by the stream and I had to hail her three times before she realized that I was there. When I finally got her attention she just kind of stared at me. I swear it took her a while to remember who I was."

Aderyn felt fear like the tip of a cold needle just pricking at his mind.

"Of course," Enabrilia went on, "she might be pregnant. I mean, you two have only been together for four years, hardly any time at all, but you are—well, no offense intended—but you are a Round-ear, after all. They always say things are different with Round-ear men."

Aderyn hardly heard her chatter. Her concern was forcing him to see something that he hated. When Dallandra returned to the camp, he was in their tent and waiting for her.

"You've been riding off to see them again, haven't you?" He blurted it out straightaway.

"Yes. I never said I wouldn't."

"Why haven't you told me?"

"Why should I? It only upsets you. Besides, I never go to their country. I always make them come through into ours."

He stood groping for words while she watched, her head tilted a little to one side, her steel-gray eyes utterly calm and more than a little distant.

"Why are you so afraid?" she said at last.

"I don't want you to go off with them and leave me."

"Leave you? What? Oh, my beloved! Never!" She rushed to him and flung herself into his hungry arms. "Oh, I'm sorry. I didn't know you were worried about something like that." She looked up, studying his face. "For the work's sake I might have to go off alone for a few nights, maybe, but that's all it would ever be."

"Really?" He wanted to beg her to stay with him every minute of every day, but he knew that such a plea would be ridiculous as well as impossible, given their mutual work. "Promise?"

"Of course I do! I'd always come home to you. Always."

She kissed him so passionately that he knew that she had to be telling the truth, that at the very least she believed implicitly in her own words. His relief was like a warm tide, carrying all his fears far out to some distant sea. For a long time, too, all through the cold and storm-wracked winter, she seemed to put her distraction aside and to devote as much of her attention to him as she could whenever they were together. By the time that spring came, he decided that he'd been foolish to worry about her work with the Guardians, even when she told him openly that she'd been talking regularly with Elessario.

"That child needs me, Ado. You know, I truly do think that she and her race are meant to be as incarnate as you or me. Something's gone terribly wrong, somewhere. Some of the evidence I've gathered makes me think that these beings are scattered through the universe, across several of the inner planes. I think that's what they mean. They talk about living on several worlds, you see, not one single world."

"But I've never heard of such a thing."

"No more have I. That's why they intrigue me so much. You

know, I left my parents for the dweomer because I loved hidden things, secret things."

"So did I. I can understand. But please, be careful around them. I just don't trust them."

"Neither do I. Don't worry."

"But suppose they did incarnate. What would they become?"

"I have no idea. Neither do they, truly. I think that they've been here so long now that they'd become beings much like us— like the elves, I mean, not you Round-ears."

The words rang in his mind like a shout of warning. Not since their marriage had she made that sharp distinction between herself and his kind. Yet it hurt so much that he hesitated, letting her talk on, until the moment was irrevocably lost.

"They'd have to give up a lot to become like us," she was saying. "So much, truly, that I wonder if they ever will, but if they don't, well, they're the ones who keep telling me they'll fade away and be lost forever. I'd hate to see that happen to any soul. It would be a tragedy indeed."

"Just so. But it's their choice."

"Is it? Unless they get someone to show them the way, they have no choice."

"Indeed? What do they want you for, then? Some kind of cosmic midwife?"

"Well, yes." She looked surprised that he didn't already know. "Just exactly that."

In the bright grass by the stream Evandar lounged, half sitting, half lying, his harp at his side. Up close Dallandra could see that the harp was real wood, like the arrow she'd been given, and of elven design, though more elaborate than any she'd ever seen, all inlaid with mother-of-pearl in a pattern of seaweed and sea horses. He noticed the way she studied it.

"This harp is from the lost cities, from Rinbaladelan, to be precise—a thing that doesn't come easily to my folk."

"You must have taken it away before the city fell."

"Oh yes." He frowned suddenly. "I tried to help defend Rinbaladelan, you see. It was hopeless, of course, even with me there. But it was a very beautiful place, and I hated to see all that beauty lying broken in the mud."

"Was it only the beauty? What about the elves that lived there?"

"They live, they die, they come and go, and it's no concern of mine. But stone and jewel endure, and the play of water on stone, and the play of light on jewels. The harbor at Rinbaladelan wrung my heart with its beauty, and those hairy creatures filled it with rubble and let it silt and threw corpses into it to turn the water mucky and foul. And then the crabs and the lobsters came to eat the corpses, and the furry creatures ate the crabs and got the plague and died, and I laughed to see them crawling on their bloated bellies through the gutters of the city they'd broken."

When Dallandra shuddered, he was honestly puzzled by her reaction.

"They deserved to die, you know," Evandar said. "They'd killed my city and, for that matter, all of your people. I don't know why you keep saying you don't remember Rinbaladelan, Dalla. I'm sure that I saw you there."

"Maybe you did, but I wouldn't remember from life to life. You don't remember much after you've died and been reborn. A soul that remembered everything would be too burdened to live its new life afresh."

It was his turn for the shudder.

"To forget everything. I couldn't bear it, and to live bound down the way you do!"

"Evandar, it's time for some honest talk, if indeed your folk can do such a thing. You keep asking me to help you, yet you keep saying you don't want my help."

"Well, that's because this is such a new thing for me." He picked up the harp and ran a trill, notes of such unearthly sweetness that her eyes filled with tears. "It's not myself. It's Elessario."

"Ah. You do love her, don't you?"

"Love? No. I don't want to possess her. I don't even want her at my side all the time." He looked up from the strings. "I only want her to be happy, and I'd hate to see her fade away. Is that love?"

"Yes, you dolt! It's a greater love than just simply wanting her."

His surprise was comic.

"Well, if you say so, Dalla. Fancy that." He ran another trill, faintly mocking notes, this time, and very high. "Very well, then. I love Elessario, strange though it sounds to my ears, and she's still young, so young, too young to know what she'd be giving up if she followed you people into birth and flesh and the endless wheel and all of that glittering, strange, and sometimes oddly sticky and slimy and wet world you live in. And then she'd have all we were meant to have, and I could die in peace."

"Why not come with her and live?"

He shook his head in a no and bent over the harp. The song he played was meant for dancing; she could tell by the driving chords and the way her feet demanded to move. She forced herself to sit very still until he was done, modulating suddenly into a minor key and letting the tune hang unfinished.

"You won't understand us until you come into our country," he said.

"Suppose that I came—just suppose, mind—what would happen to my body while I was gone?"

"The lump of meat? Do you care?"

"Of course I care! Without it I can never come home to the man I love."

"But why should I care?"

"Because without my body I'll die and go away to be reborn and you'll have to wait a long time and then start this all over from the beginning."

"Oh, well, that would be tedious beyond belief, wouldn't it? Let me think. I know. You can change from a woman to a bird and back again already, so if I turn the lump of meat into a jewel on a chain, and you put the chain around your neck, it shall travel everywhere with you, and you can change back whenever you want to go home. Dalla, truly, if you'd only stay a few days with us —just a few days—to see us and know us and all that we do, and then you'd see how to help my Elessario, I'm sure of it." All at once he smiled. "My Elessario. Whom I love. What an odd sound to it, but you know, I think you must be right."

He hit the harp in a discord and disappeared.

If Evandar had asked for his own sake, Dallandra might never have gone—she realized it even then—but that he would ask for the sake of another soul made all the difference. She'd seen enough of his people already, particularly Alshandra, to understand just how right Nevyn had been to wager against them having compassion. That Evandar was beginning to be capable of a love beyond wanting for himself was a momentous thing, and a change to be nurtured and cherished. Yet she was always mindful of the dangers, and she particularly hated the thought of letting Aderyn know that she was thinking of running such a risk. He'll only yell and scream, she told herself, and with the thought realized that she'd made up her mind.

Since she couldn't bear to lie to Aderyn, either, she rode out that morning without telling him anything at all. When she was a good five miles from camp, she unsaddled and unbridled her mare, turned her head in the direction of the herd, and gave her a slap on the rump to start her back home. Then she took the silver nut out of her pocket and unwrapped it from its bit of rag. For a long time she merely studied it and wondered if she truly had the courage to go through with this thing. What if Evandar were lying? Yet she had enough dweomer to tell true from false, and she knew that he'd never spoken so honestly before in all his long existence. In the end what spurred her on was her respect for Aderyn. What would he think if she acted like a squealing coward, full of big plans, empty of courage? With one last wrench of her will she touched the nut to her eyes, left first, then right.

When she lowered it, at first it seemed that nothing had happened, and she laughed at herself for being taken in by some prank of Elessario's, but when she put the nut in her pocket, she was suddenly aware of a subtle change in the landscape. The colors were brighter, for one thing, the grass so intense a green that it seemed to be shards of emerald, the sky as deep and glowy as a sunlit sea. When she took a few steps, she saw, ahead of her to the north across the emerald billows of grass, a mist hanging in the air, seemingly at the horizon, but as she walked on, it grew closer, swelled up, turned opalescent in a delicate flood of grays and lavenders shot through with the palest pinks and blues like the mother-of-pearl on Evandar's harp. Thinking of the harp, she suddenly heard it, a soft run of arpeggios in some far distance.

The mist wrapped around her in a delightful coolness like the touch of silk. Ahead she saw three roads, stretching out pale across the grasslands. One road led to the left and a stand of dark hills, so grim and glowering that she knew they had no part in Evandar's country. One road led to the right and a sudden rise of mountains, pale and gleaming in pure air beyond the mist, their tops shrouded in snow so bright that it seemed as if they were lighted from within. Straight ahead on the misty flat stretched the third. As Dallandra stood there hesitating, Elessario came racing down the misty road.

"Dalla, Dalla, oh, it's so wonderful you've come! We'll have such a splendid time."

"Now, now, I can't stay very long, just a few days."

"Father told me, yes. You have to get back to your man, whom you love. Here. Father said to give this to you."

She handed over an amethyst hanging from a golden chain. When Dallandra took the jewel, she cried out, because it was carved into a full-length statue of her, no more than two inches long, but a perfect likeness, down to the shape of her hands. She slipped it over her head and settled it round her neck.

"If you ever see me drop or lose this, Elessario, tell me at once."

"Father said that, too. I will. I promise. Now let's go. There'll be a feast tonight because you've come."

When Elessario took her hand, as trusting as a child, Dallandra realized that this spirit, at least, was still young enough to learn how to love. Hand in hand they walked on down the misty road, and when Dallandra looked back, mist was all that she saw behind her.

Three hours before sunset, Dallandra's mare came ambling into the herd. When Calonderiel, who happened to be on herd guard, saw her come home, he sent a young boy racing to camp to fetch Aderyn. In his tent, Aderyn heard the lad yelling all the way in and came running out to meet him.

"Wise One, Wise One," he gasped between breaths. "The Wise One's horse has come home without her."

Aderyn broke into a run and headed for the herd. His mind kept flashing horrible images: Dalla thrown, her neck broken; Dalla dragged by a stirrup and bruised to death; Dalla falling down a ravine and hitting the bottom dead and broken. Leading the unperturbed mare, Calonderiel came to meet him.

"She just wandered in like this, without saddle or bridle."

"Ye gods! Maybe Dalla was just doing a working, then, and the mare slipped her tether and wandered off."

Yet even as he spoke he felt a cold clammy dread, like an evil hand grabbing his heart. He was so perturbed, in fact, that when he tried to scry her out, all his skill and power deserted him. No matter what focus he used, he saw nothing, not her, not her trail, not even her saddle and bridle, which must have been lying abandoned somewhere. Finally Calonderiel saddled up three geldings and put the mare on a lead rope, then comandeered Albaral, the best tracker in the warband, to help them. On the way out, Albaral trotted ahead of them like a hunting dog, his eyes fixed on the ground as he circled round and round, looking for tracks. Fortunately, no one from the alar had ridden out that day but Dallandra, and soon enough he picked up the trail of crushed grass and the occasional clear hoofprint that led, straight as an arrow, across the grasslands.

The sun was dancing on the cloud-touched horizon when they

found her saddle and bridle. When Albaral yelled at Cal to stop
and keep the horses from trampling the area, Aderyn dismounted
and ran to the other elf, crouching in the tall grass.

"These are hers, all right," Aderyn said.

Albaral nodded, then got up to start circling again to see if he
could pick up any footprints or other traces of her leaving the spot.
Aderyn knelt down, and when he laid a shaking hand on her
saddle, he knew with the dark stab of dweomer-touched certainty
that she was gone, not dead, but gone so far away that he would
never find her. Involuntarily he cried out, a long wailing note of
keening that made Albaral spin around to face him.

"Wise One! An omen?"

Aderyn nodded, unable to speak. Calonderiel left the horses
and came running over, started to say something, then thought
better of it, his cat eyes as wide as a tiny elven child's. With a
convulsive shudder Albaral turned away.

"Found a few tracks. Wise One, do you want to wait here?"

"No. I'll come with you. Lead on."

But the tracks only led them a few yards, to a place where the
grass was flattened down in a pattern that suggested, to Albaral's
trained eyes at least, that she'd first fallen to her knees, then lain
down all in a heap. Beyond that there was nothing, no sign to show
she'd risen again, no footprints, nothing, as if she'd turned into a
bird and flown away.

"But she didn't leave her clothes behind her," Aderyn said.
"She couldn't fly with those."

"Grass is kind of damp here," Albaral said, kneeling. "Like
there was fog, maybe. Or something."

"Some kind of dweomer mist?" Unconsciously Calonderiel
crossed his fingers in the sign of warding against witchcraft.

Aderyn's fear clutched his throat and turned him mute. Had
some great bird swooped down out of that mist and carried her
away?

"We could see how far the damp grass stretches," Albaral said.
"Seems to go on a ways."

Aderyn was about to answer when he heard—when they all

heard—the sound of a silver horn, echoing from some long distance away, and looked up to see at the far horizon a line of riders silhouetted against the setting sun, the horses picked out in black against the blood-red clouds for the briefest of moments, then gone.

"The Guardians," Cal whispered. "Have they taken her?"

Aderyn dropped to his knees and grabbed handfuls of the crumpled grass, the last thing on earth her body had touched. It took the others a long time to make him come away.

All that night, once they were back in camp, Aderyn stayed in their tent and paced endlessly back and forth. At one moment he knew with a heartsick certainty that he'd never see her again; at the next, his hope would well up in a flood of denial to tell him that she'd come back, of course she'd come back, maybe in the morning, maybe in only an hour, that maybe she was walking toward camp this very moment. Then tears would burn in his throat as he told himself that she was as good as dead, gone forever. At dawn he stumbled out and actually walked off in the direction that she'd gone, but of course, he didn't find her. When he came back to camp, everyone else treated him like an invalid, speaking softly around him, offering him food, telling him to lie down, staring at him so sadly that he nearly screamed aloud and cursed the lot of them.

Aderyn slept all that day, vigiled all that night, and the next, and on and on, until seven days had passed with no sign of Dallandra. Only then, toward the dawn of the eighth night, did he finally think of the obvious and call to Nevyn through the fire. The old man responded so quickly that he must have been already awake and up. When Aderyn told him what had happened, his image above the fire seemed to grow even older with grief.

"She promised me once that she'd never leave me," Aderyn said at last. "And like a dolt, I believed her. Not for more than a few days, she said, and I believed her."

"Now here, I can't imagine Dallandra breaking a solemn promise, no matter how much glamour these Guardians have."

"Well, maybe she wouldn't. Nevyn, I just don't know what to

think! If I only knew what's happened to her, really knew, I mean. I'm only guessing that the rotten Guardians even took her."

"Why don't you ask them?"

"Ask them? I can't even find them!"

"Have you truly tried?"

Aderyn left the tent and walked outside into the rising dawn. He hadn't really tried, he supposed. In his heart he never wanted to see them again, wanted only to curse them or rage at them or in some way cause them the same heartsick pain that he was feeling. If he did, though, they would most likely never give her back. He left the waking camp and walked out into the grasslands, stumbled along blindly at first, wandering with no purpose, until he felt calm enough to think. From studying the lore, he knew something about the sort of places where the Guardians might appear: boundary places, the crossing of paths, the joining of streams, anywhere that seemed to be a gate or a ford or a marker between two different things. Following a dim memory, he came at last to a place where three rivulets became a proper stream.

"Evandar!" he called out blindly in grief and rage. "Evandar! Give me back my wife!"

His only answer was the grass sighing as it bent in the wind and the stream gurgling over its rough bed. This time his voice screamed in a berserker's howl.

"Evandar! At least give me the chance to fight for her. Evandar!"

"She's not mine to keep or give back."

The voice came from directly behind him. With a yelp he leapt straight up and turned as he came down, panting for breath, close to tears, and faced the seeming-elf. His yellow hair was bright as daffodils in the morning sun, and he was wearing a green tunic over leather trousers, a bow slung over his back and a quiver of arrows at his hip.

"She came to us of her own free will, you see," Evandar went on. "Truly she did. I asked for her help, but never would I have stolen her away."

"And I suppose you won't be able to tell me if she'll ever come back."

"Of course she will, when she wants to. We won't keep her against her will."

"But what if she doesn't want to? That's no concern of yours, I suppose."

Evandar frowned, studying the grass, and spoke without looking up.

"I have the strangest feeling round my heart, and all for your sake. I've never felt such a thing before, but you know, I do think I pity you, Aderyn of the Silver Wings. My heart is so heavy and sore that I don't know what else to call it." He looked up at that point and indeed, his luridly blue eyes glistened with tears. "I'll make you a promise. You'll see her again. I swear it, no matter how long she stays."

"Well, I believe you're sincere, but your promise may not do me one jot of good. I'm not elven, you know. My race only lives a little while, a very little while compared with them and even less compared with the likes of you. If she doesn't come home soon, I won't be here. Do you understand?"

"I do." He thought hard, chewing on his lower lip in a completely human gesture. "Very well. I can do somewhat about that. Here, let me give you a pledge . . . oh, what . . . ah, I know. A long time ago my woman gave yours an arrow. Here, take another to go with it. You have my word and my pledge now, Aderyn of the Silver Wings, that she'll come back and that you'll live to have her back."

Aderyn took the arrow and ran his fingers down the smooth, hard wood, cool and solid and as real as the grasslands under him.

"Then you have my thanks in return, Evandar, because I don't have another thing to give you."

"Your thanks will do. Oddly enough."

When Aderyn looked up he was gone, but the arrow stayed, a tangible thing in his hands. He took it back to the camp and his tent, searched through Dallandra's possessions, and found the other arrow, wrapped in an embroidered cloth in one of her saddlebags. He wrapped its fellow up with it, put the bag back, then sat down on the floor and stared at the wall, merely stared, barely thinking, for hours and hours.

To Dallandra, much less than an hour passed on the misty road. Just at sunset Elessario brought her to a vast meadow, a long spill of green flecked with tiny white flowers. Scattered all across it were tables made of gilded wood set with jewels, so that they sparkled in the light of the thousands of candles that stood in golden candelabra. It was night, suddenly, and in candlelight the host was feasting. They were dressed in green and gold, and gold and jewels flashed at throat or wrist or sparkled in their hair; all of them looked like elves but more beautiful than elves to the same degree that elves are more beautiful than human beings. Dallandra was never sure just how many people there were, a thousand maybe, but when she tried to count them, they wouldn't hold still —or so it seemed. Out of the corner of her eye she would see a table with, say, ten individuals; when she turned her head for a better look, the table might be gone, or it would seem that only two or three sat there, or perhaps twenty instead of ten. When she looked at a group from a distance, they seemed to blend together while still remaining distinct, as if they were forms seen in clouds, or flames leaping from a fire. Over the laughter rang music, harp and flute and drum, of such beauty that she felt on the edge of tears for the entire time the music played.

Elessario and Dallandra sat, one to his right, one to his left, at the table Evandar headed. He caught Dallandra's hand and kissed it.

"Welcome. And was your journey an easy one?"

"Oh yes, thank you."

"Good, but still, you must be tired. Here, have some mead."

He handed her a tall, slender goblet of pure silver wrapped with a garland of tiny roses made of reddish gold. Although she

KATHARINE KERR

admired the workmanship, mindful of the old tales Dallandra set it down untouched.

"I'm not thirsty, thank you."

His handsome face turned sharp with rage.

"Why do you turn down my drink?"

"I have no desire to be trapped here, and I won't eat your food, either."

"I've already given you my pledge: you leave when you want to leave and not a moment later. You can drink with us in safety."

"Oh, please, Dalla?" Elessario broke in. "You can't just go hungry the whole time you're here."

She hesitated, then smiled and raised the goblet in his direction. If she kept distrusting them, they would never trust her.

"To your health, Evandar, and to your continuance." She drank off the toast. "Oh, by the gods, this mead is wonderful!"

"It tastes like the mead they made in Bravelmelim."

All at once something came clear in her mind as she studied the feast and the feasters, the fine clothes, the jewelry, the gilded tableware and the intricately embroidered linens.

"All of this is modeled on the lost cities, isn't it?" Dallandra waved her hand randomly round. "Your clothes and everything else."

"Exactly that." He grinned in pleasure at her recognition. "And later we'll have jugglers and acrobats, just like the ones your kings used to watch."

The feasting and the entertainments went on till dawn, a glamour more ensnaring than any ordinary ensorcelment could have been. After all, Dallandra's own magicks would have been more than a match for any clumsy manipulation of her mind or her aura, but for that little space of time she was watching—no, she was living in—her people's lost past, religiously remembered, scrupulously re-created by beings to whom these forms meant life itself, or at the least, the only life they knew. A sheer intellectual lust to see more, to understand that missing history caught her deep and held her tight. When the feast broke up and the folk began to slip away in the pale light of a strangely twilit dawn,

Evandar took her for a long walk down to a riverbank bordered with formal gardens exactly like the ones that used to grow in Tanbalapalim. They crossed a bridge carved with looping vines, roses, and the little faces of the Wildfolk to enter a palace, or perhaps it was only part of a palace, floating in mist. Some of the rooms seemed to open onto empty air; some of the halls seemed to dead-end themselves in living trees; some of the floors seemed almost transparent, with shadows moving back and forth underneath.

The chamber that they all settled into for a talk seemed solid enough, though. It had a high ceiling, painted white and crossed with polished oak beams, and a floor of pale gray slate, scattered with red-and-gold carpets. The two walls that held no doors or windows were painted just like the outside of a tent, but far more delicately; on one was a vast landscape, a river estuary opening to the sea at either dawn or sunset; on the other, a view of the harbor at Rinbaladelan. The polished ebony furniture was all padded with silk cushions of many colors.

"Did this room once belong to a queen of the lost cities?" Dallandra asked.

"No, not at all." Evandar gave her a sly grin. "To a merchant's wife, that's all."

Dallandra gasped, properly impressed.

"You have no idea how beautiful the cities were, Dalla," he went on, and his voice cracked in honest sadness. "Your people were rich, and they lived even longer than they do now, with time to learn every craft to perfection, and they were generous, too, pooling their wealth to build places so fine and wonderful that they took the breath out of everyone that saw them, even a strange soul like me. I loved those cities. Truly, I think they were the things that taught me how to love. If they still stood, I might go to your world and live there the way you want me to do. But they're gone, and my heart half died with them."

"Well, true enough," Dallandra said. "Broken stone doesn't heal itself, and fallen walls won't rise."

"Just so." He looked away, staring out the window to a long

view of grass and flowers. "And your people never went back, they never even went back to mourn them. That was a hard thing to forgive, that and of course the wretched iron."

"Evandar, I am *so* sick of hearing you people whine about iron. Do you think we could have built those beastly cities without it? Do you think we'd live long out on the grasslands without knives and arrow points and axes?"

"I hadn't thought about it at all. Forgive me."

"If they used iron in the cities, Father," Elessario broke in, "how did you spend time there?"

"With great difficulty. It was worth it to me, the pain."

"Well, then." Dallandra pounced like a striking hawk. "If that pain was worth the beauty, then . . ."

His laugh cut her off, but it was a pleasant one.

"You're as sly as I am, sorceress." He rose, motioning to his daughter. "Come along, let our guest rest."

"Well, I am tired, truly." Dallandra suddenly yawned. "I left home—well, it must have been a full day ago now."

For the first twenty years that Dallandra was gone, Aderyn kept hoping that soon, any day, any moment, she would return. The People marveled at him, in fact, that he would be so strong, so faithful to her memory, when all those old tales said that no one ever returned from the lands of the Guardians. During that twenty years, he spent some time talking to the Forest Folk, who worshipped the Guardians as gods, and learned what little they knew about these strange beings. When their shamans—priests is a bit too dignified a word—insisted that he should be happy that his wife had been honored and taken as a concubine for these gods, Aderyn managed to be polite, barely, but he never went back to talk with them again. It was his work that saved him. At first he supervised the copying of the books Nevyn had brought and taught his new lore to those elves who were already masters of the old; then he took young apprentices and trained them from the beginning in his craft. As Deverry men reckon time, it was in the year 752 that he sent his first three pupils out to teach others, and that year, as well, when he was still looking around for his next apprentice, Nevyn rode out to the Eldidd border to visit him.

They met about thirty miles north of Cannobaen, at the place where the Aver Gavan, as men call it, joins up with the Delonderiel. That spring the elves were holding a horse fair, because the Eldidd merchants were willing to pay higher than ever for good stock, in the wide meadows along the riverbanks. What Nevyn brought with him, however, wasn't iron goods, but news. The Eldidd king wanted those horses because he'd just declared war on Deverry.

"Again?" Aderyn said peevishly. "Ye gods, I'm glad I don't live in the kingdoms anymore, with all their stupid bickering and squabbling."

"I'm afraid it's a good bit more this time than just petty quarrels." Nevyn looked and sounded exhausted. "The High King died without an heir, and there's three claimants, Eldidd among them."

"Oh. Well, my apologies. Truly, that's a serious matter."

"It is." Nevyn paused, considering him. "You know, I'm beginning to feel hideously old these days. Ye gods, there's all that gray in your hair, and here I still remember the little lad I took as an apprentice."

"I feel even older than I am, frankly."

"Ah." Nevyn was silent for a long, tactful moment. "Um, well, how are you faring these days? Without her, I mean."

"Well enough. I have my work."

"And your hope?"

"Is feeble but alive. I suppose it's alive. Maybe it's just one of those embalmed corpses you read about, like the Bardekians make of their great men."

"I can't blame you for your bitterness."

"Do I still sound bitter? Then I guess my hope truly is still alive as well." For the first time in about six years, he nearly wept, but he caught himself with a long sigh. "Well, what about this civil war, then? How long do you think it will last?"

Nevyn considered him for a long, sour moment, as if he were wondering whether or not he should let his old pupil get away with such an obvious change of the subject.

"Too long, I'm afraid," Nevyn said at last. "All three claimants are weak, which means no one's going to win straightaway. I've gotten the most ghastly set of warnings and omens about it, too. Somewhat's gravely out of balance on the Inner Planes—I'm not sure what yet. But I intend to do what I can to put an end to this nonsense. I'd wager that the war will burn itself out in about ten years."

In truth, of course, Nevyn's hope was ill founded in the extreme: the Time of Troubles was to last five and a hundred years, although of course Nevyn was indeed the one to finally and at great cost put an end to it. If either of them had known how long the wars would rage, they might well have lost heart and done nothing at all, but fortunately, dweomer or no, they were forced to live through them one year at a time like other men. Although Nevyn immediately involved himself in the politics of the thing, a story that has been recorded elsewhere, Aderyn and the People were little affected for some thirty years. Only then, after the demands of the various armies started ruining the delicate network of trade that held Deverry and Eldidd together, did the merchants stop riding west as often as they had. Iron goods were becoming too rare in Eldidd itself for the merchants to take them freely out of the country. The People grumbled, but the Forest Folk gloated, saying that the Guardians had somehow arranged to stop the trade in demon metal. Aderyn had a brief moment of wondering if they were right.

Nevyn, of course, kept him informed of the various events of the wars, but only one meant much to Aderyn personally. Indeed, he felt himself so emotionally distant from the slaughter and the intrigues that he realized that he'd become more than a friend of the People—he was thinking like a man of the People. The Round-ears seemed far away and unimportant; their lives flashed past too quickly for their doings to endure or to take on much significance unless one of them somehow touched his heart or his own life. But in 774 Nevyn mentioned, in one of their infrequent talks through the fire, that two friends of his had died. Nevyn's grief was palpable, even through their magical communications.

"It aches my heart to see you so sad," Aderyn thought to him.

"My thanks. You know, this concerns you, too, I suppose. Ye gods, forgive me! I might have told you when they were still alive. I'm speaking of the souls that were once your parents, you see— Gweran and Lyssa, reborn and then killed again so soon by these wretched demon-spawn wars. Do you still remember them?"

"What? Of course I do! Well, that aches my heart indeed. I suppose. I mean, it's not as if they were my kin anymore. Huh. I wonder if I'll ever see them again."

"Who knows? No one can read another's Wyrd. But I must say that it seems unlikely. Their Wyrd seems bound to the kingdoms, and yours to another folk entirely."

But as it turned out, Aderyn did indeed have a small role to play in ending the wars when, in about 834, he left the elven lands for a few weeks and traveled to Pyrdon, a former province that had taken its chance to rebel and turn itself into an independent kingdom. By then, or so Nevyn told him, with so many claimants to the throne in both Deverry and Eldidd, it seemed that the wars would rage forever. Nevyn and the other dweomermasters had decided to choose one heir and put their weight and their magicks behind him in a desperate attempt to bring the kingdoms to peace. Simply because he was the closest dweomermaster to Loc Drw, where this claimant lived, Aderyn went to take a look at a young boy, Prince Maryn, son of Casyl of Pyrdon, whom the omens marked as a possible future ruler of Deverry. Traveling as a simple herbman, he arrived late on a blazing summer's day at Casyl's dun, which stood on a fortified island out in the middle of a lake.

At the entrance to the causeway leading out to the dun stood armed guards. As Aderyn walked up, he wondered if he'd be allowed to pass by.

"Good morrow, good sir," said the elder of the pair. "Looks like you're a peddler or suchlike."

"Not truly, but a herbman."

"Splendid! No doubt the ladies of the dun will want a look at your goods."

"Now here!" The younger guard stepped forward. "What if he's a spy?"

"Oh, come now! No one's going to send an elderly soul like this to spy, lad. Pass on by, good sir."

The words hit Aderyn like a slap across the face. Elderly? Was he really elderly now? Since the ladies of the dun, including the queen herself, did receive him hospitably, during his stay in the dun he had many a chance to study himself in one mirror or another. Yes, the guards were right: his hair was snow white, his face all lined and sagging, his eyes droop-lidded and weary, impossibly weary from his long grief over his stolen woman. He saw then that Dallandra's loss had burned his youth away like grass thrown into a fire. During those days in Casyl's dun the last of his hope died, too, that ever he would see her again. He realized it when Nevyn asked him to stay an extra day and he agreed without a thought; he simply no longer felt the need to rush back to the alar on the off chance that she'd returned in his absence.

When he did return to the elven lands, he told the bards to add a new bit of lore to the tales about the Guardians: not always did they keep their promises.

To Dallandra, that same hundred years passed as four days, bright glorious days of feasting and music, laughter and old tales. At odd moments, she remembered Aderyn and even stored up things to tell him when she returned, because she knew that the information Evandar possessed about the lost cities would fascinate him as much as it fascinated her. Just as she never tired of hearing about the cities, Evandar never tired of talking about them, and with such affection that she began to see a possible strategy. Late on the fourth night, they sat together on a hillside overlooking a grassy meadow, where among glittering torches harpers played and the young folk danced in solemn lines, all bowing and slow steps.

"It's so different from the dances my people do," Dallandra remarked. "We like to leap and yell and dance fast as the wind."

"Oh, I remember your dances, too—country dances, they called them then."

"I see. You know, I've been thinking. I wonder if the cities *could* be rebuilt. It's too bad the Round-ears are such a treacherous folk; otherwise we could make some kind of alliance with them, or at least learn how to work iron again. I know, I know—you hate iron—but we really would have to have it to cut stone and such-like, and we'd need to know how to work mortar and weave cloth and build bridges that wouldn't fall down and streets that wouldn't buckle. It might only be one city at first, but still, it seems such a pity to think of them lying there, all broken, with only the owls nesting and the wolves prowling through to keep them company."

"You're saying that to tempt me."

"Does it?"

"Well, yes, more perhaps than you can know, because I know better than you how it might be done. If we had a place to go to, a fine, fitting place, we'd be more likely to choose your kind of life over death. Well, some of us would. The young people. It's their fate that worries me, the young people. There are fewer and fewer born, you know, as time passes by."

"I still don't understand how they're born."

"No more do I." He laughed under his breath. "No more do I, but they *become*, and they delight us. I hate to think of them vanishing away."

Out in the meadow the music sang in harmony with the sound of laughter. Dallandra glanced up and saw a huge silver moon, just wisped with cloud, at zenith. Black specks, birds, she supposed, moved across its face, then circled round, plunging down, growing bigger and faster with the rush of wings. Howling in rage, Evandar leapt to his feet.

"Run!" he screamed. "Dalla, to the trees!"

Suddenly she saw trees, some yards away at the hillcrest. As she ran she heard shrieks and squawks, the rush of wings and the cawing of angry ravens. Just as she darted under cover she realized that one of the enormous birds was a nighthawk, stooping straight for her. In the nick of time she rolled into the shelter of woody shrubs and low-hanging branches. Screaming its disappointment, the hawk veered off and flew toward the meadow, where the dancers were scattering among the torches with little cries of fear. When Dallandra risked standing up, the hawk circled back, but this time it landed to turn with a shimmer of wings and magic into Alshandra.

"I thought it would be you," Dallandra said calmly. "You should come with your daughter when she goes, and then you won't lose her."

"Fetid bitch! I'll kill you."

"You can't, not here, not in this country." She laid her hand on the amethyst figure. "What are you going to do? Tear at me with your claws?"

A shriek hung in the morning air. Alshandra was gone, and the sun was rising through a lavender mist.

As Dallandra walked downhill in that pale dawn to join Evandar, the year 854 was ending in Deverry and Eldidd. As the slashing rains of autumn drove down, it threatened to become a black new year for Eldidd at least, because Maryn, a man now, not a lad, and the High King of a newly unified Deverry, was camped in her northern fields and sieging her northern towns with the biggest army Eldidd had ever seen. Aderyn was traveling with his alar to the winter camps when he heard the news from Nevyn, who contacted him through the fire. By then, Nevyn had become the High King's chief councillor, but rather than sit and worry in the drafty ruins of the palace in war-battered Dun Deverry, he was traveling with his king on campaign.

"Not that there's a cursed lot for me to do," he said that night and with evident relief. "We're holed up in Cernmeton, and it's nice and snug, because the town surrendered without a siege as promptly as you please."

"I'm glad to hear it. Do you think the war will last long?"

"I don't. Everywhere the king rides, the opposition crumbles away. In the spring, when the towns are all running low on provisions and can't possibly stand a siege, the army will move south and take Aberwyn and Abernaudd, and that'll be an end to it. Deverry and Eldidd will be one kingdom from now on. What's wrong? Your image looks frightened."

"I am. If the wars are over, are the Eldidd men going to start moving west again and stealing my people's land?"

"I've worked so hard to end the civil wars that I forget how things must look to you. But don't let it trouble your heart." Even the purely mental touch of Nevyn's mind on his resonated with grief. "You don't understand just how horrible things have been, just how many men have died. I think me that there'll be plenty of land in the new kingdom to satisfy everyone for years to come."

Just in time Aderyn stopped himself from gloating.

"Well, let me think," he said instead. "My alar isn't very far from Cernmeton, and we'll be riding past on our way to the winter camps. Do you think we could meet?"

"That would be splendid, but I don't think you'd best ride into town. In fact, the king's quartermasters are so busy drafting every man who looks like he could fight that I think me the People should stay far away from us at the moment. In the summer, though, when the war is over—it'll be better then." Nevyn's image suddenly smiled. "And there's someone with me that you should meet, indeed there is. The soul who once was your father. He's a bard again, of a sort, but he was a mercenary soldier, too, for years and years, and a friend of mine as well. Maddyn, his name is."

By then the thought of his father was so distant that Aderyn felt neither more nor less pleased than he would at the thought of meeting any friend of Nevyn's, but once he got to know Maddyn he did indeed find him congenial. Nevyn's predictions about the course of the war proved absolutely true. When in the spring Maryn and his army moved south, the people of Eldidd scrambled to surrender and end the endless horrors of the war. Abernaudd opened its gates the moment it saw him coming; Aberwyn made a great show of holding out for an afternoon, then surrendered at sunset. While Maryn and his men hunted down the last Eldidd king, Aenycyr (who was, for those of you who care about such historical things, the great-grandson of Prince Mael of Aberwyn, later known as Mael the Seer, through the legitimate line of his first marriage), Nevyn took a leave of absence from his king's side and traveled west with only Maddyn for company to visit with Aderyn.

They met just northwest of Cannobaen on the banks of a little stream that ran into Y Brog, where the alar had set up camp to rest their horses on their way to the first alardan of summer. By then Maddyn was forty-five, an ancient age for a fighting man; his hair was thoroughly gray and his blue eyes were weary with the deep hiraedd of someone who's seen far too many friends die in far too short a time. Yet he was still an easy man to talk with, and ready with a jest, and the People all liked him immediately because among his other talents he could see the Wildfolk as clearly as they did. There was one small creature, a sprite with long blue hair and needle-sharp pointed teeth, that was as devoted to him as a favorite dog, following him around during the day and sleeping near him at night.

"I'm afraid it's my fault," Nevyn said ruefully when Aderyn asked about the sprite. "Many years ago Maddyn spent a winter with me, you see, when he'd been badly wounded. He began seeing the Wildfolk then—just because they were all around him, I suppose. His music had somewhat to do with it, too, because he's a truly fine harper."

"The Wildfolk do love a good tune. Well, there's no harm in it, I suppose, except I feel sorry for the poor little thing. When Maddyn dies, she's not going to be able to understand it at all."

"Oh, she'll probably forget him quick enough. He wasn't meant to see the Wildfolk, much less have one of them fall in love with him."

Although Aderyn normally only slept a few scant hours a

night, that evening he felt so tired that he went to his tent early and fell asleep straightaway. In his dreams the little blue sprite came to him and led him out across the grasslands—that is, he thought at first that he was in the grasslands, until he noticed the vast purple moon hanging swollen at the horizon. In his dream-mind a voice sounded, saying cryptically, "The Gatelands." When he looked around he saw two young women running toward him, hand in hand and smiling. One of them was Dallandra. He'd dreamt about her so much in the last hundred years that he felt neither pleasure nor grief at first, merely noted somewhat wryly in his dream that yes, he still cared enough about her to summon her image at times.

Until, that is, she came closer and he saw the little amethyst figurine at her throat, such a discordant detail that it made him wonder if this dream were different. He realized then that rather than appearing as a dream-image of himself, he'd somehow assumed his body of light, the pale bluish form, a stylized man shape, in which he traveled on the etheric.

"Ado, it's good to see you, even in this form," Dallandra said. "But I don't have much time. It's hard for us to come to the Gatelands like this, you see."

"No, I don't see. For the love of every god, Dalla, when are you coming home?"

"Soon, soon. Oh, don't sulk—it's only been a few days, after all. Listen carefully. You know that guest of yours, Nevyn's friend, the one the sprite loves?"

"His name's Maddyn. But it hasn't been a few days."

"Well, five days then, but do please listen! I can feel them drawing me back already. Maddyn's got a piece of jewelry made of dwarven silver. The Guardians need it. Ado, I've got so much to tell you. Sometimes the Guardians can see the future. Only in bits and flashes, but they do see it, in little tiny true dreams, like. And one of them saw that this Maddyn fellow's going to be important. So they need the rose ring." Even as she went on speaking, her form seemed to be growing thinner, paler, harder to see. "In my saddlebags are all sorts of things that you can trade him for it—take as much as you need, heap him up with it, I don't care. Just get the rose ring. Leave it in a tree near camp."

"Do what? Why should I help these rotten creatures at all?"

"Oh, please, Ado, do be reasonable! Do for my sake if you won't do it for theirs." She was a mere shadow, a colored stain on the view behind her. "The biggest oak tree near camp."

She was gone, and her companion with her. Aderyn looked down and saw the silver cord connecting his body of light with his physical body, lying in his blankets in his tent just below him. So—he hadn't been dreaming after all! The meeting was in its way true enough. He slipped down the cord, returned to his body, and sat up, slapping the ground to earth himself out in the physical. The blue sprite was crouching at the foot of his bedroll and watching him.

"Well, little sister, you were a messenger, were you?"

She nodded yes and disappeared. For a long time that night Aderyn debated whether or not he'd do what Dallandra wanted, but in the end, for her sake, he decided that he would. He found her saddlebag—he'd been carrying it around for over a hundred and twenty years by then—and the jewelry she'd spoken of. Although it was all tarnished and dusty, she had some beautiful brooches and bracelets in the elven style, and they'd polish up nicely enough.

Early that morning, he went looking for Maddyn and found him sitting in the grass and tuning a small wooden harp in the middle of a cloud of Wildfolk. Although it was all nicked and battered, Aderyn had never heard a sweeter-sounding instrument. For a few moments they talked idly while the Wildfolk settled round them in the hope of music.

"I've got somewhat to ask you," Aderyn said at last. "It's probably going to sound cursed strange."

"Ye gods, after knowing Nevyn for all these years I'm used to strange things. Ask away."

"Someone told me that you've got a silver ring with roses on it or suchlike."

"I do." Maddyn looked startled that he would know. "It was

given to me by a woman that I . . . well, if I say I loved her, don't misunderstand me. She was someone else's wife, you see, and while I loved her, there was never one wrong thing between us."

He spoke so defiantly that Aderyn wondered if he were lying, not that it was any business of his. Mentally he cursed Dalla for asking for something that probably carried enormous sentiment for Maddyn.

"Um, well." Aderyn decided that the plain truth was the best, as usual. "You see, in the dream I was told by a dweomerwoman of great power that this ring is marked by dweomer for a Wyrd of its own. She needs it very badly for a working she has underway. She's offered to trade high."

"Well, then, she shall have it. I've lived around the dweomer for years, you know. I've got some idea of the importance of dreams and what comes to you in them. I won't trade, but I'll give it to you outright."

"Oh, here, I'm sorry! I didn't mean to wheedle like a child. It must mean a lot to you."

"It did once, but the woman who gave it to me is beyond caring about it or me." The bard's eyes brimmed tears. "If you want it, you shall have it."

With the curious Wildfolk trailing after, they went to the tent that Maddyn was sharing with Nevyn. The bard rummaged through his saddlebags and took out something hard wrapped in a bit of embroidered linen. He opened the cloth to reveal the ring, a simple silver band about a third of an inch wide, graved with roses, and a pin shaped like a single rose, so cunningly worked that it seemed its petals should be soft to touch. He gave Aderyn the ring, but he wrapped the pin back up and returned it to his saddlebags. Idly Aderyn glanced inside the ring, half expecting to see the lady in question's name, but it was smooth and featureless.

"The smith who made it, and that pin, too, is a brilliant craftsman," Maddyn remarked. "Otho, his name is."

When, out of idle curiosity, Aderyn slipped the ring on his own finger, his hand shook in a dweomer-induced cold.

"Somewhat wrong?" Maddyn said.

"There's not. It's just the knowing, coming upon me. You shall have this back, Maddo, one fine day. You'll have it back in a way you never expected, and long after you've forgotten it."

Maddyn stared in frank puzzlement. There was nothing Aderyn could tell him, because he didn't know what he meant himself. His heart was bitter, too, remembering the similar promise that Evandar had made him. Apparently the Guardian had meant that he would see Dallandra again, all right, but only in that agonizingly brief glimpse on the etheric plane.

On the morrow morning, Aderyn did what she'd asked and placed the ring high up in the crotch of the oak tree while the alar was breaking camp. Although he never knew who had taken it, the next time the alar rode that way, it was gone. In its place was a small smooth bit of wood scratched with a couple of Elvish words, a simple "thank you," but in her handwriting. He borrowed an awl and bored a hole in the scrap, so he could wear it on a bit of thong round his neck, just because her hands had touched it. Seeing her again had brought his grief alive even as it had killed the last of his hope.

Early the next year, from an Eldidd port Maddyn sailed off with Nevyn to Bardek, and Aderyn never saw or heard of him again, not even to hear how he died, far off in the islands after the rose-shaped pin had been stolen from him. But oddly enough, Dallandra did hear of the bard's death, or, to be more precise, she realized what had happened when his blue sprite turned up at the court of the Guardians on what seemed to her to be the day after she'd gotten the silver ring. It was the jewelry that drew the little creature, in fact, because they found her clasping it between her tiny hands. Her face was screwed up in an agony of despair, and when Elessario tried to stroke her, the sprite whipped her head around and sank her pointed teeth deep into the Guardian's hand. Illusory blood welled, then vanished. Elessario stared for some moments at the closing wound.

"What made her do that?"

"I don't know for certain, but I'd guess that Maddyn's dead."

The sprite threw back her head, opened her mouth in a soundless howl, and disappeared.

"He seems to be, yes," Dallandra went on. "And she's mourning him."

Elessario cocked her head to one side and considered the words for some time. They walked across the glowy emerald grass in a pinkish twilight, where blue-green trees on the horizon shifted like smoke. With a howl that they could actually hear, the sprite reappeared, much larger, about the size of a three-year-old child.

"She mourns because he's gone to the place called death," Elessario said, "and she can't follow him there."

"That's right, yes."

They were sitting on the billowing grass with the sprite between them, leaning her head into Elessario's silken lap.

"Every now and then I wonder what it would be like to die," Elessario said. "Tell me."

"I don't know. I can only make guesses. I suppose it's a lot like falling asleep—but you've never been asleep—sorry."

"I'm growing very tired of finding out that there are all these things I've never done." But she sounded sad rather than cross. By then, the sprite was sitting on her lap and was larger again, like a child of nine or ten, cradled in her arms and silent. "If I go to live among the People, if I go to be born and someday die, what then, Dallandra?"

"I don't know. None of us can know what would happen then."

"I'm growing very tired of you telling me that there are all these things you don't know."

"But I don't know them. The only one who can find those answers is you."

They were walking among roses, with the sprite, tiny again, skipping ahead. All at once the little creature threw back her head and sniffed the air like a hunting dog. For the briefest of moments she froze, then darted into the air, swooped round them in joy, and disappeared.

"Something's made her happy," Dallandra remarked.

"Maybe her bard's been reborn."

"Oh no, it's much too soon! Although, I don't know about the Round-ears. It might be different for them."

The lands of the court shifted and gleamed around them in a burst of moonlight, and now and again music drifted in warm air.

"Oh, lovely—the moon's rising," Dallandra said. "It's so hard to believe that I've been here seven whole days."

All at once, just from saying the words aloud, their import pierced her mind. How could it have been seven days, only seven short days, when enough time had passed for Nevyn to travel to the elven lands and leave them again, for Maddyn the bard to appear, then die, and now, maybe—no, it was quite likely, really— be reborn again. Dallandra shrieked aloud and felt the cry tear out of her as if by its own will.

"Elessario! You've lied to me! You've tricked me!"

"What?" She spun around to stare, then suddenly burst into tears. "Never! Dalla, what do you mean?"

"How long have I been here?"

Elessario could only stare while tears ran down her cheeks. Dallandra realized that she would have no way of understanding such things as the passing of time.

"Take me to your father. Where's your father?"

"Here." In full court garb, draped in a cloak of silvery blue and wearing a golden fillet round his yellow hair, he came strolling up to them. "I'm the trickster, Dalla, not my poor little daughter. Time runs different here in our country."

"You never told me."

"You never would have come."

"If you had gods, I'd curse you by them."

"No doubt. You know, I'm rather sorry I lied. What an odd sensation."

"Let me go home."

"Of course. That was our bargain, wasn't it? Home you shall go, and right now."

"No!" Elessario howled. "Please don't go, Dalla."

"I'm sorry, child, but I have to. You can come visit me in my own country, like you used to do before."

"I want to go with you now. Please, let me come with you and live with you."

Suddenly the air grew cold, and the moon slipped behind dark clouds. In the murky light torches gleamed on armor and sword; shields clashed, men swore, banners snapped and fluttered as an army rushed toward them, Alshandra riding hard at their head. With a frown of mild disgust, Evandar threw up one hand and snapped his fingers. All the charging soldiers turned into mist and blew away. Stamping one foot, Alshandra stood before them.

"Dallandra will never leave. She's turned my daughter against me, and I shall have her in return. It's the law and it's fair and she's my prize."

"I made her man a promise," Evandar said. "And I shall keep it."

"You made the promise, Evandar Yellow-hair, not me. She shan't leave. If our daughter is going away because of her, she's staying to be my prize in return."

Dallandra found herself clutching the amethyst figurine at her throat, as if to keep it safe. Alshandra howled with laughter.

"You don't know the way home, do you, girl? You don't know which road leads home."

They stood on the misty green plain, looking into the setting sun. On their right hand rose the dark hills, twisted and low; on their left towered the high mountains, their white peaks shining in the last of the light. Before them stretched not one road but a tangle, all leading off into mist as dark as night.

"You could wander a long time here," Alshandra said. "Maybe luck would take you home straightaway. I doubt it."

Evandar grabbed her elbow. When she swung round to face him he grinned in smug triumph.

"You say it's fair that you have a prize, and so our laws run. But

217

would it be fair, my sweet, my darling, to trap and keep a soul that never took a thing from you, that never saw Elessario before, that never, indeed, saw you or me before?"

"What? Of course it wouldn't be fair, and never would I do such a thing. What does that have to do with anything?"

"Everything, my sweet, my darling. Dallandra carries a child under her heart, an innocent child that never took a thing from us, that's yet to see any of us."

With a shriek, a scream, a howl of sheer agony Alshandra swelled up huge, towering over them like storm clouds. When she cried out again her voice was a wail of mourning.

"Unfair!"

"No." Evandar's voice was cool and calm. "Very fair."

She stretched out, as thin as clouds dissolving under a hot sun, then all at once snapped back, standing before them as an old, withered woman, dressed all in black, with tears running down her wrinkled cheeks.

"Clever," Evandar remarked. "But somehow my heart doesn't ache for you the way it should."

With a snarl she stood before them, herself again, in her hunting tunic and boots, her bow slack in one hand.

"Oh, very well, show her the road home, but you're a stupid wretched beast and I hate you."

She was gone. Dallandra caught her breath in a convulsive sob.

"And what do you want from me, Evandar, in return for all of this?"

"Only one thing. After your babe is born, and if you're not happy anymore, come back." He caught her by the shoulders, but gently. "But only if you're not happy. Do you understand? Come back only if your heart aches to come back."

"I do understand, but I fear me you'll never see me again."

"No doubt. Well, I can hope—no, I'm fairly sure—that Elessario will find her way to you and to your world, sooner or later. As for the rest of us, our fate is no concern of yours. I'll take it up in my hands, the fate of us all, and see what I can do about it. Farewell."

He bent his head and kissed her, a soft, brotherly brush of his mouth on hers.

The kiss seemed to wipe away the landscape around her. She blinked, staggered, then found herself standing on the edge of a shallow cliff. When she automatically clutched at her throat, she found the amethyst figurine gone. Down below in a brushy canyon stood the painted tents of her people. Off to one side she could see the big tent, painted with looping vines of roses, that belonged to her and Aderyn, but all the designs were oddly faded and weathered. Hasn't he kept it up? she thought. Well, that hardly matters now—I'm home. Half laughing, half weeping, she ran along the clifftop until she found the path, then scrambled down, sliding a ways in her eagerness. As she got to her feet on the level ground, she heard shouts, and some of the People began running toward her, Enabrilia in the lead.

"Dalla, Dalla!" As Enabrilia threw her arms around her, she was weeping hysterically. "Oh, thank every god, thank every god! Farendar, don't stand there gaping! Go get Aderyn!"

A tall young man, fully grown and a strong-muscled warrior, ran off at her bidding. Dallandra grabbed her friend by the shoulders while the other elves stood around in dead silence and merely stared. Half of them she didn't even recognize.

"That can't be Faro!" But even as she spoke, she felt unwelcome knowledge creeping into her mind like dread. "What's wrong with you?"

"You've been gone so long." Enabrilia began repeating the same thing over and over. "You've been gone so long."

Dallandra hugged her, shook her, yelled at her, until at last she fell quiet. When the other elves moved back to let someone through, Dallandra looked up to see Aderyn. For a moment she felt as if she would faint. He was so old, so thin, his hair dead white, his hands thin, too, like sticks or claws, and his face was so wrinkled, like ancient leather left out too long in the sun, that she sobbed aloud on a note that was close to a keen.

"Oh, ye gods! I've come back just in time to help you die."

"I doubt that." His voice was soft, but strong, younger somehow than his face. "My kind ages a long, long time before they die, Dalla."

All at once her knees would no longer hold her weight, and she staggered forward, caught herself before she fell, then staggered again, letting him grab her arms and steady her.

"How long?" she whispered. "How long have I been gone?"

"Close to two hundred years."

She threw back her head and keened, howling and raging all at once, just as Alshandra had done. The other elves closed in and caught her, supported her, led or shoved her along back to the camp and her tent. Only Enabrilia came inside with her and Aderyn.

"Sit down, Dalla," Enabrilia said. "Sit down and rest. Things will be better when you've had a moment to think. At least you're free and back with us."

"Things will never be better again, never!"

Between them Enabrilia and Aderyn got her to sit on a pile of blankets. When, blind with tears, she held out her hands, he took them and squeezed them, his fingers stiff and dry and thin on hers. She realized that she would never again feel the touch of the hands she'd been remembering and burst out weeping afresh. Dimly she was aware of Enabrilia leaving and had the hysterical thought that at least Bril had learned tact in the last two hundred years. She nearly laughed, then choked, then wept again, until at last, spent and exhausted, she fell quiet and slumped down against the blankets in a sprawl. She heard him get up; then he laid a leather cushion down in front of her. She took it, sat up enough to shove it under her head, then lay on her back and watched him numbly. His face showed no feeling but a deep confusion, like a man who's coming round from a hard blow to the head.

"Ado, I'm sorry."

"It's not your fault." He sat down next to her. "I'm surprised they let you go at all."

"I'm going to have a child, and they let me go for its sake. It's your child, Ado. We made it before I left. All those years were like seven days to me, no more."

It was his turn to weep, but his tears were the rusty creak of a man who thought he would never care enough about anything in life again to weep for it. The sound made her want to scream for the injustice of it all, but there was no good in howling "It isn't fair!" like one of the Guardians. Slowly she sat up and put her hands on his shoulders.

"Don't cry, Ado, please. At least I'm back. At least we're together. I've missed you so much."

"Missed me or the young man you left behind?" The tears gone, he turned to face her, this old man who reminded her so much of her lover. "I wouldn't even be alive, you know, if it weren't for Evandar. He worked some kind of dweomer on me, to give me an elven life span, but he forgot about elven youth."

He was furious, and she knew that no matter how much he might protest, it was her that he was angry with, not the Guardians. She wanted to weep again, but she was too exhausted.

"What about our baby?" she whispered. "Are you going to hate it?"

"Hate it? What? As if I ever could! Ah, Dalla, forgive me. At first I dreamt every night about seeing you again, and I had things all planned to say to you, wonderful loving things. And then the years dragged on, and I forgot them because I lost all hope of ever seeing you again. And now, I don't have any words left that make sense." He got up, stood hesitating at the tent flap. "Forgive me."

When he left, she was relieved. Within minutes, she was asleep.

As the days passed, Aderyn came to believe that he was more furious with himself than with either Dallandra or Evandar. He began to see himself as a warrior who spends all winter drinking, feasting, and lying around in his lord's hall until, when spring comes, his mail no longer fits over his swollen belly and hefting a weapon makes him pant for breath just when the war is about to start and he's needed the most. In all the long years that she'd been gone, it had never even occurred to him to look at another woman, never crossed his mind to grow fond of someone else.

No one could ever have taken Dallandra's place in his heart, of course; never would he have thought of remarrying, even though elven law would have allowed him to do so as soon as she'd been gone for twenty years and a day. But he might have found friendship and affection, if not love, might have kept his heart alive instead of suffocating it in his work as he had in fact done. All the energy of his heart, all his capacity to love that he might have given to another woman—he'd transmuted them into something sterile and poured them into his pupils and his studies. He marveled at himself, that he had Dallandra back yet couldn't really love her again, even though she treated him with all her old affection. She would have shared his bed if he'd wanted, but he used her pregnancy as an excuse and slept away from her.

He didn't want her pity—that's how he put it to himself. He was sure that she was treating him, an old man, withered and ugly, with pity, and he wanted no part of it. Even though he'd forgotten how to love, he knew that he wanted no one else to have her heart. As the days slipped into months, and her pregnancy began to show, he turned more and more into a hideous human stereotype that he hated even as he felt powerless to stop his transformation: he saw himself becoming a jealous old man with a young wife. All his dweomercraft, all his strange lore and his great powers, his deep understanding of the secret places of the universe and his conversations with hidden spirits—none of it helped him now, when he would see Calonderiel stop to speak to her and hate him in his heart, when he would see her smile innocently at some young man and wish him dead. And what was he going to do, he asked himself, once the baby was born and she was lithe and beautiful again?

If he could have spoken with Nevyn, his old master might have cured him, but Nevyn was off in Bardek on some mysterious working of his own. If they'd lived in Deverry, among human beings in all their vast variety of ages and looks, he might have come to his senses, too, but as it was, every person they saw was young and beautiful except Aderyn himself. His jealousy ate into every day and poisoned every night, but thanks to his long training in self-discipline and self-awareness, he did at least manage one thing: he kept the jealousy from showing. Around Dallandra he was always perfectly calm and kind; not once did he berate her or subject her to some long agony of questioning about where she'd been or what she might have said to some other man. (Years later, when it was far too late, he realized that being so rational was perhaps the worst thing he could have done, because she read his careful control as sheer indifference.) As her pregnancy progressed, of course, it became impossible for her to go off on her own, anyway. The alar made a semi-permanent camp along a stream where there was good grazing and settled in to wait for the birth. More and more, Dallandra spent her time with the other women, and particularly with Enabrilia, who would be her midwife.

When she went into labor, in fact, Aderyn was miles away, showing some of his disciples the proper way to dig up medicinal roots. By the time they got back to camp, Dallandra was shut away in Enabrilia's tent with the attending women around her, and by elven custom, he would have been kept out even if he'd wanted to stay with her. All evening he sat by the fire in a circle of other men, who said little, looked grim, and passed a skin of mead around until at last an exhausted Enabrilia came to fetch Aderyn to the tent.

"A son," she said. "And he and his mother are doing well, though . . . well, no, they're both doing splendidly."

"Tell me the truth," Aderyn snapped. "What's wrong?"

"Nothing, really. Dallandra did very well, and while she's tired, she's alert and strong and all. It's just that the baby was so quiet. He never cried, not even when he started breathing."

As he hurried into the tent, Aderyn was remembering all those old stories about changelings and wondering what sort of child his wife had birthed. Yet the baby certainly looked normal enough, though much more human than elven. Although his ears were sharp and close to being slightly pointed, his eyes had human irises and pupils, and his face and hands were round and chubby rather than being long and slender. Unlike the women of Deverry, elven women never wrapped their babies in swaddling bands; propped up in a big pile of cushions, Dallandra was holding him, loosely wrapped in a light blanket, while he nuzzled her breast. Aderyn knelt down next to her, kissed her on the forehead, then merely stared for a long time at the wrinkled, reddish creature with the soft crown of pale, pale hair. His son. He had a son, and at that moment he felt young again, felt, indeed, that he'd never loved the mother of that son as much as did right then. Yet if he told her, would she only pity him the more? An old man, gloating over a child as proof that he was still a man?

"What shall we call him, Ado?" Her voice was soft, trembling in exhaustion. "I was thinking of my father's name, but truly, I haven't seen him in so long now that it wouldn't matter if you wanted to call him something else."

"I truly don't have anything else in mind. Stupid of me, but you know, I never even thought about names to this moment."

She winced.

"Are you all right? Does something hurt?"

"No, no, I'm fine." She looked up with a forced smile. "The name I'm thinking of is Alodalaenteriel. We called him Laen for short."

"Well, that sounds splendid. If you like it, why not?"

Although the baby became Alodalaenteriel in Elvish, Aderyn tended to call him by a Deverry-sounding nickname, Loddlaen, because it was a great deal easier to say and a pun as well, meaning "the comfort of learning," which amused him. As the years passed, though, it became an omen, for learning and Loddlaen both were the only comforts left to him.

Dallandra was never quite sure exactly when she decided to return to the Guardians. She realized first that she didn't particularly love this baby she was saddled with. After the birth, she was oppressed a good bit of the time with a heartsick sadness that she could neither understand nor explain away. The slightest wrong word or look would make her burst into tears, and Loddlaen's crying was a torment. Aderyn took to keeping the baby with him unless Loddlaen needed feeding. Dallandra disliked nursing him. At first, when his sucking made her womb contract in the usual manner, she felt none of the pleasure some women feel, only cramping pains; when those stopped, her milk was scant, leaving him hungry and making him cry the more. Although Enabrilia tried getting him to suck sheep or mare's milk from a wad of rag, this animal food only made him vomit convulsively. The one joy Dallandra had during those days was seeing how much Aderyn loved his son, although even this was spoiled by the bitter thought that her man no longer cared about her anywhere near as much as he did their child.

Half starved as he was, Loddlaen might have died very young from some fever or another, but when he was two months old, they traveled to an alardan, where Dallandra found a woman named Banamario who had just given birth herself. Banamario was one of those women who produce milk in great quantities, enough for her own child and two more, most likely, as she remarked, and her breasts caused her great pain unless she expressed the milk one way or another. Dallandra handed over Loddlaen without a qualm. When she saw how fondly Banamario smiled at the nursing baby, how gently she stroked his pale, fine hair and how softly she touched his little roundish ears, Dallandra felt stabbed to the soul by guilt pure and simple—she didn't care half as much for her own son as this stranger did. Since she was elven, born to a people who saw every infant as both a treasure and a weapon laid up against their extinction, the guilt burned in the wound for days. Yet even so, she took to leaving Loddlaen for long periods of time with Banamario, who was nothing but pleased to do a favor for the Wise One.

At times, as she rode alone out in the grasslands, away from the noise and bustle of the alardan, she would think of the Guardians, particularly of Elessario, whom she badly missed. She would wonder, too, if she'd love Loddlaen more if only he were a daughter instead of a son, but she knew that the real trouble lay between her and Aderyn. They should have both been young when their son was born, should have treasured him and squabbled over his upbringing and loved each other the more for it. No doubt they would have had another child, maybe two, even, over the course of years. Now, all that was denied them, and she was dragging herself through a world turned flat and sour by her memories of the splendor of life in another, easier world. She felt, too, like a person who's been forced to leave the campfire halfway through one of the bard's best tales and never gets to hear the ending: what did Evandar have in mind for his people? More and more, in fact, she found herself remembering Evandar, particularly the way he'd told her to come back if she should be unhappy. He knew, she would think, he knew that this would happen to me.

On the day before the alardan was to break up, Aderyn arranged for Banamario and her man to leave their alar and join his and Dallandra's. Knowing that Loddlaen would be fed and loved more than she could feed and love him seemed to settle the question in Dallandra's mind. That evening, when she stopped into the wet nurse's tent to kiss Loddlaen goodbye, she felt a stab of guilt at how easy it was to leave him behind, her round little baby with the solemn eyes and the perennial smell of sour milk hanging about him, but as soon as she walked free of the camp, the guilt disappeared—indeed, she never truly thought of Loddlaen again after that day. She went about five miles west until she found a stand of hazel trees, growing thick and tangled at a place where three streams came together to form a proper river. She'd known them once as rivulets, two hundred years ago and long before the hazels had grown there, but year after year of rain and runoff had deepened them down.

Among the hazels Evandar was waiting, leaning against a tree and whistling a heart-piercing melody. She found that she wasn't even surprised that he would know and come to meet her. It was so good to see him again that she also realized, with a twist of her heart, that she was beginning to fall in love with him.

"You're certain you want to come back?" he said.

"I am. It's so odd. I hate being a mother, but it's made me ready to be a midwife. I'm assuming, anyway, that some of you will have the courage to take up your birthright."

"Elessario at least, and maybe some of the other young ones." All at once he laughed. "That's a fine jest, take up your birthright. It took me a moment to understand. You know, I'm feeling solemn, and that's something I've never really done before."

Side by side they walked into the opalescent mist, where the flat road stretched out, waiting for them, between the dark hills and the fair mountains. When she raised her hand to her throat, she found the amethyst figurine hanging from its golden chain.

"And what of you, Evandar? Won't you pass into my world once and for all, when the time comes?"

"How could I, knowing what I know, having what I have?"

"If you don't, you'll lose your daughter."

He stopped walking and glared at her like a sulky child.

"I can be as underhanded as you if I have to be," she said, grinning. "But think of this. If you went first, Elessario would follow you. She loves you even more than you love her. Just think: you could save her by saving yourself."

"You wretched trickster!" But he laughed with a toss of his head. "Let me tell you something, Dalla. I know now what missing someone means, and how bitter a thing it is. Do you know why?"

"I think I do, actually. But what of Alshandra?"

"She's left me. She's gone farther in."

"Farther in?"

"It's not a good thing. But I'll explain later."

When he kissed her, the mist closed around them, and the road changed itself to sunny meadow, bright with flowers.

At that moment Aderyn knew in a stab of dweomer cold that she'd gone again. This time, he neither wept nor cursed, merely told the wet nurse that Dallandra had such important work to do that she wouldn't be back for a while. Wrapped in the joy of having two babies to love and a new alar to help with all the hard work of caring for them, Banamario merely remarked that it was all the same to her. That night, though, when Aderyn fell into a restless sleep in a tent grown suddenly huge and lonely again, Dallandra came to him in the Gatelands.

In his dream it seemed to him that they stood on a high cliff and looked off over the misty plains. They must have been on the western border of the grasslands, he realized, because he was looking east to a sun rising behind storm clouds in a wash of light the color of blood, which he knew for an evil omen. She was wearing, not her elven tunic and trousers, but a long dress, belted at the waist with jewels, of purple silk. As one does in dreams, he knew without needing to be told that her dress was of the style worn in the long-lost cities of the far west.

"I came to apologize for leaving you again," she said. "But then, you didn't really want me to stay, did you."

It wasn't a question, but his heart ached at the unfairness of it, that she would think he wanted her gone when all he wanted was to be able to love her again.

"I don't blame you for leaving," he said instead. "There was naught left for you in our world, was there? Not even the baby could delight you anymore."

"Just so. But still, I want you to know that—"

"Hush! You don't need to explain anything to me, or apologize anymore, either. Go in peace. I know I can't keep you bound to me any longer."

She hesitated, her eyes filling with tears, her mouth working in honest sadness, but at the same time her image was fading, turning faint and pale, turning into mist and blowing away into the gray and ugly light of a stormy morning. He was in his own tent, sitting up and wide awake, hearing Loddlaen cry in his big hanging cradle of leather stiffened with bone. Aderyn rose and got the baby, changed him, and took him to Banamario's tent, which stood right next to his. As she nursed him, Aderyn squatted down nearby and thought of the two ebony arrows with silver tips, lying somewhere in his tent wrapped in an old blanket, those pledges from the Guardians that had turned out sharp and deadly indeed.

"There's the good boy," Banamario was crooning. "Not hungry anymore, is he? What a good boy! Here's your papa now, Laen, go to Papa."

Aderyn took the baby and shifted him to one shoulder to burp him while Banamario took her own child, a boy named Javanateriel, and set him at her other breast.

"When do you think Dallandra will be back, Wise One?" she asked, but absently.

"Never."

She looked up, deeply troubled.

"The dweomer has strange roads, Banna. She's chosen one to walk that leads where none of us can follow her."

"I see, but, Wise One, I'm so sorry!"

"For me? Don't be. I've accepted it."

But from that day on, Aderyn could deny Loddlaen nothing, not even when he grew old enough to beg for things that he should never have had.

Part Three

Eldidd

918

AFTER SIXTY-ODD years in Bardek, Nevyn returned to Eldidd late in the summer of 918, landing in Aberwyn with some unusual cargo tucked inside his shirt for safety's sake. While he'd been abroad, studying the scholarly dweomer lore of the Bardekian priests, he'd gotten the idea of making a talisman for the High King, a magically charged jewel that would radiate the noble virtues endlessly to its owner's mind. To that end, he'd bought an extremely unusual stone and studied the various writings about such creations in the libraries of various temples, but to make the talisman, he brought the stone home. As big as a walnut, but perfectly round and smoothly polished, a tribute to the art of Bardek jewelers, the opal was shot through with pale gold veins and bluish-pink shadows, as mottled as the coat of some exotic animal. At the moment, for all its beauty, it was an ordinary jewel, a dull thing in its way, though worth a fortune. By the time Nevyn got done with it, it would be supremely interesting, and worth a man's life.

Down in the center of Aberwyn stood the hall of the merchant guild, an imposing fat tower with glass in the downstairs windows and a stout slate roof. Their official money changer held court in a bare stone room with a hearth, two chairs, and a long table, where Nevyn found a stout and gray-haired man sitting behind a litter of Bardek-style scrolls. Behind him, at the entrance to another room, an armed guard slouched against the wall.

"I'm just back from Bardek," Nevyn said to the money changer.

"You've hit the rate of exchange at a good time, good sir. Sit down, sit down."

As Nevyn pulled up the rickety three-legged chair, he noticed the guard watching with the interest of the longtime bored, a young man of about twenty, tall and well muscled, with blond hair, blue eyes, and the beginnings of a mustache blotching his upper lip. Nevyn wouldn't have given him a second thought if it weren't for the silver dagger at his belt. As it was, he took a good look at the lad's face and then nearly swore aloud, because the soul behind his eyes struck him as familiar and friendly both. Before he could observe more, the money changer's voice claimed his attention.

"We've been giving thirty Deverry silvers for each Bardek zotar of full weight."

"Indeed? That certainly is generous! Are things troubled in Eldidd?"

"Have you been away for some time?"

"Years, actually."

"Hum." The money changer reflected upon something before he spoke again. "I hope to every god in the Otherlands that these rumors are only rumors, but they say the gwerbrets are still pining for the days when they were princes. The High King's a long way away, my friend."

"Just so. Rebellion?"

"Let us merely say that Bardek merchants have never gotten rich by allowing themselves to be caught in the middle of trouble. They're not bringing as much sound coinage in as they once did."

The money changer counted out Nevyn's zotars, marked the tally on a bit of parchment, which Nevyn signed, then went back through the doorway to his vault to change the coins. Nevyn turned to the young guard and gave him a pleasant smile.

"What's your name, lad? It looks like this duty wearies you."

"Maer, my lord. But I won't be guarding this fellow's stores much longer. He just hired me to fill in, like. His regular man broke his wrist in a fall, you see, but thanks be to the gods, the splints are off now."

When Nevyn risked opening up a quick bit of the dweomer sight with the sigils that controlled memory, the silver dagger's face blurred and changed. For a moment Nevyn seemed to look into the weary eyes of Maddyn the bard. Nevyn was so glad to see him that he wanted to jump up and embrace him, but of course, since Maer would have no conscious memory left of his last life, he did nothing of the sort.

"And what will you do next?" Nevyn said. "If these rumors of trouble are true, there'll be plenty of work for silver daggers in Eldidd."

"Oh, it's all a lot of horseshit if you ask me, my lord. The gwerbrets can mutter over their ale easy enough, but getting the coin to outfit an army's a bit harder. I'll go west, I suppose. I've never ridden that way before."

It was perhaps an omen of sorts. Nevyn had no real idea of where to settle down while he performed the dweomer work on the opal, but on the western coast lay a quiet little village that held pleasant memories for him.

"I'm heading west myself," Nevyn said. "How would your captain feel if I rode with your troop a ways?"

"Captain? Troop?" Maer paused for a laugh. "The silver daggers haven't ridden together as a troop in fifty years, good sir. It was that royal decree, you know. We can only ride together one or two at time, no more."

"Indeed?" Nevyn was honestly shocked. I've stayed away far too long, he told himself. "Why?"

"I don't know. It's the king's law and so it's good enough for me. But I'm for hire, sure enough, if you need a guard."

"Feel like riding to Cannobaen?"

"Gladly. A couple of silver pieces?"

"Done. We'll leave at dawn, then, the day after tomorrow."

When the time came to leave, Maer turned up promptly. Nevyn was loading up his newly purchased riding horse and pack mule in the little innyard just at dawn when the silver dagger appeared, leading a splendid black warhorse, laden with a pair of saddlebags, a bedroll, a plain white shield, and a pot helm, all tied in a messy sort of way to his saddle. He looked over the mule packs with some interest.

"So you're a herbman, are you?"

"I am. Don't worry about falling sick on our journey."

Maer grinned and finished loading the mule without being asked. They led their horses through the busy morning streets, then mounted outside the west gate just as the last of the sea fog was burning off into a late-summer morning. To their left, the turquoise sea sparkled and churned at the foot of pale cliffs, and to their right, the winter wheat stood ripe and golden in the fields. As they rode, Maer burst into good cheer, whistling and singing in a fine clear tenor that with training could have made him a bard. Nevyn was so genuinely glad to hear the man he would always think of as Maddyn sing again that he had to give himself a stern warning. This was Maer now, not Maddyn, and it was against all the laws of dweomer as well as common sense to treat the one as the other.

When he turned in the saddle to pay Maer a compliment on his voice, he was in for a surprise. Riding behind the silver dagger's saddle and clinging to him like a child was a good-sized blue sprite. Just as he was telling himself that of course it couldn't be the same creature, not Maddyn's favorite still loyal after all these years, the sprite grinned at him in such smug contentment that he was forced to recognize her. Over the next few days, as they made their slow way to Cannobaen, Nevyn saw the sprite often, hovering around Maer during the day, cuddling up to him like a dog while he slept at night. It became obvious, though, that Maer never saw her, because often he would have stepped on her if she hadn't jumped aside. Once, when Maer was off at a farmhouse buying food, Nevyn got a chance alone with her. Talking about death to one of the Wildfolk was, of course, a complete waste of breath.

"He doesn't see you anymore, you know. He's changed since the last time you found him."

She snarled, exposing long and pointed teeth.

"It's not good for you to follow him this way. You should be off with your own kind."

At that she threw back her head and howled, a thin wisp of sound. Since normally the Wildfolk were incapable of making noise, Nevyn became even more troubled.

"I'll talk with one of your kings," he began, "and we'll see what . . ."

In a screech of fury she seemed to swell, sucking up substance from the material plane and turning for one brief moment quite solid and as large as a growing child. Then she was gone in a gust of cold air.

Besides seeing the Wildfolk, Maer had been a silver dagger in his last life, too, of course, but Nevyn tended to consider that a simple coincidence. Although he would never had pried into the reason for this dishonor, Maer himself volunteered the story as they sat round the campfire on their second night out.

"You're not an Eldidd man, are you?" Nevyn had asked him.

"I'm not. I was born in Blaeddbyr, over in Deverry, and that's where I got this blasted dagger, too. I was riding for the Wolf clan, you see, and one night, well, me and the lads got a bit drunk. So one of my friends got this daft idea. There was this lass he fancied —oh, bad it was, good sir—he was like a boar in rut over the tailor's daughter, but her da, he kept an eye as sharp as one of his needles on the lass. So my friend puts us up to helping him. We went round to the tailor's shop and Nyn calls the lass out of her bedroom window, while me and the other lad went round the front. We pretend to get into a brawl, you see, and old Da comes running out. So we led him a merry dance, insulting him and having a fine old time, and truly, we got a bit carried away." With a sigh, Maer rubbed his chin with a rueful hand. "We ducked him in the village horse trough, just for the fun of the thing, and all the time Nyn's tumbling the daughter out under a hedgerow. So Da goes complaining to our lord, and cursed if Avoic doesn't side with the old tailor and kick us out of the warband! Cursed unjust, I say. He let Nyn come back, though, because the stupid lass had to go and get a child, and so Nyn had to marry her."

Maer sounded so indignant that Nevyn laughed aloud. Maer drew himself up square-shouldered and glared at him.

"Don't you think it was unjust?"

"Umph, well. But you're the first lad I've ever met who got that dagger because of a prank."

"That's been the tale of my days, good sir. I only want a bit of fun, and ye gods, everyone goes and takes it wrong."

Late on a summer afternoon, Nevyn and his guard rode to the top of a rise and saw Cannobaen spread out along the little stream called Y Brog. At the sight of the round, thatched houses, Maer broke into a wide grin.

"Ale tonight with supper, my lord. Or do they even have a tavern in this hole?"

"They did the last time I was here. But that was a long time ago."

At a hundred families, mostly of farmers or fishermen, Cannobaen was about twice as big as Nevyn had been remembering it. There was a good-sized proper inn on the old site of the small tavern. After he rented a chamber, Nevyn ordered ale and a meal for himself and stood his silver dagger to one last dinner, too. The innkeep, a stout fellow named Ewsn, hovered nearby.

"Do you get much trade through here?" Nevyn said, mostly to be polite.

"We've got a merchant in our town who buys and sells off in the west—with those tribes with the strange-sounding names. Men from Aberwyn come through every now and then to buy the horses he brings back." He hesitated, sucking stumps of teeth. "Be you a herbman, sir? My wife has this pain in her joints, you see, and so I was wondering."

"I am at that. In the morning, I'll be glad to have a talk with her if she'd like."

The morning, however, apparently wasn't good enough for the innkeep's wife, Samwna. While she served Nevyn and Maer their dinner, Samwna also treated them to a long recital of symptoms as well rehearsed as a bard's performance. While they ate roast beef and turnips, they heard all about the mysterious pain in her joints, strange aches in the small of her back, and night sweats, sometimes hot, sometimes cold. With the apple tart, they heard about headaches and odd moments when she felt quite dizzy.

"It's all related to your woman's change of life," Nevyn said. "I've got soothing herbs that should help a good deal."

Maer went scarlet and almost choked.

"My most humble thanks." Samwna made him a little curtsy. "I've been wondering and wondering, I have. Here, you're not thinking of settling in our town, are you, good sir? It's been years and years since there's been a herbman in our neighborhood."

"As a matter of fact, I am. I'm getting too old to wander the roads, and I want a nice quiet place to settle down."

"Oh, towns don't come much quieter than Cannobaen!" Samwna paused to laugh. "Why, the big excitement lately was when one of Lord Pertyc's boarhounds killed two chickens over at Myna's farm."

Nevyn smiled, well pleased. Idly he rubbed the front of his shirt and touched the opal hidden inside. If there's trouble in Aberwyn, he thought, it can cursed well stay in Aberwyn! No doubt remote Cannobaen would be undisturbed by these rumors of rebellion.

"By every hell, how can you be so stubborn?"

"It comes with my family title." Pertyc Maelwaedd touched the device worked on his shirt. "We're Badgers, my friend. We hold on."

"By that line of thinking, we Bears would have to stay in our holes." Danry, Tieryn Cernmeton and Pertyc's closest friend, perched on the edge of a carved table and considered him. "But cursed if I will."

"Why do you think I nicknamed you the Falcon, back when we were lads? But this time you're flying too high."

They were sequestered in Pertyc's small study behind a barred door, and a good thing, too, because Danry was talking treason. Since Pertyc had a taste for clutter, the room was crowded: a large writing table, a shelf with twenty leather-bound codices, two chairs, a scatter of small Bardek carpets, and on the wall, a pair of moth-eaten stag's heads, trophies of some long-forgotten hunt of a remote ancestor. Pertyc's helm perched jauntily on the antlers of the largest stag, and his shield was propped up against a book-laden lectern carved with intertwined dogs and badgers.

"I've always liked my demesne," Pertyc remarked absently. "So remote here on the border. Nice and quiet. Easy to stay out of trouble in a place like Cannobaen."

"You can't stay out of this. That's what you don't understand."

"Indeed? Just watch."

Danry sighed again. He was a tall man, with a florid face that usually simmered on the edge of rage, and thick blond mustaches that were usually damp with mead. Lately, however, Danry had been withdrawn, and the mustaches had a ratty look, as if he'd been chewing on them in hard thought. Pertyc had been wondering what was on his friend's mind. Now he was finally hearing. Ever since the forced joining of the two kingdoms some sixty years before, there'd been plenty of grumbling in Eldidd, a longing for independence and past glory simmering like porridge over a slow fire. Now the fire had flared up; the porridge was beginning to boil over.

"I'd hoped to come around to this slowly," Danry said at last. "But it's hard to believe you'd be too blind to see the ale in your own tankard."

"I've never much liked sour ale. What does it matter to me if I pledge to a new king or an old one?"

"Perro! It's the honor of the thing."

"How are you going to have a rebellion without a king to rally round? Or have you ferreted out some obscure heir?"

"That's a rotten way to speak about him, but we have." Danry picked up a leather dog collar from the cluttered writing desk and began fiddling with the brass buckles. "The lad is related to the old blood royal twice over on the female line, and there's a lass who's related on the male line. If we marry them, well, it's claim enough. They're both good Eldidd blood, and that's the true thing." He ran the end of the collar through the buckle and pulled it tight. "You know, my friend, your claim to the throne is as good as his."

"It's not! I don't have a claim at all. None, do you hear me? My most honorable ancestor abdicated; I'm descended from his common-born wife, and that's that! No priest in the kingdom would back a claim on my part, and you know it."

"There are ways of handling priests." Danry tossed the collar aside. "But you're right, no doubt. I was just thinking of a thing or two."

"Listen, even jackals pull down the kill before they start squabbling over the meat."

Danry winced.

"When I came to my manhood," Pertyc went on, "I swore an oath to King Aeryc to serve him well, serve him faithfully, and to put his life above my own. Seems to me I heard you and the rest of our friends swear one like it, too."

"Ah, by the hells! No oath is binding when it's sworn under coercion."

"No one held a sword to my throat. I didn't see one at yours, either."

With a curse, Danry heaved himself up from the table and began trying to pace round the cluttered chamber.

"The coercion lies in the past. They stripped Eldidd of its rights and its independence under threat of open slaughter. It's the honor of the thing, Perro."

"If I break an oath, I don't have any honor left worth fighting over." Idly Pertyc touched the device on his shirt.

"Ah, curse your horseshit Badgers! If you don't come in with us, what then? Are you going to run to this false king with the tale?"

"Never, and all for your sake. Do you think I'd put my sworn friend's neck in a noose? I'd die first."

Danry sighed, looking away.

"I wish you'd stay out, too," Pertyc said.

"And I'd die before I'd do that. You can trumpet your neutrality to the four corners of the world, but you're still going to be in the middle of it. What do you think we're going to do, muster our warbands right down in Aberwyn? When the spring comes, we're meeting in the forest, here in the west."

"You scummy bastards!"

Danry laughed, tossing his head back and giving him a friendly slap on the shoulder.

"We'll do our best not to disturb his lordship or trample his kitchen garden. Now here, spring's a long way away. I have faith you'll be mustering with us when the time comes. It might be dangerous if you didn't. You know I'd never lift my hand against you or your dun and kin, but well, as for the others . . ." He let the words trail significantly away.

"Neutrals have found themselves stripped and sieged before, huh? You're right enough. You tell our friends that I'll protect my lands to my last breath, whether they claim to have a king on their side or not."

"They wouldn't expect any less from you. I warn you, though, when we win this fight, you can't expect much honor or standing in the new kingdom."

"I'll take my chances on that. I'd rather die a beggar than break my sworn oath." Pertyc smiled faintly. "And the word, my friend, isn't 'when' you win. It's 'if.' "

Danry turned red, a hectic flush of rage across his cheeks. Pertyc held his gaze until Danry forced out a wry smile.

"Let us give the gods their due," Danry said. "Who knows where a man's Wyrd will lead him? Very well. 'If' it is."

Pertyc walked outside with Danry to the ward, where his horse was standing saddled and ready at the gates. Danry mounted, said a pleasant and normal farewell, then trotted off down the road to the north. As Pertyc watched the dust disappearing, he felt danger like a cold ache in his stomach. The dolts, he thought, and maybe I'm the biggest dolt of all! He turned and looked over his dun, a small, squat broch standing inside a timber-laced wall without ramparts or barbicans. Although his demesne was continually short on coin, he decided it would be wise to spend what he had on fortifications, even if he could only afford to build some earthworks and ditches. Whatever else it may have lacked, his dun had the best watchtower in the kingdom for the Can-nobaen light, where every night a beacon burned to warn passing ships of submerged rocks just off the coast. If the rebellion swept a siege his way, it occurred to Pertyc, he could perhaps parlay keep-ing the light into a reason for keeping his neutrality. Perhaps. The dread in his stomach turned to burning ice.

Later that same day, he was drinking in his great hall when a page came with the news that there was a silver dagger at the gates. Since he had only ten men in his warband, he had Maer shown in straightaway.

"I'll take you on, silver dagger. I don't know when we'll see action, but another man might come in handy. Your keep, and if there's fighting, a silver piece a week."

"My thanks, my lord. Winter's coming on, and the roof over my head's going to be welcome."

"Good. Uh, Maer? If you shave that mustache off, it'll grow in thicker the next time, you know."

Maer drew himself up to full height.

"Is his lordship suggesting or ordering?"

"Merely suggesting. No offense intended."

Pertyc turned him over to his captain, then went up to the women's hall, a comfortable sunny room that covered half the second story of the tower. It was the domain of his lordship's old nurse, Maudda, all stooped back and long white hair these days, but still doing her best to serve the clan by tending Pertyc's four-year-old daughter, Beclya. Pertyc felt very bad about keeping the old woman working, but there was, quite simply, no one else who could handle the lass. As headstrong as her mother, he thought, then winced at the very mental mention of his absent wife. He found them sitting in a patch of sun by the window, Beclya in a chair, Maudda standing behind, keeping up a running flow of chatter as she combed the lass's hair, but as soon as Pertyc stepped in, Beclya twisted free and rushed to her father.

"Da, Da, I want to go riding. Please, Da, please?"

"In a bit, my sweet."

"Now!" She tossed back her head and howled in rage.

"Stop that! You're upsetting poor Maudda."

With a visible wrench of will she fell silent, turning to look at her beloved nurse. She was a beautiful child, Beclya, with her moonbeam-pale hair and enormous gray eyes, tall and slender for her age and as graceful as a fawn when she moved.

"Now, lambkin," Maudda said. "You'll go riding soon enough. Your da's the lord, you see, and we all must do what he says. The gods made him a lord, and we—"

"Horseshit!" She stamped her foot. "But I'll be good if you say so."

With a sigh and a watery smile, Maudda held out her arms, and Beclya ran to her. I've got to get the poor old dear some help, Pertyc told himself. He had this thought with the same tedious regularity with which he first enlisted young nursemaids, then watched them retreat.

"Maudda, I wanted your advice on somewhat," he said aloud. "I've been thinking about my son. Do you think my cousin would take it amiss if I rode to his dun and fetched Adraegyn home for the winter?"

"Ah. You've been hearing them rumors of trouble, then."

"Ye gods, do you know everything?"

"Everything what matters, my lord."

"Please, Da, go get him," Beclya put in. "I miss Draego."

"No doubt you do," Pertyc said. "I think it might be best all round if he came home. I can train him myself, if it comes to that."

"Da?" Beclya broke in. "I want to go with you."

"You can't, my sweet. Young ladies don't go riding round the countryside like silver daggers."

"I want to go!"

"I said you can't."

"I don't care what you say. I don't care what your dumb gods say, either. I don't want to be a lady. I want to go riding. I want to go with you when you get Draego." With a shriek she threw herself down on the floor and began to kick.

"If I may be so bold, my lord?" Maudda pitched her voice loud over the general noise. "Do get out and leave her to me."

Pertyc fled the field. He was beginning to wish that he'd done what his wife wanted and let her take his daughter away with her. He'd refused only out of a stubborn honor. He could only thank the gods for making Adraegyn a reasonable and fairly human being.

"Now, you know who does have a little cottage," Samwna said thoughtfully. "Wersyn the merchant. He had it built for his mother, you see, when she was widowed, but the poor lady passed to the Otherlands just this spring. No surprise, truly, because she was seventy winters if she was a day old. She always said sixty-four, but hah! you can tell those things, good sir. But anyway, it's a nice stout little place with a big hearth."

"Does it have a bit of land around it?"

"Oh, it does, because she liked her flowers and suchlike. Besides, it had to be a good stone's throw away from Wersyn's house. Moligga—that's his wife—put her foot down about that, and I can't say I blame her, because old Bwdda was the nosy type, always lifting the lids of her daughter-in-law's pots, if you take my meaning, good sir."

Nevyn began to remember why he normally avoided small rural towns.

On the other hand, the cottage turned out to be both suitable and cheap, and he rented it immediately, then spent the rest of the day unpacking and settling in. On the morrow, he decided that while he'd keep his riding horse, the mule would only be a nuisance. Samwna, that font of all local information, told him to try selling it to a farmer called Nalyn.

"He lives out near Lord Pertyc's dun. He married the farm, you see, or I should say, it still belongs to poor dear Myna—she was widowed so young, poor thing, and her with two daughters to raise on her own—but now one of the daughters is married, Lidyan, that is, and it's good for them to have a man to work the fields again, I must say, so it's Nalyn's farm in a way, like."

Nevyn made his escape at last and rode out, with the mule on a tether rope, and found the farm. When Nevyn dismounted near the shabby thatched roundhouse, he could hear someone yelling inside. A man's voice, thick with rage, drifted out, followed by the sound of a woman weeping and pleading. Ye gods, he thought, does this Nalyn beat his poor wife? A second woman's voice yelled back, cracking in a string of curses. A young heavyset man came stalking out of the house. Just as he took a step out of the doorway, an egg came sailing after him, caught him on the back of his head, and shattered. With an oath, the man started to turn back in, then saw Nevyn.

"My apologies," Nevyn said. "I just heard in the village you might want to buy a mule. I can come back later."

"No need." The young farmer was busily trying to get the egg off the back of his head with both hands. "I do indeed need a mule, though my sister's stubborn enough for a whole rotten herd of them. Let me just wash this off at the well."

Laughter rang in the doorway, and a young woman, about Maer's age, came strolling out. She was pretty, raven-haired and blue-eyed, but not truly beautiful, with her hair cropped off short in the way many farm women wore their hair, out of the way of hard work. Her dress was dirty, much mended, and hitched up around her waist at the kirtle to leave her ankles and feet bare.

"And who's this, Nalyn? Another of your candidates for my betrothal?"

"Hold your cursed tongue, Glae!" Nalyn snapped.

"He's better-looking than Doclyn, aged or not. No offense, good sir, but my beloved brother-in-law is bound and determined to marry me off to get rid of me, you see. Are you in the market for a young wife by any chance?"

"Glae!" Nalyn howled. "I said hold your tongue!"

"Don't you give me orders, you afterbirth of a miscarried wormy sow."

With an anguished glance in Nevyn's direction Nalyn walked off to the well to wash away the egg. The lass leaned comfortably against the doorjamb and gave Nevyn a brilliant smile that transformed her face for one brief moment. Then she was merely wary, and plain, her eyes too suspicious and cold for beauty.

"Here, good sir, I haven't even asked your name. Mine's Glaenara. You must've been talking with the village women if you knew we were in the market for a mule."

"Well, I did happen to speak with Samwna. My name is Nevyn, and that's a name, not a jest."

"Indeed? Well, then, Lord Nobody, welcome to our humble farm. Samwna's a good woman, isn't she? And her daughter Braedda's my best friend. As meek as a suckling lamb, but I do like her."

Glaenara ran her hands down the mule's legs, thumped it on the chest, then grabbed its head and pried its mouth open to look at its teeth before the startled mule could even object. His wet shirt in his hand, Nalyn came back and watched sourly.

"Now, I'm the one who's saying if we buy that mule or not."

"Then take a look at its mouth yourself."

When Nalyn went to do so, the by now wary mule promptly bit him on the arm. Howling with laughter, Glaenara cuffed the mule so hard that it let go. Nevyn grabbed Nalyn's arm and looked at it: mule bites could turn nasty, but fortunately, this one hadn't broken the skin. Nalyn was cursing a steady stream under his breath.

"Just bruised, I'd say," Nevyn said soothingly. "My apologies."

"Wasn't you," Nalyn growled. "Glae, I'm going to beat you so hard one of these days."

"Just try." Glaenara set her hands on her hips and smiled at him.

At that, the other two women came running out of the house.

Glaenara's mother was gray and thin, her face drawn and etched deep with exhausted lines. Her sister was pretty, with less strength but more harmony in her wide-eyed face. Sniveling, the sister caught her husband's arm and looked up, pleading with him silently. The mother turned to Glaenara.

"Glae, please? Not in front of a stranger."

With a sigh, Glaenara turned tame, coming over to slip her arm around her mother's frail waist and give her a kiss on the cheek. Nalyn patted his wife's arm, looked Nevyn's way, and blushed again. For a moment they all stood there in a miserable tableau; then Glaenara led her mother back to the house. With one backward glance at Nevyn, the sister hurried after.

"My apologies for my little sister," Nalyn said.

"My good sir, no man in his right mind would hold you responsible for anything that lass does."

As he was riding back to the village, Nevyn met Lord Pertyc's warband, coming two abreast in a cloud of dust. At the head rode the lord himself, a tall but slender man who reminded him strikingly of Prince Mael, his distant ancestor, with his raven-haired Eldidd good looks and heavy-lidded dark blue eyes. Beside him on a gray pony was a young lad of about eight, so much like the lord that Nevyn assumed it was his son. As they passed, Pertyc gave Nevyn a wave and a nod; Nevyn bowed gravely. Behind came ten men with badgers painted on their shields. At the very rear, riding alone in the dust but grinning as cheerfully as ever, was Maer. When he saw Nevyn, he waved.

"I've got myself a nice warm spot in a badger's hole. You brought me luck, Nevyn."

"Good, good! I've settled into the village. No doubt we'll see each other from time to time."

"You know what?" Adraegyn said.

"I don't," Maer said. "What?"

"Da says he wants to hire more silver daggers if he can find them."

"Does he now? Do you know why?"

"I'll wager there's going to be a war. Why else would he come fetch me back from Cousin Macco's?"

"No doubt you're right, truly."

Adraegyn considered him for a moment. He was perched on the edge of the watering trough and watching while Maer cleaned his tack. Maer enjoyed the young lordling's company; as the eldest of a family of seven, he was used to having children tagging after him.

"Do you have to polish that dagger a lot? Silver plates and stuff get dirty truly fast."

"So they do. But the dagger's different. It's not entirely made of silver, you see."

"Can I look at it? Or is that rude to ask?"

"You can look at mine, but never ask another silver dagger, all right? Most of us are a bit touchy about it. Now be careful. It's sharp as the Lord of Hell's front tooth."

Grinning, Adraegyn took the dagger and hefted it, then risked a gingerly touch on the blade with the ball of his thumb.

"Have you ever slain a man with this dagger?"

"I haven't, but then, I haven't had it very long. Maybe I'll get my chance if your father rides to war."

"I wish I could go, but I'm still learning stuff." Adraegyn sighed dramatically. "And I've got to waste all this time learning to read."

"Truly? Now that's a strange thing. Why?"

"Da says I have to. All the men in our clan learn to read. It's one of the things that make us Maelwaedds."

In a few minutes, the Maelwaedd himself came strolling over to lean on the watering trough beside his son.

"It's always pleasant to see another man work," Pertyc said. "Odd, but there you are."

"So it is, my lord. Sometimes I'd be traveling and stop to

watch some poor bastard of a farmer slaving out in the fields, just to be watching him."

"Just so. Here, Draego, what are you doing with Maer's silver dagger?"

"He let me look at it, Da. That's all."

"Careful—those things are blasted sharp."

"I know, Da!" Somewhat reluctantly, Adraegyn handed the dagger back to Maer. "Da, I want to go riding. Can I take my pony down to the village?"

"By all means. Or here." Pertyc hesitated for a moment. "Maer, go with him, will you? You can use some of the spare tack while yours is drying."

"Done, my lord." Maer looked up sharply. "Do you think there might be trouble?"

"The world's as full of trouble as the sea is full of fish. I don't think anything just yet, but listen, Draego, from now on, when you want to leave the dun, you tell me first and take one of the men with you."

"Why? I never used to have to."

"Do as I say and hold your tongue about it. I'll tell you more when there's more to tell."

There was a fair amount of activity down in Cannobaen that afternoon, because it was market day. Most of the farmers and craftsmen had their goods spread out on blankets on the ground, though the weaver and local blacksmith did have little stalls. As Maer and Adraegyn strolled around, the lad would stop every now and then and ask a villager how his wife was doing or if his children were well, and he managed to remember everyone's name in a most impressive manner. At the edge of the market, a young woman was sitting behind baskets of eggs. Maer was immediately struck by her. Although she wasn't beautiful, she was handsome, with a slightly malicious touch to her grin and life sparkling in her blue eyes.

"Who's that, my lord?" Maer pointed her out.

"Oh, that's Glae. She and her kin have the farm next to our demesne."

Maer guided the lad over to Glae and her baskets. Tied up behind her was a mule.

"Good morrow, Glae," Adraegyn said to her.

"Good morrow, my lord. Come down for a look at your market?"

"I have." Adraegyn waved at Maer. "This is Maer. He's my bodyguard now."

"Oh, is he?" Glae gave Maer a cool appraisal. "And a silver dagger at that."

"I am." Maer made her a half-bow. "But I beg and pray that you won't think less of me for it."

"Since I think naught of you one way or the other, I can hardly think less of you, can I now?"

Maer opened his mouth and shut it again, suddenly at a loss for words.

"You've got a new mule, I see," Adraegyn said.

"We do, my lord. We bought him from the new herbman in town."

"There's someone new in town?" Adraegyn was openly delighted. "Where does he live?"

"In the cottage by Wersyn's house. And he seems a wise old man indeed, from what Braedda tells me."

"Come on, Maer. Let's go meet him. Maybe he's a dweomerman or suchlike."

"Oh, now here," Maer said, grinning. "You do have a taste for the bard's fancies, don't you?"

"Well, you never know. Good morrow, Glae. I hope you sell a lot of eggs. Come on, Maer. Let's go."

Maer made Glae one last bow, which she acknowledged with a flick of her eyes, then hurried after his half-sized commander.

They found Nevyn out in the garden in front of his cottage, digging up a flower bed as vigorously as a man a third his age. Adraegyn hailed him, leaned on the fence, then gasped in sudden delight.

"Oh, your garden's full of Wildfolk! They're all dancing round and round."

Nevyn grunted in sharp surprise. Maer started to laugh, then choked it back for fear of hurting the lad's feelings—he was already blushing scarlet at his lapse.

"I mean, uh, I'm sorry, I mean, I know there aren't really Wildfolk . . ."

"What?" Nevyn's voice was perfectly mild. "Of course there are Wildfolk. And you were quite right the first time. My garden's full of them."

It was nice of the old man, Maer thought, to help the lad over his awkward moment with a little lie. Adraegyn was beaming up at Nevyn.

"You see them, too? Truly?"

"I do."

Adraegyn spun around to consider Maer.

"And you must, too. You can tell us, Maer. We all do."

"What, my lord?"

"Well, come on. That big blue sprite follows you all over, you know. She must like you. Don't you see her?"

For the second time that afternoon, Maer found himself speechless. He stared openmouthed while an awkward silence grew painful.

"My lord," Nevyn said gently. "Sometimes the Wildfolk take a liking to someone for reasons of their own. I don't think Maer does see her, or any of them, for that matter. Do you, Maer?"

"I don't, truly."

"Now tell me, Maer. Can you see the wind?"

"What? Of course not! No one can see the wind."

"Just so. But it's real enough."

For the briefest of moments Maer found himself wavering. Did Adraegyn and old Nevyn really see Wildfolk? Did those fabled little creatures actually exist? Oh, don't be a stupid dolt! he told himself. Of course they don't!

Later, when they rode back to the dun, Lord Pertyc happened to be walking across the ward just as they trotted in the gates. A servant came running to take Adraegyn's horse. As soon as he was down, the lad ran, dodging away from his father's affectionate hand and racing for the shelter of the broch.

"Somewhat wrong?" Pertyc said to Maer.

"Uh, well, my lord, your lad wanted to go meet the new herbman in town, so I took him, but truly, I wonder if the old man's daft."

"Daft? Did he scare the lad or suchlike?"

"Not at all, but he scared me. Here, my lord, I don't mean to open old wounds or suchlike, but does young Adraegyn talk about the Wildfolk a lot?"

"Oh, that!" Pertyc smiled in open relief. "That's all, was it? Did the herbman tease him about it? Well, no doubt the fellow was startled to hear a lad his age still babbling about Wildfolk."

"Er, not exactly, my lord. The old man says he can see them, too."

Late on the morrow morn, Nevyn was working out in back, planting a few quick-growing herbs and hoping that they would reach a decent size before the days turned short, when he heard a horseman riding up to the cottage. Trowel in hand, he hurried round and saw Lord Pertyc dismounting at the front gate.

"Good morrow, my lord. To what do I owe this honor of a visit? I hope no one's ill at your dun."

"Oh, thanks be to holy Sebanna, we're all healthy enough. Just thought I'd have a chat, since you're new here and all."

Nevyn stuck the trowel in his belt and swung open the gate. Pertyc followed him in, looking wide-eyed round the garden as if he expected to see spirits leering out from under every bush. The place *was* full of spirits, of course, little gray gnomes sucking their fingers, blue sprites, ratty-haired and long-nosed, grinning to show pointed teeth, sylphs like airy crystals, darting this way and that. Inside, near the hearthstone, Wildfolk sat on the table and the bench and climbed on the shelves full of herbs. On the table a leather-bound book lay open.

"Ye gods!" Pertyc said. "That's my most illustrious ancestor's book!"

"One of them, at least. Being here made me think of it. Have you ever read it?"

"I take it on, every now and then. When every Maelwaedd man comes of age, his father tells him to read the *Ethics*. So you plow through a bit, and then your father admits that he could never finish the wretched thing, either, and you know you're truly a man among men."

"I see. Won't you honor me by sitting down, my lord? I can fetch you some ale."

"Oh, no need." Pertyc had an anxious eye for the shelves of strange herbs and drugs. "Can't stay more than a minute, truly. Er, well, you see, there was somewhat I wanted to ask you about."

"The Wildfolk? I figured that Maer would tell you what happened."

"He did indeed. Um, you were just humoring my lad, weren't you?"

A yellow gnome reached over and closed the book with a little puff of dust. Pertyc yelped.

"I wasn't, actually," Nevyn said. "Does his lordship truly doubt that young Adraegyn can see the Wildfolk?"

"Well, I can't say that I do, but I like to keep it in the family, you know."

"Ah. I take it that his lordship's wife is a woman of the Westfolk."

"Well, she was."

"My apologies, my lord. I didn't realize that she'd ridden through the gates of the Otherlands."

"Naught of the sort, if you mean did she die." A tone of injured pride crept into Pertyc's voice. "As far as I know, anyway, she's alive and well and no doubt as nasty and strong-minded as she ever was. I suppose I'm being unfair. I don't know how I ever thought she could live in a dun and be the proper wife of a noble lord, but by all the ice in all the hells, she might have tried!"

"I see." Nevyn suppressed a grin. "I take it that you didn't stand in her way when she decided to leave."

"It wouldn't have mattered one jot if I'd gone down on my knees and begged her to stay." All at once he turned faintly pink. "But why I'm burdening your ears with all of this, I don't know. You seem to be an easy man to talk to, Nevyn."

"My thanks, my lord. It's a valuable thing in a herbman, being easy to talk to."

"No doubt. Herbman, huh? Is that all you are?"

"And what else would my lordship think I am?"

"Now, I know that most men would mock the dweomer, good sir, but we Maelwaedds don't. There's bits and pieces about it in Prince Mael's books, for one thing, and well, we pass the lore along. We're like badgers, truly. We hold on."

"Even to your oaths to a foreign king?"

Lord Pertyc's face went dead white. Nevyn smiled, thinking that this exercise in logic must seem an act of magic.

"We do," Pertyc said at last. "Aeryc's the king I swore to serve, and serve him I will."

"With only ten men, it's going to be hard to stand against the king's enemies."

"I know. A badger can tear one boarhound to pieces, but the pack will get him in the end. But a vow's a vow, and that's that. They just might honor my neutrality, or so I can hope, anyway." All at once his lordship grinned. "Besides, I've already hired one silver dagger, so I've actually got eleven men now. Maybe more will ride my way."

"That reminds, my lord. Do you know why the silver daggers never ride together as a troop, the way they did in the old days?"

"Well, one of the kings forbade them to. I suppose they were too dangerous. The kingmakers—that's what they were called, you know. A warband that's made a king can unmake one just as easily." Pertyc frowned, remembering something. "Let's see, in this book I have at home it says that after the civil wars all the free troops were banned. That's right! I remember now. It was Maryn's son. His councillors wanted him to ban the silver daggers, too, but he refused, because of the service they'd paid his father. But he didn't want an independent army riding round causing trouble, either, so he ruled that they could only hire out as one man or two together."

"Ah, I see. Well, too bad in a way. You could hire them if only they still existed, eh? But then, maybe this rebellion will stay in Aberwyn."

Pertyc looked away so fast that Nevyn knew that he had information to the contrary.

"There are times when trouble spreads like fire in dry grass," Nevyn said. "No one knows which way the wind will blow."

"Just so. Well, no doubt I'm keeping you from your work. Good day."

All summer, Glaenara had been curing cheeses in round wooden molds. When the four biggest wheels were ready, she loaded them on the mule and took them to Lord Pertyc's dun as part of their taxes. Since it was drowsy-hot, she went barefoot, saving the leather of her one pair of shoes for the winter. Although Nalyn kept urging her to get some boots made down in the village, she preferred to scant herself rather than take what she thought of as his charity. Until Nalyn appeared, Glaenara had been the strong one in the family, keeping up her mother and sister's spirits after her father died, working harder than most lads to scrape a subsistence living out of their farm. Just when I'm old enough to plow like a man, he comes strolling in, she thought bitterly. But there was no doubt that Mam and Lida were happier now. Perhaps that was the worst blow of all.

The gates to Dun Cannobaen stood open, and the ward was its usual slow confusion—servants strolling about their tasks, the riders sitting out in the sun dicing for coppers, Lord Pertyc himself lounging on the steps with a tankard of ale. Glaenara dropped him a curtsy, which he acknowledged by getting up. Although she considered herself a world below him, Glaenara was fond of her local lord because he was a kind man, and his unfortunate marriage had given everyone something exciting to talk about for years now. Rulers have been loved, after all, for a good deal less.

"Looks like cheese," Pertyc said. "What kind, yellow or white?"

"Yellow, my lord. It's awfully good."

Pertyc set his tankard down on the ground and drew his dagger to cut himself off a slice. When he took a bite, he nodded in satisfaction.

"So it is. Goes well with ale, an important thing round here, truly."

Pertyc cut himself another, thicker slice, retrieved his ale, and returned to his steps. Glaenara led the mule round back to the kitchen door and began unloading the cheese. She'd just swung two wheels out when Maer the silver dagger came running up and made her a low bow.

"Now here, fair maid, those look heavy. Let me carry them for you."

"Not heavy at all. Only twenty pound each."

Maer, however, insisted on hefting three and leaving her only one to carry into the kitchen. As he laid his wheels down on the long wooden table, it occurred to Glaenara that he was trying to be polite to her. The idea came as a surprise.

"Well, my thanks," she said.

"Oh, I'd pay you any service gladly."

Another surprise: he was flirting with her. Caught off guard, Glaenara turned away and began talking with the cook, an old friend of her mother's, leaving Maer to hover helplessly in the doorway. She was hoping that he would just go away, but he waited until she and the cook were done with their chat. As she was leaving, Maer grabbed the mule's lead rope and led him to the gates for her.

"Truly, it was good to see you," Maer said.

"Was it? Why?"

"Well, uh." Maer began fiddling with the end of the lead rope.

"Well, it's always good to see a pretty lass, truly. Especially one with spirit."

Glaenara snorted and grabbed the rope back from him.

"My thanks for helping me haul the cheese. I've got to get back to my work."

"Can I walk with you a ways?"

"You can't. Or . . . wait a minute. You said you'd pay me a service?"

"I will. Just name it."

"Then shave that beastly mustache off. It makes your face look dirty and naught more."

Maer howled, clapping a hand over his upper lip in self-defense. Glae marched away, sure that she'd seen the last of him. Yet that very afternoon, she was taking a couple of buckets of vegetable scraps out to the hogs when she saw him leading his horse in through the gates. She stopped and stared: the mustache was gone, sure enough. Nalyn came strolling over with a hoe in his hands and gave Maer a cold looking-over.

"Good morrow, sir," Maer said. "I was wanting to speak to Glaenara, you see."

"Oh, were you now? And just what do you want with my sister?"

"And what's it to you who I talk with?" Glaenara snapped.

"Now hold your tongue. I just want to get a look at a man who comes courting you with a silver dagger in his belt."

"Now here!" Maer put in, but feebly. "I've got honorable intentions, I assure you."

Nalyn and Glaenara both ignored him and turned to glare at each other.

"You're too young to judge a man," Nalyn snarled. "I've had the experience to know a rotten apple from a sound one."

"Who are you calling rotten?"

"No one—yet. Maybe I'm only married kin, but I'm the only brother you've got, and cursed if I'll let you hang about talking with silver daggers and other scum of the road."

"Don't you call Maer scum! I won't stand for it."

"Oh, won't you now?" Nalyn said with a smug little grin. "And how do you know his name, and how come you're so quick to defend him?"

Glaenara grabbed one of her buckets of pig slops, swung, and emptied it over Nalyn's head.

"I'll talk to who I want to!"

Predictably, the noise brought Lidyan running—and shrieking at the sight of her husband covered with carrot peels and radish leaves. Maer doubled over laughing.

"Flowers to the fair," Maer choked out. "And slops to the hogs. Ye gods, you've got a good hand with the bucket. He should be glad you weren't sweeping out the cow barn!"

A piece of carrot peel had flown his way and stuck to his shirt. He plucked it off and handed it to Glaenara with a courtly bow.

"A small token of my esteem. Now I'd best get out of here before your brother takes a hoe to me."

"Brother-in-law, that's all. And don't you forget it."

The next time Glaenara went to market, she sold all her cheese and eggs early in the day, then went over to the inn. As she was tying the mule up out back, Braedda, Samwna's pretty blond daughter, came running out to catch Glaenara's arm and lean close like a conspirator. They were exactly the same age, although Braedda looked younger, just because her hands were soft and her face had been spared the rough winds of the fields.

"Ganedd and his father got home last night," Braedda said, giggling.

"Oh, wonderful! Is your father going to go ask about the betrothal?"

"He's going over this evening, right after dinner. Oh, Glae, I can hardly wait! I want to marry Ganno so bad."

Out in the back of the stables was a shed, filled with sacks of milled oats and tied shooks of hay. Glaenara and Braedda went there, as they usually did, to talk out of the hearing of her parents. They'd barely started their gossip, though, when Ganedd himself appeared, opening the door without knocking. He was a tall lad, filling out to a man built more like a warrior than a merchant, with pale blue eyes and golden hair, a sign that somewhere in his clan's history was some Deverry blood.

"I'd best go," Glaenara said. "I'll be in for the market next week, Brae."

Ganedd smiled briefly, then gallantly opened the door for her. As she led the mule out of the village, Glaenara was wishing she felt less jealous of her friend's good fortune. Although she rather disliked Ganedd, he was a far better catch than any man that was likely to come courting her. Just as she was turning into the road, she happened across Nevyn, riding in. He made her a bow from the saddle, surprisingly limber for one who looked so old.

"In for the market, were you?"

"I was, sir. And a good day to you."

He smiled, then suddenly leaned forward, staring into her eyes. For a moment she felt as if she'd been turned to stone and his cold gaze was a chisel, slicing into her soul; then he released her with a small nod.

"And a good day to you, lass. Oh, wait, I just thought of somewhat. Would you like to earn four coppers a week, doing my laundry and sweeping out my cottage and suchlike?"

"I would indeed."

"Splendid! Then come in tomorrow, because I'm afraid I've let things pile up a bit. After this, two mornings a week should do it."

"Well and good, then. I'll be in before noon."

As he rode on his way, Nevyn was thinking of the strange vagaries of Wyrd. The last time he'd known this woman, she'd been queen of all Deverry and the virtual regent of Cerrmor while her royal husband was on campaign. The oddest thing of all, though, wasn't the obvious change in her fortunes; it was that he'd pitied her even more when she'd been queen.

Out in the paddock behind the merchant's big wooden house, twelve Western Hunter colts nibbled at the grass or stood drowsing head down in the warm sun, blood bays and chestnuts, mostly, but off to one side was a perfect strawberry roan, Ganedd's favorite. When he leaned on the fence, the roan came over to have his ears scratched.

"I'm thinking of giving that colt to the gwerbret in Aberwyn," Wersyn said. "It's been a while since I've given his grace a token of our esteem."

"This lad will make a good warhorse, truly."

"Just so. You know, I think I'll let you be the one to deliver him to his grace. It's time he knew your name as my heir."

"Uh, well, Da, I've been thinking, and . . ."

"You're not going to sea! I'm sick to death of having this discussion. You're my son, and we deal in horses, and that's that."

"You've got Avyl! He's your son, too, isn't he? He'll make a fine horse trader! You say so yourself."

"You're the eldest son, and that's that."

Wersyn had his arms crossed over his chest, a sure sign that arguing was futile. Ganedd turned on his heel and stalked off in the direction of town. At times he wished that he had the guts to just run away. If he could only find a merchant captain who wouldn't mind offending his father . . . but that was worse than unlikely down in Aberwyn, where Wersyn was an important man in the guild. His aimless walk brought him to his grandmother's cottage and the new herbman in town, who was grubbing away in the garden. When Ganedd leaned on the fence to watch, the old man straightened up, wiped his hands on a bit of rag, then strolled over to say good morrow.

"And does the cottage suit you, sir?" Ganedd said. "If it needs repair, I can try to set things right."

"Good of you, lad, but so far, everything's just fine. I hear you and your father are going to Aberwyn soon."

"Tomorrow morning, actually, with the dawn. We've got some tribute to pay to Gwerbret Aberwyn, and then there's going to be a big meeting of the merchant guild."

"Interesting. What about?"

"I'm not allowed to discuss it, sir, with someone who isn't in the guild."

"All right, then. I'll wager you enjoy going to Aberwyn, though."

"Oh, I certainly do! Ye gods, life is so beastly boring here in Cannobaen."

"No doubt, but don't you go with your father when he trades with the Westfolk?"

"Of course, but so what? They're just the Westfolk."

"Ah. I see."

And Ganedd was left with the infuriating feeling that the old man was doing his best not to laugh at him.

That very evening their two fathers arranged the wedding pact, but the formalities of life demanded that Braedda's father come ask Lord Pertyc's permission to formalize the betrothal of his daughter to Ganedd the merchant's son. Technically, Wersyn should have come with him, but he was already on his way to Aberwyn with his son and the loan of his lordship's silver dagger as well, for a guard. Pertyc approved the betrothal, stood the man a goblet of mead in celebration, then sent him on his way with his best wishes. The innkeep was only a few hours gone when Tieryn Danry turned up at Pertyc's gates with an escort of ten men.

All that afternoon, while they drank together in the great hall and talked idly about everything but the rebellion, Pertyc was aware of Danry studying him like a tactical problem. Over breakfast the next day, when Danry suggested that they go hunting alone rather than organizing a full-scale stag hunt, Pertyc felt a confrontation coming, but he agreed simply to have it over with. When they rode out, they took only a lad with a pack mule and some dogs with them. Danry carried the usual short hunting bow; Pertyc had a yew longbow, mounted with silver, that had been a wedding gift from his wife's brother.

At the edge of the forest, they left the lad with the horses and went alone on foot to see if they could flush a deer. The dogs, a pair of the sleek gray breed called gwertrae, were eager, whining as they sniffed round for tracks and nosed their way through the bracken and fern. Above them rose the ancient oaks, casting a shade cold with a hint of winter coming. Pertyc and Danry had hunted together this way a hundred times, picking their way down narrow trails as silently as the wild animals they sought. Pertyc found himself wishing they were both lads again, too young to be troubled by obligations and vows and the need to ride to war. When at length they came to a clearing where the sun came down in a long golden shaft onto the leaf-littered ground, Danry whistled sharply to the dogs and brought them back to heel.

"They haven't even found us a trail yet," Pertyc said.

Danry turned to him with a faint smile.

"My answer's still the same," Pertyc went on. "I won't ride with you in the spring."

"As stubborn as a badger, truly. But I came to tell you somewhat, and if you love me, then never say where you heard it."

"You know I'll keep silent."

"Well and good. Then listen, Perro, things are growing nasty. You were wise to bring your lad home. I'm not the only man who had thoughts about your claim to the throne. There are some who'd be glad to put little Draego in your place."

"They'll have to kill me to get at the lad."

"That's just what they might do."

Pertyc went cold, standing in the warm shaft of autumn sun.

"He wouldn't be the first child to have a throne won for him by grown men," Danry said. "Now listen, I don't know any more than rumors. No one's going to speak honestly of such things in front of me, because they know you're my oath-sworn friend. It would be a long sight easier to stop this talk if you were one of us."

Pertyc looked away.

"If they come for the lad, how are you going to stop them?" Danry said. "You can't afford an army. Ah, ye gods, I feel torn apart, Perro."

"Then maybe you should join me and the king."

Danry winced, shaking his head in honest pain.

"I can't. My honor would never let me rest."

"No more would mine if I joined the rebels. I'll warn you somewhat. If your allies decide to try for my lad, then get ready to watch me die."

Danry came close to weeping. At his feet, the gwertroedd whined, dancing a step away, then coming reluctantly back to heel. Far off in the forests, a bird sang, a flood of defiant melody in the shadows.

"And if I die, and you live," Pertyc said slowly, "I'll beg you to watch over Adraegyn for me. He'll need a faithful dog if he's surrounded by wolves."

Danry nodded his agreement. Pertyc hesitated, considering saying more, but there was nothing to say. He wanted to have one last day with his friend when they could pretend that things were as they'd always been.

"Let's get on with the hunt, shall we?"

Danry threw up his hand and sent the eager hounds forward. They coursed slowly through the woods for another hour, neither of them speaking, the dogs growing sullen and frustrated, until at last the lead gwertrae stiffened, tossing up its head. An arrow nocked ready in his bow, Pertyc jogged after until, all at once, they heard a crash and rustle as a deer broke cover, and the hounds shot forward as fast as arrows, yapping after a young doe. An arrow whistled: Danry's first shot, bouncing off a tree, way too short. Pertyc fell into his stance, raised his bow, and loosed all in one smooth motion. The doe reared up and fell, stumbled a few steps, then fell again as the dogs threw themselves upon her. Drawing his dagger, Pertyc ran for them, but she was already dead, skewered neatly through the heart. Shouting, Pertyc kicked the gwertroedd away. Danry came running, tossing his bow down, and grabbed the whining hounds by the collars.

"Ye gods, man!" Danry said, grinning. "You've got the best hand with a bow in all of Eldidd."

Pertyc merely smiled, thinking that his wife could best him without half trying. While Danry was forcing the dogs to lie down away from the kill, he set his foot against the doe's neck and pulled the arrow out with both hands. Unbroken, it was worth straightening. As he examined the fletching for splits, he was thinking of his wife, remembering the stories she'd told him of wars long fought and over. His heart began to pound in a sudden gruesome hope. When he looked up to find Danry watching him, he felt as guilty as a caught burglar.

"Perro? I'll beg you. Please join us."

"I can't. I'm too much of a badger, my friend."

"Ah, by the hells! Well, so be it."

Their afternoon was over, the last time they could love each other without the love turning to nightmare. Pertyc turned away before he wept.

Late that night, when the rest of the dun was asleep, Pertyc went up to his study and lit a pair of candles in a silver sconce. As a draft caught the flames, shadows flew back and forth across walls and filled his mind with thoughts of winter, his last winter alive, or so he was counting it. He was determined, though, that his death would cost his enemies a price as high as he could set it.

"And would it be a true dishonor," he said to one of the stag's heads on the wall, "to bring longbows back into Eldidd? I've always been told so. The question is, do I give the fart of a two-copper pig about the dishonor? Our rebels, my cervine friend, are being a good bit more dishonorable with their wretched plots."

In the blown shadows the stag's eyes seemed to move, pondering his logic, but he never did answer. Pertyc found his ancestor's books, actually a collection of treatises, bound up for the clan in two volumes, stamped with the clan device on the pale leather covers, and massive things, weighing a good fifteen pounds each. He propped the second one up on the lectern, lit more candles, and stood to turn the pages. Touching the book was a comfort all its own, because it gave him palpable contact with his history, all those other Maelwaedd lords, going back a hundred years to the disclaimed prince himself. He doubted, though, that his clan would live after his own coming death. Once a rebel faction proclaimed Adraegyn royal, the High King would have no choice but to kill the boy.

"Ah, stuff the dishonor then!" he said to the stag's head. "They're murdering my lad, just by trying to put him on a throne that isn't his. I've got every right to skewer as many of the miserable bastards as I can before the end. We'll see if I can get those merchants to ride west for me—well, once they get themselves back home, anyway."

Then he returned to his reading, which gave him a surprise of quite another sort.

In the morning, Danry took his leave, riding out at the head of his escort with a cheery wave of his hand and a jest for his last farewell. Pertyc had the groom saddle him up a horse, then rode straight to Nevyn's cottage. As he walked through the garden, hot and hushed in the sunlight, Pertyc had the uneasy feeling that eyes were watching him, but although he peered into every shadow, he saw nothing but turned earth and growing things. When he knocked, Nevyn opened the door and ushered him in with a bow.

"Good morrow, my lord. To what do I owe this honor?"

"Oh, I just wanted a word with you."

Nevyn smiled, waiting pleasantly. Pertyc glanced round the room, filled with the rich mingled smell of a hundred herbs and roots and barks, bitter and sweet, dry and sharp all diffusing together in the sunlit air.

"I was reading my ancestor's book last night, you see, and I came across a most curious passage about the dweomer. It was in the book of *Qualities*. Have you read that, by any chance?"

"I have, but it was a very long time ago."

"No doubt. Let me refresh your memory about this one bit, then. The most noble prince was discussing whether dweomer exists, you see, and he remarks that he once knew a dweomer-man."

"Oh, did he now? I think I begin to recall the passage."

"No doubt. It would be a great honor to have one's name recorded in a book for men to remember down the long years."

Nevyn considered him with a small frown, then suddenly laughed.

"His lordship has quick wits. He's most worthy of his noble ancestor's name."

"By the hells! You mean I've guessed right?"

"About what? You don't really think that I'm the selfsame man that knew Prince Mael, do you?"

"Er, well, it did seem too fantastical to be true . . ."

"Indeed." The old man considered for a moment, as if he were debating something in his mind. "Here, if you promise to keep this to yourself, I'll tell you the truth. The name of Nevyn is a kind of honorary title, passed down from master to apprentice just like a lord passes his title to a son. When one Nevyn grows old and dies, then a new one appears."

Pertyc felt as embarrassed as a page caught in some lapse of etiquette. Nevyn grinned at him in an oddly sly way, as if the old man had just done something that pleased him mightily.

"And did you come to ask me that, my lord, and naught more? His lordship seems troubled. Is it all because of the dweomer?"

"You'll have to forgive me, good sir. I have much on my mind these days."

"No doubt. So must every lord in Eldidd."

If it weren't for Danry, Pertyc would have told the entire tale to the dweomerman there and then, but his oath-sworn friend was up to his neck in treason.

"Eldidd is always full of troubles." Pertyc chose his words carefully. "Few of them come to much."

"Those few that do can be deadly."

"True-spoken. That's why our Mael listed prudence among his noble qualities. It pays to be ready for trouble, even if none comes."

Nevyn's eyes seemed to cut through to his soul, as sharp as a sword thrust.

"I'm well aware that you and your son have a tenuous claim to the Eldidd throne."

"I have no claim at all in any true or holy sense of that word."

"Qualities such as the true and the holy are held in general disrespect in most parts of the kingdom. That's a quote from your ancestor's book. It seems he was farsighted enough to deserve the name of Seer."

Pertyc rose, pacing restlessly over to the hearth.

"Let me guess what you're too honorable to tell me," Nevyn went on. "Every friend you have is in this rebellious muck too deep to get out again, and so you're being torn to pieces between your loyalty to them and your loyalty to the king."

"How—ah, ye gods, dweomer indeed!"

"Naught of the sort. Mere logic. Let me ask only one thing: are you going to fight for the king or try to stay neutral?"

"Neutral, if only the gods will allow. And let me ask you the same. Are you a king's man or neutral in this scrap?"

"I belong to the people of this kingdom, lad, not king nor lord nor usurper. And that's all the answer you're going to get from me."

The great guildhall of Aberwyn was hot. Every one of the long rank of windows held diamond-paned glass—an enormous luxury but a stifling one as the sun poured through onto the packed crowd. A hundred men sat solemnly on long benches down on the blue and gray slate floor, while up on the dais stood a row of carved chairs filled with the guild officers, all in their ceremonial cloaks of brightly colored checked wool. At one end of this impressive line, the guild's chief scribe snored shamelessly. In his seat down on the floor, Ganedd wished that he could do the same, but every time he nodded off, his father elbowed him in the ribs. All afternoon, the debate raged over the matter of loaning two thousand silver pieces to the gwerbret of Aberwyn. Although no one ever mentioned why the gwerbret wanted the coin, the knowledge was as cloying as the heat, making it hard to think clearly. A successful rebellion meant freedom from Deverry taxes, freedom from the Deverry guilds, and a certain heady rush of pride in independence. Failure, of course, meant losing the money down to the last copper. After the formal meeting droned to a halt, close to sunset, the debate continued in private inn chambers or over dinner tables in wealthy merchant houses. There, in whispers among a few men at a time, rose the simple question: could the gwerbrets win or not?

"And even if they do win, what next?" Wersyn said. "There's two great gwerbrets in Eldidd and only one throne. Ye gods, it gives me a headache, thinking about them turning on each other once the first war is won."

"Well, we've got to start thinking about this kind of thing, Da," Ganedd said. "We're going to vote on the loan tomorrow."

"True enough, but you'd better vote the way I tell you when the time comes."

They were in their luxurious inn chamber, waiting for two of Wersyn's old friends to join him for another private discussion. Among flagons of Bardek wine a small cold supper was laid out on a linen-covered table.

"If I'm voting the way you say, can I go down to the tavern room tonight? No need for me to listen, is there, if you're going to make up my mind for me."

"You nasty little cub." Wersyn said it without real rancor. "Just don't come in staggering drunk until my guests have gone. Ye gods! Sometimes I wonder where I got a son like you. Wanting to go to sea! Drinking! Humph!"

Since they were staying in an expensive inn, the tavern room was big and clean, with glass lanterns hanging every few feet along the whitewashed walls, but all the serving girls were respectable and watched over by a paternal tavernman who seemed determined to keep them that way. Down in one corner, out of the way near the kitchen door, Ganedd found Maer, drinking ale alone and doing his best to behave himself.

"Aren't you going to discuss grave affairs of state with your da and his friends?"

"I'm not. They won't listen to me, and it drives me half mad. This scheme is daft, Maer. They keep talking about how many riders the rebels can raise when what they need to be talking about is ships."

"Huh? What have ships got to do with it?"

"Not you, too! Look, as the king marches south from Dun Deverry to Cerrmor, what does he find along the way? Loyal vassals, that's what, with nice fat demesnes that support big warbands. Then when he gets to Cerrmor, what does he find?"

"Ships." Maer sat up straight and began thinking. "Ships to deliver all those men to Abernaudd and Aberwyn in about half the time they could ride."

"Right. And the rebels don't have a third of the galleys they need to stop him."

"Hum." Maer thoughtfully chewed on his lower lip. "Too bad you can't go for a marine officer, Ganno, on one of his grace's galleys. You've got the mind for it."

"That's a splendid idea, you know, and one I never thought of. I wonder . . . but we won't be in Aberwyn much longer this trip, so I can't go ask his grace. What do you say we go see what kind of lasses work in the taverns closer to the docks? I nipped some of Da's coin from his pouch when he wasn't looking."

"Did you now? Well, if you don't mind me helping you spend it, I'm on."

It was well into the third watch when Ganedd came stumbling up the stairs of the inn. As he let himself into their chambers, he tripped, falling onto his hands and knees with a curse and a clatter. Just as he was picking himself up, Wersyn came out of the bedchamber with a candle lantern in his hand. Ganedd grabbed the edge of the table to steady himself and forced out a weak smile.

"I can smell the mead from way over here," Wersyn announced. "And a good bit more than mead, I must say. Cheap perfume, is it?"

"Well, I waited until your guests left, didn't I?"

"I suppose I should be thanking the gods for giving you one little crumb of good sense. Look at you—like a prize bull, properly bred and twice as sweaty! And you're drunk, and you stole from me, and—" He sputtered briefly, then took a deep breath. "Ye gods, Ganno! Do you know how late it is? You've been out carousing most of the night. And now you're going to go staggering into the guildhall, I suppose, with your eyes as red as a weasel's, and everyone will know what you were up to. By the Lord of Hell's black ass, what will people think of me for having a son like you?"

Wersyn strode back into his bedchamber. When he slammed the door behind him and his candle, the reception chamber went dark. Stumbling over furniture, Ganedd found his way to his own bedchamber, fell down on the bed fully dressed, and passed out.

But he woke in the morning in a sullen temper. During breakfast, which he could barely eat, he had difficulty looking at his father, who prattled on about lower taxes as if the rebellion were already won.

"Now remember what I said about the vote this morning," Wersyn announced finally.

Ganedd tried to swallow a spoonful of barley porridge, then shoved the bowl away as a bad job.

"The loan's going through no matter what we think about it," Wersyn continued. "So when it comes to the vote, we're giving our approval, too."

Ganedd started to argue, then got up and rushed out of the room. He never made it to the privy, but no one cared when he heaved the contents of his stomach onto the dungheap out back of the inn.

The vote on the loan was the last item on the guild's agenda, rather as though the master were putting it off as long as possible in the vain hope that some omen might make the decision easier. Ganedd sat sullenly on his bench—way at the back since he'd come in late—and nursed the mead-sick throb in his temples and the queasiness in his stomach. All at once, a bustle on the dais caught his attention. The guildmaster rose, tossed his cloak back from one shoulder, and blew on his silver horn to bring the meeting to order, the long sweet note echoing through the abruptly silent hall. Sunlight hung heavy on the sea of color that was the finery of the guild: gold-shot banners, checks and stripes of all colors on cloak and brigga, rainbow-hued tapestries on the painted walls.

"We come now to the matter of the loan of two thousand silver pieces to his grace, Gwerbret Aberwyn," the guildmaster called out. "Is there any more debate to be laid before the convocation?"

Silence, stillness—no one spoke or moved. The guildmaster raised the horn to his lips and blew again.

"Very well. Those in favor, to the right. Those against, to the left. Scribe, stand ready to count and record the numbers."

Slowly, a few at a time, the men rose, starting in the front of the hall, and walked to the right, so unanimously that the motion was as smooth as uncoiling a rope. Ganedd watched as first his father took a place at the right, then his father's close friends trotted meekly after. His row, the last, began to get up. Ganedd followed them free of the benches, then abruptly turned and marched to the left side of the hall. He'd be cursed and frozen in the third hell before he'd back a doomed scheme like this one. It was also the sweetest pleasure he'd ever tasted to see his father's face literally turn purple with rage. Ganedd crossed his arms over his chest and grinned as the entire guild gasped and stared: whiskered faces, lean faces, shrewd eyes, watery eyes, but all of them outraged.

"Done, then," the guildmaster called. "Scribe, what is your count?"

"Ninety and seven in favor, two members missing from the count, and one against."

"There's one man in Eldidd who'll hold for the true king," Ganedd yelled. "You stinking cowards!"

At the shriek that rose he felt as if he'd heaved a rock into the middle of a flock of geese. The men swirled round, nudging each other, whispering and cursing, then shouting and cursing, louder and louder as they milled through the hall. Ganedd had said it out, the one unsayable truth: they were voting treason. Ganedd started laughing as the guild broke, hurrying away, muttering among themselves as they all tried to pretend they'd never heard a thing. Wersyn came running and slapped him so hard across the face that Ganedd staggered back against the wall.

"You foul little cub!" Wersyn howled. "How could you? Ye gods, I'll kill you for this!"

"Go ahead. I won't be the last man to die in the war."

Cursing a steady stream, Wersyn grabbed his arm and dragged him across the hall. Ganedd followed meekly, laughing under his breath. He'd never had such a splendid time in his life. But his pleasure ended once they were back in their inn chambers. Shaking in fury, Wersyn shoved Ganedd into a chair and began pacing around, his hands clenched, his eyes snapping.

"You rotten little bastard! This tears it once and for all! I'm sending you straight back home. I can't hold my head up if I've got a son like this at my side. How could you? Why? Ganno, for the love of every god—why?"

"Just to see what would happen, mostly. You all looked so wretchedly pleased with yourselves."

Wersyn strode over and slapped him again.

"You're taking Maer and getting out of here today. Get your things and go! I want you out of my sight."

All the time Ganedd packed, all the time he was saddling his horse, Wersyn went on yelling at him, calling him a fool and a demon-spawned ungrateful whelp, a worthless dolt and a turd dropped by a spavined mare. The entire innyard and Maer as well listened to this lecture with visible curiosity. Once Wersyn had stormed inside, and they were leading their horses out into the town, the silver dagger could stand it no longer.

"Ye gods, is he that blasted furious over one whore?"

"Last night's got naught to do with it. Remember the gwerbret's loan? It came to a vote today, and I was the only man who voted against it."

Maer stared at him with a sudden flattering respect.

"Here, that took guts."

"Did it? Maybe so."

At the west-running road the city gates were standing open. Just outside they found another merchant, an old family friend named Gurcyn, standing by his horse and yelling orders as his muleteers organized his caravan. Ganedd threw his reins to Maer and strode over to speak with him, just as a last defiance.

"Good morrow," Ganedd said. "Leaving so soon?"

Gurcyn looked him over, not anywhere as coldly as Ganedd was expecting, but he said nothing.

"Go on," Ganedd went on. "Tell me what you think of me. I'm giving you the chance, rebel."

"All I think is that you're a bit lacking in wits, though long on nerve. This thing's going to be remembered. Here, did your father send you home in disgrace?"

"Just that. And what about you? I'm surprised you're not staying to celebrate your treason with the rest of them."

"Oh, hold your tongue! Roosters who strut too much end up in the soup kettle. As for me, my wife's been ill, and I've got to get home straightaway. Good morrow, lad, and by the gods of our people, watch what you say, will you?"

As Gurcyn walked away, shouting to his men, Maer led their horses over.

"Who was that? One of the guild?"

"Just so. Why?"

"I've seen him before." Maer's eyes narrowed in hard thought. "Probably in some tavern, but you know, I think it was up in Dun Deverry, right after my lord kicked me out of Blaeddbyr, like, and I was riding west."

"Maybe it was. A good guildsman rides wherever the coin calls, and Dun Deverry calls in a lot of coin. Come on, let's get on the cursed road."

Although Ganedd was usually good company, on the ride back home he fell into long cold silences and refused to be drawn out, not even by jests, thus leaving Maer with a lot of time to think—an unfamiliar activity and one that he preferred to avoid whenever possible. Now, however, he had a number of strange things to think about, starting with old Nevyn the herbman. When they'd first met back in Aberwyn, Maer had barely noticed him, but as they'd ridden west together, Maer had found himself oppressed by the growing feeling that he'd known the old man before, an acquaintance that was logically impossible because Nevyn insisted that he'd never been anywhere near Blaeddbyr in all the years since Maer was born, and while Maer was traveling as a silver dagger, the old man was over in Bardek.

Added to that, of course, Lord Pertyc thought that Nevyn was a sorcerer, which meant Lord Pertyc believed that the dweomer craft was a real thing. Every now and then Maer would bring this idea to mind, like taking a strange coin out of a pouch, and turn it over and over between mental fingers, wondering at it. Since Maer had been raised to follow the noble-born without doubt or question, he supposed that if Pertyc said the old man was a sorcerer, then sorcerer he was. He supposed. He held the thought up to the mental light one more time, shook his head, and put it away again. Maybe sometime soon it would make sense. Maybe.

Finally there was the matter of the Wildfolk. Ever since young Adraegyn and the old man had discussed them that one afternoon, Maer had, again quite against his will, found himself thinking that perhaps they did indeed exist and that just maybe one of them was following him around, just as the lad said. His evidence for this was thin, and he did his best to ignore it. It was just that every now and then he felt something touch his arm or his hair; even more rarely, when he was riding, he felt tiny arms clasp his waist as if someone sat behind him on the saddle. Occasionally he saw a bush or branch move as if something stood within or upon it, or one of Lord Pertyc's dogs would suddenly leap up and bark for no reason, or one of the horses would suddenly stamp and swing its head round to look at something that Maer couldn't see. Once, when he was drinking a foaming tankard of ale and all alone at table, a tiny breath had blown the foam off right into his face as he went for a sip. It was beginning to make his flesh creep, all of it. He would have wished that they'd stop and leave him alone, except wishing meant admitting that someone existed to do the stopping. He wasn't ready to admit that, not in the least.

Yet he kept gathering new evidence in spite of his attempts to ignore it. As their horses ambled the last few miles to Cannobaen, Ganedd's silence grew as black and cold as a winter storm. Maer amused himself by looking at the now familiar scenery: off to his left the clifftop meadows and the sparkling sea, the rich fields to his right, striped here and there with strands of trees, all second growth planted for firewood. Scarlet and gold, the leaves already hung thin and bare along the branches, especially on the trees planted next to the road that received the full force of the sea winds. It was in one of these that Maer saw, clear as clear, a little face peering at him. It was a pretty face, obviously female, with long dark blue hair and big blue eyes, staring at him wistfully. When Maer stared back, she suddenly smiled, revealing a mouthful of long pointed teeth. Maer yelped aloud.

"What?" Ganedd roused himself. "What's so wrong?"

"Don't you see it? Look! Right there, on that low branch."

"See what? Maer, are you going daft? There's naught there."

"It's a windless day and the leaves are shaking."

"Then some bird flew away or somewhat. What are you doing? Falling asleep in the saddle and dreaming?"

"Well, I guess so. Sorry."

With a melancholy sigh Ganedd went back to his brooding. Maer cursed himself for a fool and took up the job of convincing himself that he'd seen nothing. He'd just about succeeded when he noticed Nevyn, some hundred yards away, digging for roots out on the clifftops. As they passed, the herbman straightened up and waved, just pleasantly, but his simple presence suddenly struck Maer like an omen. It was all he could do to wave back.

It was the next market day that Glaenara sold the last of the cheeses. She was just packing up to go home when she saw a rider leading his horse through the crowded square: Maer, his silver dagger bright at his belt. She wasn't sure if she hoped he'd stop or not, but he took the matter out of her hands by doing just that.

"And is your bilge-mouthed brother in town today?"

"He's not. What's it to you?"

"Well, I brought you somewhat of a present from Aberwyn, and I didn't want him to see me give it to you." Maer took a packet wrapped in a bit of white linen out of his shirt and handed it over.

"My thanks, Maer. Truly."

He merely smiled, watching as she unwrapped the cloth and found a small bronze mirror, a circle that fit neatly into the palm of her hand. On one side was a bit of silvered glass, held in place by a band of knotwork wires; on the other was a fancy design of laced spirals.

"I wanted to get you the silver one," Maer said, sighing, "but coins flee from silver daggers like chickens run from foxes."

"It doesn't matter. This is lovely. Ye gods, I've never had a mirror before. My thanks. Truly, my thanks."

Glaenara held the mirror up. By angling her head, she could see her reflection a bit at a time, and a lot more clearly than in the reflection from a bucket of water. Much to her horror, there was a bit of dirt on her cheek. Hastily she wiped it off.

"A pretty lass like you should have a mirror of her own."

"Do you truly think I'm pretty? I don't."

He looked so shocked that she was embarrassed.

"Well," Maer said thoughtfully. "Truly, pretty isn't the right word, is it? As handsome as a wild horse or a trout leaping from a stream, not pretty like a rose in some lord's garden."

"Then my thanks." Glaenara busied herself with wrapping the mirror up in the cloth again, but she felt herself blush in sheer pleasure. "And what errand are you running?"

"Well, our Badger wanted a word with Ganedd the merchant's son. Cursed if I know why, but I'm taking the lad a letter. I can't read, or I would have sneaked a look. It's not sealed."

"It would have been dishonorable."

"Of course, but ye gods, I've always been a curious sort of man. Ah, well, it's beyond me anyway, all this wretched writing. Will you come into town next week?"

"I might, I might not. It depends on the chickens."

"Then I'll pray to the Goddess to let them lay more eggs than your family can possibly eat and that my lord will let me come down to town."

After Maer left, Glaenara counted up her coin. She had just enough to buy a length of cloth to make herself that new dress that Nalyn had been nagging her about. If she worked hard, sitting outside every evening to get the last of the sunlight, she could have the dress finished by next market day.

Ganedd sat uneasily on the edge of his chair and held his goblet of mead in nervous fingers. The lad was wearing a pair of blue-and-gray-checked brigga and a shirt heavily worked in flowers—his best clothes, Pertyc assumed, for his visit to the nobleborn.

"No doubt you're wondering why I asked you up here. I'll come straight to the point. My silver dagger told me that you voted against the rebellion in Aberwyn. I'm holding for the king myself. It gladdens my heart that you do the same."

"My thanks, my lord, but I don't know what the two of us can do about it."

"Naught more than what we can, truly, but we've got to try. I want to ask you to take my service. There's going to be a war in the spring, lad, and I've no doubt that our rebels will want me dead before they march against the king."

"I'm no warrior, my lord, but if you want me to join your men, I'll do my best to fight."

Pertyc was both surprised and ashamed of himself. He'd been dismissing this young man as nothing but a merchant, little more than a farmer and most likely a coward to boot.

"Well, actually," Pertyc said, "I was hoping you'd run an errand for me. You deal with the Westfolk all the time, don't you? You must know where to find them and all that."

"I do, my lord." Ganedd looked puzzled; then he grinned. "Longbows."

"Just that. If I load you up with every bit of iron goods and fancy cloth and jewelry and so on that I can scrape together, do you think you could get me enough bows for the warband? I wouldn't take a few extra archers amiss, either, if you can recruit some."

"Well, I'll try, my lord, but I don't think the Westfolk are interested in hiring out as mercenaries. The bows I can most likely get, though."

"Well, that'll be somewhat to the good." Pertyc hesitated, struck by a sudden thought and then surprise, that he'd never had the thought until this moment. "You know, I wonder just how proud a man I am."

"My lord?"

It took Pertyc a long time to answer, and in the end, the only thing that brought him round was his love for his children. While no rebel lord would ever have knowingly killed his daughter, terrible things happened in sieges, especially if they ended in fire. If Pertyc lost the battle but the rebels lost the war, Adraegyn of course was quite simply doomed. The king's men would smother the boy, most like.

"Tell me somewhat, Ganno. Do you think you could find my wife?"

Ganedd stared openmouthed.

"Well, she won't lift a finger for my sake," Pertyc said, "but for Beclya and Adraegyn, she just might raise a small army."

"I'll do my best, my lord, but the elven gods only know where she might be, and the Westlands are an awfully big place. The sooner I leave, the better. Can you give me a guard and some packhorses? The less of Da's stock that I use, the fewer questions Mam will ask."

All that afternoon, while Ganedd gathered supplies, Pertyc

agonized over the letter to his wife. Finally, when he was running out of time, he decided to make it as simple and as short as he could:

"Our children are in mortal danger from a war. My messenger will explain. For their sakes I'm begging your aid. I'll humble myself in any way you want if you'll just come and take them to safety."

He rolled it up, sealed it into a silver message tube, then without thinking kissed the seal, as if the wax could pass the kiss along.

Just at sunset, Ganedd and his impromptu caravan assembled out in the ward, a straggling line of packhorses and mules along with two of Pertyc's most reliable riders for guards and the undergroom for a servant. Pertyc handed Ganedd what coin he could spare and the message tube, then walked to the gates to wave his only true hope on its way until the caravan disappeared into a welter of dust and sea haze. As he turned to go inside, the ward flared with yellow light. Up on the tower the lightkeeper had fired the beacon.

In every warband, Maer reflected sadly, there was always an utterly humorless man like Crindd. If you said it looked like fair weather, Crindd saw rain coming; if you said a meal tasted good, Crindd remarked that the cook had filth under her fingernails; if you liked the looks of a horse, Crindd insisted that he had the legs to come up lame. On a bad day Crindd's little black cloud of gloom could make even Garoic the captain groan under his breath.

"Ye gods," Maer said to Cadmyn one morning, "I'd drown the man except it would give him too much pleasure to have somewhat go wrong."

Cadmyn, an easygoing blond who was Maer's only real friend in the warband, nodded with a faint look of disgust.

"True-spoken. We all used to mock him, but it wasn't truly satisfying. He never seemed to notice, you see."

"Really? Well, just you leave this to me."

That afternoon Maer asked for and received Lord Pertyc's permission to leave the dun, then rode over to Glaenara's farm. Much to his annoyance, she was gone, and her brother-in-law refused to tell him where.

"Just what do you want anyway, silver dagger?" Nalyn snarled.

"To buy a pint of dried beans or peas from you and naught more. I'll give you a copper."

Nalyn considered, greed fighting with dislike.

"Oh, I'll sell you a handful of pulse gladly enough," he said at last. "But I don't want you hanging round Glae."

After dinner that night, two of the other lads kept Crindd busy in the great hall while Maer and Cadmyn sneaked out to the barracks. They stripped Crindd's bunk of blanket and sheet, and while Cadmyn kept watch at the door, Maer sprinkled the dried peas over the mattress before he made up the bed again. When the time came, everyone in the warband went to bed full of anticipation. In the dark they could hear Crindd squirming this way and that. At last he got up, and they heard the sound of him trying to brush the sheet clean with his hands. When he got back into bed, the squirming picked up again. Finally one of the men broke and sniggered; the entire warband joined in. Crindd sat up with a howl of rage.

"And just why are you bastards all laughing?"

Silence fell, except for the sound of Crindd getting up and messing with something at the hearth. At great length, he struck a spark into tinder and lit a candle. Everyone else sat up and arranged innocent smiles while he stalked over to examine his bunk.

"There's somewhat in my bed!"

"Fleas?" Maer said. "Lice? Bedbugs?"

"Oh, hold your pus-boil tongue, you whoreson bastard!"

"Nasty, isn't he?" Cadmyn remarked.

Crindd shoved the candle into a wax-crusted holder and began hauling the sheet off.

"Dried peas!"

"And how did they get in there?" Cadmyn said.

"Must be the Wildfolk," Maer answered.

The moment Maer said the name he regretted it, because they came at the sound, or so he assumed, not knowing that the Wildfolk love a good prank, the meaner the better. Although it was hard to be certain in the flickering candlelight, Maer thought he saw them as little shapes of shadow, thicker than smoke but just as unstable. When Crindd began gathering the pulse and throwing it impartially at every man within range, the Wildfolk helped the warband catch what they could and throw it back. Maer, however, sat stone-still on his bunk and merely stared, wondering if Nevyn could make a potion that would bring him back to normal. At last Garoic rushed in, wearing a nightshirt over his brigga and swearing at the lot of them to restore order.

The prank brought Maer so much glory that of course he wasn't going to stop there, Wildfolk or no Wildfolk. On the morrow he filled a bucket with water, threw in a handful of mucky straw from the stable, and balanced it on top of the half-open door of the tack room. When young Werryc maneuvered Crindd into going to fetch something from this room, Crindd flung the door open and dumped the foul and by then chilly water all over himself. For the rest of the day, he strode around in a humor as foul as his bath, and his mood wasn't sweetened any when Maer barred the privy door from the outside and trapped him in it. He must have banged and yelled for a good hour before Adraegyn heard him and let him out. Crindd grabbed a rake from the nearby dungheap and came charging for the barracks; he might well have killed someone if Garoic hadn't calmed him down.

Although Crindd had no idea who was persecuting him, Garoic wasn't so dense. That very evening, he caught Maer as he was leaving the great hall and hauled him off for a private word.

"Listen, silver dagger, a jest's a jest, and I have to admit that I've had some good laughs out of all this, but enough's enough."

"But, Captain, sir, what makes you think I've got anything to do with it?"

"My eyes and ears. A warning, silver dagger: the long road might be calling you soon."

Since being kicked out of the warband would mean disaster, what with winter coming on, Maer swore that the pranks would end. Unfortunately, Cadmyn came up with an idea that was too good to resist, and he also offered to take the blame for it if worse came to worst. Crindd had a pair of new riding boots, worked in two colors of leather, which had cost him all his winnings from a particularly lucky dice game. Maer and Cadmyn went down to a pond not far from the dun and found the two last frogs who hadn't dug themselves under the mud for the winter. One fit neatly into each boot. Although Maer and Cadmyn were outside when Crindd went to put on his new boots, they could hear his shriek quite clearly. They were laughing themselves sick when Crindd found them.

"You foul bastards! I can see the mud on your brigga."

From inside his shirt the frogs croaked.

"You've got a pair of pets, have you?" Maer said. "Well, flowers to the fair, and frogs to the warty."

Crindd hauled back and hit him in the face. With a yell, Maer swung back, but he was so dizzy that he missed. He could hear Cadmyn shouting, and men running; just as Crindd hit him again, hands grabbed them both and hauled them apart. Although Maer's right eye was already swelling and dripping, he could see Lord Pertyc and Garoic strolling over, both of them scowling.

"It was all my fault!" Cadmyn squeaked. "Crindd hit the wrong man!"

"He would," Garoic said.

"What is all this?" Pertyc snapped.

"Frogs, my lord! They put frogs in my boots. This very morning." Crindd reached inside his shirt and hauled out the terrified creatures. "Here's the evidence. And they put dried peas under my sheet and doused me with rotten water and . . ."

"Enough!" Pertyc took the frogs, contemplated them briefly, then handed them to a grinning Adraegyn. "Go put these back in the pond, will you? Right now, please. Now. Maer, Cadmyn. Why did you two commit this list of heinous crimes?"

Cadmyn groped for words and gave it up as a bad job.

"Well, my lord," Maer said. "Just for the jest of the thing. You see, Crindd makes a splendid victim."

Crindd squealed in outrage, but his lordship laughed.

"I do see, indeed. Crindd, it looks to me like you've already gotten your revenge on Maer's right eye. Let this be a lesson to you: never be a splendid victim again. It gives people ideas."

"But, my lord—"

"Just think about it, will you?" Pertyc turned to the two male-factors. "Maer, you'd better go down to the village and have the herbman look at that eye. I don't like the way it's swelling."

When Maer rode up to the herbman's cottage, he received a surprise bigger than the one the frogs had given Crindd. Out in the front garden Glaenara was spreading laundry to dry. Pretty in a new dress of woad-blue wool, she was singing to herself, her raven-dark hair gleaming in the sunlight. The sight of her made him feel warm all over.

"And what are you doing here?" he called out as he dismounted.

"Keeping up Nevyn's house for him." She strolled over to open the gate. "Oh, Maer! Your eye!"

"I just got into a little scrap with one of the lads."

He found Nevyn sitting at a table inside and sorting out various herbs and dried barks. The old man got up and caught Maer by the chin, tipping his head back for a look as if the silver dagger were a child, and his fingers were surprisingly strong.

"Well, that's a nasty mess, isn't it? I'll make you up a poultice. Sit down, Maer."

When Maer sat, a pair of big-bellied gnomes appeared on the table and considered him. He scowled right back. Nevyn went to the hearth, where an iron pot hung from a tripod over a small arrangement of logs. When the old man waved his hand at the wood, it burst into flame. Maer felt so sick that he slumped against the table behind him like a lady feeling a faint coming on. Nevyn picked up a handful of herbs from the table and stirred them into the water simmering in the pot.

"I'm assuming someone's fist gave you that black eye."

"It was, sir. Not long ago."

"Ah." Nevyn turned from his stirring and fixed Maer with one of his needle-sharp stares. "Glaenara's a nice, decent lass, Maer. I would absolutely hate to see her dishonored and deserted."

"Would you, sir?" Maer paused to lick dry lips with a nervous tongue. "Er, ah, well, I imagine you're not a pleasant man to face when you're angry about somewhat."

"Not in the least, Maer lad, not in the least."

When he waved his hand again, the fire went out cold. So Lord Pertyc was right about the old man, Maer thought. I wonder if sorcerers can really turn men into frogs? I've no desire to find out the hard way, that's certain.

Yet, as he was leaving, so was Glae, and he decided that it would be dishonorable to let her walk when he was riding her way. He lifted her to his saddle, then mounted behind, slipping his arms around her waist and taking the reins.

"What were you fighting over?" Glaenara said. "Some lass, I'll bet."

"Naught of the sort! It's a long story."

During the ride home, he told her about his persecution of Crindd, and she laughed as much as the lads in the warband. He decided that one of the things he liked best about her was the way she enjoyed a good laugh; so few lasses seemed to appreciate his sense of humor. When they got about half a mile from the farm, she insisted that he let her walk the rest of the way to keep her brother-in-law from seeing them together. As he was lifting her down, he tried kissing her. Although she laughed and shoved him away, she let him steal a second kiss. Just as his lips touched hers, he felt a sharp pain, like the pinch of bony fingers, in the back of his left thigh. He yelped and jumped.

"What?" Glae snapped. "What happened to you?"

"Er, a muscle cramp, I guess." He rubbed the spot gingerly— it still hurt, all right. "I'm sorry."

"Humph, well, if that's the way you're going to be!"

But she was smiling as she turned away and ran off, heading for the farm. Although Maer waved goodbye, he was completely distracted. For a few moments he could see in a tangle of bushes nearby a small creature, as solid and distinct as she could be, with long blue hair and a face like a beautiful child, scowling at him in jealous rage. Suddenly she disappeared, leaving him wondering if he were going mad.

Yet he saw her again, the very next time he rode down into town in hopes of meeting Glaenara. Sure enough, he found Glae selling eggs and turnips in the market, but just as he was striking up a conversation, the blue-haired creature appeared, standing directly behind Glae and snarling like a jealous lover. Maer completely forgot himself.

"Now don't you hurt her!"

"What?" Glae said. "Hurt who? The chicken?"

"My apologies. I wasn't talking to you—I mean—oh, by the hells!"

Glae swiveled around to look behind her. Although Little Blue-hair, as he started calling her, stamped a foot and shook a small fist in Glae's direction, it was obvious that the human lass saw nothing.

"Maer, you *are* daft! That's the oldest prank in the world, making someone look and find naught there. And I must be a lackwit to fall for it."

"Ah, er, sorry. Truly, I shouldn't have . . . uh, well. Here, I've got to go, uh, er, run an errand, but I'll be right back. Don't leave without me."

Leading his horse, Maer hurried off through the sparse crowd in the direction of the blacksmith's shop, but he turned off before he got there and found a private spot behind the inn. Little Blue-hair appeared, sitting on his saddle and smirking at him. Although he felt more daft than ever, he waggled a finger at her.

"Now listen, you, you can't go around pinching people and suchlike."

She held up one hand and made a pinching motion with her thumb and forefinger.

"Like that, truly. Don't do it again, especially not to other people."

She stuck her tongue out at him.

"If you don't behave, I'll . . . I'll . . . I'll tell Nevyn the dweomerman on you."

He made the threat only because he could think of none better—after all, Nevyn terrified *him,* didn't he?—but it had all the force he could possibly have wanted. She leapt to her feet, opened her mouth in a soundless shriek, flung both hands into the air, and disappeared. For a moment Maer felt almost guilty; then he decided that she'd brought it on herself and hurried back to take up his courting in peace. For some weeks afterward, all the Wildfolk stayed far away from him, and he was glad of it.

"Now listen, Glae," Nalyn snapped. "You know as well as I do that Doclyn's a decent young man and a good hard worker. His father's asking me for the smallest possible dowry that can stand up in a lord's court. We won't do better than that. Why won't you marry him?"

Glaenara looked up from the bowl of dried beans she was sorting and simpered at him.

"He doesn't please me."

"Oh, my humble, humble apologies, my fine lady! It's not looks that matter in a man."

"Obviously, or Lida never would have married you."

"Glae!" Myna spoke sharply from her chair by the fire. "Please don't start things up again."

Glae banged the bowl onto the table and stalked outside, sweeping her skirts around her as she hurried across the muddy farmyard. The bitter truth, she supposed, was that unless she married someone, she'd go on living here, under her brother-in-law's thumb, working hard all her life, never having anything resembling her own house—not that she'd ever have the lovely things and leisure that Braedda would. When she reached the cow barn she paused, looking up at the sky, where the moon sailed free of a wisp of icy cloud. She shivered, wishing she'd brought her shawl. Over by the chicken coop something moved: a man shape, detaching itself from a shadow: Maer. She hurried over to him and whispered when she spoke.

"What are you doing here?"

"Trying to figure out how to get a word with you. Are you cold? You can have my cloak. Here."

Bundled in the heavy wool, she walked with him a little ways back into the woods, where he'd left his horse. The moon streamed through the bare-branched trees and made little patterns on the ground.

"Suppose I came out here tomorrow night," Maer said. "Would you meet me?"

"It's going to rain tomorrow night. Samwna's joints ached all day today, and that's always a sure sign of rain coming."

"Well, then, I'll come out here anyway and keep a hopeless vigil in the pouring rain and get a horrible fever and maybe die, and it'll all be for love of you."

"Oh, don't talk daft."

"I mean it. Glae, truly, I'm half out of my mind for love of you."

"Oh, don't lie to me!"

In the moonlight she could just make out the shock on his face. Half afraid she'd cry, she sat down on the ground under a tree. In a moment he joined her.

"I'm sorry," he said. "You're right. But I'll say this, and it's not fancy words but the truth. I don't think there's another lass like you in all Deverry and Eldidd."

"Is that good or bad?"

"A little of both. How's this? I'm not mad for love of you, but I blasted well like you a whole lot, and every now and then, I think maybe I do love you."

"That I can believe, and my thanks. I like you, too."

Somewhat hesitantly, Maer slipped one arm around her shoulders and kissed her. She let him steal another, found herself thinking of the future, and kissed Maer instead to drive the thought away. When he started caressing her, she wrapped her arms tight around him in the spirit of someone gulping a particularly bitter healing decoction and let him lie her down in the soft leaves.

The medicine worked. Having a man of her own made the rest of her life easier to take, as did the coppers Nevyn gave her for tending his cottage. Once she set her mind to ignoring Nalyn's insults and keeping peace between them, they got through whole days without squabbling, and Mam and Lidyan began to relax into a pleased relief. When the explosion came, then, it was twice as bad as it might have been. One evening, just at sunset, Glaenara was chasing the chickens back into the coop for the night when Nalyn came walking out of the house. She could tell something was wrong just from the cold look in his eyes.

"And what's eating at you?"

"I was down in town today, that's what, and everyone was telling me I should be keeping an eye on my little sister. That silver dagger's been riding into town to fetch you, hasn't he?"

"And what if he has?" Glaenara set her hands on her hips. "It's decent of him to give me a ride when I'm tired."

"Ride—hah! Who's riding what, Glae?"

"You little pus boil! Don't you talk to me that way!"

Nalyn grabbed her by the shoulders and shook her.

"You tell me the truth."

Glaenara twisted free and kicked him across the shins. When he grabbed her again and held tight this time, she was shocked at how strong he was—towering over her, causing her pain with an easy masculine strength.

"You've been rolling around with that lad, haven't you? He wouldn't want naught else out of the likes of you."

This very real possibility made Glaenara burst into tears.

"Oh, ye gods!" Nalyn snapped. "It's true, isn't it?"

"So what if it is? Can't I have one thing in my rotten life that I want just because I want it?"

With an oath, Nalyn let go of her, then slapped her hard across the face. Glaenara slapped back without thinking, and at that, the long bad feeling between them erupted. He grabbed her by the shoulder, twisted her around, and slapped her hard across the behind. As hard as she fought and kicked—and she landed some bruises on him—she couldn't get free. The pain of his slaps was nothing compared with her terror at feeling so helpless. She was sobbing so hard that she could barely see. Dimly she heard her mother screaming and Lidyan's voice calling out. All at once, Nalyn let her go. Glaenara staggered and almost fell into her sister's arms.

"Nal, Nal," Myna whined. "What are you doing?"

"Beating a little slut," Nalyn sputtered out. "Lida, let go of her! I won't have my wife feeling sorry for a slut like this. Her and her cursed silver dagger! Ye gods, I'm never going to be able to make her a decent match now."

Lidyan started to cry, her hands slack on Glaenara's arm. Still terrified, Glaenara turned to her mother to find Myna staring in paralyzed disbelief, her thin lips trembling, her patient eyes full of tears. Glaenara tried to speak, but she choked on pure shame.

"Glae," Myna whispered, "tell me it's not true."

Glaenara wanted to lie, but she was shaking too badly to speak. Myna reached out her hand, then drew it back, staring at her all the while with aching eyes.

"Glae," Lidyan wailed, "how could you?"

But Lidyan was watching her husband; Myna turned toward him, too, a final slap sharper than any hand. They were both going to let him pass the final judgment on her.

"It's true enough," Glaenara spat out. "Go on! Call me what you want. I won't be here to listen!"

Glaenara barreled through gate, raced as fast as she could down the road, kept running even when she heard them call her back. She hardly knew what she was doing; she only wanted to run and run and never see any of them again. Her mother was siding with Nalyn. At the thought tears came to choke her and leave her gasping, forcing her to fling herself down into the tall grass to

weep. By the time she'd wept herself dry the sun was setting. She
got up, expecting to see Nalyn coming after her to beat her some
more, but the twilight road was empty, the house far behind. She
wiped her dirty face on her sleeve and began running again,
heading for town and Braedda, who would maybe forgive her—
perhaps, she thought, the only person in the world who would.

At last, just as the stars were pricking the velvet sky, Glaenara
reached the village. As she stood behind the inn and wondered if
Samwna would even let her inside, once she knew the truth, the
tears rose up again, hot and choking. She had no place in life
anymore, nowhere to go, nothing to call her own; she was a
shamed woman and a slut and naught more. She was still weeping
when Braedda's enormous cousin, Cenedd the blacksmith's son,
came strolling through the innyard.

"Glae, by the gods!" Cenedd said. "And what's all this?"

"Nalyn turned me out, and I deserved it. All because of
Maer."

When Cenedd caught her by the shoulders, Glaenara flinched
back, expecting that he would beat her, too.

"Bastards, both of them," Cenedd said matter-of-factly. "Now
don't cry like that." He turned his head and yelled. "Braedda, get
out here!"

When Braedda and Samwna hurried out, Glaenara blurted
the truth between sobs, simply because there was no use in lying.
Braedda began to cry, too, but Samwna took charge—again, as
matter-of-factly as Cenedd.

"Now, now, it's not the end of the world. Oh, Glae, you've
been such a dolt, but truly, I was afraid this was going to happen.
Here, you're not with child, are you?"

"I don't know. It's not been long enough to tell."

"Well, then, we'll know when we know and not a minute later.
You come inside where it's warm, and we'll all have some nice hot
ale."

As the two women led her into the kitchen, Glae looked back
to see Cenedd standing and talking urgently with Ewsn and Selyn,
the weaver's son. She and Braedda sat huddled together on a

bench in the corner of the kitchen while Samwna bustled around, pouring ale into a tall metal flagon and settling it into the coals on the hearth.

"Mam?" Braedda said. "Can Glae sleep here tonight?"

"Of course. There's no use in trying to talk sense to Nalyn until he's had a chance to cool off a bit."

"My thanks," Glae stammered. "Why would you even help me? You should just let me sleep in the road."

"Hush, hush! You're not the first lass in the world to make a fool of herself over a good-looking rider, and doubtless you won't be the last."

Ewsn stuck his gray head into the kitchen and caught Samwna's attention.

"Be back in a bit. Just going for a ride with some of the lads. We've been thinking about poor Myna, you see."

"So have I," Samwna said. "It aches my heart."

"You're not going to the farm, are you?" Glaenara blurted out.

"Not just yet, lass," Ewsn said. "We'll let your brother think things over before we do that."

After dinner, Pertyc's riders were welcome to sit in the great hall and drink while they gossiped or watched what little there was to see. Maer and Cadmyn were playing dice when Ewsn the innkeep, Cenedd the blacksmith's son, and Selyn the weaver's son came into the great hall, stood looking around them for a hesitant moment, then went over to whisper urgently to Pertyc.

"Wonder what they're doing here," Cadmyn remarked.

"Who knows? Seems a strange time of day to pay your taxes."

In a few minutes a smirking Adraegyn came skipping over to the riders' table.

"Maer, Da wants to see you. You're in real trouble, Maer."

"Am I now? Then why are you grinning like a fiend?"

"You'll see. Come on, Maer. Da wants you right now."

Up by Lord Pertyc's carved chair stood Ewsn, Cenedd, and

Selyn, all of them with their arms crossed over their chests and their mouths set in tight lines. Pertyc himself seemed to be smothering laughter. Maer shoved a couple of dogs out of the way and knelt at the lord's feet.

"I wanted to tender you my congratulations, Maer," Pertyc said.

"Congratulations, my lord?"

"On your coming marriage."

Utterly puzzled, sure that this was a prank, Maer glanced this way and that. Cenedd stepped forward, looking somehow even more enormous than usual.

"Marriage," Cenedd said. "You've been trifling with Glae, you little bastard, and now her brother's kicked her out."

"Marriage isn't as bad as all that, Maer." Pertyc leaned forward with a look of bland sincerity on his face. "Why, I did it myself once, and it didn't kill me—though in all honesty it came blasted near."

Maer tried to speak and failed while the warband snickered among themselves.

"I guess I'd best give you a permanent place in my warband," Pertyc went on. "Can't have poor Glae riding behind a silver dagger."

"Now here," Maer squeaked, "I haven't even said I would yet."

Cenedd flexed his massive muscles.

"Now look, I'll make a cursed rotten husband. Glae deserves better than me."

"So she does," Ewsn put in. "But it's a bit late for that now, lad. You're the one who's been lifting her skirts, and you're the one who's marrying her."

Ewsn and Selyn stooped like striking hawks, grabbed Maer one at each arm, and hauled him to his feet.

"Now listen," Cenedd said. "You've lost Glae her home. Either you give her another one, or I'll pound you into slime."

Maer had the sincere feeling that he was going to faint.

"If she comes to live with you here in the dun," Pertyc said, "I've got just the place for her. I've never known as strong-minded a lass as our Glae, so she can be my daughter's nursemaid. Here, you've gone all white, lad! You'll like being married. It just takes a bit of getting used to. We'll see what we can do about getting you a chamber to yourselves here in the broch." He glanced at a smirking servant. "Go saddle Maer's horse for him. He's riding down to the village to see his betrothed."

Catcalls, cheers, and jeers—the warband exploded into laughter.

"Hey, Maer!" Crindd called. "Now this is truly funny!"

With a deep involuntary groan, Maer shut his eyes and let Cenedd drag him out into the ward. Adraegyn came running after and gave Maer's sleeve a tug.

"But, Maer, what did you do to Glae?"

"Go ask your father, lad. It's too complicated to explain right now."

A grim procession of three villagers and one newly betrothed silver dagger rode round to the back of the inn to dismount. When Maer hesitated, Cenedd pulled him bodily from his horse, shook him hard, and set him on his feet again. When Maer groaned at the injustice of it all, Cenedd gave him a shove and sent him staggering inside, where Ewsn, Selyn, Samwna, and Braedda were all waiting and, just behind them, Nevyn stood and glowered. Maer went cold all over in sheer terror, remembering two very salient facts: Nevyn had taken Glae under his wing, and he was a sorcerer, capable—Maer was suddenly positive on this point—of turning men into frogs. No hope now, Maer thought; it's marriage or the marsh. Glae herself was huddled on a bench in a corner. He'd never seen anyone look so miserable as she did then, her eyes swollen from weeping, her pretty dress torn and dirty, and on her cheek a flat red welt. All at once, Maer realized that her brother must have beaten her, and he felt himself to be the most dishonorable wretch in the entire kingdom. Glae raised her head and looked at him, her mouth trembling with tears.

"You don't have to marry me if you don't want to." Her voice was dry and cold. "I'd rather starve than take that kind of charity."

"Oh, hold your tongue! Of course I want to marry you!" He hurried over and threw himself down to kneel beside her. "Here, my sweet, forgive me. I've been cursed rotten to you."

Glaenara stared as if she couldn't believe her ears. When he held out his hand, she let hers lie limply in his, as if she hardly cared what he did to her.

"Glae, I truly want to marry you. Now come on, give your man a smile, won't you?"

At last Glaenara did smile, shyly at first, then blossoming into the brilliant grin that made her look beautiful. Nevyn pushed his way through the gathering crowd and fixed Maer with an ice-blue stare.

"You'd best be a good husband."

"The best you've ever seen. I swear it."

"Good." Nevyn started to say more, then glanced to one side, frowning.

When Maer followed his gaze, he saw Little Blue-hair sitting cross-legged on the floor like a child. That night she seemed about three feet tall, and more solid than he'd ever seen her before. She pointed to Glae, wrinkled up her nose in scorn, then began to weep. As Maer watched horrified, she slowly vanished, fading away, turning transparent, then gone, tears and all. Yet somehow, he knew she'd be back. When he glanced Nevyn's way, he found the old man troubled, and that was the most frightening thing of all.

That year, which was 918 as Deverry men reckon time, Loddlaen turned three, a slender, solemn child with pale hair and enormous purple eyes. Although the other children treated him as one of their own, he always seemed set apart from the games and the general shouting, preferring to cling to his father's trouser leg and merely watch the goings-on or to play quietly with his foster brother, Javanateriel, in the safety of a tent. In his better moments Aderyn wondered if the time he'd spent trapped in his mother's womb off in the Guardians' strange country had affected him in some way, but usually he refused to believe that anything could be wrong with his beautiful son. Even when Loddlaen woke in the night screaming from horrible dreams, Aderyn told himself that all children dreamt of monsters and suchlike at his age.

The autumn alardan that year was one of the largest Aderyn had ever seen. Since all summer the weather had been exceptionally fine, the grass was exceptionally lush, meaning that there was enough fodder near the campground to feed the herds for a few days longer than usual, and the elves took advantage of it for a long week of feasting and good company. Although Aderyn didn't bother to count, it seemed to him that at least five hundred tents sprang up along the stream chosen for the great meeting. At night the tiny cooking fires looked like a field of stars. There were so many horses and sheep that the mounted herders had to take them out a long way round the camp, half a day's ride in some cases.

It was no wonder, then, that Ganedd and his small caravan stumbled across the alardan, especially since the young merchant had enough sense to realize that the elves would be traveling south by then instead of camping near the usual trading sites. Aderyn had met Ganedd several times before; he rather liked the lad, and he could sympathize with his desire to break free of his family's constricted life and see something of the world. It was Aderyn that Ganedd sought out, in fact, once he and his men had been fed and given a place to set up their own tent, because Ganedd knew elven ways well enough to come to the Wise One first. As soon as Aderyn heard his story, though, he sent for Halaberiel. The banadar was beginning to show his age; there were deep crow's-feet at the corner of his eyes, and in certain lights you would have sworn that you could see streaks of gray in his pale hair.

"Hal, you'd best listen to this," Aderyn said. "There's trouble in Cannobaen, and two half-elven children are involved."

"Pertyc Maelwaedd's offspring?" Halaberiel glanced at Ganedd.

"Yes, Banadar." The boy's Elvish was not good, but adequate. "He sent me here with a letter for his wife. He needs help badly. His enemies are threatening to burn his stone tent and kill him and his children. He has eleven men and no archers. They have hundreds and hundreds of men."

"Well, how like the cursed Round-ears, to count on unfair odds like that." Halaberiel changed to Deverrian for the sake of their guest. "I doubt me if you can find his wife, lad. The last I saw of her, she was heading west with her alar to the far camps. I'll send out messengers, but we don't have a blasted lot of hope of catching up with her in time."

"Well, I was afraid of that, sir," Ganedd said. "But what we really need are bows, and extra arrows, and maybe an archer or two to show us how to use them, though truly they'd best be gone again before the siege starts. It would ache my heart to have your people slain in what's most likely a hopeless cause."

"I remember Pertyc from his wedding." Halaberiel glanced at Aderyn. "As I remember, you missed that particular celebration, Wise One. He's a good man, the only Round-ear I ever really liked—well, besides you, but then, you're not really a Round-ear. Never were, as far as I can tell. I don't see why Annaleria ever married him, mind, but I liked him as a man. I may be getting old, but cursed if I'll sit here while a man I like gets himself murdered in his tent."

"You'll help us, sir?" Ganedd broke into a grin.

"I will. Bows you shall have, and arrows, and me and some of my men, too. Calonderiel's always spoiling for a good scrap, and I think Farendar and Albaral will ride with us for the excitement of the thing, and then there's young Jennantar, who needs to learn Eldidd speech. I'll pass the word around and see if anyone else's heart burns to come with us, but truly, Ganedd, I don't want to risk many more men than that."

"Banadar, you're worth a hundred Round-ear men by yourself alone."

Halaberiel laughed.

"Put me up high on a stone wall with a good bow and someone to keep filling my quiver, and you might just be right, lad. We'll find out soon enough."

Although Aderyn's first reaction was a sick feeling at this elven interference in human politics, in the end he decided that there was nothing he could do to prevent it. As the Wise One, Aderyn could have overruled the banadar, but only at a great social cost; there would have been arguments for days, and the entire alardan would have lined up on one side or the other, leading to further trouble for years to come. Besides, he considered that indeed Pertyc Maelwaedd had every justice on his side and deserved defending, as he remarked to Nevyn when they talked later that evening through the fire.

"I agree, actually," Nevyn thought back to him. "But do you think archers are going to make much of a difference?"

"I do. I mean, Hal tells me that in an open field the rebel army could easily wipe out a small squad of archers, but this isn't going to be an open field, is it? The banadar's bringing two fletchers with us, and I gather he's going to have them spend all winter making arrows while he trains Pertyc's men."

"I see. Wait—did you say with *us?*"

"I thought I'd best come along. I'd like to bring Loddlaen, so you could see him, but it's just too dangerous."

"On that, at least, I couldn't agree more. You know, there's a thing going on here that I'd like you to take a look at, too. Do you remember Maddyn?"

Aderyn thought for a long moment.

"Oh, the bard! The one who had the silver ring with the roses on it."

"Exactly. Well, he's been reborn, and he's here, and that wretched little blue sprite is still hanging around him. You know, I think she honestly loves him. I didn't think the Wildfolk were capable of that."

"No more did I."

"And now Maer's starting seeing her and all of her kin, for that matter. He came to me the other day, poor lad, quite troubled about it. I made a little speech, all pompous and vague, about the magical nature of borderlands in general and this one in particular, and I dropped a few harmless hints about the Westfolk. Blather, it was, but he was impressed and felt much better. I could hardly tell him that being around me was awakening his deepest memories of his last life."

"If that's all it is. The sprite may have somewhat to do with this, too. I'm on my way, then. We leave at dawn tomorrow, and since we have a pack train to contend with, it'll probably take us a fortnight at the very least to reach Cannobaen."

"Well and good. I'm looking forward to seeing you again."

"And I, you. It's been too long."

On the day that the caravan arrived in Cannobaen, it poured rain, one of those quiet storms that without any pompous show of thunder and lightning settle in to soak everything. Since Maer had drawn stable duty that morning, he was out in the ward, wrapped in a greased cloak with the hood up, sweeping the stable leavings into a mound for the gardener. The rain had just finally found its way through the heavy wool to run down his back when he heard a clatter of hooves and a shout at the gates. Delighted with the distraction, he dropped his rake and trotted over just as Ganedd led his men and laden mules inside. Maer whooped in delight and yelled at the gardener to run and fetch his lordship.

"Maer!" Ganedd sang out. "Gladdens my heart and all that! We've done it, Maer! We've got bows and the men to teach us how to use them."

Maer whooped again; he'd been rather looking forward to living longer than one winter more. All at once he realized that Wildfolk were swarming around the tiny caravan, and that he could see them all more clearly than ever before. Sylphs hung in the air, delighting in the rain; undines rose up out of puddles and grinned at him; sprites and gnomes thronged around the animals and sat on the saddles and mule packs; some of the bolder creatures were even perched on the shoulders of the men or rushed to greet them as they dismounted. Nevyn's impressive remarks about the Westfolk and their affinities began to take on actual meaning.

"Come on!" Ganedd called. "Take our guests inside to meet Lord Pertyc. Here come the servants to tend the stock."

With Ganedd in the lead they all dashed into the great hall, which was hot and smoky from the fires roaring in both hearths. Immediately everyone threw off their cloaks and dropped them into a wet and smelly heap for a serving lass to deal with later. Maer received his second shock of the day, because he'd never seen an elf before, never even knew that they existed, in fact. Cat-slit and enormous eyes of green and purple and indigo blue, hair as pale as moonlight, and the ears—try as he might, he couldn't look away. Finally a tall fellow with violet eyes took offense.

"And just what are you staring at, you Round-ear dog?"

"Cal, hold your tongue!" As fast as any lord to break up a brawl, the eldest of the lot stepped in between them. "You can't blame the lad for being surprised. He can't be such a bad fellow, anyway, since he's friends with the Wildfolk."

Maer glanced down to see Little Blue-hair. She'd come up beside him and taken his hand in one of hers; now she leaned against his trouser leg and stared at the visitors like a shy child.

"You see them, too?" Maer whispered.

"Of course." The man called Cal smiled and held out his hand. "Friends?"

"Done."

They shook hands solemnly; then Cal hurried after the others to be presented to the lord.

"Ganedd, my friend, if it were in my power to ennoble you, I would," Pertyc said. "Since it's not, and since I don't have more than a handful of coin to my name, I don't really know how I'll ever be able to repay you."

"Well, my lord, if we all get ourselves killed in the spring, repayment's a moot point, anyway."

Pertyc laughed and gave him a friendly slap on the shoulder. "I like you merchants. So hardheaded, so practical. Well, if I can figure out a way to do it, I'll repay you anyway, especially if by some miracle we do live through the spring."

"Then I'll take it gladly, my lord. Here, the servants should have brought those bows in by now. If his lordship will excuse me, I'll just go hurry them along."

"Please do. I don't think I've ever waited more eagerly for anything than I've been waiting for those bows. And I need to have a word with my old friend Halaberiel anyway."

As Ganedd was leaving the great hall, he came face to face with a young woman. With Glaenara—Ganedd stared open-mouthed. All bathed and civilized as she was, he hadn't recognized her for a moment. Even her hair was glossy-clean and growing longer, curling softly around her face. Her hands were clean, too, and her nails nicely manicured.

"What's wrong, Ganno? Fall off your horse and hit your head?"

"Oh, my apologies, Glae! I, uh, well, just didn't recognize you. I mean: I wasn't expecting to see you here."

"I'm married to Maer now."

"The silver dagger?"

"Well, he isn't that anymore." She hesitated, suddenly distressed. "Ganno, do you still want to marry Braedda?"

"What? Of course."

"Then you'd best get down to the village today. When your da got back from Aberwyn, you know? He went straight to Braedda's father and tried to break off the betrothal, but Ewsn, bless him, said he'd wait to speak with you about it."

Ganedd took her advice and rode down as soon as Pertyc gave him leave, much later that day. The rain had rolled on its way by then, leaving the sunset clean and bright, with a snap of the sea wind and the tang of salt in the air. Round back of his parents' house he tethered his horse, then climbed over the garden wall and let himself in the back door. Twelve-year-old Avyl was in the kitchen, badgering the cook for a piece of bread and honey. When he saw Ganedd, he smirked. The cook threw her apron over her face and began to weep.

"Oho, so you came home, huh?" Avyl said. "Wait'll you see Da."

When Ganedd stalked by, Avyl followed, snickering. The noise brought Moligga out into the corridor. She took one look at Ganedd and began to tremble. Avyl abruptly held his tongue.

"I'm sorry, Mam," Ganedd said. "But I had to do what I think is right."

She started to speak, then merely shook her head in a scatter of tears. When Ganedd went to lay his hand on her arm, she drew back.

"Ganno, get out," Moligga said, almost whispering. "I don't want your father even seeing you."

"Indeed? Well, I want to say a thing or two to him. Tell me one thing: how do you feel about this rebellion?"

"Do you think I care one way or another? Oh, ye gods, that ever it would come to this: my lad and my man, at each other's throats, and all over a king I've never even seen!" Slowly the tears welled, running down her cheeks. "Ganno, he made a declaration before the whole guild and cut you off."

"I knew he would. Where is he?"

"Don't." Moligga caught his arm. "Just leave."

As gently as he could, Ganedd pushed past her and walked on down the corridor. He flung open the door to his father's study and marched in without knocking. Wersyn rose from his writing desk, his fingers clasping a leather-bound ledger, and gave him a sour little smile.

"Who are you? Strange—you remind me of my dead son."

For a moment, Ganedd couldn't breathe. Wersyn went on smiling. The silence hung as thick as sea fog in the tiny chamber.

"Then count me his spirit come back from the Otherlands for

a little while. And I'll give you a warning, like spirits do. If I live through this winter, then I'm going to see to it that you never trade in the Westlands again. They're my friends, Da, not yours, and you cursed well know it."

With a gasp, Wersyn hurled the ledger straight at his head. Ganedd dodged, laughing.

"But it's for the king's sake, Da. Not mine."

His face scarlet with rage, Wersyn rushed him, his hand raised for a slap. Ganedd heard Moligga scream. He dodged, caught his father's wrists, and grimly held on. No matter how much Wersyn struggled, he couldn't break free. He was panting for breath and weeping in frustration at the inescapable truth: his little son was the stronger man now. When Moligga started to sob, Ganedd let him go.

"You can't hit a dead man. Farewell."

Ganedd turned on his heel and walked slowly out, strode down the corridor, and opened the front door. His brother's skinny little face stared at him wide-eyed.

"I'm the heir now, Ganno. What do you think of that?"

"They should have drowned you young. Like the rat-faced weasel you are."

Earlier that day Aderyn had ridden down to see Nevyn in his cottage, where they could talk privately of things that would only unsettle ordinary men. Nevyn was surprised by just how glad he was to see his old pupil in the flesh rather than through a scrying focus, enough so to make him wonder if he were growing old and sentimental or suchlike. For hours they talked of everything and nothing, sharing news of the craft and the various apprentices they'd taken in the past or, in Aderyn's case, that they had now.

"The Westfolk are really amazing when it comes to magic," Aderyn said at last. "They have more of an affinity for it than we do."

"No doubt. Look at how vital they are, living so long while

keeping so young-seeming and all. It seems to me that they must be far more open to the flow of the life-power than humans are."

"They're far more in harmony with life itself, actually. Well" —Aderyn's expression suddenly turned blank and closed—"most of them."

Nevyn could figure out that somehow the conversation had brought Dallandra to his mind.

"Ah well," Nevyn said, and a bit hurriedly. "I take it then that your larger work is going well, too. Restoring the full dweomer system to the Westfolk, I mean."

They talked for a good long while more and parted with arrangements made to meet on the morrow as well. After Aderyn went on his way, Nevyn went into his bedchamber and sat down on the floor to lift up the loose board and take out the small wooden casket where the opal was hidden. It was wrapped in five pieces of Bardek silk: the palest purple-gray, a flaming red, a deep sea blue, a sunny yellow, and then a mottled bit, russet, citrine, olive, and black. He laid it in the palm of his hand and considered the stone as it gleamed softly in the candlelight.

Since any good stone will pick up bits of emotion, dream-thought, and life-force from its owners and the events around it, Nevyn had postponed starting his work upon it. His own will and feelings were troubled and clouded by what he referred to as "this stupid rebellion," and if his mind wasn't utterly clear, he would inevitably charge the opal with the wrong thoughts. The last thing he wanted his talisman to radiate to the High Kings of All Deverry was a self-righteous irritation. They doubtless could summon enough of that on their own. One way or another, he'd have to settle things here in Cannobaen before he could get down to work. Ah well, he told himself, if you'd wanted an easy life, you could have been a wretched priest and been done with it!

IN THE GREAT dun of Elrydd, looming over the town on a high hill, Danry of Cernmeton was drinking with its lord, Tieryn Yvmur. By the honor hearth they sat round a beautifully carved table with the young pretender to the throne, Cawaryn. Although he was only sixteen, he would impress the men who would have to serve him; with raven-dark hair and cornflower-blue eyes, every inch an Eldidd man in looks, he walked with an easy grace, stood arrogantly, and had all the mannerisms of a man born to command. A hard-bitten fox of a man in his thirties, Yvmur sported long dark mustaches, and his pale blue eyes glanced at his elder sister's son with a genuine fondness, as if inviting Danry to share it.

"I'm truly grateful that you'd ride to take our hospitality." Cawaryn spoke carefully in what sounded like a prepared speech. "I value your skill on the field highly, Your Grace."

"My thanks, Your Highness."

Yvmur and Cawaryn shared a brief smile at the honorific.

"But I'm hoping there'll be no need to demonstrate that skill before spring, when the Deverry king arrives," the pretender went on. "I'd hate to see us wasting our strength here in Eldidd. It would be a pity to have factions before we even have a throne."

"Just so," Danry said. "Pertyc Maelwaedd has a good saying

about that: even jackals bring down the kill before they squabble over the meat."

At the mention of Pertyc's name, Yvmur stiffened ever so slightly. Danry decided that it was time to end the fencing match.

"You know, with my own ears, I've heard Pertyc belittle and disclaim his right to the Eldidd throne. He's quite aware that he descends from the bastard of a common-born woman."

"Pertyc's always had a wit as sharp as a razor," Yvmur put in, before the king-to-be could comment. "He's a man I honor highly."

"So do I," Danry said, "for all he's an eccentric sort. It's rare that you meet a man with no desire to rule."

Cawaryn merely listened, his head tilted to one side like a clever dog.

"You know our Perro better than any man alive," Yvmur said.

"I do, and I've never met a man who fits his clan's device better. Pertyc can be as stubborn as a badger, all right, once he takes an idea into his head. He wants to stay in Cannobaen, and he'll hang on with all his claws."

Yvmur nodded, thinking, but Cawaryn moved restlessly in his chair.

"That's all very well," Cawaryn snapped. "But why won't he pledge to the true king?"

Yvmur turned smoothly and shot a glance of warning.

"Oh well, I mean, er," Cawaryn stammered. "Doubtless he will once the war's over. I mean, he doesn't even have many men to bring to the army, so maybe he just doesn't want to fight or suchlike."

Danry smiled, pretending to take no insult.

After the meal that night, Yvmur insisted on taking Danry out to the stables to see a particularly fine horse, and he carried the candle lantern himself instead of bringing a servant. They went down to the stall where a handsome gray stallion was drowsing over his manger. Danry made the obligatory compliments and waited.

"Cawaryn's not old enough to understand a man's desire for neutrality," Yvmur said at last. "But I am."

"I understand it, too. I wondered if anyone else did."

"A few. A very few. By the by, it's time to celebrate Cawaryn's wedding. Once the two thin lines are joined, they'll look thicker."

"Just so. My lady is looking forward to coming to Abernaudd for the festivities."

"It gladdens my heart to hear you plan to attend."

"And why wouldn't I? I intend to show every bit of support for our liege that I can."

Yvmur lowered the lantern and looked Danry full in the face.

"There are some who assumed you'd support your friend over the king. I begin to think they're wrong."

"Dead wrong. My sword and my men are marching behind Cawaryn."

"Well and good, then, and my thanks." Yvmur considered briefly. "Is it a wrong thing for me to ask why?"

"Not in the least. I want to save Pertyc's life and Pertyc's son. Any man who considers Adraegyn a better claimant than Cawaryn will have me for an enemy—for Pertyc's sake and for your sake, too."

Yvmur nodded slowly, considering the lantern in his hand.

"Then a friendly word. You'd better keep your eyes on Leomyr of Dun Gwerbyn. That's where I've been keeping mine."

Out behind Dun Cannobaen in a wild meadow, where scruffy grass grew tall, bent continually by the sea wind, Halaberiel made an archery range for Pertyc's warband with targets out of painted wood—to begin with; later they would stuff old shirts with straw to look like men. Maer found archery practice the most boring thing he'd ever done in his life, and the rest of the warband grumbled with him. All morning, every day, wind, rain, or shine, Halaberiel lined his new recruits up at the marks, subjected them to intense sarcasm, and made them draw and loose arrow after arrow. Even with the leather guards and gloves, fingers blistered and wrists bruised. Halaberiel handed out elven herbs for soaking hands and told them to be back at their marks promptly on the morrow.

Maer, of course, was the only man in the warband who saw the congregation that assembled to watch them. The Wildfolk came in swarms, lining either side of the practice ground like onlookers at a contest, crawling all over the targets, standing behind the men and mimicking everything they did, ruffling the fletching on the arrows and occasionally even pinching the archers themselves, just to see if they could spoil their aim. The first time Maer saw an arrow skewer one of the Wildfolk he nearly shouted aloud—he could feel his face turning pale—but the little creature merely disappeared, then popped back into manifestation a few feet away, no worse for the experience. Every now and then he saw the blue sprite, standing nearby and watching him sadly. The reproach in her eyes was so human that he almost felt guilty, as if he'd actually betrayed her.

The rigorous training left Maer little time for his new wife, which to his surprise annoyed him. He had to admit that being married was turning out to have advantages. It was nice to have Glaenara whenever he wanted, and in the warm comfort of their own bed, not the hard ground. At dinner, when they sat together at the servants' table and shared a trencher, Glaenara would smile and listen with a flattering intensity to his account of his day until she had to go help old Maudda in the women's hall. Since Maer would go drink with the rest of the warband at that point, he found himself thinking that he'd lost very little by marrying compared with what he'd gained.

One night, when Maer had a little less ale than usual, he found himself thinking about his new wife's sweet body and left the table early. When he went to their bedchamber, he found her sitting up on the edge of the bed and mending a rip in his spare shirt by candlelight. Maer sat down on the floor and watched her sew, frowning a little at her work in the uncertain light.

"My apologies for that," Maer said. "I lost one of those cursed arrows in a hedge, you see, and our cat-eyed friends made me fetch it out again. I guess the fletcher can straighten them if they're not too bad."

"I'd rather mend for you than anyone else."

She looked up with a smile that Maer found sweetly troubling. He wondered how long it would take her to get the blasted shirt finished so they could go to bed.

"Maer? Are you happy with me?"

"Happy?" Maer was taken utterly off guard. "Well, now, I don't truly think much about things like being happy. I didn't think you did, either."

"I never have before." Glaenara was concentrating on knotting her thread. "But I'm starting to."

"Well, I like being part of the warband a lot more than I liked being a silver dagger, even with the archery practice." He put his arms around her and kissed her. "Come lie down, and I'll tell you some more."

"Gladly. When are you going to give me a baby, Maer?"

"When the Goddess wants me to give you one, I'll wager, and not before, but come lie down, and we'll give her a chance at it."

On the morrow morning, after archery practice, he lingered behind to walk back to the dun with Pertyc.

"My lord, somewhat I wanted to ask you. You're a married man and all, so you'd understand. I've been thinking that we might get besieged. There's your daughter, and now my woman, and then the old nurse and the serving lasses. What's going to happen to them?"

"I'm sending them away long before the trouble starts. I wondered if you'd been worrying about that."

"I have. Glae might be a widow soon enough, but I couldn't bear it, watching her starve with us."

"You're a good lad in your way, Maer. It's too bad your Wyrd was harsh enough to bring you to Cannobaen. But don't trouble your heart about the women. I'm going to ask Nevyn for help."

Maer was much relieved, willing to trust blindly in his lordship and the sorcerer. As they walked through the gates, they saw a fine horse, laden with beautiful red leather and silver trappings, standing outside the doors. Pertyc swore under his breath.

"Here, Maer," he said. "Grab some of the lads. Run out and take down those targets and hide them. Hide the bows, too. I'll pray it's not too late to distract this bastard."

While Pertyc ran for the hall, Maer ran for the barracks. He rounded up six men and followed his orders, stowing the targets and the bows up in the hayloft. When they returned to the great hall, Maer saw a young man kneeling by Pertyc's chair and talking gravely with him. Maer found Glaenara over by the servants' hearth and caught her arm.

"Who's that, do you know?"

"One of Tieryn Yvmur's riders. He came with a message for our lord about the royal wedding."

Right then Maer discovered the value of having a wife in the confidence of the most knowing gossip in all Cannobaen.

"It's ever so exciting," Glaenara went on. "This lad who's going to be married is the one the rebels say is the king of Eldidd. So if our lordship goes, he's saying he's a rebel, too, but if he doesn't go, it'll be an insult. If he goes to the wedding but won't declare for the king, they'll kill him right then and there. Maudda says she's ever so worried. After all, our lord was like a son to her."

"What's our Badger going to do?"

"Stay home. He told her that he's already insulted everyone once, so why not twice?" Glaenara sighed, troubled herself. "I wish they'd just be content with the king we've got. He doesn't even come to Eldidd and bother the pack of them."

"True-spoken. Pity they don't see it your way."

On the morrow, the messenger rode out again, and archery practice resumed. But from then on, they practiced far away from the dun in the woods, where no casual visitor would see the telltale row of targets.

Since Cawaryn's father was dead, the marriage took place in the gwerbret's palace in Abernaudd. A gray-haired, blustery sort of fellow, Gwerbret Mainoic was related to Cawaryn by blood several times over and devoted to his cause. As a particular mark of favor, Danry and his family were invited to shelter in the main broch of the many-towered dun itself for the long round of entertainments—hunting in Mainoic's park, bardic performances in the great hall, displays by the war galleys down in the harbor. Late one afternoon, Yvmur suggested that they go for a stroll out in the gardens behind the broch complex. It was a drizzly sort of day, with the flower beds turned under for the winter and the trees dripping gray drops from bare branches. Out in the middle of the browning lawn stood a small fountain, where the dragon of Aberwyn and the hippogriff of Abernaudd disported themselves under a spray of clear water. Yvmur studied the statues for a moment.

"You'll notice how they've made the dragon a bit smaller than the hippogriff. There's a fountain in Aberwyn to match this. Ever seen it?"

"I have. Odd: there the dragon is a noticeable bit larger."

"Just so. By the by, Leomyr's arrived. He came by way of Aberwyn."

They let their eyes meet for a moment.

"Chilly out here," Danry said. "Shall we go in? I truly should pay my respects to Leomyr."

Leomyr, Tieryn Dun Gwerbyn, had been given a pair of splendid chambers up on the top floor of the main tower. When Danry found him, he was eating an apple, holding it in his hand like a peasant and taking neat bites with his prominent front teeth.

"I was going to seek you out." Leomyr paused to toss the core into the fire blazing in the hearth. "It gladdens my heart to see you, my friend."

"My thanks, and the same to you. A tardy arrival's better than none at all."

Leomyr took another apple, then offered the silver bowl to Danry.

"None for me, my thanks. I've just eaten. The gwerbret sets a good table. There should be enough on it for any man."

His eyes faintly mocking, Leomyr bit into the second apple.

"You're turning into quite a courtier," Leomyr said with his mouth full. "I never knew you could fence so well."

"Practice always sharpens a man's hand."

"Did you learn from Pertyc? He seems cursed coy these days, as bad as a young maid."

"There's nothing coy about Perro. If he tells you a thing, he means it from his very heart."

Leomyr took another bite and considered him.

"Most maids like a brooch as a courting gift," Leomyr said at last. "And usually, the bigger the better, especially when it's a ring brooch."

"For the shoulder of a plaid cloak? Pertyc's never cared for jewelry."

"Well, of course, what Pertyc does is no concern of mine, as long as he doesn't fight for the Deverrian."

"Of course."

"You'll notice I'm here for the wedding. I brought our liege a splendid gift, too."

"Well and good, then. I hope he and the new queen treasure it for a long time in good health."

By a mutual, if unspoken agreement they sat down in facing chairs. Danry rested his hands on his thighs and waited.

"I'm mostly surprised at you, my friend," Leomyr said. "I know you love the Maelwaedd like a brother."

"I do, which is why I'm willing to let him do what he wants, not what I want him to do."

"Umph, well. You know, I have only thirty men, not exactly enough to make a king."

"And how many men do they have in Aberwyn?"

"A hundred and ten, which is no more than you do, Falcon, as you cursed well know. But I wonder if you know just how much the success of this rebellion turns on your loyalty."

"I can count up the men available for an army as well as anyone else."

"It's beyond that. I've seen you fight, you know. You look like one of the gods themselves out there when the steel starts flashing. Men will follow you anywhere."

Danry turned away in sincere embarrassment. When he spoke again, Leomyr sounded, oddly enough, amused.

"I hope the day doesn't come when both you and our stubborn Badger regret this decision. I've never trusted Yvmur for a minute."

"Neither has Mainoic." Danry turned back. "I've no doubt things can work out to your satisfaction—if you care to spend a bit of time in Abernaudd."

Leomyr looked at him sharply, then smiled. Danry smiled in return. One king's enough for the jackels to fight over, he thought, as long as the blood smells fresh enough to attract them.

Later that afternoon, a page summoned Danry to the great hall to attend upon Cawaryn and his uncle. Most of the lords sheltered in the dun were there, seated at long tables in order of rank with Cawaryn at the head of the gwerbret's own table, even though he was only a tieryn's nephew, a gesture lost on no one. When Leomyr came into the hall and made a bow to the lad that was as close to a kneel as circumstances would allow, Danry was satisfied with the results of their conversation. Gwerbret Mainoic rose and cleared his throat for a speech.

"I called you together, my lords, to witness somewhat that might gladden your hearts. The merchant guilds of Abernaudd and Aberwyn have banded together to bring our Cawaryn a gift for his marriage."

The guilds never wasted their coin on gifts for minor lords, only for gwerbrets—and kings. Slowly, gravely, in measured step, four pairs of merchants came in, carrying, on a sort of litter improvised from a plank, an enormous red velvet cushion, and on the cushion, a golden cauldron, all graved and worked in bands of interlace and spirals, that would hold a good twenty skins of mead. Danry caught his breath in a low whistle—the thing was worth a fortune! At his uncle's prompting, Cawaryn rose to receive them just as they set their burden down.

"My humble thanks for this splendid gift," Cawaryn said, with a sideways glance at his uncle. "To whom do I owe this honor?"

"To all the assembled trade guilds of Eldidd, Your Grace."

The merchant who stepped forward was old Wersyn of Cannobaen. Well, well, well, Danry thought, and does Perro know about this? When Wersyn began a long and somewhat tedious speech, which skirted without saying that everyone knew Cawaryn for the new king, the assembled lords allowed themselves small smiles and sidelong glances at one another. If even the common folk stood behind the rebellion, the omens were shaping up favorably indeed.

As Danry was returning to his chamber to fetch his lady down for dinner, he saw another merchant, standing in a corridor and talking idly to a servant lass. At the sight of Danry, the merchant bowed, smiled, and hurried quickly away, a little too quickly perhaps. Danry stopped and caught the lass by the arm.

"And who was that?"

The lass blushed scarlet as she dropped him a curtsy.

"Oh, his name is Gurcyn, and him a married man and old enough to know better, too, Your Grace, than to bother a lass like me."

"I see. Well, get on about your work, then."

Late that night, once the feasting was over, Danry retired to his chamber. Since he was Pertyc's foster brother, raised by Maelwaedds in the eccentric Maelwaedd way, he could read and write. That night he was glad of it, too, thanking Pertyc's father in his heart for making him independent of another lord's scribes. He wrote Pertyc a long letter, telling his friend all the doings round the new king, but stressing in several different ways that he was to beware of Leomyr of Dun Gwerbyn. Early in the morning, when the sun was just rising, he went to the barracks complex, roused his captain, and gave the letter to his most trusted man to take to Cannobaen. He even walked down to the main gates of the dun with the rider and saw him on his way, but as he walked back, Leomyr met him.

"Sending a letter off?"

"Instructions for my steward at home. You've got sharp eyes for another man's affairs."

Leomyr shrugged and bowed. Danry had no doubt that Leomyr believed him as much as he believed Leomyr.

"Pertyc, listen," Nevyn said. "You've asked me to help, and I've promised I would, but there's blasted little I can do for you if you're not honest with me. How soon are the rebels planning to declare themselves?"

Pertyc hesitated, visibly torn. They were up in his cluttered chamber, Pertyc slouched in a chair, Nevyn standing behind the lectern and resting his hands on the cover of Prince Mael's book.

"I know you have your friends to consider," Nevyn said.

"Well, one friend. I'd be willing to die for his sake, but I'm not about to let the women and children die, too."

"Decent of you. How can I advise you when I don't know what's causing the trouble? Suppose you were ill, and you refused to tell me where it hurt. How could I prescribe the right medicinals?"

Pertyc hesitated, staring into empty air.

"Well, the trouble won't come till spring, most like." The lord spoke slowly at first, then with a rush of words. "Most of the rebels are rallying around one claimant, Cawaryn of Elrydd, but there are those who'd start a second faction because they don't trust the men behind Cawaryn. This faction wanted to put me forward as a claimant, but I refused. Naught's been said outright, mind, but I'll wager we can both guess what they're thinking. Kill the Maelwaedd, and we can take his son for a candidate."

"Of all the stupid . . . ! Ye gods, but I should have known! That's Deverry men for you, so busy fighting the battles among themselves that their enemies march in and win the wars. I see you have Mael's old copy of the *Annals of the Dawntime* here. Have you read the tales of Gwersingetoric and the great Gwindec?"

"About how their own allies betrayed them, and so the cursed Rhwmanes drove King Bran and our ancestors to the Western Isles? No doubt this rebellion is as doomed as the one Gwindec led. Ye gods, my poor Danry! I—" He caught himself, wincing at his slip.

"So. Tieryn Cernmeton is the sworn friend, is he? Does he love you enough to send you warnings?"

"He does, and he has, because he's doing what he can to bring the second faction over to Cawaryn so they'll leave me alone. He told me they're installing the new king as soon as they can. He has great hopes that everyone will support the lad once the priests have worked their ritual and all. I keep having doubts, myself."

"Wise of you. Very well; I know enough to get on with. I'll stop putting hot irons to your honor. For a while, anyway."

That evening, Nevyn enlisted Aderyn's help to guard his body while he went scrying in the body of light—a dangerous business, but he had no choice; since he'd never seen any of these men in the flesh before, he couldn't simply scry them out through a fire or other such focus. They went into his bedchamber, which was pleasantly warm from the small charcoal stove in the corner. Nevyn lay flat on his back on the hard straw mattress while Aderyn sat cross-legged on the floor nearby. The little room was silent, dark except for the faint reddish glow from the coals. At this time of day, there was little chance that one of the villagers would come knocking, but Aderyn was there to fend them off if they did.

"Where will you go?" Aderyn said.

"Aberwyn for starters."

Nevyn folded his arms across his chest, shut his eyes, and concentrated on his breathing. Quickly his body of light came, a simple man shape, built of the blue light, bound to him by a silver cord. He transferred over, hearing a rushy click as his consciousness took root, and opened his astral eyes. When he looked at

Aderyn, he saw his friend's body only dimly, like a wick in a candle flame, obscured by the blaze of his gold-colored aura.

Slowly Nevyn let himself drift up to the ceiling, then brought his will to bear on a thought of the coast road. Abruptly he was outside, hovering in the blue etheric light above the cliffs. Across the beach, the ocean was a silver and blue turmoil of elemental force, surging and boiling in vast currents, swarming with Wildfolk and spirits of all types. Although the sand itself, and the stone and dirt cliff faces, appeared black and dead, they were dotted here and there with the reddish auras of the clumps of weed and grass caught in cracks and crannies. The meadows at the clifftop glowed a dull orange, streaked by the dead road. As Nevyn rose higher, the Wildfolk clustered round him, some in the form of winks and flashes of refracted light; others, as pulses of glow, bright-colored as jewels. When he glanced over his etheric equivalent of a shoulder, he saw the silver cord stretching behind him and vanishing into mist.

With the Wildfolk swarming after, Nevyn rushed in long leaps of thought over the sleeping countryside until he came to Aberwyn. Far below him lay the town, a haphazard scattering of round dead shapes—the houses—lit by the occasional patch of reddish vegetable aura. Here and there some human or animal aura wandered through the dark streets like a mobile candle flame. Wreathed and misted in a veil of elemental force, the dangerous river ran like a streak of cold fire down the middle. Nevyn drifted over the city wall, but he was careful to avoid the river's surge as he flew to the gwerbret's dun.

Since he'd only been inside this dun once, and that nearly seventy years ago, he was lost at first until a small garden caught his attention. In the midst of the bright auras of well-tended plants stood a fountain in the shape of a dragon and a hippogriff, illuminated by the etheric glow of the water playing over them. He focused down until it seemed that he hovered only a few inches off the grass. Nearby was the jutting round wall of the main tower. Candlelight and firelight, forming pale reflections in the overall etheric glow, flickered out of the windows in such profusion that

Nevyn could assume the great hall lay inside. He could also pick up a welter of ancient emotions: blood-lust, rage, the exhilaration of war and the stink of treachery, all lingering as faint, nearly unreadable traces in the blue light.

He walked right through the wall and found himself standing, or rather floating, on the dais at the honor end of the great hall. Gwerbret Gatryc was dining with his lady and an honored guest, a lord whom Nevyn didn't recognize, a brown-haired fellow with prominent front teeth. The currents of feeling emanating from them were as tangled and sharp as a hedge of thorns, but one thing was clear: although they hated each other, they needed each other. They spoke only of trivial things for a few moments; then by mutual agreement left the table and went upstairs, calling for a page to follow them with mead and goblets.

Nevyn floated right along after them to a small chamber hung with tapestries, as dull and dead as painted parchment to the astral sight. Gatryc and his guest sat in carved chairs by a small fire, took the mead from the page, and sent the boy away. In this plane, the silver goblets, bathed in the bluish aura of the moon-metal, seemed as alive as the hands which held them. Carefully Nevyn focused his consciousness down one degree, until the chamber barely glowed with the etheric light and he could, with great effort, discern their thoughts.

"That's all very well for now," the guest was saying. "But how will you feel when Mainoic is controlling the throne?"

"That will be the time to make our move. Listen, Leomyr, a prize like this is worth waiting for."

"True-spoken, Your Grace. But if we don't advance the Maelwaedd claim now, men might have grave doubts when we do. And why did you swear to Cawaryn, they'll say, if you never believed him a king?"

Gatryc considered, rolling his goblet between the palms of his hands.

"True-spoken. It's a vexed situation, truly. We don't have enough men behind us to make Adraegyn king by force. That's why Danry was so important."

"I know. But maybe we should have the lad now, for safekeeping, shall we say?"

"If we move on Pertyc Maelwaedd, we might as well refuse to swear to Cawaryn and be done with it. Everyone will know why we're doing it."

"I see naught wrong with crushing the only king's man in our territory before the war comes. He's an enemy at our flank, for all his supposed neutrality."

"Perhaps." Gatryc had a swallow of mead. "But with ten men or whatever it is he's got, no one's going to believe he's a dangerous threat to the rebellion. And then there's Danry. And his hundred and twenty men. And his allies."

Leomyr considered.

"Well, Your Grace," Leomyr said at last, "you're exactly right about one thing: it's too soon to move, one way or another. I only want to keep these questions alive in your mind. When it comes time for the new king to be proclaimed, we'll have to sniff around and see what we can pick up. I think a few more lords may join us, once they see Yvmur all puffed up and prancing round the king."

Nevyn had heard enough. He thought himself outside, flew over the dun walls, and headed home. On the morrow, he left Aderyn at the cottage and rode out to the archery ground, where he found Lord Pertyc practicing with his men.

"News for you, my lord," Nevyn said. "Let's walk a bit away, shall we?"

Pertyc followed him into the trees, where the fog hung in clammy gray festoons from the branches.

"Tell me somewhat, my lord. What do you know of an Eldidd peer named Leomyr?"

"Tieryn Dun Gwerbyn? Why do you ask?"

"Do you think him a friend that needs protecting? I'll swear to you that he's the worst enemy you have."

Pertyc went a little pale, staring at him like a child who fears a beating.

"How do you know that?"

"Ways of my own. Do you honor him?"

"Not in the least. Danry warned me about him, you see. I'm just cursed surprised you know, too."

"And did Danry tell you that Leomyr's as close as two cows in a chilly field with the gwerbret of Aberwyn?"

"He only hinted about it. He didn't know for sure."

"I do know. Listen, if either of those two ride your way, or if they send you messages, don't believe a word they say. And send Maer down to the village to tell me straightaway, will you?"

Over the next week Nevyn spent many a long and dangerous night traveling through the etheric until he knew the names and images of the men he needed to watch. From then on, he could scry more safely in the fire. He saw Leomyr busy himself with his demesne and his family, as if factions were the farthest thing from his mind despite the string of messengers coming and going between him, his allies, and Gwerbret Aberwyn. He overheard Gatryc exchange weaseling words with men loyal to Cawaryn. He saw Cawaryn himself and pitied the lad, pushed by his ambitious uncle into danger. Even more to the point, he saw Yvmur consulting with priests of Bel, pondering the calendar and the omens as they discussed the most favorable day to proclaim the new king, that crucial day which would mark not only the beginning of Cawaryn's reign but of open rebellion.

Hatred, however, is a very poor reason to start a war, for the simple reason that it makes a man blind to his enemy's good qualities. The Eldidd lords were so intent on thinking King Aeryc a dishonorable usurper that they forgot he was no fool. For years he'd seen trouble coming in that distant province, and he had spies there, paid in good solid coin to send him what news there was to know. Even as Yvmur and the priests chose a night for pronouncing Cawaryn king, one of those spies was receiving his pay, up in Dun Deverry, for some very interesting news.

Although a fire of massive logs burned in the hearth, it was cold at the window, an exhalation of chill damp from the stone walls and an icy breath from the glass panes. Outside the royal palace in Dun Deverry, the first snow lay scattered on dead brown grass. The king was restless, pacing idly back and forth from window to hearth. A handsome man, with striking green eyes, Aeryc stood over six feet tall, but he looked even taller thanks to his mane of stiff pale hair, bleached with lime and combed straight back in the Dawntime fashion. Since he was on his feet, Councillor Melyr was forced to stand, too, but the old man kept close to the fire. His lean face was drawn with worry—reasonably enough, Aeryc thought, since it was a dangerous point that they were discussing.

"We're simply sick of waiting," Aeryc said. "If the king is going to tolerate rebellion, then the king deserves rebellion."

"No doubt, my liege, but does the king truly think he should take the field himself?"

"We have yet to make up our mind on this point."

Out of pity for the councillor's age, Aeryc sat down. With a grateful sigh, Melyr sank into a chair opposite.

"But if we ride to Eldidd, then we must ride soon," Aeryc went on. "Hence our haste."

"Just so, my liege. The roads will be bad soon."

"Just that." Aeryc considered, too troubled to keep up the proper formalities. "Cursed if I'll let this pack of Eldidd dogs enthrone their usurper without any trouble. They'll all be in Abernaudd with their warbands, then, anyway."

"If this information you've received is accurate."

"Why should Gurcyn lie? He's been loyal to me—or to my coin, more like—for years. He gathered news from all over the province, to say naught of what he saw with his own eyes. The cursed gall of those whoreson merchants! Celebrating this piss-poor excuse of a lad's wedding with a royal cauldron."

When in sheer rage Aeryc got up from his chair, creaking at the joints, Melyr rose to join him.

"But, my liege, will a spy's word be sufficient proof of treason in the eyes of the rest of the kingdom? Some of the Eldidd lor 's may have individual alliances in the western parts of Deverry. A king whom men secretly call unjust is a king with many troubles on his hands."

"True-spoken. From the point of view of war, it would be better to fall on them straightaway and wipe them out one at a time. But from the point of view of rulership, you're right. It's better to wait. But I see naught wrong with being close enough to march as soon as this impious farce of a ceremony is done with. Cerrmor's never snowbound. I intend to take an army down while the roads are still clear. Then we can take ship for Eldidd when the time comes."

"A brilliant stroke, my liege. There remains the question of whether the king himself will ride with his men. It seems unnecessary to me. I have every faith that your captains honor you enough to fight as bravely for your sake as they would with you at their head."

"Of course. So what? I'm going, and that's that. I want to grind their faces in the mire myself. The gall of this piss-proud whoreson excuse for a nobility! Didn't they think I'd be keeping an eye on them? I—" Aeryc stopped in mid-tirade and grinned.

"My liege?"

"Somewhat just occurred to me. Since they don't seem to think in terms of spies, I'll wager they don't have any of their own. How unfair of me, to keep all the spies to myself! I think I'd best send them one with some special information, all nicely brewed—like a purgative."

It was about a month later when Yvmur showed up at Danry's gates for a visit. All that day, they both kept up the fiction that Yvmur was paying a mere social visit to satisfy the tieryn's natural curiosity about the preparations for the kingship rite. Late that evening, though, when Danry's family had retired to their chambers and the warband was back in the barracks, they lingered at the table of honor in the great hall and drank a last goblet of mead by the dying fire.

"I've had no word at all about Leomyr's doings," Danry said. "Have you?"

"None, which worries me. It's been a long time since he rode to Aberwyn last, but I doubt me if he's been thinking only of his own affairs. I've sent him a message, just a friendly sort of thing, wondering if we're to have the honor of his taking part in the ceremonies. There's always room for another honored equerry or escort in affairs like this if he does agree."

"Good. Let me know how he answers."

On the morrow, when the pale sun dragged itself up late, it glittered on frost, a white rime thick on fallen leaves and dying grass alike. With a pack of dogs and a band of beaters, Danry took his guest hunting, but just as their little procession reached the edge of a leafless woodland, a rider came galloping after. It was a man from the dun, yelling Lord Danry's name over and over.

"Your Grace," the man panted out. "Urgent news. Your lady sent me to fetch you. A messenger at the keep."

With a wave of his hand, Danry turned the hunt around and galloped for home. As they rode, he felt a foreboding, as icy as the morning, clutching at his very heart, an omen that was more than justified by the message from Mainoic.

"It's truly urgent, Your Grace," the carrier told him. "I beg you, fetch your scribe straightaway."

Instead, Danry broke the seal and pulled out the roll of parchment himself. As he read, he could feel the blood draining from his face. The merchant Gurcyn had come rushing back from one last trading trip with horrible news. The king had men in Cerrmor—worse yet, the king himself was in Cerrmor, and everyone said that he was riding for the Eldidd border with his entire army behind him before the rebels could declare Cawaryn king. Mainoic was begging every man in Eldidd to collect his warband and muster in Aberwyn, where they would declare the lad and march to meet the invader.

"Ah, ye gods," Danry said. "Well, your nephew won't have the splendid ceremonies we'd planned, my friend."

"As long as he's king, the Lord of Hell can take the ceremony.

So—the cursed Deverrian thinks he can beat us out like stags from a wood, does he? We'll be fighting on our ground, not his, and we'll give him the same fight of it now as we would later."

Danry nodded in agreement, but he knew, just as Yvmur doubtless knew, that the words were bluster. They'd held no councils of war, planned no supply lines, done no work on their fortifications. Here at the edge of winter's famine Aeryc could depend on the surplus of a rich kingdom while they would be extorting provisions from a reluctant populace.

"I'd best leave straightaway," Yvmur said.

"Of course. We've all got our preparations to make. I'll see you in Aberwyn as soon as ever I can."

All that day and on into the night Danry worked side by side with his chamberlain and captain to ready his warband and procure supplies. He slept for a few fitful hours, then rose long before the tardy dawn to finish. Just as the sun was breaking over the horizon he ran upstairs for the last time to say farewell to his wife. Ylanna threw herself into his arms and wept.

"Here, here, my love," Danry said. "You'll see me again soon enough. The gods will fight on the side of a just cause and a true king."

Although her pale face was wet with tears, she looked up and forced a smile.

"So they will. Then fight to a true victory, my love, and bring our lad home safe to me."

"I'll swear it. Someday you'll have the favor of a true Eldidd queen."

Out in the ward their elder son, Cunvelyn, paced back and forth while he waited, grinning as if his face would split from it. At fifteen, the lad was riding to battle for the first time.

"And who are we riding for, lad?" Danry said.

"The true king. The one true king of Eldidd."

The warband broke out cheering: to the king, the king! Danry was laughing as he mounted his horse. As they trotted out of the gates, the sun was just beginning to rise, a new day dawning for Eldidd.

By riding hard they reached Aberwyn in three days, and as they rode, they picked up men and allies until Danry, by a mutual consent among the lords, led an army of close to four hundred into the city. They found the gwerbret's dun a seething confusion of men and horses. Supply carts clogged the main ward, horses stood tethered in walled gardens, bedrolls lay scattered on the floor of the great hall, battle gear overflowed the tables while warriors stood to drink and eat, servants ran endlessly back and forth with food and messages and spare bits of armor. Danry shoved his way through and found a council of war in progress in the gwerbret's private chambers at the top of the main broch. Ordinary lords hovered outside while tieryns crammed the half-round room; Mainoic and Gatryc stood at either side of the pretender and talked urgently, often at the same time. Danry sought out Leomyr and found him leaning into the curve of the wall out of the way. Danry was tired and exasperated enough to dispense with fencing.

"There's no time now for your cursed factions. Let the Badger stay in his den."

"I know it as well as you do, but it might be too late for the Maelwaedd anyway."

"What do you mean?"

"Listen. Just listen to the talk, Falcon."

Danry left him and worked through the crowd, stopping to say a word here and there to a friend. Everyone was full of the same question: how did Aeryc come to know so much about their plans?

"He even knew about that blasted cauldron the guilds gave the king," Ladoic of Siddclog said. "Treachery, lads."

The men around nodded grimly, staring at Danry in a decidedly unpleasant way. Danry was struck breathless, wondering if they doubted him, but then Ladoic went on.

"Neutral, was he? This Badger friend of yours, I mean. I think Pertyc has blinded you good and proper, Danry. We should have ridden to Cannobaen and wiped him out the day he refused to join us."

Most of the room was turning to listen. When Danry glanced

around, he saw cold eyes, grim eyes, eyes filled with a bitter hatred.

"Pertyc swore a vow to me," Danry snarled.

"Oh, no doubt," Ladoic said. "No one's blaming you, my friend. Vows have been broken before, haven't they? Someone sent the pus-boil Deverrian all the news he needed."

Nods—grim smiles—Danry felt as if he were being cut with a thousand knives.

"By the hells, Pertyc would rather die than lie to me. It must have been someone else!"

"No time for that now, anyway!" Yvmur came striding down the room, pushing men aside to reach Danry. "It doesn't matter who slit the wineskin—what counts is stitching the leak. Later we can deal with whoever this traitor might be."

More nods—a few mutters—a sullen defeated agreement. For the rest of the day, Danry kept to himself. Although he refused to believe Pertyc capable of treachery, the wondering ate at him like poison.

Instead of the feasts and entertainments, instead of a hall draped with blue and gold and filled with lovely women, instead of the long processions and the temples, Cawaryn was declared king in Gwerbret Gatryc's ward on a dark cold morning. Torches flared, sending their scarlet light over the grim faces of the men, lords to the front, riders to the rear, packed close together, armed for war and ready to ride. Up on an improvised dais, the lad stood straight, flanked by the gwerbrets and his uncle, while the priests of Bel draped the blue, gold, and silver plaid of Eldidd round his shoulders. Cawaryn knelt while the priests lifted up their hands and prayed over him. Danry listened grimly, glad of every prayer they had on their side. At last, the head priest took from its coffer the massive ring brooch of Eldidd, kept hidden for over fifty years in the vaults of his temple. It was eight inches across, solid gold, chased and worked on both sides with delicate knotwork fit for a king, and bearing in the middle the locked dragon and hippogriff twined round an enormous sapphire. As he held it high in both hands, the crowd gasped. Slowly, with due ceremony, the old priest pinned it to the shoulder of the cloak.

"Rise, Cawaryn," the priest called out, "king of all Eldidd in her hour of need."

As the lad stood, the men cheered and howled. Wave after wave of shrieking, hysterical laughter echoed off the walls as the sun rose on the war.

The army rode out that very morning. Besides the easy coast road, there were two mountain passes into Eldidd from Deverry. The one to the north was high, doubtless choked with snow. The southern pass was just barely open to a determined army. Although scouts had been sent out long before, everyone was assuming that the Deverry forces would come along the coast from Cerrmor.

Two days' forced march brought an Eldidd army of nearly a thousand men close to the mountain border. On that first march, there was hope. They had plenty of men, who would fight not merely at orders but because they believed in the fight. They'd been warned of Aeryc's advance in time to take up a good position of their choosing for the first confrontation. They had, for a couple of weeks at least, plenty of food and fodder to keep the army strong. Scouts rode out and returned from the southern pass, bringing the news that, as yet, there was no sign of the Deverrians. Late on the second night, after a weary army had made camp, Yvmur summoned Danry to a small council of war round the fire in front of the king's tents. While the older men talked, Cawaryn paced, his brooch bright at his shoulder.

"If we catch Aeryc on the sea road," Yvmur said, "we've got him in a cursed bad spot. We can pin him against the cliffs where there's no room to maneuver."

"And shove him over the edge, may the gods allow," Gatryc said, grinning. "Have those scouts come in?"

"Not the last lot." The king finally spoke. "We have sent men across the border, you see, in hopes that they can tell us how far away the enemy lies."

The men nodded gravely, trying to ignore the king's frequent glances to his uncle for reassurance.

"My liege?" Danry said. "And what of the scouts from the north?"

"No word," Yvmur put in. "We've sent men after them, but I'll wager that Aeryc's not risking that pass."

Yvmur was right about that, but the rebel lords had overlooked what, in fact and to be fair, everyone in Eldidd but Ganedd of Cannobaen had overlooked: the king had ships in Cerrmor, a vast fleet of ships, enough to ferry him and an army of over fifteen hundred to Abernaudd. The rebels heard of the landing round noon on the morrow, when a hysterical rider on a foundering horse caught up with the rear guard as the rebel army marched east. Danry rode back with Yvmur and Leomyr to see what the shouting was about and found one of the men left behind on fort guard in Abernaudd.

"My lords, he's invested the city. I got out just in time."

"What?" Yvmur snapped. "Who?"

"The king. The Deverry king. Aeryc. With a fleet. They landed in the harbor at dawn yesterday. They've got the harbor, my lords, but the city's holding firm. They haven't even tried an assault. They're just camping at the gates."

Even as the men around him swore and wondered, Danry knew with an awful certainty why Aeryc was biding his time.

"Then we've got to ride back straightaway." It was Mainoic, pushing his way through the knot of men around the messenger. "My city! He'll burn it to the ground."

"Naught of the sort," Danry snarled. "That's what he wants us to think and the worst thing we can do."

"Hold your tongue, *Tieryn* Danry! I say we ride back straightaway."

"Let Danry finish." Much to everyone's surprise—even his own, perhaps—Leomyr was the defender. "He knows war, my lord, in his heart and blood and bone."

There was a moment's silence; then Mainoic made a grudging nod and let Danry speak.

"He only wants us, my lords. He doesn't want to harm one soul in that city and turn Abernaudd against him. He wants to break us and the rebellion, and then offer his ever so majestic pardons to everyone else in Eldidd, so there'll never be a rebellion here again. If we go rushing back to Abernaudd, he'll be waiting on ground of his choosing with well-rested men."

The arguments broke out like a summer storm, thundering, violent, and over very fast.

"True enough, Falcon," Mainoic said at last. "What shall we do, then? Find a good position and wait for him to come after us? Our men could starve before he decides to move."

"I know that, Your Grace. I say we march for Aberwyn. Let Aeryc sit on his behind in 'Naudd and wait for us. By the time he moves, we'll be entrenched in a walled town with fortifications that seal the harbor off from the countryside. We can send ships out for provisions if we need to, or use ships to get men in and out safely. Then we can try to rally the countryside."

Everyone turned to look at Gatryc. He shrugged and turned both hands palm upward.

"Leomyr was right," Aberwyn's lord remarked. "The Falcon lives and breathes war. My lords, allow me to offer you the hospitality of my dun."

There was laughter, but it was only a grim kind of mutter. Even so, as they dispersed to give orders and turn the line of march, there was still hope. The men and horses were fresh, and even if they rode by a long route to throw Aeryc off, Aberwyn was only some hundred miles away while the Deverry king was stuck holding Abernaudd. Unfortunately for the rebellion, Abernaudd, guarded only by some fifty aging or ill culls from the rebel army and a reluctant and whining citizen watch, surrendered that very afternoon.

When the town militia threw open the gates of Abernaudd, Aeryc suspected a trick, but a carefully chosen detachment occupied the city with no trouble. Leading the rest of the army, Aeryc rode through unmanned gates and down silent streets where the few townsfolk he saw were huddled behind upper windows. Finally, near the gwerbret's dun, he saw one old woman standing openly on the street corner. As he started to pass by, she grabbed her rags of a skirt and dropped him a perfect curtsy. Aeryc threw up his hand and halted the march. While the army milled around and sorted itself out, he bowed gravely from the saddle to the wrinkled old crone.

"Good morrow. And what makes you curtsy to the king?"

"Simple manners, my liege. Whether or not everyone else in this cursed town's forgotten their courtesy or not, and truly, so they must have, to shut a door in the face of a king. Always curtsy to a king, my mam told me, and so I do."

"Indeed? And what's your name, pray tell?"

"Oh, they call me Daft Mab, and it's true enough, my liege. Are you going to burn the place down? I do like a good fire, I do."

"Well, you'll have to watch your fires in a hearth, Mab. Tell anyone who asks you that the king says there's mercy for all, as long as they took no hand in the actual plotting of the rebellion. I'll put out a proclamation soon enough."

"Then I'll tell them first, my liege. You look like a good king, truly." Daft Mab considered, her head tilted to one side. "Oh, that you do, and polite to your mother, no doubt."

"I try my best to be. Good day, Mab."

When Aeryc rode up to the dun, which stood on the highest of Abernaudd's many hills, he found a squad of his men waiting at the gates. The place was deserted, they told him, stripped bare of every man, horse, and most of the food. Not even the servants were left behind, though they might be mingling with the townsfolk.

"I don't care about the cursed servants," Aeryc said to the reporting captain. "Well and good, then. Mainoic's wife must have gone elsewhere, which is fine with me. I can't be bothered sorting out hostages at the moment."

Aeryc turned his horse over to his page and went into the great hall with Gwenyn, the captain of his personal guard. Aeryc was honestly surprised at how small and shabby it was, not much better than the hall of a tieryn down in Deverry. The tapestries were old-fashioned, the furniture was worn, and there wasn't room to seat more than two hundred men.

"Well, my liege," Gwenyn remarked. "The only thing the false king is going to do in this dun is hang. It's magnificent enough for that."

One of the men did find a pair of fine maps, treasure enough since neither the king nor any of his captains had ever been in Eldidd before. Aeryc sat on the edge of the table of honor and spread them out himself. While he and his staff ate a hasty meal of cheese and bread, washed down with a forgotten barrel of Mainoic's ale, they studied the long curve of the Eldidd coast, marked with all the villages and demesnes of the various noble lords. Far to the west stood Cannobaen, where his one loyal vassal was holed up like the badger of his device. Aeryc pointed to the spot with the tip of his dagger.

"One way or the other, we eventually want to sweep by the Maelwaedd's dun," Aeryc said. "I have every intention of rewarding him for his loyalty, so it'll be best to let him join his men up with the army. Our spies say he has only ten or eleven riders, but it's the honor of the thing that matters to a rustic lord like the Maelwaedd."

"No doubt, my liege," Gwenyn said. "Ye gods, there's not a cursed lot out there on the western border, is there?"

"Forest and fog, or so I hear. I'm in no hurry to march to Cannobaen. There's no real need. First we'll wait here in the trap and see if our rebels take the bait."

Just after sunset, however, a pair of scouts rode in with the news that the rebel army seemed to be swinging toward Aberwyn. Aeryc woke his staff and gave orders to have the men ready to march well before dawn.

Danry, of course, had sent out scouts of his own, and that night, when the rebel army halted, he made sure that guards ringed the camp round on a double watch as well. After a quick and futile conference with the demoralized king, Danry went back to his own fire and found his impatient son waiting up for him.

"Da, I don't want to sit in Aberwyn all winter! Aren't we going to get to fight?"

"Eventually. Once the countryside's roused, and a relief army's marching our way, we'll sally from Aberwyn."

Cunvelyn's disappointment was almost comical.

"Waiting's a part of war, lad. Whether you like it or not, you're a real soldier already."

At that point, the rebel army had forded the Aver Dilbrae some twenty miles upstream from Abernaudd and camped on its western banks. If they headed southwest on a reasonably direct line, they were only about forty-five miles from Aberwyn. Since even in good summer weather, twenty miles was a solid day's march to an army of those days, and here in the short damp days of midwinter they were lucky to do twelve, Danry considered that they were safely out of the king's reach. He quite simply had no way of knowing that the king's crack cavalry, rigorously trained and drilled, riding the best horses with extra mounts at their disposal, backed by an elaborate supply system that was, ironically enough, one of Nevyn's legacies to the kingship, could in emergencies cover twice that distance.

Yvmur himself unknowingly made the situation a bit worse on the morrow by insisting that the army swing a few miles out of its way in the direction of another holding, Dun Graebyr, to pick up the twenty men he'd left on fort guard. Since Aeryc would be marching after the main army, Yvmur reasoned, he wouldn't be attacking the dun, and they might as well have the men and the fresh horses. Although Danry wanted to scream at the man that they had to make all possible speed, he was painfully aware that he was no cadvridoc, only a councillor of sorts, and very much on sufferance. So he held his tongue and let the army angle sharply west, heading for Dun Graebyr, instead of angling south, as Danry wanted, on the road to Aberwyn.

In the end, Yvmur's twenty extra men made no difference, because Aeryc caught them on the road on the second day after the surrender of Abernaudd. Since the rebels had scouts riding out on the flanks, Danry wasn't taken entirely by surprise. They had about an hour to find a good defensible position and arrange the army in it. A broad meadow eased into a low rise, just some twelve feet high, but enough to guard their backs, and on the top of the rise was a loose stand of scattered trees to protect the supply wagons and suchlike. And the king—Yvmur and the two gwerbrets agreed with Danry without one cross word or argument that the lad had better stay safely out of the way for this first, crucial battle. While they waited for Aeryc's army, Danry collared Cunvelyn.

"Now listen, lad, it's your first real scrap. You're going to be one of the men protecting the king."

"Hiding in the forest, you mean!"

Danry slapped him across the face, but he held his hand a bit, since he was only teaching manners.

"You do what I say."

"I will, sir."

"Good." He allowed himself a smile. "Now come on, Bello, most men would be begging for a chance to ride next to the king. You're being honored, you silly young cub, and trust me, there'll be more than enough battles later on to satisfy you."

Rubbing his face with one hand, Cunvelyn managed a smile at that. His father clapped him on the shoulder, then sent him on his way after the supply wagons and the rest of the king's guard.

By the time Aeryc's army came into sight, the sun was as high as it was going to get. When the plume of dust appeared, heading straight for them, horns blared up and down the waiting rebel line. In the clink and rustle of metal, men pulled javelins and readied shields. Danry arranged his men, with himself at their head, in the center of the lax crescent formed by the army. He offered one prayer to the gods for Cunvelyn's safety; then the Deverry horns shrieked a challenge, and there was no time for prayer or thought. Aeryc's army turned off the road, came free of a stand of trees, and paused about a quarter mile away to draw their javelins. There were about a thousand of them, Danry estimated, very fair odds indeed. Although his scouts had set the number higher, he put the discrepancy down to the fears and excitements of untried men. It was the only mistake he made in the whole campaign.

The Deverry army bunched into a loose wedge for the charge. The Eldidd line inched forward, gathering itself as the enemy walked their horses a few hesitant yards closer to get a little momentum. At last, when they were close enough for Danry to see the golden wyverns on their shields, their horns blew for the charge; the line surged; the wedge leapt forward and raced for the rebels. With a shout to his men, Danry flung his javelin and drew his sword on the smooth follow-through as the Deverry wedge flung up shields. A few men went down. Danry shrieked a battle cry and spurred his horse forward. Behind him his men plunged after, turning, as they'd been trained, to smash into the flank of the leading riders and scatter their force. Behind them the field exploded in shouting and the clash of weapons.

Danry faced off with one man, killed him, spun for another— then heard horns—a lot of horns—bellowing above the war cries and the shouting. The Deverry line ahead was wheeling back, almost as if to retreat. Riding hard, his captain, Odyl, fell in beside him.

"My lord! Look back!"

With Odyl there to guard his flank, Danry could turn his head for a look just as a plume of dust began to rise among the trees, and a new set of horns and shouts broke out. The rest of the Deverry army was battling up the other side of the rise. Doubtless they'd merely been trying to hit the rebel army from the rear, but all at once Danry realized that they were getting themselves a splendid prize indeed.

"The king!" he screamed. "Odyl!"

Screaming and cursing, they tried to turn their horses and rally the rest of their men to get them up the rise, but the Deverrians were all over them. Aeryc's men fought well, cursed well; Danry had just time for that grudging thought before he found himself fighting for his life, mobbed by three of them. Odyl went down, stabbed in the back. Desperately Danry fought to stay mounted, parrying more than attacking, dodging his way free only to find himself in a new mob. His heart went cold as he realized that Aeryc's men were deliberately going for the leaders, the noble-born and the captains, the better to crush the common-born. As silent as death itself he went on striking, slashing, dodging, working his horse back and back till at last they reached the rise. There what had been protection became a trap. He was so hard pressed that turning his horse and climbing the rise meant death. He could only fight on and hope for a chance to break out to the side.

The Eldidd horns started shrieking retreat. Everywhere Danry saw the gold wyvern coursing the field. Danry knocked one off his horse, killed another, drove forward, and by a stroke of sheer luck leapt past a pair of Deverry men so fast that they had no time to react. Just as he got through, he saw three Eldidd shields galloping to meet him, Leomyr and two of his men.

"Get out of here, man!" Leomyr screamed at him. "It's lost!"

"My son! I've got to get to the trees!"

"There's no hope of it. It aches my heart, but for god's sake, ride! Here the bastards come!"

A squad of some twenty men were bearing straight for them. Only the thought that the king and Cunvelyn might by some miracle be alive and need him made Danry retreat, but he followed Leomyr as they galloped across the field and dashed for the safety of a distant woodland. Later Danry would realize that they'd been allowed to escape by men turned indifferent to their fate by some great victory; at the time he could only thank the gods that they made it out.

On the other side of the woods they found a scattered remnant of Eldidd riders. They herded them up like cattle and led them on, galloping until their horses could gallop no more, then letting the horses stumble to a walk. When Danry turned in the saddle and looked back, he saw no pursuit behind them. The only thing they could do was head for the nearest loyal dun and hope that the rest of the army would have the same idea. On the way, they gathered stragglers, until at last they brought sixty weary men to Lord Marddyr's gates. In the ward they found a confusion of wounded, panting horses. Danry turned his contingent over to the frantic servants and led his men inside.

The hall was a sea of riders, sitting on the floor, lying in corners, nursing wounds or merely weeping from the defeat. Marddyr's lady and her serving women rushed back and forth, tending the wounded. Up on the dais was a huddle of noble lords. When Danry and Leomyr joined them, Danry realized with a sinking heart that the king was not among them, nor Mainoic or Yvmur. There's time yet, he thought, or maybe they went elsewhere. But Ladoic grabbed him by the arm and spit out the news.

"The king's captured! Ah, ye gods, they took him prisoner like a common rider!"

Danry began to weep, shaking with the death of all his hopes and his honor, as the grim tale went on, and he wasn't the only man in tears. One lord saw Mainoic fall, another saw Yvmur slain, a third had seen Cawaryn dragged out of his saddle. As they talked, a few other stragglers staggered into the great hall. At every new arrival, Danry looked up, praying it would be his son. It never was. As servants crept round, lighting candles and torches against the setting of the sun, the lords began arguing over what to do next. Every lord had left men behind on fort guard; if they could gather them, they could field a strength of close to four hundred. The question was how to go about it. Finally Gwerbret Gatryc, wounded though he was with a slashed right arm, rallied his strength enough to take command.

"We've got to get out of here, or we'll be penned in a hopeless siege. Start kicking your men onto their horses. I know it's bad, but we've got to ride west. We'll have a better chance of hiding in wild country."

The logic was irrefutable. While Danry was separating his men from the general mob, one of Yvmur's riders came up to him. "My lord? I saw your son fall. He's dead."

Danry could only stare at him for a long, numb moment. The lad wasn't much older than Cunvelyn himself.

"We'll all be dead soon enough," Danry said at last. "I'll see him in the Otherlands."

That night, about two hundred men out of the original thousand took the cold ride west. The horses were too weary to do much more than walk, and no one pushed them, because they had little hope of finding more if they foundered them. They rode until they could ride no more and made a camp of sorts in the wild forest around midnight. Around a sputtering campfire of damp twigs and sticks, the remnants of Eldidd nobility gathered and tried to plan.

"We've got to find shelter away from the coast," Gatryc said. "We'll stretch his cursed supply lines thin that way. He won't dare follow us all the way into our territory. Let him take Aberwyn! We'll take it back again."

"True-spoken," Ladoic put in. "And Danry here knows the wild forest around Cannobaen."

Danry realized that everyone was turning to stare at him. In his numb grief he couldn't understand why.

"So I do. And that's our best hope, right enough."

They all nodded. With a sigh, Gatryc cradled his bandaged arm and stared at the ground. While the others talked, Danry began thinking about his son, remembering the little lad who used to toddle to him with outstretched arms and lisp a few words. When someone caught his arm, he looked up dazed.

"Did you hear that?" Leomyr said to him.

"What? You'll forgive me, my lords. Cunvelyn fell in that battle."

There was a quick wince of sympathy from every man there. Leomyr let him go.

"We were wondering how soon the Deverrian will hang the king," Leomyr said. "I'm wagering he won't wait."

"Oh, I agree with you, for what my opinion's worth."

"And the king has no heirs." Gatryc's voice was faint. "If we want to keep the throne in Eldidd, we'd best have a man to sit on it, hadn't we?"

Like a hot dagger through wax the words cut through Danry's exhaustion.

"It's a noble thing to honor a friend," Gatryc said. "But Pertyc Maelwaedd holds the future of Eldidd in his Badger's claws. Do you think you can persuade him to the right way of thinking?"

When Danry hesitated, Gatryc gave him a thin smile.

"I doubt if you can," the gwerbret went on. "Danry, believe me, it aches my heart to say what I have to say. But we have to have his lad. Adraegyn's the king of Eldidd the moment Cawaryn dies. I've no doubt that the Deverrian knows it as well as we do. We're sending a warband ahead of us, the men in the best shape on the best horses to go fetch him from his father's dun. Leomyr will captain them, because that way he can stop at Dun Gwerbyn and pick up his fresh men and suchlike. The rest of us will follow and fight a rearguard action. Keep the Deverrian too busy to make a quick strike west. And you're staying at my side. We need your battle wisdom. Besides, I have no desire to make you watch the events at Cannobaen."

Although it was nicely said, Danry knew that he was being put under arrest.

"My thanks, Your Grace. Though he's betrayed us, Pertyc was my friend once. I don't want to see him die."

This was just unexpected enough to put everyone off guard. As they stared at him, Danry summoned a bitter smile.

"Well, by the black ass of the Lord of Hell, what do you think? That I can see the death of all my hopes, of my king, and of my own son, and still love the traitor who brought this all down upon me?"

"I think I've misjudged you, my friend," Gatryc said. "Well and good, then. Here, my lords, there's nothing more to be said. Get what sleep you can."

As he strode off, Danry was aware of Leomyr watching him, but he had no strength to worry about the man. It's all lost anyway, Danry thought, all we can do is die with a little bit of honor. Around three campfires huddled the thirty-seven men he had left out of his warband of a hundred and twenty. Danry spoke a few words to them, then rolled himself up in his cloak. He fell asleep on the icy ground to dream of his son and Pertyc, the two things he loved most in the world, one already lost, the other doomed.

Danry woke long before the rest of the camp, when the moon was setting among the icy stars. He got up, moving stiffly, and looked round for the guard that he knew Gatryc had posted over him. In the dim light, he could see the young rider huddled on the ground and snoring. Danry crept past without waking the lad. In a clearing the horses were tethered; the guard there was asleep, too. Danry found his own chestnut gelding, still bridled, and led him away through the forest. Once they were clear of the camp, he set the horse's bit and mounted bareback. He was going to have a long, hard ride to Cannobaen, but he was determined to warn Pertyc and die at his side. In his muddled state of mind, it all seemed perfectly just: he was leaving his men and horses with his allies to make up for this betrayal.

Since the horse was tired, Danry let it walk along the west-running road while he tried to think. He could lie his way across Eldidd, he supposed, claiming fresh horses and food from his erstwhile allies' duns on the pretext of bringing them the terrible news. The road here ran through trees, which soon would thicken into a remnant of the wild forest. He would cut straight across country, he decided, to the dun of Lord Coryn, one of Mainoic's vassals. Then he heard the sound behind him: men and horses, coming fast. He clung to his horse's neck and kicked it as hard as he could, but the horse could only manage a jog. When he looked back he could see a squad gaining on him.

At first Danry thought it was Deverry men, closer than any of them had expected, but as they approached, he recognized Leomyr in the moonlight. It was a pathetically ridiculous race of exhausted men on exhausted horses, trotting after one another with barely the strength to yell. Sick in his heart of the farce, Danry turned his horse and rode back to meet them. Leomyr's smirk made him draw his sword. The six riders ringed him round, jostling uneasily for position in the dim light.

"I thought so," Leomyr said. "You're a good liar, Danry, but not quite good enough. You're never reaching the Badger's hole."

Danry shouted and kicked his horse straight for him, but a rider intervened. With two quick cuts he killed the man, swung round him, got one good blow on someone else—he couldn't see who—before he felt the fire, slicing open his back as the five remaining riders mobbed him from flank and rear. The pain came again, burning through his shoulder to the bone, then stabbing from the side. The dim night road was swimming and dancing around him, spinning, spinning, spinning as horses reared and men yelled. The trees were swooping and falling. Danry hit the road hard, tasting dust and blood as he choked. The road went dark. He saw a light burning in the dark, but it was a light that never shone on land or sea. In it he saw his lad, reaching out to him.

The news was such a shock that for a long while Pertyc felt as muddled and sick as someone suffering from a bad fever. He was lingering over his breakfast that morning, dreading the thought of archery practice in the rain, when Nevyn came striding into the hall. The old man pulled off his wet cloak and tossed it to Adraegyn.

"They're coming, my lord. Leomyr and eighty men, but the rebellion is over, whether the idiots will admit it or not."

When Pertyc tried to speak, no words came. Nevyn went on, rattling off the news: the king had marched, caught the rebels by surprise, and torn them to pieces. A few desperate men were left to regroup out in the forest and fight to the death.

"And this morning, King Aeryc hanged young Cawaryn," Nevyn finished up. "Ye gods, this all took me completely off guard!

I was only idly looking for news, and found a boiling kettle spilling soup into the fire. Here I thought we had another month before the king even arrived in Eldidd."

"So did I," Pertyc stammered out. "How close is Leomyr?"

"A day's ride."

Pertyc could only shake his head in bewilderment. Halaberiel, who'd apparently seen Nevyn's arrival, came hurrying up to the table of honor.

"And what are we going to do about the women?" the banadar said. "It sounds like there's not a dun in Eldidd where they'd be safe."

Pertyc nodded, glancing around. Aderyn was standing in the doorway and watching Nevyn with his blank owlish stare.

"We can't send them into the forest," Nevyn said. "Well, I guess they'll just have to stay here, and we'll simply have to hold the siege until the king can lift it."

Pertyc found his tongue at last.

"Easy to say, not so easy to do. If the archers hold them off, they'll probably try to fire the dun. You know, ride as close as they can and sling torches over the wall. We've got mounds of firewood stacked all everywhere, you know, for the beacon."

"I sometimes marvel at the gods." Halaberiel was grinning to take the sting out of his words. "Here they gave you Round-ears heads that are as big as ours, but they forgot to put any brains in them. You've got two dweomermen on your side."

"And what does that have to do with anything?"

Halaberiel rolled his eyes heavenward to beg the gods to bear witness to the aforementioned lack of brains.

"He means that if Leomyr tries to fire the dun," Nevyn broke in. "It won't burn."

"Now here, are you telling me you can command the fire?"

Nevyn glanced around, pointed to a wisp of straw on the hearth, and snapped his fingers. The straw burst into flames. When he snapped his fingers again, it went quite stone-cold out. Pertyc felt like fainting dead away.

"I thought I'd shown you that trick. Now, my lord, I suggest we prepare for the siege."

At last Pertyc rediscovered how to talk.

"One last question. Have you seen Danry in your scrying?"

"Well, I have, my lord. It aches my heart to tell you this, but Danry's dead, and so is his elder son."

Pertyc wept, tossing his head to scatter the tears away.

"Ah, ye gods, I knew it would happen when he chose this rotten road, but it hurts, my lord. Was it in battle?"

"For his son, it was. But Danry . . . well, Leomyr and six men murdered him on the road. I think that Danry was trying to get free and warn you the rebels were coming, but of course, I can't know for certain."

"It would be like him, to think of me." He heard his voice shake and swallowed hard, then turned to face the great hall. "Men, listen! When the rebels start riding for the gates, Lord Leomyr of Dun Gwerbyn is mine. Do you hear me? No man is to send an arrow his way until I've had my chance at him. Now let's get to work. We've got to warn the villagers and farmers, and we need to start distributing the arrows to our stations on the walls."

The day passed in a confusion too frantic to leave Pertyc time to mourn, but late that evening he walked alone in the dark ward and thought of Danry. He would have given his right arm for a chance to kiss him farewell. His wife had always accused him of loving Danry as much as he loved her; it was true enough, he supposed, although he'd never loved Danry more, either, not that she'd believed him. Wrapped in the loss of both of them, he climbed up the hundred and fifty steps of the Cannobaen light, because the tower view could often soothe him. On the platform up top, the beacon keeper crouched beside the fire pit and fed split chunks of log into the leaping flames. At the far edge Halaberiel was leaning on the protective stone wall and surveying the dark swell of the ocean, spattered with silver drops of moonlight. Pertyc leaned next to him and watched the waves sliding in, touched with ghostly foam, so far below.

"Well, Perro, looks like you're ready for your uninvited guests."

"As ready as ever I can be. There's still time for you and your men to head home, you know."

"There's not enough time in a hundred years for that. I was thinking about your wedding, and . . ."

"You know, Hal, I don't really want to remember just how happy I was then."

"Fair enough. We should probably be thinking about our enemies instead. Nevyn says they're still a good bit away, camped by the road to the north."

"Well, I take it the old man knows what he's talking about."

"He's keeping a strict eye on them." Halaberiel turned slightly, and in the leaping light from the beacon fire behind them Pertyc could see that he was close to laughing. "Nevyn says to me, 'That bunch of bastards took me by surprise once, and I'll be twice cursed if they do it again!' The old man's a marvel, isn't he?"

"You could say that twice and only be half true."

Long before dawn, Pertyc got his men up and positioned them by the glow of the Cannobaen light. The line of archers sat on the catwalks, hidden behind grain sacks stuffed with wet beach sand for want of a proper rampart. When he gave the signal, they would stand up, ready to attack, and hopefully, surprise the enemy good and proper. Pertyc took the position directly over the gates, but although he kept his bow out of sight, he leaned on the wall as if he were waiting to parley. As they waited, no one spoke, not even the elves. Slowly to the east the sky lightened; slowly the beacon fire paled and died away. Up on the tower, the lightkeeper gave a shout.

"Dust on the road, my lord. It's coming fast."

In a moment or two, Pertyc heard horses trotting along, a lot of horses. Leomyr, insolently unhelmed, riding easy in his saddle, led his warband of eighty men off the coast road and toward the dun. When they stopped, some hundred yards away and just out of bowshot, Leomyr had the gall to wave, all friendly like, before he rode a little closer and yelled at the top of his lungs.

"Open your gates. Don't be a fool, Badger! This is your chance to be king of Eldidd."

"Eldidd already has a king. His name's Aeryc."

With a shrug, Leomyr turned in his saddle and began shouting orders to his men. By chance, most like, they kept out of range as part of the warband peeled off and ringed the dun round while the rest bunched behind Leomyr on the path up to the gates. Toward the rear of the line, men dismounted and hurried to a pair of pack mules. They brought down a ram—a rough-cut tree trunk tipped with iron, which Leomyr must have fetched from Dun Gwerbyn on his way. Obviously he'd never even considered that Pertyc would surrender. Eight men, dismounted but still in full armor, caught the handles of the ram and stood ready.

"One last chance," Leomyr called to Pertyc. "Surrender?"

"You can shove that ram where you'll enjoy it."

Leomyr shrugged, settled his pot helm, then turned to wave his men forward. Slowly the line advanced, the armed riders escorting the ram with Leomyr off to one side shouting orders. The men moved cautiously, slowly, since they and Leomyr expected that at any moment the gates would burst open for a sally out. Pertyc smiled, judging distance. As the riders came closer, they drew their swords, but they kept looking up at the walls, as if they were puzzled.

"Pertyc, curse you," Leomyr called out. "Won't you even parley?"

"Here's my parley."

Pertyc raised his bow, aimed, and loosed, all in one smooth motion. The arrow sang as it flew, striking Leomyr in the shoulder. Pertyc grabbed another, nocked it, loosed again, and saw Leomyr reel in the saddle as the arrow bit through his mail and sank into his chest. With a shout the other archers rose, nocked, and loosed in a slippery whisper of arrows. Pertyc heard Halaberiel laugh aloud as his shot knocked another man clean off his mount.

"Try to spare the horses!" the banadar yelled in Deverrian, then howled out the same order in Elvish.

In the boiling panic that erupted out on the field, Leomyr

tumbled over his horse's neck to the ground. Horses screamed and reared; men shrieked and fell and rushed this way and that. The men carrying the ram threw it to the ground and raced for the road, but only two of them made it. Pertyc was only aware of the dance of it: loose, pull an arrow, nock and loose again, leaning effortlessly, picking a target, bracing himself as the last of the enemy warband charged the gates, simply because they could think of nothing else to do. As the wave swept forward, Pertyc had the satisfaction of seeing Leomyr's body trampled by his own men. Halaberiel yelled in Elvish; his men swung round to aim directly into the charge. The arrows flew down; men and horses dropped and whinnied and swore and bled. Finally Pertyc could stand this slaughter of the helpless no longer. He lowered his bow and began screaming at the enemy.

"Retreat, you stupid bastards! You can't win! Retreat!"

And simply because he was noble-born and they were hysterical, they followed his orders and wheeled round to flee. With shouts and curses Halaberiel called off the archers and let them go, flogging a last bit of speed out of their sweating horses as they galloped for the road. Swearing, Pertyc realized that it was over. Nothing moved on the field but wounded horses, struggling to rise, then falling back.

"Open the gates, lads!" Pertyc yelled out. "Let's see what we can do for the poor bastards they've left behind."

His men cheered, laughing, slapping each other on the back. Pertyc fought to keep from weeping. He'd never expected his idea to work so well, and as he looked at the carnage below him, he suddenly understood why Eldidd men had ignored the existence of longbows for so many hundreds of years. With one last convulsive sob, he slung his bow over his back and climbed down the ladder to the cheering of his men.

Pertyc set some of the men to carrying what few wounded there were into the dun, then ordered others to start burying the dead and putting badly wounded horses out of their misery. He himself found Leomyr's mangled body and dragged it free of a tangle of dead animals. He laid Leomyr out flat, crossed his arms over his chest, then rose, staring down at the corpse.

"I hope you freeze in the hells tonight."

He kicked Leomyr hard in the side of the head, then went back inside the dun. Adraegyn came running and grabbed his hand.

"Can I come out now? This isn't fair, Da, shutting me up like one of the women!"

"Tell me somewhat, Draego. Do you want to be king of Eldidd?"

"I don't. I'd only be a usurper, not a king. Isn't that what you said, Da? You're always right, you know. Oh, this is splendid. Glae said you killed them all. Did you truly?"

"Most. Come along. There's a lesson my da taught me that it's time to teach you."

Pertyc led him to the area just beyond the gates where the warband was piling up the bodies of the dead. Pertyc held Adraegyn's hand tight and dragged him over to the heaped and contorted corpses. When Adraegyn tried to twist free and run, Pertyc grabbed him by the shoulders and forced him round to face the sight. The lad burst out weeping.

"This is what glory means, Draego," Pertyc said. "You've got to see it. Look at them."

Adraegyn was sobbing so hard that he could barely stand. Pertyc picked him up in his arms, carried him over to Leomyr, then set the weeping lad down.

"Do you remember Tieryn Dun Gwerbyn, Draego?" Pertyc said.

His face streaming with tears, Adraegyn nodded.

"I killed him," Pertyc went on. "I stood on our wall and hit him twice and knocked him off his horse. You know why? Because he killed Danry. That's what having a blood-sworn friend means, lad. Look at him. Someday you'll be Lord Cannobaen, and you'll have a friend you love the way I loved Danry."

Slowly, a sniffle at a time, Adraegyn stopped crying.

"What happened to his face?" the boy whispered.

"The horses kicked his body a lot."

Adraegyn turned away, pulled free of Pertyc's hand, and began to vomit. When he was finished, Pertyc knelt down beside him, pulled a handful of grass, and wiped the lad's mouth.

"Do you still think it's splendid?"

Adraegyn shook his head in a mute no.

"Well and good, then. Once, when I was your age, your gran did to me what I just did to you. It's part of what makes us Maelwaedds."

Carrying shovels, servants trotted past. Adraegyn turned his face away from the sight.

"You can sleep in my bed with me tonight," Pertyc said. "Doubtless you'll have bad dreams. I did."

That evening, Pertyc shut his gates again, posted guards, and called the rest of his men into the great hall. He ordered mead poured all round, then had the servants ceremoniously chop up the captured ram and feed it into the fire. The men cheered, calling out to him and laughing, pledging him with their goblets as the best captain they'd ever seen. Pertyc merely smiled and called back that they deserved all the glory. On the morrow he would make a grim speech, but for now he wanted them to taste their victory. The elves were another matter. Pertyc called them together out of the hearing of the rest of the men.

"You can leave tomorrow at dawn if you'd like, with as much booty as your horses can carry. There's no need for you to see the defeat. The rest of the rebels are on their way here as fast as they can ride, or so Nevyn tells me, and they've picked up some reinforcements."

"Well, Perro," Halaberiel said. "That's honorable of you and all, but we don't ride into a race only to ride out again at the first taste of dust."

"Are you certain? Look, you know enough about bowcraft to know that sixteen archers can't repel an army of three hundred."

"Not forever. But there'll only be a hundred and fifty left by the time we're done with them, if we have the least bit of luck."

"Bound to have luck," Calonderiel broke in. "The Wise One

of the West is here, and so's the Wise One of the East. Ye gods, if we've got so much evil luck coming our way that those two can't turn it aside, then we'll only fall off our horses on the journey home and break our necks."

Late that night, once the wounded men were tended and asleep, Nevyn climbed up to the top of the tower. Since the beacon keeper was used to his eccentric ways by then, he merely said a pleasant "Good evening" and returned to chopping some of the continual firewood for the light. Nevyn sat down comfortably with his back to the guard wall and studied the fire, a splendid, large luxury for scrying. In a few minutes, a portion of the Cannobaen blaze turned into a tiny campfire, and round it paced Gatryc and Ladoic, talking in hushed voices. Nevyn focused his will and brought himself closer to the vision, until he could see Gatryc's grayish face. Every time the gwerbret moved his arm, he winced and bit his lower lip. The wounds were infected, most like, Nevyn thought with a professional detachment. Nearby two of the men who'd ridden with Leomyr sat on the ground, slumped and exhausted. So the lords knew that Leomyr was dead and that if they wanted Adraegyn they'd have to come get him themselves.

Nevyn widened the vision until it seemed that he swooped over the countryside from a great height and found that the rebels were less than a day's ride, perhaps twelve miles, away. What counted more was the king's location. That search took a little longer, but eventually Nevyn spotted the royal army some fifty miles away, camped on the road just outside the western gate of Aberwyn. A flash of gloom cost him the vision. From what he understood of Halaberiel's talk, their small squad of archers would be unable to turn back the newly augmented rebel army before they managed to ram open the gates. The rebels were warned, now, that archers with elven longbows held the walls, and they wouldn't be stupid enough to come charging right in as Leomyr had. Well, if the king won't arrive in time, Nevyn told himself, we'll just have to slow the rebels up, then. The question is, how? He leaned back against the wall and considered the play of flames while he weighed possibilities.

All at once the wind gusted, and the lightkeeper swore and coughed, rubbing his eyes with the back of his hand.

"Cursed smoke!" he muttered.

Just in time Nevyn kept himself from laughing, because, of course, it wasn't the poor man's stinging eyes that were amusing him. He got up and bade the lightkeeper good night, wondering what the man would think if he knew his small misfortune might have just saved the entire dun. For this work, though, he would need privacy. He hunted up Aderyn, who took him to his chamber at the top of the broch.

"I'm not sure I can really pull this off," Nevyn said after he'd explained his plan. "According to the Bardek scrolls that I've been studying, it's theoretically possible, but theory's one thing and practice another."

"Well, if you can't, we'll try to think of somewhat else. Are you ready to go into trance? I've got the door barred."

"I am, at that. If I start flopping around, hold me down, will you? I do that sometimes in deep trance."

As soon as Nevyn assumed the body of light, he left the dun, hovered high above it for a moment to gather strength, then flew off to the rebel camp. By the time he reached it, most of the men were already asleep, but Gwerbret Gatryc was awake and sitting by his council fire with a handful of the noble-born and what few captains remained. What infuriated Nevyn was that they knew their cause was already lost. They were planning on making Aeryc pay high for his peace and naught more, just so they could die with what they called honor, no matter what the cost to the farmers and villagers of Eldidd.

After a few moments of rest, Nevyn floated close to the fire, which welled and purled with golden currents of pure etheric energy and thick blackish smoke, because the lords were burning damp and moldy wood culled from the forest floor. Nevyn prepared his mind in the way his theoretical scrolls recommended, called on the god-names they suggested for good measure, then slowly sucked up the energy, drew the fine particles of smoke to himself, and bound them round him by force of will. With one sharp thrust, he called on the Lords of Fire for aid. The smoke particles rushed and clung, caught in the stresses of his body of light the way iron filings arrange themselves around a lodestone. Gatryc yelped in terror and scrambled to his feet, his rotting arm dangling useless at his side. When the other lords all leapt up, too, cursing and staring, Nevyn could assume that yes, he was quite visible as a ghost-creature of smoke. Since he had no throat to speak with, he sent thoughts to their minds.

"Beware," Nevyn intoned. "Beware! Beware, O impious men! The gods have lost patience with your cause. Beware, lest you feast with me tomorrow in the Otherlands."

Nevyn could see their auras draw in sharply, a panic reaction as the fine forces rushed back to the body. In one convulsive step the pack of men fell back. Nevyn noticed that behind them, a couple of the riders had woken and sat up to stare.

"Who are you?" Gatryc stammered.

"I am the spirit of Aenycyr, last king of Eldidd. Be you mindful of my tragic tale?"

"We are."

"For this little while, the Lord of Hell has allowed me to walk upon the earth, that I may warn you men who love Eldidd so greatly." He hesitated, trying to remember more of the old saga that he was quoting. "Though your cause is just, your Wyrd is harsh. Not even the dead know when the time will come for Eldidd to rise again. Beware!"

The strain of keeping the smoke-built body was growing too great. Nevyn could feel his improvised form swirling and wavering over the fire. He decided that specifically warning them off Pertyc might be too blatant for an omen and allowed most of the form to drift back into smoke, but he did keep the face intact for a few moments longer.

"Even as I speak the Lord of Hell recalls me. Throw this folly aside, men of Eldidd, or on the morrow night you'll dine with me in the Otherlands."

As the last bit of smoke swirled away, Nevyn sent out an exhalation of pure panic. Just as the scrolls predicted, the men thought they heard an actual shriek, a grating, blood-freezing howl like a banshee's, as he raced through the camp in his body of light, thrusting that thought into the minds of the sleeping riders as well as those of the lords. The men threw off their blankets, stumbled to their feet, cursing, swearing, asking each other what that ungodly wail might have been.

The Wildfolk heard it, too. Radiating distress, which the more sensitive of the men dimly felt as their own, they materialized into physical form but clustered round Nevyn's body of light, which they of course could see, in an enormous pack. All at once, he got another inspired idea.

"See those men?" Nevyn thought to them. "They're very bad men. They want to kill Aderyn and Halaberiel."

If they could have screamed in rage, they would have as they swept off through the camp. They pinched and kicked and bit, hammering the men, grabbing the horses. In a yelling, neighing, swatting, kicking chaos, the camp erupted. At this point, Nevyn realized that he was dangerously exhausted. He rushed back along the silver cord to the dun and slipped into his body. As he woke to normal consciousness, he found that he was lying all in a heap in the curve of the wall. Panting for breath, Aderyn had his arms around him.

"By the gods!" Aderyn snarled. "If I'd known how strong you are in trance, I'd've got Maer up here to help hold you down."

"You have my sincerely humble apologies. Are you all right?"

"You gave me a clip on the jaw, but otherwise I am. How did it go?"

"Taking the smoke into the etheric mold worked splendidly. Humph, I certainly wish I'd known this trick during the civil wars! As for the results, well, let's take a look in the fire and see, shall we?"

But when they scried out the camp, they saw only trampled

blankets, scattered gear, broken tether ropes, and Gwerbret Gatryc, sitting alone at the fire and cradling his inflamed arm while he stared into the face of despair. If it weren't for the death he would have brought to the people of Eldidd, Nevyn might have found it in his heart to pity him.

In effect, the rebellion ended that night. Most of the common-born riders disappeared into the countryside, slinking back to their families and taking their old places on their father's farm or in his shop to wait and see just how lenient Aeryc was going to be. To protect their families, the remaining rebel lords and their last few loyal men surrendered to Aeryc, who pardoned the riders and hanged the lords. Gatryc committed suicide, but his infected wounds would have killed him in a few days anyway. While Aeryc rode at a leisurely pace to Cannobaen, all Eldidd waited and trembled. With their fathers slain, boys were the only lords the province had, but everyone knew that Aeryc would attaint the rebel duns and redistribute them to loyal men from Pyrdon and Deverry itself.

Pertyc wasn't in the least surprised when Halaberiel announced that he and his men would be leaving before the king arrived. There was no need, as the banadar remarked, to turn his highness's whole view of the world upside down over a petty little rebellion like this.

"But I thank you from the bottom of my heart for coming, my friend," Pertyc said. "And it gladdens my heart that none of your men were killed over this."

"Mine, too." But Halaberiel spoke absently. "And I'll be seeing the rivers of home soon enough."

"You must be glad of it."

"I suppose."

Pertyc hesitated on the edge of comment.

"I'm growing old." Halaberiel said it for him. "I think that somewhere deep in my heart I was hoping for a glorious death in battle, clean and sudden. And now it doesn't seem likely, does it? I see naught but peace ahead for my last few years. Ah well, what the gods pour, men must swallow, eh?"

"Just so. I understand."

"I thought you might. Well, if I see your wife, shall I give her any message from you?"

"That the children are well. That I wish she still loved me."

"She never stopped loving you, Perro. She just couldn't bear to live with you. It was the Round-ear ways, not you."

"Oh." Pertyc considered this revelation for a long moment. "Well, then, tell her that if she wants, she can come and take Beclya away with her. And as for me, say that I never stopped loving her, either."

Surrounded by an honor guard of a mere four hundred men, King Aeryc arrived at Cannobaen on a day that threatened rain but never actually delivered it. Although Pertyc suspected that Nevyn had something to do with the accommodating weather, he never had the nerve to ask the old man. Even though the king had left most of the army back in Aberwyn, there still, of course, was no room inside Dun Cannobaen's walls for those that he had brought; they made a camp in the meadow where the villagers grazed cattle in the summer while Aeryc, Gwenyn, and an escort of fifty rode on to meet Lord Pertyc at his gates. For the occasion Pertyc insisted that every member of his warband, all eleven of them, take a bath and put on clean clothes; he followed his own order, too, and went over protocol with Nevyn, who seemed to know an amazing amount about dealing with kings.

When Aeryc arrived, dismounting some feet away and striding up to the gates, Pertyc was ready. He and Adraegyn both bowed as low as they could manage; then they knelt, Pertyc on one knee, the boy on both.

"My liege, I'm honored beyond dreaming to welcome you to my humble dun."

"It is small, isn't it?" Aeryc looked around with a suppressed smile. "It won't do, Lord Pertyc."

"My apologies, then, from the bottom of my heart."

"No apologies needed. But I suggest that we repair as soon as possible to your other dun."

"My liege? I have no other dun."

"Indeed you do, Gwerbret Aberwyn."

Pertyc looked up speechless to find the king grinning.

"Pertyc, my friend, thanks to this rebellion there are exactly two men left on the Council of Electors for southern Eldidd: you and me. If I nominate you to head the gwerbretrhyn, and you second the motion, well, then, who's to say us nay?"

"My liege, my thanks, but I'm not worthy."

"Horseshit. Rise, Aberwyn, and stand me to some of your mead. His highness is as thirsty as a salt herring."

When, much later that day, Pertyc consulted with Nevyn, the old man told him that the king was invoking an ancient law. Any member of the Council of Electors who backed a rebellion against a lawful king did by holy charter forfeit his seat upon the council. Although Pertyc was frankly terrified by his sudden elevation, he knew in his heart that he'd regret it the rest of his life if he turned it down. Besides, he realized soon enough that as gwerbret he had considerable say in the disposition of the rebellion's aftermath. Since the king was minded to mercy—he was farsighted enough to be more interested in preventing future rebellions than in punishing the current one—he granted many of the petitions to mercy Pertyc was minded to make. Not all, of course—the families of the rebel gwerbrets would be stripped of lands and title both, as would Yvmur's clan and Cawaryn's clans, by birth and marriage both. His young widow, barely a wife, was allowed to live, but only as a priestess, a virtual prisoner in her temple.

But Danry's widow and his younger son stayed in possession of Cernmeton, as did Ladoic's of Siddclog, and so on among almost all the minor lords. Pertyc was finally able to repay Ganedd, too, when the young merchant came to him to beg mercy for his father. Dun Gwerbyn, however, was a different matter. When

Aeryc wished to dispose it upon a loyal though land-poor clan of western Deverry, the Red Lion, Pertyc had not the slightest objection to make.

And such are the twists of the human mind that from then on, the Red Lion clan felt nothing but friendship toward the Maelwaedds, while the Bears of Cernmeton, worn down by gratitude, came to hate them.

WHEN PERTYC, GWERBRET Aberwyn, and his family and retinue were ready to take up residence in their new city, the gwerbret insisted that Nevyn stay in Cannobaen as its virtual lord for as long as he liked. When the spring came, the place settled down rapidly into the drowsy routine of keeping the light burning and the lightkeeper's family fed. Nevyn poked around the broch and finally decided to use a chamber up on the top floor for his work. After he got it swept and cleaned, it was pleasantly sunny—when Cannobaen had sun, a rare thing in the summer—and its three windows gave him a dramatic view of the sea and the countryside. Once it was furnished with a long table, a set of bookshelves, a charcoal brazier, and a comfortable chair, he could pick up his interrupted work on the talisman again, though he did set mornings aside to tend the ills of the local folk. Every now and then a letter came from Aberwyn, either telling him what news there was or asking his advice on some small matter. Nevyn would answer promptly, then return to reveling in his solitude.

It was on a warm morning in late summer, just about the time of the last apple harvest, that Nevyn saw from his tower room a horseman riding toward Cannobaen. Thinking that it was the usual messenger from Pertyc, and that the servants would see to it that the man had a meal and a place to sleep, he went on studying some diagrams of sigils that he'd brought from Bardek. In a while, though, there was a cautious tap at the door. Swearing under his breath, he opened it to find Maer. His eyes were so weary, and his face so thin and pinched, that he seemed to have aged ten years. Nevyn was shocked to see the silver dagger back in his belt.

"If I'm disturbing you, my lord, I'll just ride on."

"What? Of course not! I take it you're not here as Pertyc's man."

"I'm not." He looked down at the floor and bit his lower lip as if he were fighting back tears.

"Well, let's go down to the great hall and have some ale, and you can tell me what's gone wrong."

"It's simple enough, my lord. Glae's dead."

Nevyn stared, gape-mouthed.

"Childbirth?" he said at last.

"Just that, and our son dead with her. The baby was just too big, the midwife said, and it was like the birthing beat them both to death." His face went dead white, and he trembled, remembering. "Ye gods, I had to get out of Aberwyn. His grace asked me to stay, but I just couldn't bear it. So I thought I'd come tell you the news and say farewell, and then it's back on the long road for me."

"My heart aches for you, and more for Glae." Nevyn felt a stab of guilt, a wondering if he could have saved her if only he'd been in Aberwyn, but at that time, he had none of the knowledge nor the surgical tools of a Bardek physician to cut open a womb and try, at least, to save the babe if not the mother. "But don't make some hasty move, lad."

"That's what Lord Pertyc said, too, but I know my own mind, my lord." He looked up with the faintest ghost of a smile. "But I'll take that ale, sure enough, if you wouldn't mind."

Over the ale Maer told Nevyn more details about Glae's death, but as he rehearsed what had been for everyone concerned a time of horror, his voice stayed cold and flat, his eyes fixed and distant. Only his bloodless face betrayed the effort it was costing him to stay calm. During the story the blue sprite appeared to sit beside him on the bench. She was frankly gleeful, clapping soundless hands and showing her mouthful of pointed teeth in a wild grin. Yet when at the end Maer glanced her way, she stopped grinning abruptly and arranged her face into a decent imitation of sadness.

"Does she understand what's happened, Nevyn?" Maer said.

"She doesn't, lad. She doesn't have a real mind, you know. So don't be harsh with her if she's glad her rival's gone."

"I was furious at first. But then I started thinking about some of the things you'd told me, and I figured well, she's like a clever dog, no doubt, and naught more."

"Brighter than that, because she can understand speech even if she can't use it. Have you ever seen a monkey or an ape?"

"A what, my lord?"

"Animals they have in Bardek. But if you haven't seen them, my comparison won't do you any good. Think of her as a little child, then."

By being persuasive enough for a Bardek politician Nevyn managed to get Maer to stay for three more days, but nothing he said would change the silver dagger's mind about leaving Pertyc's service. The gwerbret, it seemed, had told him that he could come back anytime; the most Maer would allow was that someday, if the long road got too cold and hungry, he might think about returning.

"If you live that long, I suppose," Nevyn remarked one night at dinner. "What are you planning on doing? Getting yourself killed in some battle straightaway?"

"I'm not, my lord. If it was suicide on my mind, I'd have drowned myself in Aberwyn Harbor, but I'm not the sort of man for that. It's just that, well, what else can I do to earn my dinner but fight?"

"Have you thought of riding west and finding the Westfolk? Calonderiel gave you an invitation, you know, when they were leaving."

"So he did. Do you think he meant it, my lord?"

"The Westfolk never say anything unless they mean it."

A flicker of life woke in Maer's eyes.

"Ganedd's going to be making one last trading trip west soon," Nevyn went on. "Why don't you go with him?"

"He's got his father's business now? I thought Ganno would go to sea for sure once he had the chance."

"Well, his father's a broken man, you see. He sits and stares all day at the ocean and naught more. So Moligga and the younger lad need Ganedd, and then there's Braedda." Abruptly Nevyn caught himself and shied away from the subject of happy marriages. "But you could stay in the Westlands for the rest of the summer, say. Then see how you feel in the autumn. My heart aches for you, but you know, Glae wouldn't have wanted you to throw your life away."

Maer started to speak, then wept like a child. Nevyn flung an arm around his shoulders and let him sob, so long and so hard that Nevyn realized he'd kept himself from weeping during all the long weeks since Glae's death.

In the normal course of things Nevyn's cure would have worked. Maer would have visited the elven lands, a world different enough to completely distract him, then most likely returned to Aberwyn with his mourning behind him. But Nevyn hadn't reckoned with the blue sprite, or, rather, with Elessario.

In the endlessly shifting land of the Guardians, the seeming of only a few hours had passed since Dallandra left them to return to Aderyn. When she saw her friend walk down the road toward home, Elessario rushed blindly away. Her feeling of pain was too ill defined to be called grief, but it was bitter enough to make her throw herself down in the grass and weep. At about the time Dallandra was giving birth to Loddlaen, she stopped weeping, the pain forgotten as fast as it had come, and went in search of company. When Dallandra was returning, Elessario was far away, sitting by the soul of a river and watching her friends dance. It was there that the blue sprite found her, at roughly the same time as

Maer and Ganedd were joining the fall alardan out in the Westlands.

Although Elessario had forgotten her grief already, she did remember Dallandra and all the things they'd discussed. One of those discussions involved compassion and the helping of others for no reason beyond their hurting. Somewhere in her growing core of mind, Elessario wanted to please Dallandra so badly that she was willing to follow her teachings, even though, unfortunately, she remembered them by rote rather than understanding their basic principles. When she saw the sprite's honest pain, and once she understood what caused it, she decided to help the poor little thing to the best of her abilities in the hopes that Dallandra would be proud of her. Child though she was, Elessario's abilities were considerable.

When the fall alardan was preparing to disperse, and Ganedd was talking of riding back home with his newly acquired horses, Maer was faced with the choice of going with him or of riding with Aderyn and his alar down to the winter camps. He was still so grief-struck and lonely that the choice was a hard one simply because making any decision was hard. Every day he woke to the irony, still fresh and ghastly after all this time, that he'd never realized how much he loved Glae until he lost her. If you could go back, he would think, just for one day, just one rotten day, and live it over, knowing what you know now . . . ! Then he would shake his head hard, as if he could physically throw off his Wyrd, and get up to face another morning. A further irony vexed him, too. Now, when he would have been grateful for a little company, the blue sprite seemed to have deserted him. In all his long weeks in the elven lands, he never saw her once.

Finally, though, the morning came when the Westfolk were striking their tents, and Ganedd's men were linking the horses on lead ropes. Maer walked through the falling camp with Calonderiel and tried to make up his mind. South with the Westfolk or east with Ganedd?

"Tell me," Calonderiel remarked. "If you do go back with Ganno, what'll you do then?"

After six weeks among friends, the idea of riding the long road again looked less appealing than it had in the heart of his mourning.

"Ah well, go back to Aberwyn and tell Gwerbret Pertyc he was right after all."

"And then sit around in his stone tent all winter long?"

"I catch your drift, all right. Well and good, then. I'll stay with you, if you'll have me."

"Naught I'd like more."

At that time Aderyn's alar consisted of himself and his son, the banadar, his warband of twenty and their families and tents, and a dozen other families as well, all of them, of course, owning flocks and herds. With so large a group they needed a winter campground to themselves and finally found one in a deep canyon about two miles from the sea. As usual, they set up the tents along the riverbank, but the herds would graze at the canyon's rim. Since Calonderiel's current woman friend rode off in a huff soon after they arrived (his women tended to come and go as frequently and as fast as the Wildfolk), Maer moved into his tent with him. Maer insisted on taking his turn at riding herd; he may have been a guest, but he disliked eating someone's food and doing nothing in return. When he wasn't on watch, and on the increasingly infrequent sunny days, he would often go riding, climbing out of the canyon, then letting his horse amble across the grasslands for aimless hours.

It was on one of these solitary rides that he saw the sprite again, not that he recognized her at first. On a sunny morning he came to clump of hazels standing where three streams joined to make a proper river. Since his horse was thirsty, he dismounted, slacked its bit, and let it drink while he looked idly around. Sitting among the trees was an elven woman, dressed in a long tunic, or so he thought at first.

"Greetings." He trotted out one of his few Elvish words, then switched to Deverrian. "Am I disturbing you?"

With a shake of her head and a toss of waist-length blue hair, she stood up and took a few steps toward him. Her skin was a deadly sort of pale, but otherwise she was very beautiful, with enormous blue eyes and a full, soft mouth. When she smiled, her teeth seemed on the sharp side, but they were white and no longer pointed. He was intrigued enough to drop the horse's reins and go to meet her. Close up, she smelled of roses.

"Maer?" she said.

"How do you know my name?"

"I've known you for ever so long. *She* said you wouldn't recognize me, though. I guess you don't."

"I don't, truly. She? Who's she?"

"Just she. A goddess." She paused for a slow seductive smile. "I can say words now. I love you, Maer."

It was her remark about the words that made him recognize his blue sprite, somehow transformed. With a little yelp he stepped back.

"What's wrong? I'm a real woman now."

"Not by half you are!"

Her eyes flooded tears. Maer turned and ran for his horse, but as he was mounting, he could hear her sobbing. He was just frightened enough to keep riding, but her tears echoed in his memory and hurt. He knew what it was like to lose a beloved, didn't he? The poor little thing, he would think. Trying to turn herself into a woman to please me! It was grotesque, really, and embarrassing as well as frightening—or so he saw it. As he did some hard thinking on the ride home, he decided that this mysterious "she" couldn't possibly be a real goddess. Most likely she was just another member of the Wildfolk, unless she was something far worse. Like everyone else he knew, Maer believed in all kinds of spirits and ghosts, off in the Otherlands somewhere, who could at certain ill-omened times come through to his world. Meeting one was geis, and bad luck, and so many other awful things that he refused to tell anyone about his experience out of the real and honest fear that everyone would shun him from then on.

That night he fell into an uneasy sleep and immediately dreamt of her. In the dream, it seemed that he was lying, wide awake but unable to move, in his usual blankets in Calonderiel's tent. She materialized through its side, scorning the tent flap, and sat down to stare at him, merely stare in a teary-eyed reproach until he could no longer stand the silence.

"I'm sorry I made you cry."

"Please come talk to me, Maer. That's all. Please come back and talk to me."

"Do you live in those hazels?"

"I live in *her* country. I visit the hazels. And I can visit the camp, but not when the mean old man's around."

"Who?"

"The owl."

Maer supposed that Aderyn did rather look like an owl, now that he thought of it. Automatically he went to sit up, only to find himself awake in a dark tent with Calonderiel snoring over on the other side. A dream, was it? But a cursed real one! When he fell asleep again, he had only his usual dreams of Glae.

What with the continual wash of quick autumn storms and his herding duties, it was some weeks before Maer saw Little Blue-hair again. She'd been on his mind, though, out of simple guilt. He felt like a man who's come home late at night without bothering to light a lantern and in his blind progress through the house manages to trip over and injure his faithful dog. Finally, on a sunny morning between two storms he rode out looking for her. When he found no trace of her in the hazel thickets, he rode upstream a ways through grass so tall and wet that it clung to his horse's legs as they rode through. Still no sign of her. With an anxious eye for the dark clouds building and piling to the south, Maer considered turning back, but up ahead was another thicket. Sure enough, when he rode up, he saw her, standing between two trees and smiling, so brilliantly happy to see him that it ached his heart.

"You did come. Finally."

"Well, the weather's not been the best, you know."

Maer slacked his horse's bit and as an afterthought unsaddled him to let him roll and rest. Leaving the animal peacefully grazing, he walked into the thicket. She sat down on the ground, gracefully spreading what seemed to be a long blue skirt out around her like a gracious lady. Automatically Maer sat, too, facing her.

"Now, I can't stay long."

"Why not?"

"Because it's growing late, and there's a storm coming. I don't want to get soaked, and I don't want to stay out in the cold all night, either."

"Oh." She tilted her head to one side and considered. "I can understand that."

"Good. Now look, little one. We've got to talk about somewhat that you're not going to like. You've got to find yourself a man from your own people and leave me alone."

"Won't!" Her eyes flashed in rage. "They're all ugly and warty."

Maer had to admit that the gnomes he'd seen—and they were the only ones who seemed to be male—weren't the handsomest lot around.

"That's too bad, truly, but it's the way these things go. You know, I don't think you should be listening to this 'she' you keep talking about. I think me she's leading you down the wrong paths."

"Not!"

"Oh, indeed? Then why is she messing about with the way you look? I'll wager Nevyn and Aderyn wouldn't be very pleased to hear about this."

"Don't tell them, Maer! Oh, please, don't!"

She threw herself forward, so that she was crouching in front of him like a suppliant, and looked up teary-eyed. When she clasped his hand in both of hers, her flesh felt as cool and soft as silk from Bardek. Since he couldn't manage to think of her as truly real, it was impossible for him to realize that she was dangerous. He smiled and patted her on the cheek.

"I won't, then. But I still don't like this so-called friend of yours. I doubt me if she's a goddess. I'll wager she's some spirit or ghost, and she shouldn't be leaving the Otherlands to mess about here."

"Not a ghost. Not the Otherlands." Her hands tightened on his as she stared up into his eyes so sadly, so wistfully, that his heart went out to her. "Would you kiss me, Maer? Just one little kiss?"

With a smile he bent his head and gave her a brotherly brush of the mouth across her lips. When he raised his head again, the hazels were gone. All around them in a glowy purple twilight stretched a meadow filled with summer roses, blooming in a drunken exhalation of scent. Maer shoved her away and lurched to his feet with a yelp. She laughed, rising, dancing around him in a swirl of skirt.

"You're mine now, and we'll be ever so happy."

"Here, now! You take me back!"

"In a little while." She stopped, smiling at him so winsomely that he would have been suspicious if only he hadn't been frightened out of his wits. "Of course we'll go back. In just a little tiny while."

Since Maer doubted that she was capable of an outright lie, he was reassured enough to look round him. Some quarter of a mile away stood what seemed to be a dun far more elaborate than the palace of Aberwyn, maybe twenty fine towers, all joined together in a pattern that he couldn't decipher and rising out of mist.

"Let's go see her, and then you can go home," the sprite said. "Please? Just for a little while?"

Maer let her take his hand and lead him toward the many-towered dun as the twilight turned all blue and silver. As they walked on, he could see it ever more clearly; a square sort of building, unlike any he'd ever seen, supported the towers, and a square wall, turreted at the corners, surrounded it, made of many kinds of stone, pink sandstone, gray limestone, the occasional decorative touch of green marble. He could see the windows turning golden with candlelight and hear music playing of such a sweetness that he felt he could weep. But at the same time, the castle seemed to stop drawing nearer. Each step he took was like raising a foot made of lead; his legs turned numb, too, and he felt that he could barely breathe. The light began to fade in the windows ahead, although he was suddenly aware of another light, all golden and blinding, opening like a tunnel before him.

The last thing he heard before his etheric double broke up completely was the sprite, shrieking in agony.

Maer fell into trance just after noon, not long before the storm broke with all the fury of the first full tempest of winter. Lightning stroked down; thunder rumbled; his horse panicked and fled out across the grasslands. Unfortunately, since it was the horse he'd brought from Aberwyn, it couldn't find its way home to the herds round the winter camp. (In time, it did wander into the herd of another alar, far to the west, but that was months later and an event of no importance at all.) All afternoon it rained as the storm proceeded slowly and majestically north, but Maer, entranced in the true and technical sense of the word, lay sprawled among the hazels. By sunset, the river was brimming in its banks, and still the rain poured down. Maer's body, in a convulsion of cramped muscles that had nothing to do with mind, flopped over onto its back, then lay still. All evening clouds rolled in from the sea, rained, and moved on north. The river rose steadily, then round midnight spilled over and flooded, sending a first a thin sheet of water trickling through the grass and swirling round the knobby roots of the trees, then a pour, a spill of water traveling out and out and swelling as it ran. It covered Maer's face some three hours before dawn and kept rising, but the rain stopped before the flood was deep enough to float his corpse more than a few feet away, where it fetched up against a tree and stuck.

Under normal circumstances, Calonderiel would have re-
cruited the entire warband and gone to search for his guest when
Maer didn't return for the evening meal, but the floods were rising
along the river that flowed by the camp, too. As soon as the
swirling brown water started churning downstream, Aderyn and
Halaberiel ordered the alar to begin packing. In an organized
frenzy the People rushed round, stuffing tent bags, loading the
travois, collaring dogs and children. By the time the water came
within a few inches of the riverbanks, just at sunset, everyone's
portable goods had been hauled up to the canyon rim. Halaberiel
and Aderyn walked along by the surging water and studied it in
the last light fading from the clouds. Twisting and bobbing like
some many-armed animal, an entire gnarled tree raced past.

"It's going to keep rising," Aderyn remarked. "I don't need
dweomer to tell me that."

"Just so, Wise One. Very well. Let's give the order to strike the
tents."

As they turned to head back to camp, they heard a woman
shriek, a howl of terror and agony. A chorus of voices cut through
the pound of rain: "He's gone in!" Cursing under his breath,
Halaberiel dashed to the river's edge. Aderyn could just barely see
a small blond head bobbing toward them some five feet from
shore. Howling and keening, the child's mother tried to throw
herself into the river after the boy. Her man grabbed her and held
her back just as the banadar dove, as smoothly as a seabird, into the
torrents. Aderyn heard himself yell aloud, invoking the Lords of
Water, as he ran downstream. At first he could see nothing but the
surging brown and silver race; then two heads popped up, a small
blond and a larger gray one.

"Hal! I'm keeping pace with you! Oh Lords of Water, help me
now if ever I've aided you!"

With one arm crooked round the boy's neck Halaberiel was
struggling to swim with the other even as the raging current swept
them both inexorably out to the estuary and the pounding, foaming sea. Although Aderyn never actually saw the Lords of the
Elements, they must have appeared in answer to his cry, because

Hal never would have been able to reach shore without some supernormal aid. As it was, he managed to struggle to within a bare foot of the muddy bank and thrust the boy into Aderyn's grasping hands. Then the current grabbed him in turn and swept him on, swept him under in the churn and mill of white water pouring down to the waiting sea waves. Aderyn clasped the shrieking child in his arms and wept until the others caught up to him. Sobbing hysterically, the mother snatched the child from him as if he'd been the one who nearly drowned it.

"The banadar!" Calonderiel came running. "Hal! Hal!"

"He's gone." Aderyn caught his arm. "You're the warleader for this alar now."

Calonderiel threw his head back and screamed his grief into the howling wind. Aderyn grabbed him by the shoulders and shook him.

"The tents! You've got to order the alar to strike the tents!"

With one last convulsive sob Calonderiel pulled himself together. As he ran off, he was shouting orders in a voice of command.

It was close to dawn, and the rain was slacking to a drizzle, before anyone said, "By the way, where's Maer?" With a lot of snapping and cursing the warband rushed around through the sopping, improvised camp. Just as the gray and sullen dawn was breaking they returned with the news that Maer and his horse both were missing. Aderyn felt an icy finger of dread run down his back.

"He must have been caught in the storm," Calonderiel said. "And these wretched Round-ears don't know how to take care of themselves in open country. We'll have to start searching for him right now."

"If you'll wait for five ticks of a heart together," Aderyn said with some asperity, "I'll scry for him and make your task a good bit easier."

Since fires were out of the question, he used water for a scrying focus, appropriately enough, and saw Maer's heaped and tumbled body against a hazel. With a high-pitched keen he broke the vision.

"Dead?" Calonderiel said.

"Drowned. But I don't understand why. I found him in the midst of trees. Why didn't he climb one? Ye gods, the water's only a foot or so high around him."

At the head of a grim procession Aderyn led them to Maer's body. Calonderiel was as overwhelmed as he'd been by losing the banadar, but in this case, it was guilt as much as grief that was ripping at his heart. Maer was his guest-friend, and he'd failed him —that's how Cal saw it, no matter who tried to argue otherwise. While Calonderiel wept and stormed, and Albaral wrapped Maer in a blanket with the ritual prayers, Aderyn left the hazel thicket and walked a few feet downstream to the place where three streams joined for the river. Three streams. The hazels. Aderyn swore under his breath.

"Evandar!" he yelled. "Evandar, can you hear me!"

No one answered, no one came. Only the wind blew over the rain-soaked grass in its endless sigh.

It was some days before Aderyn discovered what had really killed Maer. He scried by every method he knew, consulted Nevyn and learned two new ones, invoked the Kings of the Elements and the Lords of the Wildlands both, assumed his body of light and journeyed long and hard through not only the etheric but various portions of the astral plane as well until, a few scraps of information at a time, he pieced together the story of the transformed sprite's unwitting murder of the only thing she loved. Eventually, many weeks later, he found and confronted her among the hazel thicket by the joining of three streams.

He went there on an impulse so strong that he knew someone was sending him a message, whether the Lords of the Wildlands or the King of Water he wasn't sure, but either way, he wasn't disposed to ignore it. As he rode up, he saw her pacing back and forth by the stream, head down as if hunting for something. To avoid frightening her, he dismounted and walked the rest of the way.

When she saw him, she snarled and swiped at him with one hand, curled into claws like a cat's.

"I didn't take Maer away."

"You did! I saw you take him. You came with some of the elder brothers, and they wrapped him a blanket, and you all took him away."

"His soul was already gone by then. He was dead. Do you know what dead means?"

She merely stared, then wept in a numb scatter of tears.

"Give him back."

"There's nothing to give back."

"Yes, there is! You took him away. Where did you put him?"

Aderyn debated, then decided that he was desperate enough to bargain.

"I'll show you his grave if you answer me three questions."

"His what?"

"The place where we put his body. I warn you, though, that he can't speak or move anymore."

"I want to see him."

"Then answer me the questions. First, who taught you how to speak?"

"She did. The goddess who helped me."

"What did this goddess look like?"

"All sorts of things. She comes and goes and changes like I do."

"Does she have a name?"

"A what?"

"A name. Like Maer. A word that belongs only to her."

"Oh." For a long moment she wrinkled her nose in thought. "Elessario. That's her special word. Now show Maer to me. You promised, and I've answered all three."

"So you have. Follow me, but I warn you, he's all different now."

With a rustle like grass in the wind she vanished, but her voice lingered briefly.

"Ride, and I'll follow."

As he rode back to the pretty spot in the canyon where they'd buried Maer (since Calonderiel had decided that his guest would have preferred the burial of his own people rather than a burning), Aderyn was considering strategies. Although he was afraid to openly contact the Lords of the Wildlands, apparently they'd been keeping an eye on him, because when he reached the grave, they were there, tall slender pillars of silver light, barely visible as a shimmering in the air. He felt rather than heard their thanks, knew wordlessly that they'd come to claim the sprite as one of their own so that they could heal her.

But she never came. All that day Aderyn and the lords waited, and all evening, too, until the last quarter moon rose to announce that it was midnight.

"She's been too clever for us," Aderyn remarked in thought. "I think she knows you'll take her away."

He could feel them agree in an exhalation of worry. One by one they winked out, like stars disappearing in the light of dawn, leaving Aderyn with the feeling that he wasn't to trouble himself with the sprite any longer, that they would, one way or another, find a way to deal with her.

Maer, however, or, rather, the soul of the man who'd once been Maer, was another matter altogether. Nevyn agreed that his Wyrd might well have become tangled with things that were, at root, no affair of his. After all, the sprite had found him once before when he'd died and been reborn; now she had even more reason to search for him, her lost beloved.

"I take the responsibility onto myself," Nevyn said through the fire. "Because of Maddyn. I never should have let him make a link with the Wildlands."

"Oh, come now, you had no way of knowing where it would lead."

"True. But still, I might have done some meditating. I might have gotten an inkling of what would happen, or at least that it was a wrong thing."

"It might not have been a wrong thing if it weren't for the Guardians. Let's not forget that one of them's been meddling in this mess. And that, somehow, is partly my fault. I shouldn't have left them to Dallandra. I should have tried to know them myself, and maybe then—"

"All these maybes ill become us, my friend. What is, is, and we're not the men to unweave Time and pluck this strand out again."

"I know. Well, I suspect that when he's reborn, Maer will come my way again. We'll see what we can do for him then."

It was a long time before Aderyn met that soul again, though, some three twenties of years, and even then it was only by chance. Late one summer, when the days were already growing short and the trees on the tops of hills and in other exposed places were turning yellow, his alar was traveling up in the northern plains, not far from the Deverry province of Pyrdon. One of their horses, a young stallion, got it into his head to break his tether and run off, following his natural instincts to get away from the reigning stud of the herd. A couple of the men went after him, of course, and out of a sentimental desire to see his own people again Aderyn left Loddlaen in charge of their tent and herds and rode off with Calonderiel and Albaral. The stallion's tracks were easy to follow; in fact, in a few miles the tracks of another horse, one carrying some kind of load, joined them, and the two sets marched east in such a straight line that it was obvious that the stallion had either been stolen outright or picked up by a mounted rider while wandering loose. Since the second horse was shod, it was easy enough to guess that the rider was a human being.

Sure enough, the trail led them straight to the town of Drwloc, where it joined a welter of other tracks and petered out, but by asking around they discovered that one of Lord Gorddyn's men had found a Westfolk horse and brought it in to the dun. Calonderiel was furious, swearing to slit the fellow's throat for a stinking horse thief, but Aderyn ordered him to hold his tongue.

"We could at least go ask the lord about the matter first,

couldn't we? If you'd only traded the stallion off to a herd that needed a stud, he never would have broken tether."

"Well, you've got a point, I suppose. But this wretched rider could have come looking for the horse's owner."

"Would you have ridden alone into a Round-ear camp?"

Calonderiel started to snarl an answer, then stopped to think. "A second point, truly. Let's go talk to Lord Gorddyn."

The lord's dun was about three miles out of town, a solitary broch behind earthwork walls set up on a small hill. As they rode up to the gap in the earthen mounds that did duty as a gate, they saw a strange woman—or at least she seemed to be a woman at first—lounging on the grassy wall. She was slender and pale, dressed in a dirty, torn smock, but as they came closer, they saw that her long unbound hair was a deep blue, the color of the winter ocean. At the sight of Aderyn and the elves she leapt to her feet, then suddenly vanished clean away.

"What?" Calonderiel hissed. "What was that? One of the Wildfolk? It looked so cursed human!"

"So she did, indeed." Aderyn felt a premonition of trouble coming. "Cal, I have the wretched feeling I've seen her before. This might not be a pretty thing we've stumbled onto."

Lord Gorddyn turned out to be stout, balding, and good-humored, greeting them with no more fuss and as much friendliness as if they'd all been human beings. He insisted that they sit at his beat-up table of honor by the smoky hearth and drink mead out of dented silver goblets, then listened to their story of the lost horse.

"Well, he's here, sure enough, lads. A beautiful animal, beautiful. What do you say I trade for him? Under Deverry laws he's mine, because my man found him wandering loose, but under Westfolk laws he's yours, so let's not have a fight over it, eh? I've got two fine dun mares out in my stable, and you shall have both if you want."

Faced with this utterly unexpected fairness, Calonderiel could do nothing but agree to look them over, and everyone trooped out to the stables. The mares were indeed fine breeding stock, young, healthy, and handsome.

"Done, then, my lord," Calonderiel said. "I'll take them gladly in trade for the stud for the sake of peace between our two peoples."

"Splendid, splendid! That gladdens my heart, good sir. Here, lad!" This to a stable boy, who was hanging round to stare goggle-eyed at the elves. "Get those mares on lead ropes and bring them out to the courtyard."

As they were leaving the stables, Aderyn noticed a young man lying on the straw in an empty stall. Even though the day was warm, he was wrapped in a blanket, and his face was a deathly sort of pale.

"My lord?" Aderyn said. "What's wrong with that fellow?"

"He's dreadfully ill, I'm afraid, and it aches my heart, because he's one of my sworn riders and a good man, too. Our local herbwoman has him lie out here during the day, you see. She says he'll soak up the vitality from the horses, and it'll help him."

Superstitious nonsense, that, but Aderyn refrained from saying so outright.

"I happen to be a herbman, my lord. Would you like me to have a look at him? Maybe I'll see somewhat she missed, like."

"Gladly, good sir, gladly. His name's Meddry. I'll just take our other guests on into the great hall."

For all that Lord Gorddyn called him a man, Meddry was really little more than a boy, about fifteen and most likely brand-new to the warband. He was far too thin and hollow-eyed, with his pale blond hair sticking with sweat in wisps to his pinched face. When Aderyn knelt down beside him, Meddry propped himself up on one elbow, tried to speak, then began to cough, the most horrible hacking deep cough Aderyn had ever heard a man give. He threw one arm around Meddry's shoulders and supported him until at last he spat up—not rheum, but blood, bright red and clotted. Aderyn grabbed a twist of clean hay and wiped his mouth for him.

"Dying, aren't I?" Meddry whispered.

"Not just yet, and maybe not at all." Aderyn came as close to an outright lie as he could get. "We'll see what we can do for you, lad."

"I can spot false cheer by now, herbman." With a sigh he flopped back down into the warm straw.

Mostly to check how much vitality his newfound patient had left, Aderyn stared into his eyes, then nearly swore aloud as he recognized the soul who in his last life had carried the name of Maer. At that point he remembered the strange womanlike sprite he'd seen hanging round Lord Gorddyn's gates, and his blood ran as cold as the sick boy's.

"You've got a strange sort of lover, don't you, Meddry?"

His face turned first so white, then so fiery with shame that Aderyn knew that his loose arrow had hit the mark.

"You've got to leave her alone. She's what's killing you. Hush! Don't try to argue with me. Just listen. She's so desperate to please you that she wants to look like a real woman. She's doing it by feeding off your life. I can't explain any better than that, but it's making you ill."

In a stubborn burst of energy he shook his head no.

"We'll talk more later. You rest here for now, and I'll send one of your friends to you."

Aderyn hurried into the great hall, where Calonderiel and the other elves were just finishing up their mead and preparing to leave. He took Lord Gorddyn to one side for a hurried talk.

"My lord, your rider's close to death."

Gorddyn swore and stared down at the floor.

"I might—just barely might, mind—be able to help him. Tell me, how long has he been ill?"

"Well, he didn't come down with the actual fever until the spring, and he's only been spitting up the blood for the last few weeks, but truly, he started acting strange months ago. Last winter, it was, just after Samaen."

"Acting strange? How?"

"Oh, keeping to himself a fair bit, when he was always the soul of good company before. He used to go for long rides out in the snow, and I think me that's when his humors started to wither, out in the cold and wind and all. That's what the herbwoman in town calls it, withering humors. And every now and then one of the other lads would find him talking to himself. Just talking to the empty air as if there was someone there."

Aderyn felt the savage sort of annoyance that comes from seeing your worst fear confirmed.

"Well, my lord, I ride with the Westfolk these days, but our camp is only a couple of days from here. I need to ride back and fetch my medicinals and suchlike, but I'll be back as soon as ever I can. Now, listen carefully. I know what I'm going to say will sound strange, but please, my lord, if you value your man's life, do as I say. While I'm gone, set a guard over Meddry. Never let him be alone for a minute. He's more than ill; he's being troubled by an evil spirit, but one of the lesser sorts that walk abroad on Samaen. She must have fastened herself onto him then. It's the spirit that's drying up his humors. If there's people around him—or so I hope, anyway—the spirit will be puzzled at first and leave him alone for a few days."

Lord Gorddyn's eyes went as a wide as a child's, but he nodded a stunned agreement. Out in these isolated settlements, people took talk of spirits seriously.

When they left, they rode out fast, and Aderyn pushed everyone along as they traveled back to the camp. There he loaded up his medicinals, took a couple of fresh riding horses, and rushed back again. Although Aderyn wanted Loddlaen to come with him to study this interesting medical case, the boy—well, a young man by then, really—insisted on staying home, and as usual, Aderyn refused to cross his will. Aderyn was, of course, as worried about the spirit as he was about Meddry, no matter what he'd said to Lord Gorddyn. As he rode, he was planning how to approach her, and how he'd invoke the Lords of the Wildlands to help him catch her, but in the end, and for all his speed, he was too late. He rode up to Lord Gorddyn's gates just in time for Meddry's burying, out in the sacred grove of oaks behind the dun.

"Ah, ye gods, what happened?" Aderyn burst out. "I truly thought he had a couple of weeks left, my lord."

"Good herbman, I've failed him badly, I'm afraid. Here, after this sad thing, we'll talk. Go on into the dun and have the stable lads take your horses and suchlike."

Later that afternoon, over mead Lord Gorddyn told Aderyn the tale. After the dweomermaster left them, they'd followed his orders exactly. The men in the warband took turns sitting with the lad and making sure that he was never alone for a minute during the day. At night they carried him to his bed in the barracks, where he slept surrounded by other men. Since he was so deathly ill no one even considered the possibility that he might get up and slip out on his own.

"But that's just what he did, good sir." Lord Gorddyn looked sick to his stomach. "Two nights ago, it was. All that day he'd been begging the men to go away, and he was raving, too, saying 'I've got to see her' over and over. They thought maybe he meant his mother, but she's been dead these two years." Suddenly he shuddered. "Maybe he did mean his mam, because truly, he's seeing her in the Otherlands tonight, isn't he? But anyway, they wouldn't leave him. So when night came, they put him to bed in his bunk and brought him some broth and suchlike, but still they didn't leave him alone. They took turns, like, eating dinner in the great hall so he always had company. Sometime in the dead of night, when everyone was sound out, he must have escaped. It's cold these fall nights, Aderyn. Winter's coming early this year, I swear it, to judge from the frosts we've been having. But be that as it may, Meddry got the strength from some god or other to get out of the barracks and walk all the way out of the dun. He didn't get much farther, though. We found him not more than a quarter mile from here, up in the birch groves."

"He was dead, I take it."

"Just that. He had one of his coughing fits and bled to death." Lord Gorddyn's pudgy face turned a sudden pale. "But here's the cursed strange thing. He was lying on his back with his hands crossed over his chest. Someone had laid him out, like, for burying.

And me and my men asked around in town and in all the farms, and we never found anyone who'd even seen him that night, much less anyone who'd admit to doing such a thing, and frankly, I know my folk, and none of them would have done it without fetching me first."

Although Lord Gorddyn wanted Aderyn to take his hospitality for the night, he made a raft of polite excuses and left well before the dinner hour. A farmer he met on the road told him exactly where young Meddry's body had been found. On the far side of a meadow from the dun stood a copse of pale birches, standing silently now in the chill of an autumn afternoon as if they mourned the boy who'd died there. Since there was a nearby stream to water his horses, Aderyn made camp in the copse. He had a light meal, then drew a magic circle round the camp, sealed it with the pentagrams, and waited.

She came with the moonrise, an hour or so after sunset that night, came walking up to the trees just like a human woman, but her long blue hair waved and drifted around her face as if it blew in some private wind, and she was barefoot, too, in the rimy frost. Unlike a human woman, she could see the magic sphere glowing golden over the camp. She greeted it with a howl of rage that sounded more like a wolf than a human. Slowly and carefully, so as not to frighten her, Aderyn walked to the edge of the circle and erased a portion to welcome her in. She refused to come any closer, merely balled her fists and made a show of threatening him.

"Where is he?" she snarled.

"The boy you love? He's dead, child."

She stared with mindless blue eyes.

"You killed him, child. I know you didn't mean to hurt him, and indeed, you need my help, too. Come now, let's talk."

Again she stared, her mouth slack.

"He's gone away." Aderyn tried to make her see. "Gone far, far away under the ground. He did that once before, remember? When you tried to take him to see Elessario."

Her howl took him by surprise, because it was such a human

sound, that time, as if all the grief and pain and mourning of the world were tearing her heart.

"I'm sorry. Please, child, come in and sit by my fire. Let me help you."

She howled again, then vanished, leaving him to curse himself for a clumsy fool that he should let her escape so easily. Never had he expected her to love her victim so deeply and so well that she would react with true grief. He camped there in the copse for a fortnight, and every night he went searching the etheric plane for her, and during the day he meditated upon the matter and discussed it with the Lords of the Wildlands, but never did he or they find her again. (He did find out, though, that it was the lords who'd laid the poor lad out properly, as a small token of their desire to make amends.) Finally he was forced to admit defeat and leave to rejoin the People out in the grasslands, because winter was coming on, driving them down to the south coast. He reproached himself with his failure for years.

And for years the folk around Drwloc heard a banshee, or so they called it, wailing in the lonely places whenever the moon was at her full. At length she came less often, and finally, after a long, long time, she vanished, never to be heard again.

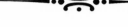

Epilogue

The Elven Border

Summer 1096

F OR SIX NIGHTS the alar camped near the ruined dun and waited for news of Rhodry's father. Because of the stock, they did have to move on the seventh day, heading north a day's ride to fresh pasture. After two days there, though, the alar split up for Rhodry's sake. Calonderiel and his warband, with their women and children, along with Aderyn's magical company and of course Rhodry himself, drove off a herd of extra horses to leave the best grazing for the sheep. They made camp back on the Eldidd border and set a guard every night to keep watch for any hated Round-ears. Every day the dweomermasters would scry for Devaberiel; they always found him easily enough, but he always seemed to be traveling idly north, unaware that his long-lost son was waiting for him on the border.

During all this time Rhodry found himself drawn to Jill in spite of all his best efforts to leave her alone. He had never wanted to lose her, had always planned, from the moment he first met her, to spend his entire life in her company, and now that he'd found her again—or so he thought of it—all that old devotion came back in the same way as a fire, banked with sod for the night, flares up when a servant knocks the lumps of earth aside and lets the fresh air in. He found himself courting her as if she were a young lass, turning up at her side whenever she went walking, bringing her flowers, angling to sit next to her at every communal meal. Although she was mostly cold to him, every now and then she warmed, when they were talking about something they'd done or someone they'd known, all those years ago in his other life on a silver dagger's long road.

One morning, when Rhodry went looking for Jill in his usual way, he found her sitting on the streambank near Aderyn's tent. Apparently she'd just bathed, because she was combing her wet hair while Salamander sat with her and talked. When Rhodry joined them, his brother turned to him.

"I'm going to leave today and go look for our father. Obviously Cal's messengers haven't caught up with him yet, and I can just see us all wandering back and forth across the grasslands for years and years, passing close by but never meeting, endlessly wondering where the other one is—that sort of thing."

"I was beginning to worry myself, and you have my thanks, but maybe I should just go with you. I'm the one who wants to see him, after all."

"Aderyn says your place is here," Jill broke in. "He doesn't want you wandering all over the grasslands just yet."

"Very well, but why not?"

"He didn't tell me that."

"Well, I'd like to know—"

"Hold up, brother of mine." Salamander intervened. "Among the People we have a custom. What a Wise One—a dweomermaster, that is—says, we do. That's one reason why I've never aspired to that exalted title myself. Some small dweomer I have, but the wisdom to lead my people—well, I'd just as soon not put myself to the test."

"Which shows," Jill said. "That you have a little bit of wisdom at least." She rose, still holding the bone comb. "I'm going back to camp."

"I'll come with you."

Rhodry started to get up, but she scowled and waved him back down.

"Would you stop following me everywhere?"

"Oh, here, my love—"

"Never call me that again."

There was the crack of command in her voice, so cold, so harsh that he sat down and said nothing, merely watched her walk away while Salamander pretended to look elsewhere.

"Ah well," Salamander said at last. "I'm going to take a pack-horse with me. Going to come help me load up?"

"Of course. Let's go get the parting over with, shall we?"

"Ah, you're beginning to think like an elf, sure enough."

On the morrow, Rhodry went riding by himself out to the edge of the wild plains, very much like a green sea indeed, with the grass bowing and sighing like waves under the touch of the wind. For a long time he sat on his horse in the hot spring sun, watched the grass ripple, and thought of very little. All at once he realized that he could no longer remember his name. He swore, slapped his thigh hard with the reins, shook his head and swore again, but the name stayed stubbornly hidden until in frustration he started back toward camp.

"Rhodry Maelwaedd," he said aloud, then laughed. "Or it isn't truly Maelwaedd—never truly was—and I suppose that's one reason I couldn't remember. But Rhodry ap Devaberiel still sounds passing strange to me. What do you think? Which one should I use?"

The horse snorted and tossed its head as if to say it didn't care either way.

When he rode back to camp he found Calonderiel waiting for him out by the hobbled herd. The warleader helped him unsaddle his horse and turn it out with the others, in a silence so profound that Rhodry knew something was wrong.

"What's happened?" he said—and in Elvish, without really thinking about the choice.

"Oh, well, nothing much, really. Aderyn wants you to come share his tent instead of mine, that's all."

"All right. But why do you—oh, by the Dark Sun! Jill's left, hasn't she? That's what this means."

"I'm afraid so. She's like all the blasted Round-ears—as impatient as babies, all of them! She announced this morning that if

Devaberiel couldn't be bothered to hurry, then she couldn't be bothered to sit around and wait for him." Calonderiel frowned down at the ground. "She could have had the decency to wait and tell you goodbye."

"She's leaving because of me, you know, no matter what she told you."

"Oh." A long pause. "I see."

Rhodry turned on his heel and strode off alone to the camp. At Calonderiel's tent he found all his gear gone—moved already, he supposed, at the Wise One's command. When he went to the old man's tent, he found the dweomermaster sitting by a banked fire with Wildfolk all around him. In a curve of the wall not far from Gavantar's place, his bedroll and other gear were neatly laid out below a new pair of tent bags. Aderyn looked up with a wary cock of his head.

"Jill's gone, then, is she?" Rhodry said, falling back into Deverrian.

"She is. Did you truly think she'd stay?"

Rhodry shrugged and sat down on his blankets. From outside the normal sounds of the camp drifted into the tent—children laughing and running, a horse whinnying, a woman singing as she strolled by—but all the noise seemed strangely far away.

"I don't know what I thought," Rhodry said at last. "I do know it doesn't matter. Not to her, not to the gods, not to my Wyrd or the wretched dweomer either."

"Well, that's probably true enough."

Rhodry nodded and began pulling off his boots. In a few minutes he looked up to find the old man gone.

That night, some time when his sleep was deepest, Rhodry had a dream. He was walking across a meadow on a night when the full moon shone overhead, guarded with a double ring, and the grass crackled with frost under his feet, but in his dream he was too fevered to feel the cold, his cheeks burning in the icy air. Every step he took drove pain like a knife into his lungs. Yet he kept walking, never considered turning back, forced himself on a step at a time until he reached a copse of birches, white as frost in the moonlight, dancing and trembling with his fever. Among the trees a woman waited. At first he thought it was Jill, but when he went to meet her, he saw that she was neither human nor elven, with her flesh as pale as the birch bark and her waist-length hair as dark blue as a winter sea. She threw her arms around him and whimpered like an animal as she kissed his burning cheeks with cold lips, but when he kissed her mouth, he had to fight for breath between each kiss. Then he started to cough. He shoved her away, turned away and clasped both hands over his mouth while he choked and coughed in spasms that made his entire body rock and tremble. She wept, watching him. When he took his hands away they were covered with blood, dark and fresh, but thick with clots of gore. With a cry the woman flung herself against him and kissed him. When she pulled back, her pale lips were bright with his blood.

He couldn't breathe. He was choking, drowning in his own blood—Rhodry sat up with a cry and heard the woman's answering wail echo around him. Yellow dweomer light danced on the walls of the tent. Aderyn was standing over him.

"What were you dreaming?"

"I was choking. She kissed me and killed me. In the white birches." Then the dream faded and blurred, like a reflection on water as the wind blows across. "I don't remember any more of it."

"I wondered what being back on the border would do to you. Come, get up, and we'll have a bit of a talk."

At the old man's bidding Wildfolk made the dead fire leap up with flame. Rhodry was shivering.

"You know, I used to have a nightmare somewhat like that when I was a child, but I don't remember it very well. This one was blasted real, though. Ye gods, it still hurts to breathe."

"When you had the dream before—as a child, I mean—did your lungs hurt when you woke?"

"Don't remember, but I doubt it, because I do remember screaming my head off, and my old nurse running over with her nightdress flapping around her. What does it mean?"

"Most dreams have as many meanings as an onion has peels. I wouldn't venture to say what the right one might be."

Rhodry hesitated on the edge of asking more. Although he knew that Aderyn had sworn a sacred oath never to tell an outright lie, he could sense that the old man was leaving a great many things unsaid. *And do I want to force them out into the open?* Rhodry asked himself. There in the middle of the night, miles and miles away from his old home and his old life, the answer was a decided no. Yet all the next day, he kept thinking about the dream, and every now and then, it seemed he could remember a little piece of it, just a visual image of the woman or the feel of a kiss, until he realized just how familiar to him she was, this White Lady, as he found himself calling her for no particular reason at all.

At dinner that night Aderyn announced that he'd scried Devaberiel out and found him traveling by himself and quickly, heading south through the grasslands but a good many miles away. He'd seen Salamander, too, hurrying to meet him. Since the dweomermaster could assume that one of Calonderiel's messengers had finally tracked the bard down, he decided that the alar should ride in his direction. When they headed north, though, they kept to the borderlands, because Devaberiel was expecting to find them somewhere near Eldidd. For the same reason they didn't ride far, finally making a semi-permanent camp not far from the Peddroloc.

Once he was well away from his old rhan, Rhodry turned melancholy. It was one thing to think of having an entire new life ahead of him; another to leave the old completely behind. Much to his surprise, he realized that he missed his kin far more than he missed the power of rulership. At odd moments of the day he would find himself wondering how his sons fared, and their children, too; he even had the occasional fond thought of Aedda. He took to riding alone to ease his hiraedd, and the elves were willing to leave him alone with his solitude.

One day he borrowed a particularly fine gelding from Calonderiel and rode farther than usual in the simple pleasure of getting to know a new horse. After some hours he came to a little stream that led back to a marshy, spring-fed pond, surrounded with scrubby hazel thickets and some willows. Rhodry dismounted, and as he led his horse to the pond for a drink, he saw a white heron, standing on one leg in the shallows and regarding him with one suspicious round eye. All at once the bird shrieked its harsh cry and flapped off. Rhodry spun around, thinking that someone else had crept up behind him, but he saw no one, not even one of the Wildfolk. Since his horse was elven-trained, he left it to drink without him and walked back into the trees. The golden sunlight of late afternoon came down in shafts, solid with dust; the silence felt just as palpable. Then he saw her standing between two willows and watching him sadly.

Although he knew at once that she wasn't truly substantial, she wasn't an illusion, either: a real enough woman but lighter, somehow, than the solid trees around her. Tall and lithe, she was wearing a loose blue dress that left her arms bare and hung in torn dags around her ankles. Her dark blue hair flowed like water over her pale shoulders and curled close to her pale, pale face. When she spoke, he heard her language as Elvish, but it seemed that she wasn't truly speaking at all.

"You heard me this time." Her eyes filled with tears. "I've been calling and calling, but you didn't come. You always used to come to me."

"Please don't cry. I'm sorry. I couldn't hear you, that's all."

"Ah. That must be because of the old man. He's a mean old man. I hate him. Why are you staying in his tent?"

"I've got to stay somewhere. Do you mean Aderyn?"

"An aderyn? Yes, the owl."

"No, no, no, he's a man—Aderyn is just his name."

She looked so puzzled that he gave up trying to explain.

"Why do you hate him?"

"He lied to me. I knew you weren't truly gone far away and under the earth. That's what he said, you know. Far away and under the earth." She paused, tilting her head to one side in thought. "But it's taken me so long to find you again. Why?"

"I don't know."

She pouted like a child, then laughed, tossing off the mood as she sauntered all sway-hip over to him. Her eyes were the same dark blue as her hair, and they were utterly mindless, like pools of water, glittering and vacant.

"You look so cold." She was staring at him, studying his face. "You don't love me anymore, do you? You've forgotten."

Big tears rolled down her cheeks, but rather than falling, they merely vanished. Yet her sobs, the big gulping gasps of a heartsick child, were real enough.

"I'm sorry." Rhodry felt her grief like a stab to his own heart. "Please, don't look so sad. I just don't understand."

The tears stopped. Again she tilted her head to consider him, then suddenly smiled.

"I know what you'll remember." She caught his face between her hands and kissed him on the mouth. "Oh, you're warmer now, truly. Come lie down with me. I want to hold you just like we used to. Do you remember that? I'll wager you do. Men seem to like it so much."

As she ran her hands through his hair, Rhodry did remember it, a slow, sensual kind of pleasure, utterly different than being in a human woman's arms. Yet as he drew her close, as he kissed her, he remembered something else as well: her lips, bright with his blood in the moonlight. That was only a dream, he told himself, it all meant somewhat else. He took another kiss, then another, tipped her head back and softly kissed her throat. She began to laugh and cling to him, so perfectly happy, so suddenly solid and radiant in her happiness, that he laughed himself in the simple joy of finding her again. When they lay down together, he could think of her as nothing but a woman. Yet when he caressed her, his hands knew the difference in their blind way. Her skin felt more like silk; her flesh, oddly soft, without resistance or muscle. At first he was repelled, but with every kiss they shared, the difference faded. She grew warmer, more solid, heavier in his arms. The tattered dress faded away, too; he never took it off, but suddenly she was naked in his arms. He ran his hand over her breast, then cried out and pulled his hand back. She had no nipple, merely a soft curve of not quite real flesh.

It was her need of him as much as lust that kept him in her arms. When he opened his eyes and saw that she had no navel, either, he drew away. She looked up, her beautiful eyes brimming tears, and she seemed so desolate that he kissed her to keep her from weeping. Once he kissed her, he could no longer stop, though for a long time he was content with kisses alone, while he let himself forget what his hands had discovered. Finally, with a little laugh to mock his shyness, she reached inside his brigga and fondled him. At that he could think of nothing but taking her.

Yet the passion was different, a slow thing, languid, wrapping him round like warm water. It was enough to stay inside her, hardly moving, feeling her arms wrapped tightly around him. She whimpered like an animal, shifting under him, keeping him aroused for what seemed like a blissful eternity until his pleasure built close to pain. When he began to move, he nearly fainted from the agonizing delight, and as he sobbed into her shoulder, she laughed, a crow of triumph. He lay next to her, pulled her into his arms, and panted for breath.

"Shall I show you things like I used to?" she whispered. "Shall we go to the pretty places? Not the dangerous ones, not the ones where *she* is, but the safe ones in my home country."

"I don't understand. Who's this she?"

"You never did get to meet her, did you?" She frowned, thinking hard at the edge of her capacity. "You said she was a demon."

"I don't remember saying any such thing."

"You did, too! And maybe you were right, because when we went to her country, you went under the ground. So we won't go there again."

"Indeed? Well, whatever you want."

She raised her head and kissed his closed eyelids, then his mouth. He felt as if they were gliding together down a slow stream, felt sunlight, too, warm and strong. When he opened his eyes he found that they were lying in a meadow, with banks and hedges of red roses scattered through the grass. Rhodry sat up and stared around him. A flock of peacocks strutted by, led by three males in display, gleaming like blue-and-purple jewels.

"You always liked it here." She sat up and began combing out her hair with her fingers.

"It's beautiful, but where are we?"

"I don't know. Just a place." She lay down again and ran her hand down his back. "Do that to me again. It's been so long, my love."

"Much too long. Ye gods, I've missed you all my life and never known what I was pining for."

But this time, as the pleasure of their lovemaking faded, so did the meadow. They were lying among the hazel thickets on hard ground where dark shadows stretched out long in the setting sun. Only the smell of roses lingered in her hair.

"It's getting on toward night," Rhodry said. "I hate to do it, but I have to leave you."

"I know. I don't want the old man to find out, anyway. But come back tomorrow?"

"I will. I promise."

With a scatter of dead leaves she vanished. Rhodry stood up, only to stagger out of sheer dizziness. Cold sweat streamed down his back as he grabbed at a tree to steady himself. It was a long time before he could summon the strength to walk back to his horse, grazing patiently in the long grass. Yet, exhaustion or no, he knew he would come back to her, and not only for the strange sexuality she offered. It was the marvels. Somehow he'd been stupid enough to forget how she could take him to the Wildlands and show him the marvels there. All during his long ride back to the camp, he was wondering how he could have forgotten her at all. Her warning stayed with him, too: don't let the old man find out.

Aderyn was gone when he returned to their tent, off somewhere in the main camp. Rhodry sat down, planning on resting for a few minutes, only to fall asleep where he sat. He woke once and had just enough energy to crawl into his blankets. When he woke again, sunlight was filtering through the tent walls, and Gavantar was crouching by the fire and stirring something spicy-smelling in an iron pot.

"Morning," Rhodry said with a yawn. "Where's the Wise One?"

"Oh, he took a packhorse and went down to the sea. There's a variety of red seaweed ripe for harvest—good for stomach troubles, he told me."

"And you didn't go with him?"

"I'm going to leave this afternoon. Bronario's daughter is still a little bit sick. Aderyn wanted me to stay with her this morning, just to make sure the fever doesn't come back."

"All right. I'd best eat and get on my way myself. It's my turn to help lead out the herd."

"You're too late for that." Gavantar sat back on his heels and grinned at him. "It's nearly noon. I was going to wake you, but Cal said not to bother. You can take a turn tomorrow, he said."

"Noon? Nearly noon?"

"Just that." His smile faded. "Rhodry, are you all right? You look pale."

"Do I? No, I'm fine. I just . . . I just had the strangest dreams last night, that's all. Well, I think I'll ride out and catch up with the herd, anyway. I feel like a cursed fool, sleeping when I should have been riding!"

But of course, instead of guarding the horses, he rode back to the willows and the hazel thickets, and without the slightest remorse over lying to Gavantar, either. She was waiting for him at the streamside, sitting on the ground and running her fingers through her long blue hair. He dismounted some yards away and began to unsaddle his horse.

"You didn't tell the old man, did you?" she said.

"I didn't. He'll be gone for a few days, anyway."

With a laugh she glinted away like a flash of light from a mirror and reappeared standing next to him.

"Then stay here with me until he gets back."

"I can't. I've got to go ride with the herd tomorrow. It's my turn. We have to keep moving the horses around, you see, so they get enough to eat."

With a puzzled frown she reached up to drape her arms over his shoulders, as light and languid as a bit of cloth. When he kissed her, suddenly he could feel her weight.

"There's lots of food for your horse right here."

"True, but we've got lots more horses back at camp."

"You're one of the elder brothers now. Isn't *that* odd."

"Is it? Why?"

"I don't understand you people. You change so much." She pressed herself close to him and kissed him. "Come lie down. Then we'll go somewhere nice."

Over the next few weeks, Rhodry grew very sly and very clever about stealing time for his White Lady. He did his share of the alar's work, spent just enough time with Calonderiel and his other friends to allay any suspicion, and dug up one good excuse after another for his fits of melancholy and long solitary rides. Every now and then he noticed Aderyn studying him, but he always managed to display enough good cheer to put the old man off. Everyone assumed that he was still pining for Jill on the one hand and adjusting to his new life on the other. After all, to go from being the most powerful human being on the western border to just another man of the People—and one without even any horses of his own—was the kind of change that would leave most men brooding. No one suspected the truth, that he was as much in thrall to his White Lady as any Cerrmor brothel lass ever was to her opium pipe.

Yet of course, she was as much in thrall to him. Every time he left her, she begged him to stay, and no matter how much he tried to explain, she could never understand that he needed food and shelter. When he tried offering to take her back to camp with him, she turned furious, screaming at him and clawing his face like a cat. He had so hard a time explaining those scratches to Aderyn that he resolved to stay away from her, but the next time that he had a chance to slip out and ride her way, he took it. She was waiting for him, as sunny and loving as if they'd never fought. Indeed, he had the feeling she'd forgotten all about it.

That day she took him to a place that she called, quite simply, the sea caves. Enormous amethysts, jutting crystals as big as a horse's head and sparkling with mineral fire, lined those caves, and turquoise water as clear and warm as liquid light filled them. Together they drifted down winding halls through chambers walled with gold where creatures spoke to them in voices sweeter than any harp. At times it seemed to him that they were asking his help, begging him to stay and rid their country of some evil, but he could never quite understand the sense of their words, only its emotional tone. At other times he and his White Lady were left alone to satisfy his desire. When at last the vision faded he was too exhausted to raise his head from the grass at first, but then he became aware of thirst, so urgent it was like a burning in his mouth. He hauled himself up, staggered out up to his knees in the pond, and gulped water until he could hold no more. She came to sit beside him and stroked his sweaty forehead with a pale, cool hand.

"The sun's in the east," he said at last. "It must still be morning. But it seemed we were gone a long time."

"What? I don't understand."

"Just time passing, that's all. It seemed like days, but it couldn't have been more than a few hours."

She stared at him, her eyes narrow, her lips a little parted, in utter confusion.

"Well, don't worry about it, my love. It doesn't matter."

Yet, when he reached camp, he found that it did matter. As he rode up, a couple of men came running, asking him where in the hells he'd been for the last two days. He realized, then, just how long he'd been gone—lost in her strange world and without a bite of food or a mouthful of water. He ducked into Aderyn's tent to find Aderyn, Gavantar, and Calonderiel discussing how many riders they should take to search for him. A crowd of overexcited Wildfolk swarmed and roiled round the tent. At the sight of Rhodry, Calonderiel jumped to his feet and grabbed him by the shoulders while the Wildfolk rushed over to grab his ankles or dance around him in glee.

"By the Dark Sun herself!" Calonderiel said. "I thought you'd fallen down a ravine and gotten yourself killed! You dolt! Riding out alone like that! There's poisonous snakes out there, you know! You ever do this again, and I'll break your neck myself!"

Rhodry could only stare openmouthed at him.

"Cal? Gav?" Aderyn's voice was so cold that Rhodry suddenly realized that the old man knew the truth. "Out."

Sweeping up the Wildfolk, they went without a word of protest. Sick and shivering, Rhodry knelt by the fire and held his hands over the warmth. Aderyn watched, more troubled than angry.

"I'm sorry," Rhodry blurted at last.

"Don't be. It's mostly my fault, because I should have warned you. I was going to warn you, once I figured out how much I could say. I never dreamt she'd find you this quickly, that's all. To tell you the absolute truth, I was hoping she'd never find you at all. Stupid, wasn't I?"

When Rhodry started to feed a few more twigs onto the fire, his hands spasmed and sent the twigs flying. Aderyn got to his knees and laid one hand on the back of Rhodry's neck. Warmth flowed from his fingers and drove the chattering cold from his veins.

"Where did you meet her?"

"I won't tell you. You'll hurt her."

"That's not true."

"You'll keep us apart."

"Now that *is* true."

Without thinking Rhodry turned and swung at him, an open-handed sweep of an arm intended to knock the old man's hand away and nothing more, but Aderyn merely swayed back and let him fall spraddled onto the floorcloth. Only then did Rhodry realize just how exhausted he was. He lay doubled over for a long moment, summoning the energy to lift his head up and struggle into a sitting position. Aderyn sat down facing him.

"I'm sorry," Rhodry whispered. "I don't know what's gotten into me."

"She's like a fever, or a poison in the blood, but it's your mind and soul that's infected. And truly, you've done it to yourself. She can't help herself or stop what she's doing, any more than a fire could stop burning your hand if you were stupid enough to stick it into the flames."

"How did you know?"

"For the past few weeks I thought you had a love affair going and were just too embarrassed to mention the fact. My age seems to take people that way." Aderyn smiled briefly. "It was obvious you were hiding somewhat, and every now and then I'd see you smiling to yourself like any man will do when he's been with a woman he fancies. But then you disappeared, and I was worried sick, fearing the worst, and sure enough, you come staggering in here, drained of your very life and pale as a birch tree—all at once I remembered the dream you had. I should have known she was close by. I've been much distracted these days, and busy with my apprentice, too, but I should have seen it then."

"Well, it's my shame, not yours. You're not the one who's been—" The words stuck like thorns in his throat as he finally saw just how unnatural his lust was. "Oh, ye gods, I'm sorry."

Aderyn said nothing, staring into the fire as if he could read the flames like writing. Rhodry was only aware of his shame, burning in his face worse than any fever. Yet even in his dishonor he knew that the marvels had snared him more than the sex. He could remember them so vividly, those bejeweled caves deep under waves that never broke on any earthly shore, or the rose meadows, breathing perfume in a golden sunlight. He could hear the harsh shrieks of the peacocks, strutting through the emerald grass, and see just beyond them a ruby mound of roses, big as a dun. He got up and began walking over to those roses, drawn by the scent

until a stinging pain flooded his face. He tried to ignore it and keep walking, but the pain came again. The vision vanished with a rushy hiss like water dropped into a pot of hot oil. Rhodry found himself staring up at Aderyn, who was leaning over him, one hand still raised.

"This is very bad," the old man said. "She's come right after you."

Aderyn stepped back, stretched out his hand, and began turning slowly in a circle while he chanted under his breath in some language that Rhodry didn't recognize. It seemed that he was using his pointing finger to draw a big invisible circle around the tent and to scribble some sort of figure at each quadrant, too. As soon as he'd gone round three times, Rhodry felt as if he'd been suddenly shaken awake after a night of vivid dreams. While he could remember that he'd seen marvels, he couldn't remember a single detail, and the tent seemed far more real and solid than it had in weeks. Yet the world around him was also strangely bleak—tawdry, somehow, and dirty round the edges, as if it were some rich and beautiful shirt, all embroidered in Bardek silk, that he'd worn and worn until it was frayed bald and stained, fit only for giving to a beggar to keep off the cold.

"You've got to give her up." Aderyn's voice was cold and harsh. "Do you understand me? She'll kill you if you don't."

The anger he felt caught Rhodry by surprise. He wanted her, wanted the marvels, wanted them so badly he had a brief thought of killing anyone, even Aderyn, who stood in his way. The old man stepped back so sharply that Rhodry knew his rage must have shown on his face.

"Please, Rhodry, listen to me. You've touched on the edge of forbidden things, and it's hard for me to explain, but—wait, I know. Think of it this way. That dream you had? It's an omen. She'll kill you without even meaning to do it if you keep going to her. She's sucking the life-force out of you, and soon enough your body will weaken and die, because there won't be enough force to sustain it. I know that doesn't make a lot of sense, but—"

"Cursed right it doesn't! Ye gods, don't you understand? Dying seems a small price to pay for what she gives me."

Aderyn stared, simply stared at him for a long time.

"Things are worse even than I feared," the old man said at

last. "But there's one last thing you don't understand. Maybe you're willing to die, but what about her? Are you going to drag her down with you? She thinks I hate her, but she's as much my charge as you are. She has no mind to understand what happens between you. She loves you, and that's everything and all that she knows about this world."

Almost against his will Rhodry was remembering her confusion over simple things like names and time passing.

"She's become the way she is because she knows you want her that way," Aderyn went on. "You're doing this to her, Rhodry Maelwaedd. If she goes on trying to please you, she'll be utterly ruined, caught between the lands of men and elves on the one side and the Wildlands on the other. The Wildlands are her true home, but soon she'll lose them, get herself shut out of them, and all because of you. Do you want that? She'll be doomed, a bit of cosmic refuse, suffering for half of Eternity, and all because of—"

"Stop it! Oh, ye gods, hold your tongue! I could never do that! I'll give her up, then! I swear it on the gods of both my peoples!"

"And I'll hold you to that vow. Good. Well, then, let me just call Gavantar back in. Looks to me like you could use some dinner."

Rhodry forced down food that was strangely tasteless, then went to his blankets and fell asleep without even bothering to undress. Almost at once he was dreaming so vividly that he knew it was no ordinary dream, that she'd come to him when he could set no guard against her, because in the land of dream she was the lord and he the vassal. When she reproached him for betraying her, he fell to his knees and begged her to forgive him, groveled at her feet like a bondsman until she graciously reached out a hand and bade him take it. She swept him back to the rose meadows, where even in dream the perfume hung thick in the golden air, and led him to a stream, where fish as bright as jewels slipped through golden rushes and emerald water weeds. As they sat down together in the warm and sweet-scented grass, Rhodry knew that if he made love to her there, he would never wake, that his body would sleep entranced while his mind roamed free in dream.

Until, of course, he died, but her smile was sweet, so sweet that the price seemed very low. He would seem to live for a long time, perhaps, here with her, and they would share a glorious day before the gray night inevitably fell. When she leaned toward him for a kiss, he smiled, welcoming her—then caught her wrists and held her back.

His death would doom her. Aderyn said so, and he knew in his very heart that the old man would never lie. Pouting, she slid closer, sensing his coldness, smiling again, slipping her hands free of his weakening grasp and moving closer yet to run her hands through his hair and waken a desire that made him gasp for breath, just from the sweetness of it. He was about to kiss her when she screamed. Rhodry spun around and saw Aderyn striding across the meadow, his face as grim and set as a warrior's, and right behind him came a presence. At moments it seemed to be a slender young man, but with flesh and clothes of palest silver; at others, a misty, swirling tower of moonlight. With a howl and shriek of rage the White Lady vanished, sweeping all color from the world along with her. Over a corpse-gray meadow Aderyn came stalking, the ground shaking, rumbling, the trees trembling, rocking

and Rhodry woke to find Aderyn shaking him by the shoulders. Although Aderyn's face was every bit as grim now as it was in the dream, there was no sign of the Silver Lord of the Wildlands.

"By the Dark Sun herself," Aderyn said. "This is going to be a battle and a half. You're not leaving the camp alone until we've won it. I'm going to find Cal and ask him for some guards."

Rhodry's first and immediate thought was to slip out while the old man was gone, but Gavantar was standing by the door with his arms folded over his chest and a grim look of his own carved onto his young face. When he snapped his fingers a horde of Wildfolk materialized to sit on Rhodry's lap, grab his arms, weigh down his shoulders, and generally do whatever they could to keep him in place. Rhodry studied the floorcloth and tried to ignore her voice, whispering, begging, calling to him like the murmur of a distant sea. Now that he was awake, he could argue with her, warn her, tell her of the evil fate that waited for her if she persisted in loving him, but she only said that she was as willing to die for him as he was for her.

"You don't even know what death means."

He realized that he'd been speaking aloud and looked up to find Gavantar listening in a horrified fascination. He felt tears brim in his eyes and spill beyond his power to stop them, but he couldn't say one word more until Aderyn returned. As soon as the dweomermaster slipped through the tent flap, she fled with one last whisper of desire.

"I don't sleep as much as most men do," Aderyn said. "But I do need some rest every now and then, and Gav is only a beginner at this sort of thing. Thanks to the warleader and his men, your body's going to stay right here, but your soul's somewhat of a problem. I think me I'd best send for some help."

After she left the encampment, Jill rode southwest, heading for the seacoast and the islands of Wmmglaedd, which at that time was a small temple complex dedicated to the gods of knowledge and learning. Already, though, a long stone building, where peat fires always smoldered to keep off the damp, held the core of what was to become its famous library. With the help of a young priest Jill settled in, hunting through its collection of some five hundred books and scrolls for any scrap of information that would help decipher the mysteries of Rhodry's Wyrd in general and the rose ring in particular. Her problem was simple. At that time the entire Elvish heritage of literature and history appeared lost. Although some of the People out on the grasslands could read, and a few more were trained as sages to memorize vast amounts of oral tradition, only two Elvish books were known to have survived the Great Burning. Apparently lost with this heritage was the meaning of the word engraved inside Rhodry's ring.

Scattered here and there through books in other languages, however, were the occasional reference to Elvish lore and learning, written down by the rare scribe who considered the People worth listening to. Jill was determined to see what she could glean from these less than fertile fields. Since she'd learned to read so late in life, understanding Deverrian text was still a slow process for her, and she had to pause often and ask one of the scribes the meaning of an obscure word. Puzzling out Bardekian was even slower.

After about two weeks of frustrating and unprofitable research, Jill was ready to pack it up as a bad job and depend entirely on meditation for her information, but just as she was about to give up she came upon a passage that made her struggles seem worthwhile. "When our people first came to the islands," wrote a certain Bardekian historian, "they found other refugees there ahead of them, a strange people who had no name for themselves but who said they came from across the northern sea. There were never very many of them, so the old tales run, and they either all died or sailed south." That was all, just a tantalizing scrap of legend passed down by word of mouth and quite possibly unreliable—but one that would fit the elvish refugees from the Great Burning of the Cities. What if it were true? And what, furthermore, if descendants of those refugees still lived, off in the little-known islands far to the south? The very thought drew to the surface of her mind long-forgotten memories, little scraps of knowledge about Bardek that had never seemed very important before, such as a certain style of wall painting that reminded her of the decorations on elven tents.

Late one evening she was sitting in the tiny guesthouse, going over a list of names of the more obscure islands and hoping to find some similarities to Elvish words, when she felt Aderyn's mind tugging on hers. She sat down on the floor by the fire and stared into the glowing coals until at last his face appeared, floating just above the flame.

"Thank god I finally reached you. I've been trying to attract your attention for hours."

"My apologies, but I've been on the track of some very peculiar information, and it's a fascinating puzzle."

"Could you see your way clear to laying it aside for a while? Somewhat's dreadfully wrong."

"What? Of course! I mean, what is it?"

"I need your help. I hate to ask, truly, because I know how you feel about Rhodry, but you're the only one I can turn to. I beg you, if ever you've honored me, ride back to us."

"I'll leave on the morrow. Where are you?"

The vision changed to show her the camp, nestled in a valley up at the northern end of the Peddroloc; then Aderyn's mind left hers in a gust of anxiety, as if every moment was so precious that he simply couldn't stop to explain.

When she rode out, Jill left her mule and packs of medicines behind, and she borrowed an extra riding horse from the priests, too, so that she could switch her weight back and forth between her two mounts. For the first three days she traveled fast and smoothly; then a summer storm boiled up out of the west. On the fourth morning she woke to a sky as dark as slate and a pair of horses turned jumpy and foul-tempered by the thick and oppressive air. Late in the day it broke, a few fat drops at first, then a hard stinging slash of storm and the crack of lightning. Jill was forced to dismount and calm her trembling pair until at last the lightning moved off and the rain settled to a steady drizzle. Although she made a few more miles, shoving a way through the soaking-wet grass was so hard on the horses that she stopped early, making a wet camp in a little clump of willows by a stream.

Just before dawn she woke, cramped and shivering, to the distinct feeling that someone was watching her. Although the rain had stopped, the clouds still hung gray and lowering over the plains, bringing a dark and misty dawn, but as she looked around, she could just make out a woman, standing among the trees.

"Well, a good morrow to you," Jill said in Elvish. "Is your alar nearby, or are you riding alone?"

The woman tossed back her head and wailed, one high keen of a spine-chilling note, then vanished. Slowly Jill got to her feet, and she was shivering from more than the damp.

"A banshee, was it? Oh, ye gods! Rhodry!"

Immediately she tried to scry him out, but she could find no trace either of him or the elven camp. Just before she panicked she realized that Aderyn might well have set seals over them all for some reason of his own—if so, a portent of horrible trouble indeed.

All that day, while the storm cleared and the sun and wind dried the tall grass, she pushed herself and the horses mercilessly, but even so, it was on the morrow noon—the fifth day after she'd left the islands of Wmm—that she finally saw the elven camp, a huddle of round tents on the horizon, and the horse herds, spread out and grazing peacefully. The young elf on watch greeted her with a shout that brought Calonderiel and half a dozen men riding hard to gallop her into camp.

"Take her horses," the warleader called. "I'll escort her to the Wise One's tent. Jill, by every god, I'm glad to see you!"

"Is Rhodry dead?"

"No. Aderyn didn't tell you? Rhodry's gone mad. Straight off his head, raving, seeing things—I don't understand it one bit, but it's terrifying, truly. Just trying to get him to eat is a battle and a half."

Aderyn's tent was standing in the middle of the camp instead of at its usual distance. With Calonderiel right behind her and a crowd of Wildfolk shoving and pushing round them, Jill rushed inside. Aderyn was standing by the dead fire and waiting for her. The dweomermaster looked exhausted, pale and stooped, with dark circles round his eyes that were worthy of a drunken warrior. Behind him, crouched in the curve of the leather wall like an animal at bay, sat Rhodry. At first she barely recognized him, just because he sat so quietly, his eyes stripped of all feeling and fire.

"What's so wrong?" Jill snapped.

"I haven't slept much in a week, for starters," Aderyn said. "But I'll wager you mean our Rhodry."

Rhodry never moved or looked up at the mention of his name.

"I was afraid he was dead. I met a banshee on the road."

"It wasn't a banshee. It—she—was the trouble." Aderyn turned to the warleader. "Cal, stay here with him, will you? Yell at the first sign of the usual madness. We'll just be outside, where we can talk privately."

They went round to the side of the tent, and Jill noticed that no one dared come near, not even the normally curious children, not even one of the dogs.

"It's a woman from the Wildlands." Aderyn wasted no time on fine phrasing. "The little bitch has gone and ensorceled him, but it's hurting her worse than it is him, truly. She's linked to him from other lives, and there was no way for me to warn him adequately without spilling truths he shouldn't hear."

"We've got to trap her and turn her over to her lords."

"Easier said than done. I've been trying, but she's a wily little thing."

"Look, Rhodry's a man of honor. Can't you explain that he's hurting this poor innocent spirit, and—"

"I did, and that's the only reason he's still with us at all. He did his best to resist her, but in the end, she pulled him back."

"I still don't see how—"

"She's his lover. And I mean exactly that. As much his lover as ever you were."

Her sudden anger caught Jill by surprise—nothing so strong as rage, no, but a definite resentment, a flickering of old jealousies. Aderyn misunderstood her silence.

"You do know about such things, don't you?" the old man said. "She's one of the Wildfolk, but many years ago she ran afoul of one of the Guardians, who gave her a false body of sorts. Ever since, she's been working on becoming a physical being, sucking magnetism from him and other lovers to—"

"Of course I know what she's doing! Oh, my apologies, Aderyn, I didn't mean to snap at you. How long has this been going on?"

"A couple of hundred years, more or less and all told."

"She must be quite . . . well, convincing by now."

"Very, and beautiful, too, or so he says, but in this case beauty's certainly in the eye of the beholder. I never cared for the pale and pouty type myself, all wide eyes and simpers, when I was young."

"Neither did Rhodry. Ych, this is revolting, isn't it? It's hard to believe it of him, but here we are. How are you guarding against her? The usual seals?"

"Just that, but she keeps calling to him, particularly when he's asleep, and I can't watch him every moment of every day. Gav can help set the seals, but that's all. In fact, with you here and all, I was thinking that I might just go to Cal's tent right now and get some sleep. Ye gods, I'm tired!"

Leaving Gavantar just outside the door on watch, Jill went back to Aderyn's tent. Rhodry never even glanced up when she came in, nor did he say a word to her as she helped herself to bread and smoked meat from the basket lying by the hearthstone. She sat down some feet from him and studied him while she ate, since he didn't seem to care whether she did or not. He looked his age, she realized with a shock. Even though he didn't have a single gray hair or a pouch or bag in his weather-beaten face, he looked old, slumped down, drained of the immensely high vitality and magnetism that keeps those of elven blood so "young" by human standards. Since in her mind she always held the image of him as *her* young lover, she felt that she hardly knew this middle-aged man. The estrangement hurt.

"Rhodry? Don't you have one word to say to me?"

He looked up, his mouth slack, his eyes narrow, as if he were trying to puzzle out who she was.

"My apologies," he said at last. "I thought you'd prefer it if I just held my tongue."

"Why would I do that?"

"I must disgust you."

She considered the matter with the care it deserved.

"You don't, truly. But I'm afraid for your life."

"Does it matter if I live or die?"

"Of course it does. Your Wyrd—"

"Ah, curse my wretched Wyrd! I mean, does it matter to *you?*"

Another question that deserved a careful answer, not some unthinking reply.

"It does matter. I may not be in love with you anymore, but I like you. I always have, really. Liked you as a friend and admired you, too, and over the long years that's more important than love."

"Is it? I—" He froze in mid-sentence.

Jill felt at the edge of her mind the touch of crackling energy that means the Wildlands are lying close by. Her gray gnome popped into manifestation and pointed, all big eyes and gaping mouth, at something behind her. Opening up the second sight, she slewed around and looked. The first thing she saw was the smooth curving wall of the golden sphere of force that Aderyn and Gavantar had set over the tent and marked with flaming pentagrams. Just beyond, though, she could dimly make out a female shape, all wavery like a woman seen through bottle glass. When she rose to her knees, the shape vanished.

"She knows I'm here."

"Actually, she told me you were coming. I mean, she didn't know who you were, but she told me that the old man was bringing another dweomermaster. I figured it was you."

"You knew she knew, and you never told Aderyn?"

When Rhodry blushed with shame she realized for the first time just how divided his loyalties were.

Over the next few days Jill and Aderyn worked out a strange sort of watch. While Rhodry was awake and thus fairly safe, they both rested, too, but the minute he fell asleep, one of them would watch his body while the other stood watch out on the etheric plane. The White Lady was forced to stay far out of reach of his dreams, although Jill did catch a glimpse of her one morning. Normally, on the etheric plane an elemental spirit appears as a nexus of lines of force or as a crystalline brilliance, much more a bit of geometry than a person, but the creature that Jill saw hovering on a billow of blue light seemed caught in between. She'd put on a half-human face, but it kept forming out of and dissolving into a burst of green light and line. At the sight, Jill's abstract compassion solidified into real sympathy; the poor spirit was being dragged from her own line of evolution and trapped where she didn't belong. If things went much farther, she wouldn't long survive her displacement, either, especially without Rhodry to feed upon. Jill sketched the sigil of the Kings of Aethyr into the blue light, then started forward—but the spirit fled from her with an exhalation of rage like a physical howl surging round the etheric.

Jill returned to her body and sat up, stretching and yawning a little, to find Rhodry wide awake and staring at her.

"What did you do to her?" he snapped.

"I was trying to help her, you dolt."

He did have the grace to look shamed.

All that day Rhodry was painfully restless. He paced back and forth across the tent, then started round and round, until Jill felt half dizzy from trying to watch him. When she suggested that they fetch Calonderiel and go riding, he didn't even answer.

"Are you going to start chewing your manger next?" Jill snarled.

"What?"

"You're acting just like a stud being kept from a mare in heat. It's not very pretty to watch you rut."

He stopped pacing and swirled around to face her.

"Aderyn's kinder than I am," she went on. "He sees you as the poor innocent victim. I know you better than that. I'll wager this phantom lover of yours didn't have to drag you into her bed. I'll wager she didn't even have to ask twice."

Blushing scarlet, Rhodry took a furious step toward her.

"Just try," Jill said, grinning. "I haven't forgotten how to fight, and I'll wager I can throw you all over this tent."

He spun around, hesitated, then flung himself face down onto his blankets. She watched his shoulders shaking for a couple of minutes before she realized that he was weeping. She knelt down and began rubbing the back of his neck, letting a little of her own magnetism flow out to soothe him. In a few moments he stopped crying and rolled over.

"Rhodry, please, I don't want to see you die. Do what Aderyn and I say. Please?"

He sat up, wiping his eyes on his shirt sleeve.

"My thanks," he whispered. "I just feel torn in pieces, and I don't know how to—"

The shriek sounded like a panther's howl, blind-wild and feline, filling the tent and sweeping round. The slap came out of the shriek, a vicious blow across Jill's face with the stinging rake of claws. All of Jill's long years of dweomer training seemed to vanish. Without thinking she was on her feet and hitting back, automatically grabbing for an arm that wasn't truly there, reaching for an enemy she couldn't see. Her fingers closed on something more solid than air but not quite real; another slap caught her across the mouth; then she heard Aderyn yelling. Her enemy vanished.

"And don't I feel like a fool!" Jill burst out. "Here I had my chance to put the sign of the kings upon her, and I lost my head completely."

"I can't say I blame you," Aderyn said. "Instinct and all that. Gavantar felt her presence and woke me, but by the time I got here it was too late."

"Doesn't matter." Jill glanced around to see Gavantar standing just inside the tent flap. "Gav, stay here. Aderyn, let's go talk where we can't be overheard. I'm sorry, Rhoddo, but I can't really trust you."

Since they could count on the spirit being too frightened to come back immediately, they walked a little way from the camp. Even though the grasslands were silent and sweaty in the heat of a windless summer day, being out of the tent and away from Rhodry's obsession felt as good as a plunge into a cool river.

"She's as desperate as a wolf in winter if she'd risk breaching the seals," Aderyn remarked. "It must have taken every bit of courage and power she has. I can't believe she misses him as badly as all that."

"It's somewhat else entirely. She's jealous of me, and I think me we can use that to our advantage. Look, the Lords of the Wildlands should be willing to help in this."

"I've already made contact with them. It's just that she keeps leading them a merry little dance, dashing away every time they get near her."

"What we need is somewhat to occupy what little mind she has, and I think we've found the perfect bait for our snare. Watching us catch her is going to be hard on Rhodry, but he's brought it on himself, after all."

"Forgiving sort, aren't you?"

"And there you've put a finger on my weakness. Compassion doesn't come easy to me, Aderyn. I'm not like Nevyn that way, or like you, either. Maybe it's because I've survived my own hard times, but I don't have much patience for someone else's."

"Just so long as you know."

Two days later a summer storm whistled in like a curtain of rain moving across the grasslands. Aderyn announced that he was going to talk with Calonderiel and left the tent, ostentatiously taking Gavantar with him. Jill made a ball of dweomer light, hung it near the smoke hole in the ceiling, then brought out a pouch of elven "dice," tiny wooden pyramids, painted a different color on each side. To play you shook ten pieces in your cupped hands, then strewed them out in a line; how many sides of each color came up, and the pattern they made, determined the winner, with the top score being a highly improbable straight of ten reds. Since the pyramids never fell plumb on tent cloth and grass, usually the players ended up arguing—not that Rhodry seemed to care one way or the other, though. Half the time he barely watched her pieces fall, and she had to remind him when it was his turn.

"We can stop if you want," she said at last.

"My apologies, but my heart's not in it."

"Is she calling you?"

"She's always calling me these days."

"Ah, Rhoddo, my heart aches for you."

At the sound of his nickname he looked up and smiled with such a profound melancholy that for a moment she truly did feel sorry for him. She reached out and ran her hand through his hair and caressed the side of his face, and at her touch he turned his head and kissed her fingers, an old gesture, a habit from their time together long before.

The blow from behind slammed into her so hard that Jill nearly fell right into his arms. She heard Rhodry yell; then a slap hit her hard across the face. With a wrench of will she kept herself from using magic and fought back with both hands, blindly grabbing and slapping this way and that like a cat batting at a mouse. At last one hand landed on something fairly substantial with a squishy thwack.

"You bitch! You leave Rhodry alone!"

Her only answer was another slap. Jill made a two-handed grab and caught something slick and cool but shaped much like an arm. There was a shriek, a slap, and suddenly Jill saw her, writhing in her hands: pale, lovely, but furious, her mouth twisted, her teeth pointed and sharp, her long blue hair waving in a private breeze of its own. She flung herself on Jill and tried to bite her, then disappeared, slipping through her hands as easily as water. Jill turned and made a blind grab, catching what felt like a handful of long hair. With a yelp the sprite reappeared, screaming and clawing at Jill's face.

"Enough!" Aderyn called. "We've got the circle drawn."

The sprite froze in Jill's hands, then moaned, such a pathetic little sound that Jill let her go. She was trapped beyond her power to disappear, anyway, because not only had Aderyn and Gavantar slipped in when she was distracted by the fight, but a Lord of the Wildlands had come through to the physical plane. He seemed to be a thickening of the light, a silver shaft that barely hinted of a man shape caught within it. Her eyes springing illusionary tears, the sprite fell to her knees at his feet and buried her face in her hands.

"It's all over now." The presence had a voice as soft as water slipping over rock. "You're coming home with me, child."

The sprite moaned and raised her head to look desperately at Rhodry. When she held her arms out to him, he took one step forward, but Jill grabbed him and shoved him back.

"I hate you!" the sprite hissed at Jill.

"I don't hate you, little one."

Just beyond the lord another presence appeared like a beam of light thrown from a slit in a lantern, enclosing a female form this time. Although Jill heard Aderyn gasp aloud, she kept her attention on the tormented being kneeling in front of her.

"Go with your lord. He'll make you well again."

The silver shaft glowed with warm light, then glided forward to envelop the sprite. The vague man shape within stretched out one hand to stroke her hair; then they both vanished. Rhodry fell forward, fainting, into Jill's ready arms. Swearing a little at his weight, she laid him down on the floor, then grabbed a blanket and covered him, because he was dead pale and icy cold, shivering at the loss of the magnetic link he'd made with his White Lady. When she looked up to say something to Aderyn, she realized that the female presence was still there, in fact more substantial than before. As she stepped free of the pillar of light, her flesh seemed almost solid, though translucent. She herself seemed elven and very beautiful, with hair so pale that it was almost silver and eyes of a cold storm gray. As still as stone, Aderyn watched her, his expression forced into such a hard-set indifference that Jill suddenly realized who she must be.

"Dallandra?" she whispered.

The presence turned her head and considered her unspeaking for a long moment.

"Do you follow the paths of the Light?" Her voice was more a thought touching the mind, but Aderyn heard her, too, judging from the flicker of pain that crossed his face.

"I do." Jill spoke aloud.

"Good." She turned to Aderyn. "Elessario's sorry now. She didn't realize what she was doing. She was trying to help the poor thing when it loved the man called Maer."

"I assumed your friend was guiltless."

Aderyn's voice was so cold that Jill was honestly shocked, but Dallandra ignored him.

"There is a child that will be born," she said to Jill. "Soon. Or soon as we judge time. It might be a long time in your world."

"Does this child concern me?"

"I'd hope so. I see danger all round her."

"I'll help if I can."

She nodded in a sort of wordless thanks, but her attention was drifting already to some other world. She was growing thinner, like a smoke curl in the wind.

"What of the ring?" Jill put all the urgency she could into her voice to try to pull her back. "Do you know the meaning of the rose ring?"

For the briefest of moments she smiled, and for that instant she seemed mortal again and solid.

"I don't. They never did tell me. They're like that, you know."

Her chuckle seemed to hang in the air. She was gone. Aderyn let out his breath in one sharp sigh, tossed his head, and knelt down beside Rhodry as if nothing had happened at all.

"Jill, you'll stay here for a few days, won't you? I could use your help."

"Of course. I'm always glad to pay you a service, and I'd like to see him well again, too. I loved him so much, once."

"Once and not now?"

"Once and not now." Jill got up with a sigh. "And I regret it, in a way, losing a love like that, but it never should have been, and now it's gone, and that's that."

Aderyn was silent for a long moment. When he spoke his voice cracked with unnatural calm.

"Too bad you never knew Dalla. I think you two would have gotten along quite well."

When Rhodry woke from that faint, some twenty minutes later, it seemed to him that he'd slept for days. He was muddled, too, wondering what he was doing, lying in Aderyn's tent with Jill and Gavantar standing round, as solemn as priests.

"What's wrong?" he mumbled. "Have I been sick?"

"You might say that." Aderyn handed him a cup of hot liquid. "Drink this, will you?"

The water tasted faintly of herbs, and drinking it made his head clear enough for him to remember the White Lady. All at once he couldn't bear to look at any of them, and especially not Jill; he felt his cheeks burning with shame.

"Ah, the blood's returning to your face, I see." Aderyn sounded amused. "Come on, lad, it's all ended well enough. I can't blame you for losing a fight when you didn't have a weapon to your name and she had a whole armory."

For days Rhodry refused to leave Aderyn's tent except in the dead of night, when everyone else was asleep. Under the waxing moon he would pick his way through the grasslands or stride back and forth along the streambank, always hurrying as if he could leave his shame and dishonor far behind or perhaps as if he could meet himself coming in the other direction and at last know who he was. Never once in that long madness did he think of himself as Rhodry Maelwaedd. The best swordsman in the kingdom, the lord whose honor was admired by the High King himself, the best gwerbret Aberwyn had ever known—those men were all dead. Every now and then he did become the old Rhodry who was a father and a grandfather and wonder if his blood kin fared well, but only briefly. Even his beloved grandson seemed to be drifting farther and farther away from him with every minute that passed, as if the child rode a little boat sailing endlessly away down some vast river. Just at dawn he would come stumbling back exhausted from these walks to slip into Aderyn's tent and sleep the day away in a welter of dreams. Often he dreamt of old battles, particularly the destruction of a town called Slaith; that dream was so vivid that he could practically smell the smoke as the pirate haven burned to the ground. Once, just when the moon was at her full, he dreamt of the White Lady, but it was only a distant thing, a memory dream and perfectly normal. The marvels were gone, utterly gone. When he woke, he was in tears.

Aderyn and Gavantar were sitting in the center of the tent by the dead fire and studying a book together, talking in low voices about sigils and signs. From the light glowing through the walls of the tent, Rhodry could tell that it was near sunset. When he sat up, Aderyn looked over.

"Hungry? There's smoked fish."

"I'm not, but my thanks."

Aderyn closed the book and studied him for a moment, or, rather, he seemed to be studying the air all around Rhodry.

"You know, you need to get out in the sunlight more. You're pale as milk."

Rhodry looked away.

"Oh, come now," Aderyn said sharply. "No one outside of Jill and me and Gavantar even knows the truth."

"Everyone else just thinks I went mad, right? That's dishonor enough."

Aderyn sighed. Rhodry forced himself to look at him.

"Somewhat I wanted to ask you," Rhodry said. "When this, well, this trouble started, you said some strange things that I've only just remembered. She found me again, you said. What do you mean, again? I never saw her before in my life."

"Um, well, I was wondering if you'd remember that. I made a terrible mistake, saying such a thing." The old man got up and walked over, and at that moment he seemed taller, towering, threatening, his dark eyes cold. "Do you truly want to know? I'm bound to tell you if you ask, but that asking is a grim thing in itself, and the beginning of a long, long road."

All at once Rhodry was frightened. He knew obscurely that he was about to let some terrible secret out of its cage like a wild beast, knowledge that would rend and rip the few shreds he had left of his old life, his old self. He had seen too many secret places of the world, crossed too many forbidden borders already, to risk more.

"If I'm not meant to know, keep your secrets. It'd be a fine way to repay you, anyway, prying into things you shouldn't tell me."

Aderyn sighed in honest relief and looked his normal self again. It occurred to Rhodry, much later, that the old man had been as frightened as he.

That day marked a turning point, as if fear were the only medicinal strong enough to drive out his shame. That very evening Rhodry left Aderyn's tent and wandered over to Calonderiel's, where Jill was staying. As usual, the banadar had a crowd around him, young men, mostly, passing a skin of mead back and forth. While Jill watched, a little nervously, everyone greeted Rhodry without comment. He found a place to sit off to one side, took his turn at the skin when the mead came his way, and merely listened to the talk of hunting and the summer's grass. When he left, everyone said goodbye in a casual sort of way, and that night he only walked for a couple of hours under the waning moon. On the morrow he took his place guarding the horse herd, and again, no one said a wrong word to him or asked him one single thing.

That night he joined Calonderiel's men for the evening meal. They accepted him so easily that he realized he'd already been marked as a member of the banadar's warband, another swordsman attached to the only kind of magistrate the People knew. The place suited him, and he took it gratefully, doubly grateful that he never had to say a formal word in acknowledgment. Swearing fealty to a man other than the High King, even to his oldest friend left in the world, would have come hard. After the meal they sat outside around a fire, passing the mead skin around, until Melandonatar brought out a harp and struck up a song. When the others joined in, Rhodry at first only listened. The music swept around him, long lines of sprung rhythm in some minor key, then tangled upon itself in intricate harmonies as the men sang of an ancient battle, a desperate last stand at the gates of Rinbaladelan during the Great Burning long ago. The ending left everyone so sad that the harper struck up a happier tune straightaway, a simple song about hunting. This one Rhodry knew, because it had been a favorite at the Aberwyn court on those occasions when the People came to visit, and without even thinking he joined in, adding his cracked tenor to the melodic line and leaving the difficult harmony to the others. Since the song had its bawdy side, they were laughing as much as singing, making so much noise that Rhodry never heard someone walking up to kneel behind him.

All at once a new voice joined in, a trained and beautiful tenor that rang like a bell on every lighthearted syllable. When Rhodry felt a friendly hand on his shoulder, he turned and looked into a face that was more than half his. Devaberiel's hair was as pale as moonlight, but his elven-slit eyes were the same cornflower blue as Rhodry's, and the shape of his jaw and his forehead, and the quick sunny way he smiled, were as familiar as a mirror image as well. Rhodry stopped singing, feeling tears rise in his throat beyond his power to call them back. Devaberiel threw one arm around his shoulders and pulled him close. Slowly the music died away as every man in the circle turned to watch.

"Banadar?" Devaberiel called out. "Is there any man here who is so blind as to deny that this is my son?"

"I doubt it very much," Calonderiel said, grinning. "He certainly looks yours to me."

"Then here in the required assembly I claim him and present him to you."

Rhodry wept in earnest, wondering why even as the tears came. The men rose to their feet and cheered; women hurried over with skins of mead; sleepy children crawled out of tents to join the celebration. In the midst of the uproar it was impossible to hear a word anyone said. Rhodry saw Salamander standing in the shadows with Jill, and his brother was practically jigging with excitement, with Wildfolk swarming around him like bees round a hive. When Rhodry went to join them, however, Jill turned on her heel and walked away. Even though he'd expected no less, still her coldness stabbed him to the heart, and he knew better than to try to follow her.

"Well, I finally caught up with the esteemed parent," Salamander burst out. "And dragged him back just as I promised."

"I happened to be on my way here already," Devaberiel said with a certain amount of frost in his voice. "But no matter. I see you're wearing that wretched ring, younger son of mine. Has anyone figured out what it means yet?"

"Jill wants to talk with you about that, Father," Salamander put in. "The morrow will do, however. Tonight let us celebrate, and lo, the moon already rises to join us at our drinking!"

It was two days before Rhodry had a chance to speak with Jill. He was nursing a hangover in Aderyn's quiet tent when she came in, carrying a pair of saddlebags. He slipped into Deverrian when he spoke, simply because she was so much a part of his youth and his past.

"It looks like you're leaving us. When?"

"Tomorrow at dawn."

"Jill, I only wish you'd stay with me a while."

"I can't. I've told you that before often enough. We don't belong together."

"I just don't understand."

"That's true. You don't." She got up and paced to the opening of the tent, stood there listening to the sounds of the camp. "And you can't understand, truly, so for the love of every god, let it drop!"

For a brief moment Rhodry wanted to strangle her; then he wanted to weep; then he sighed and knelt down to feed a twig or two into the tiny fire.

"And where will you go, then?" he said.

"Bardek."

"Bardek?"

"Just that." She came back and knelt by the fire. "I've just time to get back to Aberwyn and find a ship, I think, before the sailing season's over."

"And why do you want to go to Bardek, or is that beyond my poor and pitiful understanding, too?"

"You're still a sulky bastard when you want to be, aren't you? Listen, you've already nearly drowned in trouble for wanting one woman you couldn't have. Why do you—"

"Oh, hold your tongue! That's a nasty weapon to use!"

"But a true-speaking, isn't it? Anyway, I'm going to find out about the rose ring. Or try to, anyway."

Automatically he glanced down at the silver stripe on the third finger of his right hand.

"Well, to be more accurate, about those letters inside it." Jill went on. "Give it over for a minute, will you?"

"I don't know what makes you think it's an island word when it's written in Elvish. Here."

"I never said I thought it was Bardekian." She held it up, angling the band a little to catch the light from the fire. "Do you remember when you were a captive in the islands? At that rich woman's house—I don't remember her name, but I do remember what you told me about her litter boys. Remember them, with the odd yellow eyes, and you were sure they saw the Wildfolk?"

"By all the gods, so I was! I wondered if they had elven blood in their veins."

"I still do. Look, I've been talking with your father about the old days. After the Burning the People fled every which way. We know they had boats. Rinbaladelan—and it was a seaport, mind—held out for a year, time enough to pack up treasures for an exile. Your ancestors—the folk who fled east—were country people; they didn't have the time or the inclination to rescue books and scrolls as they ran. But Rinbaladelan was an ancient city of learning and every grace, or so the story runs, and you can carry books a cursed sight easier in a boat than in a saddlebag."

"And after all this time, do you think any of those books still exist?"

"Not unless someone copied them a couple of times over twixt now and then, no—not in the jungles of the southern islands with all the damp and mildews. But if—what if, just what if some of the People reached a haven there, and survived to build a city, and what if they've kept the old lore alive?"

Rhodry sat back on his heels and considered the flames. It seemed that he saw towers of gold rise among them, and the glitter of mighty palaces.

"Jill, let me go with you."

"Ye gods, you're as stubborn as a terrier with a dead rat in its mouth! I won't, and that's that. Your place is here. I don't even know why, but it is."

"Oh, is it now? And I suppose I'm just supposed to sit here and wait for you to come back! Cursed if I will!"

"You might be cursed if you don't." Oddly enough, she grinned at him. "If you're going to keep company with sorcerers, you'd better watch what you say. But truly, I doubt if it matters.

Run where you will, Rhodry ap Devaberiel, but the dweomer will catch you when it wants you."

He tried to think of some clever retort. There was none. She held the ring up to the fire again, and the silver sent a long wink of light into the shadows.

"It's got to be a name," she said at last.

"What?"

"The lettering, you dolt! If it was an ordinary word, someone would be able to translate it. Between them your father and brother took it to every sage in two kingdoms. Someone would have recognized it. But a name—well, anyone can call themselves what they like, particularly if they're neither elf nor human, can't they now?" She frowned at the writing, then sounded it out. "Arr-soss-ah soth-ee lorr-ess-oh-ahz." She paused, then spoke it again in a strange tight voice, almost a growl, that seemed to vibrate through the tent and spread out to the ends of the earth. "Arzosah Sothy Lorezohaz!"

And far away to the north, on a rocky ledge high up a mountain that no human eyes had ever seen, a sleeping dragon stirred and whimpered in a sudden nightmare.

APPENDICES

Incarnations of the various characters throughout the Deverry series

(Each column is one soul; each line, one story.)

643	Brangwen	Blaen	Gerraent	Madoc	Rodda	Ysolla	
696	Lyssa	Gweran	Tanyc	***	Cabrylla	Cadda	
720	***	***	Cinvan	Addryc	***	***	
773	Gweniver	Ricyn	Dannyn	Glyn	Dolyan	Macla	Dagwyn
835	Branoic	Maddyn	Owaen	Caradoc	***	Clwna	Aethan
918	***	Maer	Danry	***	***	Braedda	Leomyr
980	***	Meddry	***	***	***	***	***
1063	Jill	Rhodry	Cullyn	Blaen	Lovyan	Seryan	Gwin

Political Chronology
of the Kingdoms of Deverry and Eldidd

—8. The People of Bel flee Northern Gaul by magical means after Vindex's failed rebellion against the Emperor Nero and arrive in their new world.

—5. The destruction of the Seven Cities of the western elves by the people known as the Gel da'Thae, the Horse Kin.

Year 1. Founding of the Holy City of Dun Deverry after King Bran sees the omen of the White Sow.

2–254. Dynasty of the White Mare. Direct rule of King Bran's descendants as the small colonies around Dun Deverry spread and expand up and down the Belaver. Cerrmor founded in 25, Lughcarn in 106.

54–297. First Interregnum. Death of Bran's last lineal descendant touches off the fighting, which eventually the Striking Wyvern clan wins. In disgust, the Hippogriff clan, accompanied by the men of the Dragon, leaves to found its own kingdom in Eldidd.

98–402. Dynasty of the Striking Wyvern. Expansion continues rapidly. Colonies in Cantrae and Gwaentaer as well as the founding of many cities and towns in Deverry proper. By the 380s the population spread reaches the Eldidd border. Bitter fighting over the defining of that border brings down Wyvern rule.

301. After much searching for omens, Cynaeval of the Hippogriff clan founds a royal city in Abernaudd.

302. Cadvaenan of the Dragon founds Aberwyn. Since he is Cynaeval's foster brother and much the younger to boot, he cedes the kingship to the Hippogriff. This arrangement lasts until Cadvaenan's death in suspicious circumstances some fifteen years later.

317–322. Civil war in Eldidd. At the end, the Hippogriff clan is the sole royal clan in Eldidd, but the name of the Dragon is allowed to live on for sentimental reasons.

403–600. Age of the Warring Clans. To some scholars, the Second Interregnum, it is not so much a true civil war, as there is always a titular king in Dun Deverry, as a time when the Great Clans do pretty much as they please. There is enough empty land available to make the constant fighting possible without tearing the society apart, as those who prefer peace simply move away from disputed territory. In this period Gwaentaer is heavily colonized; the population builds along the iron routes down from Cerrgonney; there is even limited settlement in the Auddglyn.

Early 400s. In Eldidd, settlers to the north and the far west make the first contact with the elves, who withdraw to the west rather than fight over territory that they've barely settled.

558. First contact with Bardek, when a group of Deverry merchants, bound for Eldidd, are blown off course and carried to the far islands.

602. After many years of fighting, Adoryc I founds the dynasty of the Blue Wyvern, the first effectual dynasty in some two hundred years. His power is based

on a coalition of the rising new merchant class, the priests of Bel and Wmm, and the lesser clans. Concessions to his allies include royal support of the new Bardek trade and a royal ban against head-hunting. He also divides the estates of some the conquered Great Clans to reward the lesser, among them the Falcons, Boars, and Wolves.

621. Adoryc II, Galrion's father, ascends the throne.

655. Last time a warrior is ritually beheaded for taking an enemy head.

610–664. In general, this is a time of prosperity, relative peace, and growing trade with Bardek. The kingdom of Eldidd, however, begins to spread east rather than north, and border clashes are common along the Girysbel range.

665–676. First Eldidd War. The boundary is eventually settled as running down the middle of the mountains, a compromise that pleases no one. During this period Eldidd begins expanding to the west and comes into the first true conflict with the elves.

720–728. Second Eldidd War. Liddmaryc of the Hippogriff lays claim to Cenerrpaen, the odd triangle of coastal plain by the Girysbel. Eldidd wins and forces a humiliating treaty, one provision of which is the betrothal of Covramur of Deverry's infant daughter to Liddmaryc's grandson, Waryn. This marriage gives Eldidd a distant claim to the Deverry throne.

750. Covramur dies, ushering in the Time of Troubles, as his daughter's husbands all lay claim to the throne. There are three claimants, one in Cerrmor, one in Cantrae, and one in Eldidd. While Cerrmor and Cantrae fight over the Holy City, Eldidd fights a war of attrition on the border.

773. Capture of Mael, Prince Aberwyn, produces a twenty-year truce between Cerrmor and Eldidd.

793. The province of Pyrdon rebels from Eldidd and de-

clares itself a kingdom. The effect on the wars is a bloody stalemate that drags on for years of raiding, feints, but no decisive action.

828. Birth of the boy destined to be king of all Deverry, Maryn, son of King Casyl of Pyrdon.

843. Glyn II of Cerrmor dies without a son. Maryn evades those seeking to harm him by posing as a silver dagger and arrives safely in Cerrmor to claim the throne.

849. Maryn takes the Holy City. The Boars flee to Cantrae and attempt to establish a rival royal city there.

851. Maryn I, true king of all Deverry, is crowned in the Holy City.

852–855. The Final Eldidd War. When Eldidd refuses to make peace, Maryn conquers the kingdom and reduces it to the status of a province.

853. Casyl of Pyrdon abdicates in favor of Maryn; Pyrdon becomes part of the newly unified kingdom.

862. Maryn I dies of the aftereffects of many old wounds, leaving behind him peace and the dynasty of the Red Wyvern. The common people are convinced that the gods called him to the Otherlands so young in order to make a god out of him.

856–900. In general, a time of reconstruction. When Maryn gives the gwerbretrhyn of Cantrae to the Southern Rams, what's left of the Boars as well as other disgruntled losers flee north to Cerrgonney and found a loose coalition of independent lordships, who then spend most of their time squabbling over who will be gwerbret. The kings ignore them, except for punishing the occasional raid down into Gwaentaer. Population generally begins to rebuild after the long bleeding of the wars.

918. Abortive rebellion in Eldidd. King Aeryc crushes it with the aid of the loyal Pertyc Maelwaedd, Lord

Cannobaen, who is rewarded with the gwerbretrhyn of Aberwyn.

921. A flare-up of war with Cerrgonney when the newly determined gwerbrets attempt to impose their own taxes on the towns of the Camyn Yraen near their rhans. Aeryc crushes them within a few months.

936. All trade treaties with Bardek are reviewed and brought directly under the control of the king. Those between Bardek and Eldidd are made consonant with those in Deverry proper.

962–984. The Cerrgonney wars. In 962, King Maryn II, infuriated by the continuing efforts of the northern gwerbrets to control the iron trade to their own advantage, declares the rank of gwerbret abolished in Cerrgonney. His son, Casyl II, finally brings the matter to a successful conclusion. Thereafter, all Cerrgonney lords swear direct loyalty to the king.

1007. Gwardyn II, who has no sons, marries his daughter to his brother Savyl's son, Lallyn, who becomes Lallyn I of the new dynasty of the Gold Wyvern. Although such a marriage is legal, the inbreeding takes its toll in succeeding generations.

1039. The founding of the province of Cwm Pecl. The Stallion clan is given the gwerbretrhyn.

1057. Lallyc II ascends the throne.

Glossary

Aber (Deverrian) A river mouth, an estuary.

Alar (Elvish) A group of elves, who may or may not be blood kin, who choose to travel together for some indefinite period of time. Plural: alarli.

Alardan (Elv.) The meeting of several alarli, usually the occasion for a drunken party.

Archon (trans. of the Bardekian *atzenarlen)* The elected head of a city-state (Bardekian *at).*

Astral The plane of existence directly "above" or "within" the etheric (q.v.). In other systems of magic, often referred to as the Akashic Record or the Treasure House of Images.

Aura The field of electromagnetic energy that permeates and emanates from every living being.

Aver (Dev.) A river.

Bara (Elv.) An enclitic that indicates that the preceding adjective in an elvish agglutinated word is the name of the element following the enclitic, as can+bara+melim = Rough River (rough+name marker+river).

Bel (Dev.) The chief god of the Deverry pantheon.

Bel (Elv.) An enclitic, similar in function to *bara*, except that it indicates that a preceding verb is the name of the following element in the agglutinated term, as in Darabeldal, Flowing Lake.

Blue Light Another name for the etheric plane (q.v.).

Body of Light An artificial thought-form (q.v.) constructed by a dweomermaster to allow him or her to travel through the inner planes of existence.

Brigga (Dev.) Loose wool trousers worn by men and boys.

Broch (Dev.) A squat tower in which people live. Originally, in the Homeland, these towers had one big fireplace in the center of the ground floor and a number of booths or tiny roomlets up the sides, but by the time of our narrative, this ancient style has given way to regular floors with hearths and chimneys on either side of the structure.

Cadvridoc (Dev.) A warleader. Not a general in the modern sense, the cadvridoc is supposed to take the advice and counsel of the noble-born lords under him, but his is the right of final decision.

Captain (trans. of the Dev. *pendaely)* The second in command, after the lord himself, of a noble's warband. An interesting point is that the word *taely* (the root or unmutated form of *-daely)* can mean either a warband or a family depending on context.

Conaber (Elv.) A musical instrument similar to the panpipe but of even more limited range.

Cwm (Dev.) A valley.

Dun (Dev.) A fort.

Dweomer (trans. of Dev. *dwunddaevad)* In its strict sense, a system of magic aimed at personal enlightenment through harmony with the natural universe in all its planes and manifestations; in the popular sense, magic, sorcery.

Elcyion Lacar (Dev.) The elves; literally, the "bright spirits," or "Bright Fey."

Ensorcel To produce an effect similar to hypnosis by direct manipulation of a person's aura. (True hypnosis manipulates the victim's consciousness only and thus is more easily resisted.)

Etheric The plane of existence directly "above" the physical. With its magnetic substance and currents, it holds physical matter in an invisible matrix and is the true source of what we call "life."

Etheric Double The true being of a person, the electromagnetic structure that holds the body together and that is the actual seat of consciousness.

Fola (Elv.) An enclitic that shows the noun preceding it in an agglutinated Elvish word is the name of the element following the enclitic, as in Corafolamelim, Owl River.

Geis A taboo, usually a prohibition against doing something. Breaking geis results in ritual pollution and the disfavor, if not active enmity of the gods. In societies that truly believe in geis, a person who breaks it usually dies fairly quickly, either of morbid depression or some unconsciously self-inflicted "accident," unless he or she makes ritual amends.

Gerthddyn (Dev.) Literally, a "music man," a wandering minstrel and entertainer of much lower status than a true bard.

Great Ones Spirits, once human but now disincarnate, who exist on an unknowably high plane of existence and who have dedicated themselves to the eventual enlightenment of all sentient beings. They are also known to the Buddhists, as Boddhisattvas.

Gwerbret (Dev. The name derives from the Gaulish *vergobretes.*) The highest rank of nobility below the royal family itself. Gwerbrets (Dev. *gwerbretion)* function as the chief magistrates of their regions, and even kings hesitate to override their decisions because of their many ancient prerogatives.

Hiraedd (Dev.) A peculiarly Celtic form of depression, marked by a deep, tormented longing for some unobtainable things; also and in particular, homesickness to the third power.

Javelin (trans. of Dev. *picecl)* Since the weapon in question is only about three feet long, another possible translation would be "war dart." The reader should not think of it as a proper spear or as one of those enormous javelins used in the modern Olympic Games.

Lwdd (Dev.) A blood-price; differs from wergild in that the amount of lwdd is negotiable in some circumstances, rather than being irrevocably set by law.

Malover (Dev.) A full, formal court of law with both a priest of Bel and either a gwerbret or a tieryn in attendance.

Pan (Elv.) An enclitic, similar to *-fola-*, defined earlier, except that it indicates that the preceding noun is plural as well as the name of the following word, as in Corapanmelim, River of the Many Owls. Remember that Elvish always indicates pluralization by adding a semi-independent morpheme, and that this semi-independence is reflected in the various syntax-bearing enclitics.

Pecl (Dev.) Far, distant.

Rhan (Dev.) A political unit of land; thus, gwerbretrhyn, tierynrhyn, the area under the control of a given gwerbret or tieryn. The size of the various rhans (Dev. *rhannau)* varies widely, depending on the vagaries of inheritance and the fortunes of war rather than some legal definition.

Scrying The art of seeing distant people and places by magic.

Sigil An abstract magical figure, usually representing either a particular spirit or a particular kind of energy or power. These figures, which look a lot like geometrical scribbles, are derived by various rules from secret magical diagrams.

Thought-form An image or three-dimensional form that has been fashioned out of either etheric or astral substance, usually by the action of a trained mind. If enough trained minds work together to build the same thought-form, it will exist independently for a period of time based on the amount of energy put into it. (Putting energy into such a form is known as *ensouling* the thought-form.) Manifestations of gods or saints are usually thought-forms picked up by the highly intuitive, such as children or those with a touch of second sight. It is also possible for many untrained minds acting together to make fuzzy, ill-defined thought-forms that can be picked up the same way, such as UFOs and sightings of the Devil.

Tieryn (Dev.) An intermediate rank of the noble-born, below a gwerbret but above an ordinary lord (Dev. *arcloedd).*

Wyrd (trans. of Dev. *tingedd)* Fate, destiny; the inescapable problems carried over from a sentient being's last incarnation.